SONG
OF
KARDU

DANIEL BRADLEY

ARTHUR'S DEN

He listened again for Pegassos. Her voice never came, too hidden behind the reach of dimensions. This would have been a good time for her to pick him up. But with his mind open, he heard a song. He didn't recognize it, like it came from the world itself, alien to him, with the tremor of a woman's voice. She was the thing that had awakened. Her voice rushed over the wind, shook out of the ground, and poured molten anguish through the conduit of Seth's battered mind and overtop his heart. Whoever she was, her singing hurt him deep inside. Seth writhed as though she might kill him.

He screamed and cried out. He had no words but the universal scream of a tortured soul. It didn't let up, but he found strength in himself to stand, to look for the woman's music. He saw the cloud rising from the destroyed city had started to blot out the sun. Turning to the south, his visor caught a missile launching from the ground far away, a response to the atrocity already committed. As the missile moved into the clouds, the woman changed her song, singing straight into Seth's mind in the same way he could hear Pegassos.

Though he couldn't understand her, he felt seen by whatever the woman was. She had to be a power bigger than anything he had ever encountered, a power that invaded his thoughts like someone breaking down a door into his consciousness, Death's Door, the one that always creaked. The sky continued to darken, and under the duress of listening to the voice Seth thought he really might die. The context seemed clear. "Who are you?" repeating again and again in strange tongues.

Perplexed and beaten, Seth knelt, splashing knees into ash and sand, to witness a new world end. His skin burned from the distress of the Botistems and his thoughts were overwhelmed with questions.

He relented enough to answer the voice, "I am Seth, the son of Ashetarai, and I am alone."

—·—

Part 1

Echo Front at the End of the Bosion Advance

Of all creatures that breathe and move upon the earth, nothing is bred that is weaker than man.
    —*Homer*

1

Seth saw dark walls of living metal, and that's how he knew he was awake. A Bosion crawler had him constricted at the chest. The animal-like machine with silver- and copper-colored hide sank its jaws into his armor. Its teeth didn't penetrate, but he could feel the bruising, the pressure cracking his ribs. Botistem light within him fought against the injury while his mind searched for a solution. The last thing he remembered was being thrown from Pegassos, his ship and best friend.

"Seth, are you with me?" she called to his mind.

"Yes," he answered, struggling to think under the metallic clamp and smell. He wasn't wearing his helmet, but kept it disassembled on his back and ready to summon. The Bosions kept a climate of oxygen and nitrogen. He could breathe well enough. "Keep up the pressure. I'll find you soon."

With a burst of energy that surprised the crawler, Seth sent the creature of almost his size crashing into the living walls with a burst of bright light. The force of it shot Seth back as well. With no gravity on the ship, his attack propelled him with equal force. As he hit the walls, Seth could feel the great Bosion ship shudder, *alive*. Wounded and in self-repair, the crawler retreated into the dark corridors beyond, aided by its own bursts of light from its claws. He and the machine animal were not dissimilar, except for Seth being man. The crawler was metal. Still a machine, just like the walls. Just like this giant ship Seth had come to destroy.

With a groan, Seth clutched his healing chest.

"Keep the big ugly ship busy, Pegassos," he said. "We don't want her slipping before I can get to the..."

"...the consensus." Pegassos finished his sentence, but he ignored her.

An image of himself appeared in his way. He let go of his chest and stood upright.

"Seth Caeso," the image said. It was the consensus, the consciousness of the enemy ship reaching out to him through a hologram.

"You know who I am," Seth observed.

"The only real threat to our migration."

It wasn't unusual for a consensus to communicate by way of imitation. Seth had experienced it before, but he would never get used to the uncanny nature of talking to a replica of himself. The image didn't display itself as an exact copy, rather more like a mirror, each feature flipped from right to left. His olive skin had a purple shine in this light, and his dark hair the same. He looked young, too, like a healthy man in his late twenties. Once, Seth had read an ancient copy of Dorian Gray. He could relate a little to the impish fop-creation of ancient Earth. The stain of a hundred wars had not marked him. He wore the mask of Botistem light.

After only slight hesitation, Seth addressed the projection. "Centuries of war is hardly a migration." He drifted toward the image.

It flickered.

The real Seth pressed, "You should consider the Federacy a threat of its own. Existential. They've found ways to kill you."

"The Federacy is irrelevant, a mockery of life and nature, a relic to civilizations rightly fallen. We are machine, we will take what we wish."

Seth shot himself through the image of himself, using thrust from his hands and feet to find the object of his hunt.

"Bosion evolution is an imitation of life," he said as he flowed through the wide hall. "You are nothing new."

"What makes you different from us?" the image called after him. Its voice carried through the halls. It seemed to be everywhere, even in Seth's mind. He fought the accompanying chill.

"You are machine as much as you are a man," it continued. "We see the light that heals you. Botistem. Abomination. You have no one fooled, son of Ashetarai, prince of Libertas. You are Symbiotic. You are adjacent."

Seth searched the halls, feeling the hum of the living ship. It felt like his home, Libertas, with familiarity licking the pulsations of his perirhinal cortex. Blood and electricity worked there, the same as anywhere else in the body. That's part of what made a Bosion consensus so dangerous. The human mind was a machine. It could be manipulated. But if Seth followed the feeling well, he could find the heart of the consensus. He could find the mind of the enemy ship.

There. He found what he came for, slowing himself to slip through the veinous passage until he hovered at its edge. On a ship this big, the consensus was a vast, multicolored hall of mist and dancing light, harmonic hues in cognitive agreement, the mind and soul of the enemy as Seth's gifted eyes could see it. He took in the view, amazed at the beauty, also afraid of how it made him feel. There was no floor, just endless light brought alive with Bosion spark.

"Your storm ends here," Seth said, still at the edge, and he took a device from his belt. It was a federacy warhead, a virus to break the Bosion consensus. Many small particles that made a great intelligence would become tiny pieces of weak instinct, forever drifting apart. He set the fuse to go off after he would leave. He was part Botistem.

Botistems weren't different than Bosion by much more than defining purpose. Seth knew there was more to the story. But the longer he lived, the less he felt he wanted to know about it. All the same, in this moment of battle and flow, he knew that he shouldn't find himself near these warheads when they went off. An immortal was only such if they did what they could not to die.

"You'll see us again, Seth," said the colorful consensus, appearing again. This time it chose the face and body of a different person, standing amid the light with wearied expression. Seth almost dismissed the image until he recognized a glow in the man's eye. The glow was his own. The image was of himself, only older, without the source of power that kept him young. Seth thought of Dorian Gray, pulling the sheet off his own portrait. Dorian stabbed the heart of that image, loathing the stains upon it. Unable to look away, Seth lost peripheral awareness for a moment, tunneled by the weighty surprise.

As the image distracted him, another crawler grabbed Seth from behind, sinking its teeth into his shoulder. The same brain that the Bosions had tried to entice, had tried to distract, now filled his nerves with pain and the warm rush of blood spilling onto the black of his armor and skin underneath. The creature's bite had missed his neck by just a few inches but still found meat enough to tear. Wrestling the monster, enraged by the pain it caused and driven by the brush of death in its jaws, Seth dropped the active warhead. The small cannister drifted into the light of the consensus, nothing to stop it.

"If the virus is released before you leave the ship, you'll die with us," said the consensus, said the older version of himself. "You will lose your power."

"Can't prove that unless it happens," Seth grunted. He used his legs to constrict the crawler. His hands found grip around its head. "Now would be a good time, Pegassos."

"You'll see us again," repeated the consensus. "You'll find us at the steps of a new world. It is manifested in the Dao."

"Let me know when and where," Seth answered, popping the head off the crawler with leveraged coordination between his arms and legs. The synthetic creature twitched and curled. "I'll always enjoy frying rabid machines."

"Commander Caeso, by your bravery and skill in battle, the citizens of this sector owe you their lives and their homes."

Seth admired the award in his hand, an ornate knife with jewels on the hilt of blue and sapphire. The Federacy admiral had given it to him in formation in front of a few thousand troops on the flight deck of one of the flagships. The applause had seemed genuine. Had he not reached that last consensus, the casualties would have reached much higher. The sector chiefs would be organizing an evacuation now, rather than further settlement.

"I don't know what I could say to keep you around," the admiral said in his office. Seth sat across the desk from him. A wall-sized display of the system's sun brought in the only light to the room.

"My ship needs repair," said Seth, placing the knife again in its sheath, "and my mother has called for me."

"The Federacy won't forget what you did today."

"I'm sure they won't." Seth knew they would. Generational memory reached as far as a few narratives, but never passed opportunity. "I won't forget."

The admiral stood and saluted the commander. Seth saluted back and shook his hand. The man's hand was soft and dry at the same time. The veins were elevated, stringy and old. Seth could feel the years on the man. He wondered what the admiral could feel in his hands, if he could feel the power that made Seth different, all the reason in the power that said he couldn't stay.

The light of the sun display illuminated only half of the admiral's face, the other smiled behind a shadow. "Commander, you've been fighting this war since before even my grandfather's time. How does it feel to leave?"

Seth thought about his question for a moment, then answered, "Like it's time for a new chapter."

"Well, I'm sure I'll be long gone by the time you find it. Isn't the speed of light a bitch?" The admiral sighed, "What I would give to live forever like you."

Immortal Seth, aware of the irony behind his younger looks, smiled back. "It's longer than you might think, Admiral."

"Seth, there is another message from your mother." said Pegassos as she began to fold space, bringing herself into the Dao. He could feel the intonations in her systems change, the oscillations in her hull in intonation with the flow of the universe, of the spaces between the light and dark of the corporeal universe.

"Put it on."

Seth's mother appeared over his console, her message arriving by way of the Dao. She looked the same as she ever did. Ageless, beautiful, and terrifying. "By now you must be on your way, my boy. We're waiting for you in an uncharted system, far away from the rest this time. Pegassos will know where to go. Find me as soon as you can. You've fought the Federacy's war long enough. It's time for you to remember who you really are."

Seth leaned back, his chair retracting and preparing his body for stasis. "Close the message."

Botistems flooded into his system. They crept through his veins and tissues like a warm drug, tiny machines of light, of spirit and healing. He often contemplated them but couldn't understand them. They just made an important piece of the deeper parts of his function and consciousness, placing themselves at the heart of his unconscious identity.

Such a strange phrase, *who you really are*. Seth felt too old to know himself that way. He served the Federacy. He served his mother. He lived a continuous burn through the feathered tips of the galaxy as a lone champion for greater powers in the defense of their interest. He was a man, he was a machine. He was a leader, and a follower.

Who you really are. Symbiote.

The Botistems continued their work, healing new wounds and erasing old scars, keeping the blueprint of his perfect health as a carpenter on Theseus's ship. "What makes a human being, Pegassos?" he asked.

"Carbon and unpredictability," his ship answered.

"Right," said Seth. "I'm just wondering if I am more of what I was, or what I will be."

"Can you not just be one thing right now? Just Seth."

"No," said Seth. "We all know the present is an illusion. Isn't that the way of the universe? Who I am tomorrow exists presently. It's just outside the cone of my perspective. It's there. I can feel it."

"It's ominous, but perhaps not incorrect. But if you haven't experienced the becoming, you can't assume the identity of your destiny until you've earned it."

"Right. I'm not allowing for possibility."

Pegassos moved into the Dao. Gravity flowed to her as she did, making a small wormhole, like punching a blanket on a soft mattress, or making a whirlpool in the drain of a tub. Seth saw stars and galaxies, celestial bodies without name, time, or discovery in motion through the confines of his small ship.

"You are my friend, my vessel," the ship said. "That is your past. And your future. Don't we change each other?"

"Thank you, Pegassos," Seth breathed, falling into a stupor, ready to sleep in transit through the starlit Dao. His last thoughts were of himself, a reflection with old age, standing on invisible plane in the consensus. "Whatever happens next, whatever cruel adventure my mother has for us, whatever people we meet who shape our decisions..." he couldn't finish the thought. "That will have to do. Change is inevitable."

2

For Seth, death was a locked door with the key left inside, never there as a temptation, just a door he could see in his mind as he played games on its porch. Waking from a deep slumber at the end of his journey home, he found himself climbing outside without environmental protection. He pushed off from Pegassos's side, taking no breath in the blackness as he chose to look at death's door in a flight through nothing but the radioactive cold of space. Libertas loomed in the distance, his home.

Before long, his saliva started to boil. He could feel his body fight to hold itself together. His eyes were ready to freeze as the avarice of vacuum pulled at him one dying cell at a time. He could feel the Botistems inside him rebuilding him faster than the pull of space. They would keep him alive long enough under the spotlight of Pegassos to make it to Libertas where his mother would meet him inside.

Libertas grew larger as he flew. She was not just a ship, not just a fortress, but a guardian of worlds, not flying in the traditional sense, but looming in the shape of a woman, a grand statue over fields of Milky Way canvas. She, the ship, held a spear in one hand and a scroll in the other, two offerings of different meaning. *Servos ad pileum vocare,* her crown read. The phrase was an ancient dare. Stand with us, it seemed to say. Rise and free yourselves in the service of something great.

The stars behind Libertas curved and sloped in a river of glass, frozen in a long moment. Seth admired them as tiny memorials to faces lost in the grand tumult of time, quiet notes of memory on incomprehensible sheets of music.

Pegassos spoke through thoughts in Seth's mind, things he alone could understand. "Are we finished with the war against the Bosion machines?"

"Yes," he said in his mind, igniting Botistem light from his bare hand. He used the light's thrust to spin around and look at her. "That war is over for us now. I did what I was meant to do, and Mother has called us home. What are you thinking?"

"I'm wondering if you're going to be alright."

"I know I'll be fine out here. I have you..." He realized she wasn't talking about his unprotected spacewalk. "Oh, in there. I don't know. It's been a long time."

Pegassos murmured. Her gold feathers seemed to shimmer in the faint light of the system's distant sun and the surrounding stars. Though it didn't move, he imagined the words and sounds coming from the beak of her eagle's head. She followed him.

"You're right," Seth sighed, "I shouldn't assume anything. We'll see how long we stay this time."

As Seth drifted closer, doors opened in the folds of Libertas's robes. A woman's silhouette stood in the opening, shielded behind invisible barriers of energy and Botistem mist. Death's door seemed to disappear as Seth let himself down to touch the floor near the woman, breaking his fall with more light from his hands.

"Welcome home, my son," the woman said, her shape becoming clearer as Seth's eyes healed and adjusted. She had dark hair like his and light in her eyes, much like his, but brighter, like they were the true mark of experience, of connection to the Botistems and the way of the universe. A woman of youth and infinite age. She held out a hand to greet him. "Seth, god of war and guardian of life. Centuries apart have been too many."

"Mother," Seth said, accepting her hand. "The years seem

insignificant now that I am home."

Replenishing Botistems in the air flooded his lungs and bloodstream with the same warmth as always. In his mind, Seth could see them, working and welding at the smallest scale. He breathed them into his metabolism like a bacterial coexistence. Coming back home always drew a hyperawareness of them from his consciousness, almost like they wanted him to be thinking about them, to be grateful.

Symbiotic, he heard the Bosion consensus in his memory.

The machine collective mind wasn't wrong. With the Botistems he could live forever, just like his mother. Without them, he wondered what he would look like, how quickly he would diminish. He took a deep breath again, letting the air reach every corner of his body.

"And here she is," Mother said, "Pegassos, child of Libertas."

Pegassos flew through the hangar door and over their heads, stoic and smooth, and settled into her perch. She would spend a lot of time here to upgrade, learning and growing from Libertas. He wouldn't be able to fly her for a while. That would be alright; he was home.

Seth's mother led him up some steps and past a statue of Mercury. It was one of more than a few monuments to Old Earth and its people, everything a remembrance to the origin and ascent of Man.

"Why did you leave her and fly alone in the dark?" Mother said of Pegassos. "She's meant to protect you."

"I enjoyed some time outside," he shrugged, not explaining his kinship with death, his inner peace found in the bed of constant struggle.

A low, disapproving tone from Pegassos disturbed his thoughts.

"Sleep," he whispered.

On the lift, concentrated mist surrounded Seth's feet, carrying him and his mother into the air, stabilized on the quantum plane away from any effect of acceleration. Seth looked at his feet. The lift used a small shift in his velocity through time to accelerate his movement through physical space, pulling him and his mother through the great halls and workings of the ship as if they stood on solid ground. He'd missed that level of luxury in the war. Federacy tools usually weren't so sophisticated. A lift was a lift, all parts of ship and crew a functioning piece of Federacy influence.

Libertas was a brightly adorned, female creature of immense power. She was a nation, and an individual, the accumulation of Botistem and human community. She also gave the impression of a spirit of Yin, if one leaned into Chinese philosophy. She was contrast and balance to the regular way of the galaxy. On the lift, inside the halls of the great ship, Seth took in the might of the halls of Libertas, like great veins through her bends and hollows.

Looking a bit like a small reflection of the large, statuesque ship, mother didn't speak much as they rode the lift. Her manner seemed as pleasant as always, but time had played a factor in their relationship. It always had. Between the years grew a forest of unspoken words. Though she and he were the only two beings of alike immortality that Seth knew of, she was a stranger to him.

The lift slowed and arrived at a massive hall, a parade of sorts, above the clamor of Mother's most devoted followers. Seth didn't recognize any of them as he scanned them with his far-seeing eyes to where they gathered below in numberless crowds. As mortals, they were too young for him to have ever met. They would have lived and grown, had babies, died, all in the shadow of his legend; the faraway prince of Libertas in the struggle for humanity at the edge of the Bosion advance. Mother had collected them on her journeys, rescuing them from the shadows of empires and wars. Like him, they all called her Mother. But to him, they looked like fish in an aquarium. Less real perhaps then the men and woman of the Federacy fleets at the battle's front.

But no, more real now. Those soldiers would be dead now. They were part of Seth's past. These people. Seth needed to focus on these people.

Mother raised her hand. A hush from her gesture silenced the masses in a wave.

"Children of the Scroll!" Mother shouted. "My son has returned victorious!"

Their silence traded for erupting applause. Seth smiled at them, but didn't feel them. A small flutter puttered through his back. Fight or flight. He wanted to run. Leaping from the balcony would work. He could slow his descent, roll with the momentum hundreds of feet down. He could make it back to Pegassos, back to space.

"Alone, at the tip of the Federacy's blade, Seth has suppressed the Bosion advance. Through unspeakable toil, unimaginable ordeal, Seth and the noble Pegassos, daughter of Libertas, broke through the ranks and destroyed the Bosion consensus at the heart of the advance. The Federacy would have failed without him."

Mother turned to him, the light in her eyes aflame, her voice echoing through the wide chamber. "Thank you, Seth," she said. "You brought balance. You represented me well."

The crowd joined her in her gratitude. Drones to a collective thought.

"My children, let us remember the Bosion horde as a wayward generation, nothing like the Botistem of Libertas. One day, as long ago, we may have to face them. Libertas will raise her spear, and her daughters will pour from the folds of her robes as fire from titan core. That is why we must prepare ourselves. That is why we must grow. These halls will not always be enough."

Seth's mind tightened behind his jaw. "Pegassos, do you know what she's talking about?"

His ship didn't answer. Her refit had begun. With her gone, he felt a strange kind of chill, a feeling he could have given many names, where the simplest was loneliness. Managing a crack of a smile, Seth realized that at the head of this kind of gathering, the feeling stank of entitled irony. A short time home and he was already the prince again. Would the Federacy commander of his recent past fade? Who am I, Pegassos?

Mother continued, "We have found a new world. A world like Old Earth, a place lost to humanity, hidden from the spoil of galactic conflict. The planet is full and inhabited with brothers and sisters unaware of humanity's expansion in the stars."

Extending her hand, the world of which Mother spoke appeared in dazzling translucence, the air of its medium vibrating in colors of satisfaction. There were two moons, one large and one small. Lights flickered on the continents and ships broke water on the seas. The skies, cradled in marble clouds, held up planes. The night of space around the world coruscated with satellites trailing each other like pearls on a string. Primitive modernity.

"I would have for us such a world," Mother said, letting her whisper carry to the people. "I would take it before the rest."

A new Earth. Chills and a hundred emotions spilled from the top of Seth's head down into his hands, pulling at his fingers. She spoke of an isolated civilization of untouched humanity, a snapshot of the cyclical fulguration of Man. Mother had found what would amount to a reshaping of empirical power, a galactic gold rush. Many thought such worlds were impossible, a paradox. Earth or any place like it was nothing but legend. For the religious, human beings had lost the right to natural life.

Seth closed his eyes, imagining the conflict ahead. Death's door creaked just a little in his mind. *Time for you to remember who you really are.*

I am an emissary. I am death. He didn't want to be, but he knew it was true. Somewhere in the dark pits of his immortal soul, Seth knew that he had a place in the conquering of this world. Maybe the song hadn't played out, but it was written somewhere in notes the musicians would understand.

"Others will come for this planet," Mother said, still in her speech, "and the people. The human race in its ascended state is a well of undeserved power of destruction. On Libertas, we have the scroll of truth, we carry the wisdom of generations and the power to hold back the tides of Man, the Hordes of Bosion. Stand with me, children, and I will show you how to fight for this world, to stake the claim. As corruption finds us, let the skies over this world burn as the fields of desolation, where all will gather to conflict until victory rings over the lands in harmony of *pure* consensus."

The multitude below began a festival. Music swept the crowds into dancing and cheers. The people danced to the welcoming of a noble cause, one which would claim unto itself the rest of their lives. Seth felt his own life fall to the music, humming like Pegassos as she entuned herself to the Dao before a journey.

"How are you taking the news, my son?" Mother asked, her voice now only his to hear.

He answered in verse, "The proud heart feels not terror nor turns to run, and it is his own courage that kills him."

"Homer," she laughed.

"Who else knows about the planet?"

Mother nodded, a slight, deliberate manifestation of her power. Without warning, her nod transported him to another room.

Seth's surroundings dimmed from the gold of the chamber into a low blue, and he knew that they had gone into the Eye of Libertas, the helm of his mother's great ship. He hadn't seen it for a long time, but some of their best conversations had happened there. From the Eye, she operated the ship as if it were an extension of herself, which included the ability to fold the space inside and go wherever she liked in less than a moment. Sometimes he wondered if she ever truly left the Eye, and if all other interactions with her happened as more of an entangled projection. Most of the time, however, he acknowledged her ability that he didn't possess himself, and carried on as her son. The emissary.

"Some," she said. "My son. My beautiful son." She reached for his face with more affection than he was used to. "Shall we speak of fate? Let me show you."

3

The Eye of Libertas was a window, more than anything else, with the curvature of only a small piece of her pupil shaping a window. Seth stood at this window with Mother, gazing into a star system, outside of which Libertas now stood, and through that system to the planet of Mother's fancy. The planet spun in silent solemnity with its sun's beaming rays wrapping around the amber horizon.

Behind Seth and Mother in the dim lit room, an old man played a piano. Seth hadn't seen the man before, nor was he accustomed to his mother bringing company into the Eye. But the music accompanied the slow turn of the planet's orbit, calling Seth's mind back to when Earth must have looked just like this world. The piano's notes were the wordless voice of a muse to the story of ages past. Seth closed his eyes and drank in the song's complexity. Whoever the man was, he knew how to paint a mental picture with the art of song.

"Who is that man?" Seth asked, part of him trying to relax, the other part clinging to uneasy strings of active nerves.

She ignored his question. "Look how undisturbed this planet is," she said, her hands clasped at her core. "No orbiting empires. Nothing but the purity of human life interacting with the natural biosphere, building and shaping. It's ready for us."

Moving away from the window, Mother summoned a large display of the planet to hover above a waist-high pyramid of floating screens. With her fingers, Seth's mother spun the world like a desk globe to the rhythm of the old man's music.

Seth left the window. "Mother, how do you mean to conquer this world?"

Mother pointed to frameless, holographic images under the hovering globe. "What do you see here?"

Seth searched the images. He brought a few of them close to his face by waving his hand. "The civilization can't be very old. If it has risen naturally, maybe ten thousand years. I doubt that would be the case though."

"Go on."

"No central government. Diverse culture. Population of approximately ten billion, but it only started the breadth of its growth maybe a century ago. Space exploration is limited to lunar or planetary orbit...no, with the exception of drone programs reaching to about as far as the eleventh planet."

He swiped the air, and more images rose out of the pyramid up to his face. "Geopolitically, the balance is off. This is a population ready to destroy itself."

Mother pointed to one of the images. "What does it remind you of?"

"Twenty-first century Earth, more or less. As far as I can tell, anyway. We don't have that much data, apart from literature, of what Earth was really like before it was lost. But these reports talk most about war. There's a spirit of battle in this world."

"There's more truth to that than you know," Mother said, shifting the image of the planet to a three-dimensional graph of yin and yang. "Life exists in this world that exceeds common understanding. The planet has a complex soul. She has a life to it I can feel. Something as real as this music, entangled in the smallest pieces of her core. Her inhabitants, flora and fauna, are more genuinely earthlike than anything in the known galaxy. No terraforming. Six continents, filled with not just life, much of it Old Earth life. Have you ever seen a horse?" She pulled up another image and waved her hand. A life-sized creature of ancient regality galloped around the room and then disappeared.

Seth smiled, a sort of childlike smile that surprised himself. "So, what are we going to do? If it's really on us to save this world, we have to save it from the people, the whole galaxy. We could call the Federacy, set up an alliance–"

His mother stopped him. "The Federacy has already been here." She gestured back to the world in the window, the piano still playing along with it. "They've staked a claim that I can't tolerate."

The tone of the music was lost on Seth for a moment. He folded his arms over an ice-cold brick forming inside him somewhere.

He didn't want to have lived long enough to see the Federacy become his enemy, not after such a long effort at the expense of his peace. He thought about the admiral that gave him the ornate knife. He reached down to where he kept it in a holster in the small of his back. Though a weapon, the feel of the knife there called Seth back to a time when he could trust in the peace of humanity, not the inevitability of its conflict. That was a time of different threats. Maybe he shouldn't have beaten the Bosions so well back then. Without them, who was the new enemy? Every state needed an enemy.

"How long have they been here?" he asked.

"Not long," said Mother. "One exploratory flagship following a probe and the curiosity of a room full of scholars. I feel there are forces at work that may have drawn us here in response to their discovery, something in rise and fall of gravitational song that told me to look, to venture where I'd never been."

The man at the piano interrupted their conversation with the end of his song, rubbing his old hands together from the fatigue of playing for a long time. Getting up from the wooden instrument, he shuffled past Seth and his mother to the great window. The world turned before him, the amber of sunrise giving way to white starshine. Sighing, he pressed his aged palm over the glass.

Seth's mother graced to the man and held him by the shoulder. "What do you see, Orpho?"

"I'm thinking of my younger days," he said. Seth saw a tear welling in one eye in the faint reflection of the glass. The other held a blank and colorless stare. Orpho shuffled a turn to walk away. Before he rounded toward the doors, he disappeared, perhaps rushed away by Mother's power to some other place in the halls of Libertas.

Seth and his mother stood silent for a moment before she spoke. "You would do well to remember his music."

All of Seth's life, he had seen his mother give a new home to special souls. Not only people who worshiped her, but to those who showed insight and new light for her eternal voyage through the stars. Libertas, with the Botistems, could help them live an enlightened journey. Their genetics did not offer them the same immortality, but those she found worthy could live here, enlightened. "I see," they would often say. But something did seem different about this Orpho. Seth decided he would remember the music.

"Earth was like this," Mother whispered, palming the same spot as Orpho had, her breath fogging the glass. She searched as though to find the memory left in the print of his hand. "I will make this our home, Seth. Our New Earth. Kardu, as some have already said."

"A fitting name."

She regained her posture. "When the Federacy finds us, they will reject me because of who I am. I am a queen, Seth. Queen of the Heavens. Ashetarai. *Mother*. And I am also Libertas."

Ashetarai. Few ever spoke her name. Hearing it now invoked the name's power. He felt it inside him, a part of his identity reluctant to awake. "Will you have me fight for you? I hesitate to face my Federacy brothers and sisters. There must be a way to ally with them, to use me, a commander, as liaison."

His mother began a small pace. "We will try. But out here, far from the Bosion war, they fear you and me. The Federacy Admirals may have let you bring our Botistem power close to the Bosion hordes where they needed it. They understood their need for you. But these explorers won't allow our might here at the edge. No, too much distrust. Too much history—"

She was cut off. The image of the planet over the pyramid changed into a Federacy ship. Seth recognized the design, a military flagship from the Federacy meant for deep space exploration. The ship looked older than some he had seen, but it still held thousands of people onboard and could handle itself alone in the darkest parts of the galaxy. They hadn't taken long to detect the Libertas near the system.

The blue tint of the room changed to red. Libertas sounded the alarm. Below, in other parts of the ship, people would begin preparations for a fight. Seth felt closer to the people on the Federacy ship than he did his mother's followers, but he also knew who he was, who would be the last to stand as age marked the rest for Death and its door with the key left outside. The emissary would inherit that key.

A raspy voice reached Seth's ears. "The FFV *Marshall* broadcasts this message on all frequencies, hailing the war vessel known as the Libertas. Lower your barriers and prepare to comply. Your presence in this region is considered an act of interference to the Federacy protection of a Discovered Human Remnant Colony and violates the New Windsor Doctrine. This region of space belongs to the Federacy of Galactic Autonomy. Your technology is not permitted here as outlined in the Galactic Prohibition of Nanorobotics. In order to prevent unnecessary hostilities, lower your barriers and prepare to comply."

Seth's mother swore and shot a light out of her eyes that broke a panel across the room.

Seth grabbed his temple, swept with grief over how to react. "What do I do, Mother? What are you going to ask of me?"

His mother paced around the pyramid, her eyes glowing with white rage. "We, the gods, will have to fight in the heavens, our champions to take the struggle below."

"Am I a god or a champion?"

The Federacy ship repeated its warning, again and again, and began to deploy fighters.

"What is any man or woman except a journey?" answered his mother, ignoring the warnings. "The champion you were is not what you will become. Fight for me here and I will see that whatever you decide to be, you are forever, my son." She took his shoulders in her hands. He could feel her strength, her influence calming his emotions. He knew he didn't have a choice, but at least with her he wouldn't have to spend an eternity alone, knocking on Death's Door.

Seth knelt, the ice inside him now turning into a fire that matched his mother's eyes. "Mother, in this I am yours. I am always your son. Immortals are never alien to one another. Grant me one chance for peace."

4

— · —

On a bottom wall-bunk behind a gray curtain in the junior bridge officers' quarters on the FFV *Marshall,* young Lieutenant Arty Sato stared in excitement at the image on her mobile. Earth! That's what everyone was calling this beautiful place, a new earth anyway. She wished her aunt and uncle could see it. When she joined the Exploration, she knew it was goodbye forever. Space and time had aged them away into the afterlife before the end of her first voyage here on the *Marshall.* She swiped her finger over the oceans and continents. She'd heard theories that there may have been planets with human life cultivating outside of Galactic civilization, but people believed they were myths. They said any that hadn't been discovered would have died off.

This planet was so beautiful! Its holographic image lit up her little bunk area and she scrolled through its information in youthful delight. The mountain ranges, oceans, beaches, jungles and tundra. Scholars onboard the *Marshall* were already theorizing that civilization on the planet descended from an ark-like ship from Old Earth itself, especially given the evolutionary similarities between much of the wildlife and Old Earth records.

Besides New Earth, some proposed calling the planet Kardu, after the mountains where Noah's Ark landed in ancient literature. The human populations were as diverse as in Old Earth's history, as well. Race, language, and ethnic differences fueled thousands of years of bloodshed in the thickness of greed and distrust. Arty wondered what the Federacy would do, if they would intend to bring the Constitution of Autonomy to them yet, or if ships like the *Marshall* would only watch them undisturbed forever. She felt honored to be a part of the expedition that found this wonderful, old, and magnificent place.

Pulling her hand away from the image, Arty reached for a locket hanging around her neck. A painting of the old Shinto kami Amaterasu sat inside, the sun's rays beaming out behind her thoughtful face. Arty's aunt and uncle told stories of their ancestors in ancient Japan, a holy land blessed and made by the gods. Most of the old traditions were lost to time, but it didn't stop the adoration of the kami and a nostalgic yearning for islands on the lost world. Shinto survived after all. Arty wished she could walk in ancient Japan and feel its mountain air and sun-filled beaches. She grew up on a grain farm on a rocky planet in the middle of the Milky Way's biggest nowhere. Icy rock formations outside the thick walls of her village were all she knew. When she turned 16, leaving her aunt and uncle was hard, but leaving the icy frontier of no future was easy.

"What's that? A necklace?"

Arty tucked the locket back under her uniform and looked up at Lieutenant Lopez who had just thrown open the curtain of her wall-bunk. "Get out of here, Tessa, this is me-time." She grabbed the curtain, but Lopez wouldn't let go.

"If you ain't sleeping then it's we-time. I need to ask you something." Lopez grabbed a chair from a nearby card table and dragged it over to the protest of other junior officers playing a game. The noise grated Arty's tired ears.

"I'm not in the mood to talk about boys right now."

"Boys?" Arty's friend laughed. "I'm here to talk about nuclear physics. I have an exam coming up and I want this reactor job. I'm tired of supervising disgusting marines."

"You should come work with me in Detections." Arty swung

out her legs and grabbed another chair. This time from a card player who had just left to grab more money out of his bunk.

"Hey!"

She ignored him.

"What's the question?" Arty was smiling now, the buzzing excitement of the new planet still inside her.

The two young women talked shop for a minute and the application of the diversification of fuel sources over long voyages, redundancy being key to survival.

"It's almost like a metaphor isn't it?" said Lopez, stretching her back. Her fingertips gripped the back of her head while she pointed her elbow out, a good way to stretch out the t-spine for someone with poor posture, like Lopez.

"Metaphor for what?" said Arty, thinking about thumbing her mobile to check out the planet again.

"Systems to back up systems and documents to back up actions and people to back up ideas," mused Lopez. "Us individuals, we're cogs in the federal wheel. If one fails, send in another. We're built in, cultural redundancy, spreading Federacy love through the known universe."

"You know, I kind of like that," said Arty, chuckling to herself. "Spreading love to a new world."

A viewscreen on the barrack's wall came to life to the interruption of their study. "All hands. Report to station. Report to station. Threat level 5. Threat level 5."

Arty's mobile buzzed and she pulled it out of her pocket. It read in bold letters, "Lieutenant Sato to AIC. Threat level 5."

She sat up, annoyed. Her last rotation ended only three hours ago. They were supposed to give her the night off. "Deak is supposed to have this one!"

"Sure," said Lopez, fitting in an earpiece and tying her boots, "but they wouldn't want him for a level five."

Arty opened the locker next to her bunk and grabbed her uniform, swinging it around her shoulders and giving her pockets a single pat-down for all her inspectable gear. Notebook, field manual, mobile, med-kit, she was ready to go. She checked her side arm and personnel shield on her belt and slid out the barrack's hatch to a crowded hallway leading to the command deck.

"Lieutenant, you're already late." Commander Worley spun around when Arty entered the AIC.

"I was off duty, sir." She grabbed her earpiece out of her shoulder pocket and readjusted her chair.

"There's no such thing," replied the graying, buzz-topped XO with a half-smile. "But we weren't gonna trust second chair on this one. We need the best right now. I'm not hopeful this contact is going to work in our favor." He stormed off to the AIC war table and barked some orders at nervous crewmen.

Across the room, Arty could hear the Captain.

"Lower your barriers and prepare to comply." Captain Meskin spoke into his mobile that linked to the comms. His thick, old eyebrows were clenched into furrowed, deep lines next to beads of sweat dripping down the sides of his face. Arty hadn't seen him this nervous in a long time.

She quickly interfaced her mobile with the Detections terminal. Sergeant Lawal sat next to her, already snapping orders into his headset and ready to assist her, like a personal secretary for organizing information. Arty whispered, "What's going on?!"

"No time for a proper brief in an emergency, right ma'am? Here you go, everything I have so far." He passed her a folder. "It's the *Libertas*. I've never seen anything so big in my life that wasn't some kind of orbital station. It's like someone took a full-sized colony and covered it with a statue, and then some. How did they make that thing? Its composition is practically indestructible, and I don't even know what to make of the barrier readings." His terminal flashed red for a second and he went back to typing and speaking quietly into the headset.

"It's old," Arty replied. She put her hand up to her ear. "Say again, tower three... No excuses! I want those dishes up two hours ago. We need everything we can get on those barriers. No, we're waiting on you. Let me know when you have them, D-Tech 7 out." She could feel Commander Worley's approving half-smile from across the room. It hurt to be the favorite sometimes. Maybe she could sleep tomorrow.

Seth's eyes sparked as he kept his arms folded and moved a hand to turn the pyramid of images. Two galactic powers now had to face off and figure out who would take charge. The flagship wouldn't risk an attack just yet, and they were likely trying to figure out Libertas's unique defenses. *Marshall* command was out if its league. Federacy central government had outlawed any Artificial Intelligence governed system in regard to the use of quantum and nanotechnologies as a precaution in their war with the machines. Libertas, with her technology, contradicted their laws. They couldn't begin to know how unfair the fight was. If anything, though, they had the legends to give them some idea.

He spoke to his mother, "Once they realize they can't get a read on our energy barriers, they will attempt a summit. I say we beat them to it and order one now. We can sit down and talk this out."

Mother turned from where she'd been staring at the world through the eye to the flashing image of the FFV *Marshall* flying above the pyramid of screens. The images below the ship had changed from information on the planet to threat assessments. Seth heard in her breath a wavelength of danger.

"Our 'technology' is not welcome here," she scoffed. The image of the *Marshall* zoomed in, moving through walls and rooms until reaching the Action Information Center, the AIC. An aging captain held a transceiver, unaware he could be seen.

Seth summoned a screen from the pyramid to the front of his face. He used it to reconnoiter the AIC himself. The captain wouldn't know Seth was here, a veteran and protector of Federacy worlds, someone who suffered countless hard-fought journeys in the most hostile parts of the galaxy, all for the Federacy, part of their machine. Memories of conflict, of Bosion horde and comrades long gone climbed the walls of his memory in capillary action while he scanned the younger officers. Some were standing, passing information and buzzing back and forth like insects in a hive. Others were plugged in, sitting at stations as they commanded their own piece of the *Marshall's* function. Seth took notice of a female lieutenant near the main floor, sitting at a terminal, making attempts to coordinate readings of the *Libertas* systems. She operated with near calm demeanor, a natural leadership and striking presence that caught his attention. Sato. Seth would remember her.

Mother looked over to the occupied Seth. "You asked for a chance at peace. Talk to them. I must commune with my ship."

"FFV *Marshall*. Speaking is Commander Seth Caeso of the FFV *Luther*, Champion of Pegassos, and Heir to the Scroll of Libertas, as one speaking in the diplomatic authority of two sovereign galactic powers. *Marshall*, I query the intent and purpose behind your hostile approach on allied forces."

Arty listened to him through the AIC intercom. That voice. She had heard of Commander Caeso as a kind of legend, but one she could hardly believe. A man who fought with supernatural strength, who couldn't be killed, who piloted a ship that could read his thoughts. The legends called him ageless. Old captains like Meskin had probably heard of him as bedtime stories. But he didn't sound old. He sounded so young, so energetic. So familiar.

Shaking off the unprofessional thought tangent, Arty

poured over the *Libertas*'s schematics the sergeant had organized and sent to her terminal. As her team couldn't figure out
the barriers, she turned her attention to the hull. Barriers made
by ships like the *Libertas* were different than Federacy shields.
They adopted energy from sources unfamiliar, or perhaps a
better term would have been well-kept secrets. Most of the
Marshall's information on barriers was spotty anyway, based
on Bosion tech, rather than whatever the *Libertas* was, and up-
dates came only through entangling buoy relay systems from
outdated data packages that in this case would be irrelevant
by the time the *Marshall* could make sense of them. Ultimately,
"barriers" was a canopy of a word meant to cover everything
about a large, sentient ship and what made it hard to hit.

So, on to the hull. In leu of precision, they could always
throw a terrifying and perhaps unethical amount of ordinance
at the ship and hope for the best. Such a strategy had worked in
the past. Warheads for impact, warheads for cyber infiltration,
warheads for energy disruption, the captain could figure it out.
Maybe he could hit the ship when it wasn't ready?

Arty zoomed her terminal's view onto the *Libertas*'s face. It
appeared solid from far away, but Arty wanted to see it close up.
Closer. No. Closer again.

"I'm coming up with nothing, ma'am."

"Shut up, I'm trying to look at something."

Arty calibrated the lens, used her software to enhance the
image into a better resolution, and there it was. Sure enough,
the *Libertas*'s skin didn't look anything like metal plating at
close observation.

"What in the world?" Arty muttered.

The blueish skin oscillated, kind of like a pulse. Arty found
a weird spot on the *Libertas*'s face just under the left eye. Rising
and falling, the spot seemed metabolic, like it was interacting
with something like an aquatic animal with the ocean. But this
crazy lady-ship, alive or not, shouldn't have been interacting

with any medium. She was standing in a freaking vacuum.

The *Libertas* was breathing in the middle of space.

Arty shook her head and zoomed out to look at the face again, the complexity in its features and expression. Small electric tingles pinged at the top of her head, like *déjà vu* mixed with the first bite of something filled with sugar. Familiarity, kind of like with Seth's voice.

"...the safety of our position in this system. The Mother and Queen of Heavens Lady Ashetarai requests parley at these coordinates. Placed between these greater celestial bodies, we'll be well out of the way of the planet, but still in the system."

Arty could hear Commander Worley's complaints at the center of the room and the captain's rebuke, "Bob. Bob! I need that barrier analysis. If we're going to fight I need to know if I can find a way through!"

The approach of Commander Worley's heavy boots against the floor panels snapped Arty back from looking at the hull and onto another report from a specialist and his team on the barriers.

"Lieutenant, what do you have for me? The captain is arranging a summit with the Seth brat. We should arrive there in about an hour. Once this goes south, can we penetrate her barriers?"

Arty looked at the report without getting up, taking a moment to choose careful words. "Sir, she's next level. Like a magic kind of next level. I don't think we're getting readings because I don't think the ship is what we think it is. If you look at what I found on the hull here, it's almost like—"

The Commander cut her off with a curse. "We're all going to die, and so are the people of that planet. You're probably too young to have heard the stories about the *Libertas* that I have. Gods help us all."

Arty reached for Amaterasu under her uniform, still wondering about the sound of a voice and the face of a spaceship.

5

Seth sat at the head of the table onboard the *Tecumseh*, a Federacy ship detached from the FSV *Marshall* that served as a floating convention center. Representing Libertas, he addressed delegates from the *Marshall* in a well-lit room still looking dark in the brown aesthetic of dark-stained, wood-trimmed walls around a large brown table surrounded by uncomfortable chairs. The chairs were padded in all the wrong places. He had parleyed in similar places back when he fought for the Federacy, but usually not at the head of the table. He didn't like it.

Perhaps he had spent too much time alone on Pegassos. He missed her thoughts in his head and the silence of stars dancing in the infinite. Though this room did have a window, at least. He could see Libertas far away. Pegassos still sat parked in her hangar near the statue of Mercury. She would receive new outfitting, new growth and upgrades from the roots up. Even if she were finished, he still had to leave her there as part of the terms of the summit. The *Marshall* provided a shuttle.

Far smaller than Libertas, he could see the *Marshall* flying nearby through the same window at his left. The Federacy flagship, large as it was, looked crude in its vector, never as transfixed as Libertas. In the stillness of Libertas, Seth could see her power. The *Marshall* looked like a ship, was impressive like a ship. Libertas was a goddess, greater than him, greater than his mother, and impossible for words to cover in common language.

"Commander Caeso, as your mother's representative, perhaps you would like to weigh in on the discussion." Captain Meskin motioned to Seth.

Seth leaned forward, elbows on the table, now focusing on the ten men and women around him. Half wore uniforms, and the other half wore business attire. Sometimes it was easy to forget that flagships meant for exploration had civilian command as well. This ship, the *Tecumseh,* when deployed from the *Marshall,* was a civilian ship, which made it a better place for a peace-seeking summit. The ground, at least in principle, was neutral from military authority. Still, Seth had come wearing his sleek, dark battle armor. He wondered how they saw him in it, if he looked as different from them as Libertas did from the *Marshall.*

Mother had chosen not to come. She never left Libertas.

Seth responded to Captain Meskin's invitation, "Thank you, Captain, men and women of the board. Now, it is my understanding that under Federacy Law, my mother is within her rights to stake equal claim in this system. We are out of Federacy territory, and you have no wartime interests here in your fight against the Bosion machines."

"Of which I understand you are a veteran. Thank you for your service," said a civilian woman.

Seth glanced at her. He meant to show appreciation for her interruption, but her eyes flicked away. She looked embarrassed, like she realized that she had interrupted. If she had doubled down on the interruption, she might have succeeded in pushing him off his game, give her people an edge in the wordy game of chess they were about to play. However, maybe she wasn't here to play chess. Maybe her scholarly interest in this little planet in the middle of the galaxy's forgotten turn gave her no position except an innocent one. All of a sudden, part of Seth wished he could be her, not the man vying for rights to conquer with Federacy bombs bearing down on his home.

Holding back a sigh, he pushed on, continuing in mask of stride, "The same could be said if my mother were a representative of the Aldebaran Empire or even the Syrran Acolytes, or any other Galactic power. The Federacy has no reach here. We don't see the *Marshall* as any authority above a well-armed and over-staffed scouting vessel. In short, I move that the hostile nature of your approach on the *Libertas* is unwarranted, and a dangerous insult."

A man spoke. He sat at the other end of the table, next to Captain Meskin. He called himself the chairman. He folded his hands casually. "Commander Caeso. We recognize you, your service, and the privilege of your title in our chain of command. You speak well." He pointed at the table, as if marking it as a place to put his remarks. "However, just as it won't forget your heroics, this board also cannot forget your mother's history of conquest in other parts of the galaxy. She has destroyed entire systems in her own name. Were it not for our common enemy, I doubt any alliance would ever have come between her and the Federacy. She knows this. Is this why you've come for this world? Is your mother expanding? We're drawing historic lines here. What's happening now is absolutely of Federacy concern. Damn the territorial rights."

Seth felt himself frown. His rhetoric wasn't hitting the right mark. "With respect, Mr. Chairman, if you're here to discuss blood on the record, the Federacy isn't without its secret wrongs, is it?"

The chairman pointed at the table again, but Seth was tired of the interruptions. "Ask me sometime," he said, ice in the breath behind his words. "Ask me what your Federacy did by my hand. There were reasons they asked for me, and not all of them were Bosion." Seth stared into the Chairman's eyes, feeling their brightness as his inner emotion grew more intense. The chairman's eyes watered. At last he looked away, sneezing like he'd just taken on a staring contest with a sun. Several at the table gasped.

"Guards," someone stammered.

Seth took a breath to calm himself and held up a peaceful hand.

"I serve the Federacy," he went on. "I still do. Because I believe in your... our... ideals. I oppose the threat of Bosion advance. I believe in the free autonomy of planets. The Federacy is built on noble principles, documents, and pledges that make empires shake. But I hope you can understand, ladies and gentlemen. You've got my back against a wall here. Is this a fight you think you can win?"

No guard moved, no mouth objected.

"My mother demands that you leave this star system, as it is now claimed under the Scroll of Libertas. I can give no alternative."

Several voices protested in quick puffs of hot air but were subdued by Captain Meskin's gruff tone. There, Seth was wondering when the real voice of authority, the one behind the guns, was going to speak.

"Commander," Meskin said, "I'm going to speak to you, not as an officer of higher command, not as a man of war, but as an advocate. Men of war draw lines, give ultimatums. I'm going to speak plainly, and on behalf of citizens of the human race of not any faction yet recognized by this table. What are we calling this world now?" He gestured to one of the civilians.

"Kardu."

"Kardu. I wonder what the people of the little planet call themselves. We have big ships and missiles, advanced robotics." Meskin pointed to Seth. "But we're not them. We don't hold the ancestral bond of sacrifice and blood in the brick and mortar. We are foreigners here. Aliens. So, ladies and gentlemen, let's talk about what's fair to all of us here, in this room, *and* all the people down there."

"I'm listening," said Seth.

"Commander, the only way we will leave this system would be under the assurance, the guarantee, that the *Libertas* would also leave, that no conquering power would ever mess with Kardu again. We could leave the planet and its population to the fate of their own evolution. Independent cultural choices."

Captain Meskin shook his head, like he already thought his good idea was a bad one. "However, you and I both know that the people we represent will come back. Other, less kind governments will find a way here, too. The planet is discovered, marked. History as far back as Columbus on the beach of America can tell us what that means. It means our blood goes in the mix now too. Federacy doctrine puts us delegates of faraway frontiers in the right, and we must stake our claim. We must stake it now, without regard to our safety, whatever 'odds' we may have in the fight. As representatives of our government, we declare that it is the duty of the FSV *Marshall* to dig into this ground here and not move. Be it our victory, or our grave."

Seth studied Meskin's truth. The captain wasn't wrong. Neither was Seth's mother. Here was a good man, the kind of good that made for a stubborn fool. Young, despite the lines that wisdom bore into his face. "Captain, sir," Seth acknowledged, "I agree with you. Other governments will come. More will want a piece of New Earth. We are the first of a generational conflict, one that can't be fought on the ground, but here in the sky."

"Then what is your plan here?" Captain Meskin barked, dropping the calm in his voice for the command of volume. He stood from his chair, knocking a cushion with the back of his knees. "We are here to study this world, to reach out the hand of human fellowship with minimal interference. Your mother means to conquer it, to conquer a planet of ten billion people! Your technological interference will alter the face of the world just as any war would. Don't try to deny it. We are looking at the pure legacy of Old Earth. Conquering here shouldn't be done. It cannot be done. Appealing to the Commander of the Federacy I see before me at the head of this table, I implore you set the precedent. Leave this system. Begin a legacy of peace and leave the land to the scholars. Leave because I believe you know that it's the right thing to do. Don't give in to the promises of the sword."

Seth opened his mouth to speak. Words clawed at the walls of his mind like a webbed hand on aquarium glass. In the end, he didn't need to reply. Another delegate had arrived.

"Promises?" Mother's voice snuck into the conversation. She appeared behind Seth. He could not only hear her but feel her influence.

Captain Meskin gasped, reaching a trembling hand for the back of his chair.

Seth tried not to project his own surprise. He should have known she might make an entrance. He got out of the chair and moved to her side, feeling less outnumbered. Mother must have projected herself from a tether in the Crown of Libertas, a place she often went alone and where her power was strong. From there, she could ignore the limitations of dimension. She was on the *Tecumseh*, but she was also not on the *Tecumseh*. It was not a state of reality familiar to other people. They would simply think she had transported herself, or that they were dreaming.

"A sword is a thief. Only words contain promise. What my son has told you is in accordance with fact. Captain Meskin, your nobility could use a course correction. You've acknowledged my sword, but what do you know of the promise in the song of a living world?" Mother began to pace around the table. Her feet traced the floor with graceful license. "There may be a chance for harmony yet. We'll see who is willing to follow the score."

Captain Meskin sat to get out of her way and looked like he was about to speak, but he kept silent. Seth could hear trembling breath from around the table. Parley was over. His mother had brought the carrot. Too bad no one knew its flavor was also the stick.

With flowing robes, glow in the contour of her skin, Mother made her way around the table with the air of a goddess. Every eye in the room had to look at her, had to be afraid of her, the kind of fear that follows admiration like the shadow behind a flickering star. In the sound of her voice, the scent of her perfume, the invisible mist of her Botistem aura, the Queen of the Heavens worked the small crowd of fluttering hearts.

Seth cringed a little, tensing a few extra muscles to hide the discomfort trying to disperse up into his face. He eyed the scene as one in the wings of a magic show. If his mother could read his mind, she would probably have rolled her eyes. *Centuries old, Seth, and you're still a child. Fools are variable pieces to broader designs. Reason not the process. Do you think you know a better way than mine?*

She was as much a voice in his own head as she was in theirs. But he knew she was right. She always was. That was part of the magic. *Fine, Mother. Let's do this the easy way.*

A weighty intelligence write-up bore down on Arty's hand as she approached Commander Worley on the bridge. He had left the AIC to work with the helm and guns in Captain Meskin's absence. The bridge also had a better view around the ship. A lieutenant always stood by as helmsman so the commanding officer could post in the AIC for intelligence, but Commander Worley preferred to take leadership up here. He wanted his figurative hands at the wheel, like a captain on an old boat in a frothy sea. But Commander Worley wasn't a legend of the sea, just a seasoned man in a floating air bubble in vacuum, keeping his arms folded and one curved finger over his lips while his cloudy eyes squinted at a small tabletop screen.

Before Arty could hand him the papers, the Commander barked out another curse. "It's her! She wasn't supposed to be there! What's the point of neutral ground when your enemy can do that?"

Arty looked at the screen and saw a magnificent woman pacing around a table. The captain was there, but didn't look himself, like a combination of fear and admiration had overcome his demeanor. He sat down as though ashamed. At the head of the table, on Meskin's right, she could see Commander Seth Caeso with the familiar voice. He had a face that belonged to the voice. His body was tall and strong, and covered in black armor. The commander looked like a soldier of the night, a man who might prefer the shadows but couldn't hide from destiny, couldn't dodge the mantle of long experience. Caeso joined his mother where she faced Captain Meskin across the table. The camera view cycled as a technician searched for a better image.

"I have your report, sir," Arty interrupted.

Commander Worley didn't move his finger from his lips as he turned to face her. His eyebrows curved, signaling she could speak.

"I do think we could cause damage past the barrier. Historically, the penetrating power of human weaponry has always surpassed the capability of armor and shields. It's easier to break something than protect it. However, I'm not optimistic that this is a fight we could win. Our first barrage would have to be indiscriminate. Maybe we'll damage something vital, maybe we won't. The big girl's alive, and like the Bosion ships, can heal herself. The *Libertas* is too big and well equipped with evolving technology we don't understand."

Commander Worley took the papers. "I appreciate your confidence, and I'll use your analysis to equip the proper firing solution. This will turn into fight. Here, you have my permission to listen in."

Arty synced her mobile and earpiece to the table and

watched next to Commander Worley, hearing his uncomfortable breath. It was cheesy to admit, but she saw something of herself in the man. He had mentored her, and was the closest thing she knew to a father. The captain was more of just a captain, someone to admire from up in the cheap seats.

Onscreen the Mother's voice resounded into her subconscious with a similar familiarity to Commander Caeso's, speaking to itchy parts of her brain. Biting her cheek, she tried to ignore the feeling. Looking at the people sitting at the table on the *Tecumseh*, Arty wondered if they felt the same. The mysterious woman sure seemed to hold their attention. No one had yet seemed to have made any counterarguments.

"I fly the winds of the Dao. Libertas has led me to this world, a world which your scholars will tell you is riding at the brink of downfall. The human race is a long story of irresponsibility born of divisibility. Government, tribe, race, politics, religion... collective self-interest. All facilitate the inevitable demise. That is what is happening on this planet now. It is what has happened everywhere the human race has touched."

The people sitting around the table kept silent. Arty put her finger to her ear and turned up the sound on her earpiece. Feedback on the microphones and the static of heightened tension filled her ears with noise that for whatever reason made her think of blue.

"Let's face facts," Mother said. "The Federacy is poorly equipped to handle the opposition that will come from around the galaxy, the greed and might of distant empires. A conventional war would absolutely spread to the surface of the planet. The fighting would poison its surface and the world would die."

Commander Worley grunted.

"We must also consider the threat of the inhabitants to themselves, those lesser than we gods."

"What are you suggesting?" Captain Meskin blurted awkwardly. His forehead had beads of sweat forming at his weak hairline and his voice sounded like a person of his age attempting an extra rep on a pullup bar at positive G. It seemed he had started to shake off the Mother's shock and charm enough to try and debate again.

"Suggest?" Mother walked through the table. "I never suggest." The fabled woman took the captain's face into both of her hands and bent toward him so their faces were almost touching. The camera switched so she could see both of their faces clearly. The moment was intimate. It was also wrong.

Arty's captain began to shake. She could see a change in his face like some kind of light turned on. Sharp, quick breaths left his mouth like laughter, panting at just less than the pace of a panting dog. Arty wanted to throw up.

In the foreground of the monitor, Commander Caeso stayed upright, almost not looking. All she could see of Seth was his back, but Arty thought she could see his muscles cringe. Centuries of time fighting for her people, and now he watched the alliance come undone like an obedient little boy. The admiration inside her began to spoil.

At Arty's side, Commander Worley began giving orders to the bridge crew. "Helm, set angle of attack, starboard side to target. Give our guns a wide angle for a sweep. The captain is compromised. Action stations!"

"Action stations!" Echoed around the room with the lieutenant at the helm shouting orders. The officers and crew of the bridge took to their duties, crisp and calm, like going to war happened every day. But it didn't happen every day. The *Marshall* was a symbol of civilization. Civilization should have meant peace.

"Gods," Commander Worley muttered.

Arty held herself at the screen, unable to look away. She should go back to the AIC. She should help. There wouldn't be time now, though. Captain Meskin had lost his directive, compromised, still shuddering on the screen while the mother phased her tiny robots into his brain. Commander Worley commanded the bridge to fire on the *Libertas*.

The fatalistic fool, Arty thought. He might score some key hits, but she compiled the report herself.

The *Marshall* would not last.

Seth watched Mother's hands on the captain's face. Botistem light passed through the conduits of her fingers and lit Meskin's eyes. On Libertas, the people called this the Anointing, when a person experienced the symbiosis of man and machine for the first time. As one born in symbiosis, Seth had never experienced an anointing, but he knew something of the feeling, like when he stepped from cold space into his mother's ship, or all the times Pegassos healed him from battle. This was a vital part of the Scroll, to give the enemy the taste of an alternative.

Feeling the muscles in his back and legs tense, Seth thought about how he hadn't anointed anyone himself. Perhaps one day. A part of him accepted that, another part of him rejected it. Watching the light dance out the pockets of the captain's eyes, Seth realized not for the first time that he was afraid of his mother. He was afraid of the part of her that lived in himself. Perhaps someday he would rule from the Crown of Libertas. One day he would project himself through a table.

The captain gasped in euphoric astonishment. "I see! Oh Lords I see!"

Seth never knew what they saw, and no one could ever tell him. There were secret doors he couldn't open. Most, he imagined, involved the space between a what made a man live and what cosmic force took that life away. Something had to be there, or the Botistems would never show it. Seth didn't know them to compute anything but truth. Lies don't belong in the code of synthetic beings, however sentient. Lies must be a human thing. Botistems must have chosen humans in part for the symbiotic exchange of truth for untruth. It could give them faith. *I see,* they all said. Huh.

Mother turned to the others at the table. They continued to watch in hypnotic focus. She kept a loving grip on Captain Meskin's shoulder. "Citizens of the Federacy. I offer you a chance to redeem humanity. Fight for me here in the skies. Aid me in holding back our enemies. Under my command, in great alliance, our ships will create a home here. Children of Libertas and the FFV *Marshall* will be the balance that wakes the secrets of Kardu. The course of civilization in our universe will change. Wouldn't you like to feel this way forever?"

The *Marshall.* What was happening on the *Marshall?* There had been radio silence. They would have to have been monitoring in here. The cameras were obvious. The hair on Seth's neck started to raise, like biological cell and Botistem alike were trying to tell him that something was amiss.

Sure enough, small lights appeared in the great window, popping out of guns along the broad length of the great ship that housed them. The FSV *Marshall* had opened fire on his home.

He rushed to the window and watched the lights. Ominous fireflies at this distance, Libertas ignored them, pointing her spear downward. "Mother, it's a full battery," said Seth, the pitch in his voice elevating. "This firing solution could decimate a continent. I've seen it before. People are going to die."

In an instant, his mother was upon him, taking his shoulder. Her voice choked in his ear, only slightly, but with real emotion. "I gave them this chance for you." She stroked his hair and turned him to her, looking into his eyes with glistening sorrow. "Go now, my beautiful boy. There isn't time. Fly to Kardu. Prepare a following for me there. Don't come home. Libertas has told me of a work we can do, but not now."

Seth separated himself from her. "Mother. My ship. My home. I have nothing."

"You have a mother's love. You have a purpose. It was always going to be this way." She faded away, back through the folds of space to where she was tethered. "Find me when it's time."

Seth watched the rockets, entire light minutes away, fly toward Libertas and heard the people around the room scream. As she left, the hypnosis wore off. They came out of it like addicts from a drug. A woman tried to grab his leg. He shook her away and left her on the floor to grovel her sobbing pleas to the plastic fibers. From ecstasy to rags, not even her nice attire could allow her any dignity now. He saw her through his battle gaze, the one that overtook him when he shouldn't feel. *I'm sorry,* he could have said. But apologies weren't for the damned.

"Damn you, Mother," he said to the glass. "You've left me to die. If not here, then in my soul."

Before the rockets could hit, her queen fully aboard, Libertas sprang to life. No longer frozen as a monument, she outstretched her massive arms. Instead of turning to fight, she pulled a spherical distortion of space and time around her. The rockets and shells that threatened her stretched and the light of them extinguished as they disappeared into the warp. Alive, and surreal, the great ship surrounded herself with blackness and the bright, streaming outline of event horizon. Only matter allowed would be able to cross it.

The *Marshall,* unfit for proximity to such gravity play, careened toward the distortion and started to buckle.

Libertas had employed her time drive to create a special kind of wormhole. Libertas and her children, like Pegassos, used the drive to travel through space. It functioned like a needle on a record or a water turbine, harnessing the flow of time underneath to generate a steady stream of energy. No fuel, no antimatter or fusion reactions. That was the secret to the Life of Libertas, her tether to the bulk of higher dimensions. When applied with force, she could rupture spacetime, crumpling the flow of the universe and consuming anything caught nearby.

The helpless *Marshall* cracked. Air, cargo, and people spilling into lifeless space. Seth was blocked from empathy. All he could do was watch and know that someday he would wish to forget this.

Catching Seth off guard, Captain Meskin grabbed him from behind. Hysterical, the desperate man shoved Seth backwards onto the table, pushing him with his weight. He smelled like steamy sweat.

"My ship," he spit into Seth's face. "My family. You'll rot in Hell for this, you and your cowardly mother. You inhuman bastard." The effects of the anointing had all worn off. Love and loyalty for doomed officers and crewmen fueled the captain's rage. Seth could see everything righteous in the transparency of the captain's face. His skin shook, all the wisdom underneath it burning in the fever of a fight. Choosing a marble coaster off the table for a weapon, Captain Meskin raised it over Seth's face. Seth knew if he didn't move, the captain would try to kill him. Too bad it would take more than that.

Seth took the aged man's collar and threw him, sending him bloody through glass to a drinking bar. Caught in a heap, the captain desisted. The fight in him was gone, his legacy lost to the metal that began to twist overhead.

Gravity from the phenomenon caught up with the *Tecumseh* at the speed of light. The wormhole had found them. The framing of the room seemed to scream along with the people. Sounds of horror, of pleading, of final expressions of faith to unseen gods. The *Marshall* broke first. Seth stepped over the sobbing woman on the floor. She made no attempt to go with him.

Arty ran down the *Marshall*'s halls past a dozen other soldiers. One man in front of her slumped against a wall and started to pray out loud. He mentioned his ancestors. Almost running into him, Arty hoped they were listening.

Adrenaline pumped into her legs and kept telling her to run, even if she didn't have a place to go.

Moments before, she had been on the bridge with Commander Worley. He gave the order to fire when it became clear that the Mother onboard the *Tecumseh* was a threat to the captain. Worley fired first for tactical advantage, maybe some fighting chance, but no one anticipated the wormhole. Arty watched out the bridge window in chilling horror as the *Libertas* moved, like a living being, outstretching her arms, spear and scroll in hand with space folding around her in a dance of stars. As the enemy ship slipped into the blackness, Arty's world began to shake.

The *Marshall* could warp space for traveling faster than light, but it took a whole list of procedural preparations and valuable antimatter to make it happen. The *Libertas* just did something entirely different. She didn't just warp space; she manipulated it into a cocoon. With battle hardpoints deployed and the size of the singularity, Arty knew the *Marshall*'s structure would fail. The Federacy ship groaned like a medieval man stretched out on a rack. Without thinking, Arty just started to run. Commander Worley told her to get to the AIC, and that's where she told her legs to go, but what was the point? Her home was coming apart.

The floor whipped underneath Arty's running feet. Her boot tried to reach the ground but missed. Perturbed, hyperextended, her knee screamed when it missed the ground. The floor behind her came up and chucked her hard into the ceiling. Her back and head hit the metal, bouncing her away with ears ringing. In the disorientation, Arty realized that gravity was gone. The mechanism of it was broken. For that to go, the ship must have ruptured somewhere important. Grabbing a wall, she held herself in place long enough to gather some sense.

"God, or gods, if you're there, don't let me die." The locket in her shirt clung to her sweaty skin and wet clothes. "Ancestors be with me. Find me, please."

A soldier flew by. His uniform was half burned off and he bounced through the hall more like a dishrag than a man with bones. He must have been near an explosion. As drilled, Arty activated her personal shield from her belt. A wave of kinetic energy washed over her body and clothing, shaking the fat in her legs and chest. A rupture appeared in the ceiling, traveling down the length of her safety bubble like the end of a nightmare. The opened vacuum's jaws, ready to swallow her up. In a blink, winds of escaping air took Arty out of the ship into a streaking whirlwind of stars, debris, and wispy clouds.

In the back of her mind, she knew her shield didn't carry extra oxygen. This is where she would die.

Underneath her, the *Marshall* groaned one last time. From the belly of its redundant workings, the ship exploded into a quiet burst of flame, shimmering like a tiny sun toward the wormhole's open arms of oblivion.

6

— . —

Arty woke in a gut-bending spin. She had blacked out in the blast. As she gained enough awareness, the first thing she felt was surprise that she had woken up at all. Panic and motion sickness soon followed, making her close her eyes again. That's what the drill instructors taught her in training. If she closed her eyes, she would have no reference to her surroundings and could minimize some of the discomfort of centrifugal force. Ignorance was bliss, as the old saying went. Not seeing where she was going felt a lot better than throwing up in her shield. There wasn't any room for vomitus in a shield. For all she knew, it would come out as blood if her hollow organs had ruptured.

She felt fine, though, apart from the spinning. Arty spread out her arms. That slowed her down a little.

Personal shields like this were meant for immediate rescue in the case of an accident or... this. Technicians who worked outside of the ship needed environmental suits. Arty's work, however, only required this shield, which she now realized only delayed the inevitable. Still with her eyes closed, she thought about crying but couldn't find the tears. Instead, she just felt the pull of an end, highlighted by her spin. Images in her mind brought her back to her aunt and uncle long gone, then to her ship, now a glowing nuclear ember, and all her friends that were probably onboard, evaporated, reduced to old elements of stardust.

The *Tecumseh* might have survived, she realized. Maybe

Captain Meskin and Commander Caeso made it along with the civilians. But she doubted it. Maybe Commander Caeso betrayed them all when his mother dragged their home into a wormhole. Arty couldn't ignore the obvious. The *Marshall* was gone. Everyone was gone. The *Tecumseh* was probably gone, too, or it would be. Where could it go at this range? The planet, maybe, if it didn't suffer any damage. It must have, though. The crazy woman had used the fabric of reality like a tablecloth to clear off the dishes.

Arty's thoughts spun faster than her body, which seemed to be spinning less now. "How am I still breathing?" she asked out loud. To figure it out, she opened her eyes, done with forcing themselves shut. She had slowed down enough from keeping her arms out that she expected less of a vertiginous sky but instead found that she was slowing down more than what should have been natural. The churning in her stomach was feeling better, too.

Uncertain how, she screamed out.

As if in response, a calming sensation wrapped around her like a blanket, but under her skin. The feeling surprised her enough to know that it didn't come from herself. Unless it was the lack of oxygen. Maybe that's how asphyxiation would get her, a comfortable bleed out of awareness.

She asked again, "How am I still breathing?"

Around her, the *Marshall* had left pieces of dust and debris. She could also see the occasional frozen body, each looking like the sad part of a space thriller. Everything seemed to be holding still, having drifted past the point where the physics of objects near the wormhole made any sense. The frozen thing wasn't what she might have expected, though. Nothing was spaghettifying.

She wasn't part of anything else, though. Arty drifted backwards through the boneyard, independent and accelerating with a mysterious thrust she could see more than feel. Unsure of a lot now, she moved one of her hands to her face.

"Is this real?"

The energy shield surrounding her hand was shimmering, as expected, but with a higher intensity than she was used to.

"Keep an eye on the color of your shield," her academy instructor had drilled into her and the other cadets. "The brighter, the more time you have to live."

The one she tested on back then hadn't been this bright. She wiggled her fingers. Every muscle felt real. And the stars, they were brilliant, clearer than she had ever seen them. Had she ever dreamed of stars?

The soothing feeling inside her seemed to want her to do something else with her hand. She stretched it out ahead. The feeling said push. She pushed, blind to everything but new instinct, and a burst of light came out of her, spinning her upside and face-forward. The light felt good, like energy she hadn't known how to channel before but waited inside, waiting for the right feeling, the right moment.

"Oh, crap."

The wormhole she had nearly forgotten gaped in front of her like a celestial cave. The shield around her body shimmered even more as she picked up speed, accelerating toward it with deliberate pacing. The stars around the wormhole passed beyond her view as she moved at unimaginable speeds, not feeling any of the momentum, which should have crushed her lungs, until she could only see the elegance of a great nothing because the hole was too big to be able to look at anything else.

"This is it," she said out loud. "I'm going to die in a black hole made by a magic spaceship."

She wanted to panic, but she couldn't muster the energy beyond stringing curses that strung out behind her in the event horizon. *Oh Gods*, Arty surrendered. Oblivion didn't look so bad for a second. She had lot of people to join there. What would dying feel like? Was it scary? Was it already happening?

Her thoughts carried her back to something her aunt had told her about another world of a mirror universe.

She was small enough at the time that her legs kicked against the kitchen drawers as she sat on the counter while her aunt cleaned off dishes with a wet rag and water from the poor faucet. "Tell me again about the mirror universe," small Arty implored.

Her aunt wiped her cheek with a damp wrist, taking a quick break from cleaning. "It's where the kami live," she said.

"In the rivers and the trees," marveled Arty.

"Yes," said her aunt. "And in the mountains and the seashores, still on the earth where our ancestors worshipped them. They have Japan. When we pray to them, they also have us. We can please them wherever they are."

"I'm going to that universe someday," Arty mused. "I'm going to find the world of the kami."

Her aunt flicked Arty with water. It was warm, and made her smile, just like her aunt's words. "Your parents are there. We'll all go and meet them one day."

Drifting closer and closer to the blackness, Arty realized the warmth still on her cheeks wasn't water from the dishes. Hot tears were falling down her cheeks, free of any training or fear that may have held them in place. Silent tears for a silent goodbye. They escorted her into the darkness.

Don't fear the darkness, a voice, hardly distinguishable, told her thoughts. *Wait for the light.*

The dark of the wormhole faded like a shroud made from small shadowy fibers. At the other side, the *Libertas* came into view.

All at once, now inside the wormhole that should have killed her, Arty found herself and the ever-brilliant shield in the neck of a portal between spaces. Death had not found her here, but more life instead. Arty wasn't in control, just a passenger on one weird train.

Coming into focus, the *Libertas* stood with arms, wings, scroll, and spear outstretched in a sea of astronomical wonder. Stars and galaxies beyond danced in waves through the fabric of space, visible to Arty, whirling in rippling tides. The *Libertas* poised in contrasting motionlessness at the center. The great ship looked even more beautiful in this place, with the blue of her features now radiating full color, more alive than ever.

Arty had concerned herself over conventional things before, like barriers and armaments. Sure, she might have thought the *Libertas* was something else, but now she understood enough to no longer see a ship, to not think inside that box anymore. Here, outside the pinned viewpoint of Arty's former reality, she saw in Libertas a beautiful woman, a goddess surrounded by the ritualistic dance of heavens. The beauty caught Arty in the gut, surfacing from her emotional depth in heaving sobs of close relation to a good laugh.

Good thing Lopez wasn't with her right now. She was always a tease about crying. Arty would give it right back. But who was she kidding? Lopez would be a mess right now. She'd be overthinking the whole thing, like the way a light was growing behind Libertas's face. The scene looked like Amaterasu in Arty's locket. Arty's attention moved to nothing else and thoughts of her friend drifted behind like lost debris. The glow was mesmerizing.

The light grew until it started to overcome everything. Arty didn't know if she was having a vision or if she really was flying beyond the wormhole, flying into spaces her mind shouldn't be able to process. Either way, she gave herself to the light and let it take her further into the mystery. Not surrendering at this point could only hurt.

Follow, child. Arty heard the voice again, this time distinctly feminine. *This light is for you.*

The light strung apart, once again reminding Arty of fabric, and Libertas was lost before her. A world appeared in its place.

The planet was blue and green with vast continents and clouds like soft cotton blankets swaddling marble. There were no ships or satellites around this sacred-looking place, just green Terra. Arty knew what world it was, the turn of each piece of land something she recognized.

She was looking at Earth. The real Earth.

The woman's voice spoke into her mind again. The voice had an acoustic grandeur, even in just her thoughts. *What was lost to space has always been known to time, higher plains housed in the Dao. We cannot take you there, but we wanted you to see.*

"I see," Arty answered. "I see, but I don't understand. Who are you?"

The voice didn't answer.

The silhouette of a woman appeared in the dancing sky in front of the planet. It was a hazy vision of transparent color. The shape seemed to lift her hand and shake her head as Arty approached.

We can't keep you awake any longer, the voice said. *Remember what you saw here when it's time.*

Space grew lighter in Arty's vision, everything fading, consciousness leaving her for involuntary slumber.

No, she thought. *Let me stay.*

Do you wish to die?

What?

Death is just another door. We can open it for you but not accompany you there.

Arty thought about the question. If this wasn't death, as she had half-surmised, then that mystery would be too much for today. A moment, or perhaps a lifetime, ago, she thought she had been ready.

No, she told the voice. *Save me. Please save me.*

Earth disappeared, and the woman's shape lingered through sinking eyelids. Counterweights of exhaustion overcame Arty's consciousness. She let herself fall into white, endless nothing. For the moment, she didn't seem to care whether she woke out of this journey. She wouldn't have a choice either way.

Seth braced himself against the instrument panel as his stolen, broken shuttle plummeted through the atmosphere of the planet the council had called Kardu. He still didn't know if he liked calling it that, but he supposed that he would find out the real name of the planet soon enough. The shuttle tossed and roared, protesting the maneuver. He poured energy from himself like lightning through the maneuvering panel and into every part of the little ship, trying to save it.

"Just a little more."

Thanks to Seth's power, the energy shield held around the wings and the rest of the hull, sustaining a fiery glide. He would make it, but at higher speeds than he had hoped. He had aimed the small ship so that it would splash down in a large lake, a tiny sea in the middle of the desert. The guidance computer, now overwhelmed with energy surges, had protested. Seth resorted to manual aim through the atmosphere, long, hot flames burning in front of him in the viewer.

The computer relented, and Seth pushed on as distant landscape approached with surprising magnitude. Hills became mountains, dots became buildings, a flat skin of blue grew into a lake and then–

Darkness.

Seth regained consciousness with his Botistems reigniting his senses with electric urgency. That was the first discomfort of Kardu. The second discomfort, after the shock, was how he couldn't breathe. His surroundings felt a little like space as his nerves tried to focus. He felt warm, also cold, and he couldn't move without feeling like he was under…. water. He was underwater. His lungs seized with panic. *Up, up, swim UP.* Direction was a difficult calculation, however. He couldn't figure out which way was up. Everything was dark, and agonizing pressure made his ears feel like they would explode.

The shuttle was dark. His memory started to deliver some missing detail—he was still inside the shuttle, probably at the bottom of the lake by now. That's why he couldn't see. Seth took a moment to further gather himself. He didn't need to breathe, probably not for a long time. No need to panic just yet. He could push aside the discomfort. Later, he could allow himself to accept it. For now, he needed to make calm decisions and take in all the information he could.

The water around him tasted like iron. It was his blood. He really must have been knocked around at impact. Using his hands, he worked his way forward to find the walls that beat him up.

Finding a cabin wall, Seth navigated down the smooth plastic until he found a hatch. He thought about forcing it open with light from his hands but instead found a handle for explosive release. The force of the explosion knocked the door loose and kicked him back into the wall. A corner of something jolted a nerve behind his arm and tweaked his back.

Still, finding an opening was a victory. He ignored the pain. New wounds like this would fix themselves. Now how about the problem of up? He shook off the jolt and kicked out the open hatch, following rising bubbles brushing his skin that made their way toward the surface. A bubble's buoyancy couldn't lie.

On the surface, Seth breathed in sunlight, heat, and gravity all at once, a heavy sensation that met him with the friendliness of a hammer meeting the curve of a bent nail. He crawled out of the water and up the rocky sand. The wet grains were coarse and unclean, nothing like he'd felt in a very long time. The air was different, too. The thing about recycled air he'd been accustomed to was that it was comfortable, temperature regulated. Gravity was also different here, constant. The whole experience gave a bad first impression. Seth brought himself to his feet, uncertain what level of strength to employ. He'd expended so much power in that blasted shuttle.

The sand moved under his feet as he gave them more of his weight, giving way. *Look out, the alien is here,* it seemed to say. *He's really heavy.*

Remembering the view of the landscape, the topographical data reviewed before the shuttle really started to break apart, Seth turned east. There should be a city a day's walk from the lake. He would find people there, people who might have seen his falling shuttle. One heavy step at a time, his entire body wounded and trying to heal, Seth set out to find the city.

Every second, power seeped out of his deteriorating Botistems. In the past, he always had Pegassos or Libertas to replenish them. Now he was stuck, stuck on a world without his mother, without his rank, without his ship, far away from the source of his immortality. Stupid shuttle. Stupid *Marshall.* He couldn't know how much power and longevity he had in him, or how he might replenish it.

The desert opened in front of Seth with jaws of uncertainty. *I have found Hell where I sought Paradise.* Seth inscribed his thoughts into the air with feather-quilled imagination: Welcome to Hell, you finally made it.

Back in space, tearing away from the wormhole had taken more power than he had used in a very long time. The *Tecumseh* succumbed to flame as he took off. No one could have survived. The screams of good Federacy people echoed in his memory. Maybe he could have saved some of them. He could have stashed them somewhere. That was an unnecessary punishment of thought, however; the power he used to maneuver the ship would have killed them. Their blood was on him no matter what. The universe was cruel like that, making him live on heaps of sacrifice.

Heathen: another inscribed word for the dusty breeze.

He had almost died a moment ago, hadn't he? Seth remembered his blood in the water and inspected himself for wounds, glancing behind him at the lake nesting in its bed of hills. The hills encircled the water, except at the beach where he climbed out. Good thing he didn't have to climb over those today. An aircraft would be nice for that.

Even higher mountains loomed behind the hills. He could see green in the mountains, so this country wasn't completely desolate. Experience had made him expect desolation. Apart from a few terraformed worlds he had visited when he was younger, the worlds of the galaxy were all desolate, never abundant with this much life.

This is just the desert. Imagine the jungles.

The pulsating sunlight cooked the regenerated skin on Seth's face. His armor was intact, no shuttle crash would break it, and water had washed away most of the blood, but he could feel the newness of everything healing, the new ship smell, but the skin version. One old man, remade to order with a mask of youth included. Dorian Gray had nothing on Seth Caeso.

"Don't see my sins, new world."

Seth lumbered on, noticing the sand begin to harden into more walkable dirt. He made his way through brush and rocks, stumbling on the occasional holes left by rodents, but the terrain had improved overall. He saw a few of the rodents duck away as they sensed his alien presence. Invertebrate life eyed him curiously. They had short stingers, long legs, and they walked along thick webs where they could catch smaller prey. Some of the webs covered whole bushes, with many of the things lurking in the hot sun, waiting for something to catch. Seth had never seen a spider before, but they must have looked similar to these.

After a few hours, Seth heard something ahead of a knoll he couldn't see over. He crouched and listened, hairs on his arms and neck standing with involuntary messages of caution. Sure enough, with heightened sense, he noticed the heavy sound of breath on the other side, soft, but a lot of air. There was a predator on the other side, something big.

Once, when he was stranded on a dark and cold world in a farther reach of the galaxy, a Bosion crawler had stalked him through the rocks. He could hear it breathe in the rocks behind him, a machine's breath in whirring metabolic exchange with its environment. That crawler was a special kill. Seth had almost died in the fight, but Pegassos found him and renewed his strength. Pegassos wouldn't help today. Seth would face his first Karduan beast alone. He had faced worse, no doubt.

Stooping to a crawl, ready to summon his helmet, Seth crept over the knoll.

His instincts were right. He had found something fierce. It walked on two legs with loose black skin. Its muscular legs were clawed like a bird, with hair spiked up the back of them. Sprouting from its leathery abdomen, the beast used wide, clawed wings to fondle a large fruit. It had grabbed the fuzzy meal from atop a gray, pointed cactus plan with needles that looked like they could kill someone if they tripped. The animal's face was reptilian, with sharp teeth protruding out the front of its snout. Green, dead eyes with two slit-like pupils at the center of each looked at him. In all, the thing was ugly.

Seth stood up to face the monster, weak from depleting power, but ready.

The creature retreated.

Seth let his weight shift to one side, feeling the desert breeze wipe the sweat from under his hairline while he watched the thing's wings spread wider than Seth was tall. The monster's body looked just larger than himself, which disappointed him. Their fight might have muted the pit in his stomach. The creature screamed as it climbed, scraping a haunting sound of discord into the rippling desert horizon. The interaction almost felt like an omen.

Following nature's example, Seth shuffled through dust to where the monster had been feeding. It only took the sight of food to realize how hungry he was. He wanted the fruit. He wanted a piece of the world to digest. Maybe the food would be enough to rejuvenate some of the power he had lost by healing his body from such a power drain. The fruits were good, a fantastic first meal. The Botistems seemed to thank him for it. That could be an omen, too. He ate while staring at the city not far away, noting the wall that surrounded it. Only a place built in time of war would need such a wall.

In practice, the desert from here to there was a long stretch of nowhere. The city seemed to keep itself one distance away, like a trick to the senses. The desert kept pitching up small hills, too. With no clear path, Seth had to keep finding vantage points to get his bearings. Though he had traveled far distances across numberless stars and the infinite stretches between them, this seemed like one of the longest treks of his life. He missed his ship, and even his mother. He imagined having power like hers, bending space in the desert, zipping himself beyond the walls of the city. Once there, he could figure out what he was supposed to do.

"Prepare a following for me there," his mother had said. There could be a hundred ways to do that. He wondered how many he could live with.

After some time, the last of the moisture he gained from the fruit seemed to be dripping away in sweat from the top of his head. Sighing, wiping the salty smear from his eyes, he opened his mind to listen for Pegassos. She would say something to clarify his muddled thoughts. She would come and give him strength.

"Hey, old friend. Can you hear me?"

No reply; he had left her out of reach. His ears only picked up the warm air and rushing sage in the breeze, frightening and peaceful at the same time.

The city was finally getting closer. Its pointed buildings reached above the plain. Away, behind, towered more mountains. They were the greater monuments. No man or woman on Kardu or king or queen in the skies had made their design. Maybe that meant something, or perhaps it didn't matter. The city was impressive, but nothing against a mountain range dotted with green biology.

Seth mused, in his mind, what kind of mountain he would have to become. As much as he wouldn't want to believe it, time would move at a slower pace for him away from the cocoon of the rift surrounding Libertas. Preparing a following wasn't a short-term plan. Seth had to steel his mind for lifetimes of labor. Then perhaps Mother would come. His exile wouldn't last forever.

He wasn't sure if it was the thought of centuries in isolation, or the struggling Botistems within him, but Seth felt a fevered chill come over him. It would have felt, in different context, like something big, something in touch with his Botistem sense, had woken to his presence. Something even bigger than a consensus.

The feeling gave way, however, to curiosity for a sound. It rolled through the cloudless sky like thunder. In the sky over the city, a light appeared, falling like a meteor. He tried to focus his eyes on it, but it was moving too fast. By the sound and the look of the trailing burn, it could have been another ship, but it was falling dangerously, worse than he had fallen. No, it couldn't be a ship. The streaking light was targeting the city. It was a weapon. Seth froze, that fevered feeling upon him again, watching without time for any emotion other than raw surprise.

As the weapon struck the ground, the city shuddered. The area where the weapon hit buckled like a clay miniature, then the city exploded, shooting smoke and ash skyward in a thick mushroom plume over midday-sunset red. Seth threw himself to the ground, pressing his face into the dirt of a large rodent-made hole. His helmet deployed but captured some of the dust. The ground shook and heat rained down on him in ash-blown terror. As the blast cleared, Seth rolled over and looked into the sky. It wasn't blue anymore; it was apocalyptic dawn. He had no idea what was happening, only that fate had sent him into the grinding mill of irony. He wouldn't have to conquer anything at all; civilization of Kardu had just pulled its own life support right in front of him.

He listened again for Pegassos. Her voice never came, too hidden behind the reach of dimensions. This would have been a good time for her to pick him up. But with his mind open, he heard a song. He didn't recognize it, like it came from the world itself, alien to him, with the tremor of a woman's voice. She was the thing that had awakened. Her voice rushed over the wind, shook out of the ground, and poured molten anguish through the conduit of Seth's battered mind and overtop his heart. Whoever she was, her singing hurt him deep inside. Seth writhed as though she might kill him.

He screamed and cried out. He had no words but the universal scream of a tortured soul. It didn't let up, but he found strength in himself to stand, to look for the woman's music. He saw the cloud rising from the destroyed city had started to blot out the sun. Turning to the south, his visor caught a missile launching from the ground far away, a response to the atrocity already committed. As the missile moved into the clouds, the woman changed her song, singing straight into Seth's mind in the same way he could hear Pegassos.

Though he couldn't understand her, he felt seen by whatever the woman was. She had to be a power bigger than anything he had ever encountered, a power that invaded his thoughts like someone breaking down a door into his consciousness, Death's Door, the one that always creaked. The sky continued to darken, and under the duress of listening to the voice Seth thought he really might die. The context seemed clear. "Who are you?" repeating again and again in strange tongues.

Perplexed and beaten, Seth knelt, splashing knees into ash and sand, to witness a new world end. His skin burned from the distress of the Botistems and his thoughts were overwhelmed with questions.

He relented enough to answer the voice, "I am Seth, the son of Ashetarai, and I am alone."

—·—

Part 2

Three Centuries After the Fall of the Marshall

Like the generations of leaves, the lives of mortal men. Now the wind scatters the old leaves across the earth, now the living timber bursts with the new buds and spring comes round again. And so with men: as one generation comes to life, another dies away.
    —Homer

7

_— · —_

In the cool light of dusk and the fresh chill of the mountain breeze in a world called Kardu by some, Yurasema by others, Cash Rivers brushed the body of his horse with the care and ease of a best friend. "There, Red. I'm sorry about today."

Red flared his nostrils and nipped at Cash's shoulder. The horse's ears twitched and he stamped the ground as if to say he had even more driving left in him for the day.

"No, boy, I've had enough." Cash laughed and fed the horse a handful of sweetroot. "Rest up for tomorrow, we've got a long ride ahead. Mbe toss," he said in an old language. You're crazy.

Red answered by swishing his neck. Cash grabbed the lead rope and hitched it to a tree, smiling. Once he turned around, Cash heard the horse start to mush down on the pile of hay he had left for him. He should be alright.

"Pijare pona." Beautiful night. Cash nodded to Abelnora. She sat on a rock while chewing on a bioco leaf. She acknowledged him, smiling as the leaf stimulated her brain for the night's watch over the horses and camp. A rifle hung from a sling around her neck. She was short, but stronger than she looked. She could beat almost anyone he knew at wrestling. Abelnora had an eye for weaknesses, physical or otherwise, and could find a hole in any defense.

"Vilco, Cash. Where's your hat?" She pointed to the messy hair sticking to his sweat-drenched head.

"I don't know, Abe. Ask Red. He bucked me again."

"He's too much for you," she said through the leaf.

Cash returned the banter. "And that bioco is too much for your little head. You're gonna be nothing but snakeskin if you keep that habit up too long."

"Go find your own joy to kill, Cash. Let me have the simple pleasures."

Cash walked a short way through the brush and into the camp. Eimos and Teeg, the Hawk twins, would be watching the herd tonight, keeping an eye out for screechers and rival gangs. He felt bad for anyone who might threaten those two. The curly-haired twins were more animal than anything he'd ever encountered in the Basin. But they were kind, too, once they decided your head was worth letting you keep.

He'd lived with most of this bunch for almost his whole life, and he could tell who they all were, even in the dimming light. Chip and Ringer, the gang's youngest men, teenagers, were lighting their pipes by one of the wagons, only to be scolded by Lady Iseldris and her ladle.

"I will gut both of you and feed you to the lions, you malbred mutts. That's the powder wagon!" She threw the spoon and it bounced off the canvas. Iseldris was affectionately named the Lady of the Camp. She was also Judge's wife.

Chip dropped the match in his hand and Ringer started to laugh. Both of them darted away from the powder wagon. Fire wasn't supposed to go near it. Ringer dropped the pipe out of his mouth.

"Techa Fio," the boy cursed.

Cash found his way to the fire and sat on a log, thinking about the herd he left in the meadow behind the camp. They were lucky no trouble came from the Kona Tribe. The Tribe had a nature of unpredictability. They could go off at any time, with little provocation. Judge had given them twenty heads for passage and the promise of further taxation on their way back past Deep Lake. The only thing was, Cash wasn't sure if Judge meant to cross back that way at all. They were wanted in Ashra City, and it was Cash's fault.

Judge had raised Cash since he was born. He wasn't Cash's father, but he might as well have been. Cash's parents died in Ashra City. It seemed like everyone died in Ashra City. Worlds died in Ashra City. The Keepers had been running things a long time, and it would take an army to change any of that.

"You did it right, son," Judge said, sitting down on the same log. He brought a piece of wolf hide with him, draping it over his side of the log for a more comfortable seat. All the riding had made them all a little sore.

"I didn't see any other choice. They were just kids." Cash threw a stick into the fire.

"I meant what you did with the horse today, but if you want to talk about that again we can."

"Oh." Cash paused. "I guess it's still on my mind."

"Killing a man. That's not something that can leave anyone's mind, not anyone with any sense." Judge adjusted the wolf-hide cushion one last time. "That confounded saddle is going to kill me." A grizzled moan slid out of his goatee. "Killing many men, that turns you into something else. Something like me."

Cash let the air fill with smoke and the crackling sound of campfire instead of an answer. He had shot a few men before, in gunfights, robberies, but he hadn't in cold blood, not until last week just outside of Ashra City. Judge and the gang were planning a cattle drive with an old rancher, Ezra Steele. Steele was a chief member of the Keepers, and very powerful in the Basin. He had an army of fighters who would answer for him, and a ring of underground corruption that raised enough stink for everyone to recognize, even if no one had the backbone to make any stand against it.

Cash's trouble with Ezra started when he got curious, hearing things the way he sometimes did, coming from an inconspicuous door on the side of the manor. He burgled his way inside with a knife and a small tamping rod, of all things. The sound he heard on the other side wasn't anything more than soft crying, but it ate enough at him for him to leave his post by the horses. Judge didn't want him in on the meeting for this one, despite Cash being his second. So, Cash had time to snoop, which was also something Judge never opposed.

The door led down to a small, inactive distillery. Cash guessed that the machinery must have dated back to the time old Ashran government had tried to regulate alcohol production. Judge said that the regulation only had the appearance of trying to do good for the community, but really the powers that were wanted fingers on the kettle themselves. If they were the ones pouring the booze, that was even better than straight taxation. That was part of Ashran descent into Keeper rule. The Keepers offered better access to vice.

The tall copper pot stills were cool to the touch and turning green. Cash was admiring one of them when he heard the cry again, this time from inside the still and echoing up out of the top of the stack. Somebody was in there. It sounded like a girl, maybe, or a young boy.

"What you doing down here, outlaw?" said a man near the door. Cash didn't see him, but he heard his voice from behind the pot stills.

"Looking for a score," said Cash, turning with a smile. He wanted to know who they had inside the still. He knew why they might have someone in there.

The man laughed, stepping out where Cash could see him. He had a loose shirt on and was sweatier than the mild weather usually made someone. His skin had a slight tint of yellow that came out more in his eyes, which meant liver disease, according to the books. His beard was cut with the thickest parts of it curving from his sideburns right into his mustache. It gave him something of a dog look, mixed with pig. "You don't want to be down here, outlaw." His right hand went down to a long pistol holstered in front of his left hip.

Cash measured the man. Despite the yellow skin, he looked fit, and a head taller than him. That meant he would have to take the man to the ground. He didn't want to shoot, because Judge was upstairs talking cattle runs, "legitimate" work. He probably couldn't close the distance before the man drew. There wasn't really a scenario where Cash could win this, unless the man trusted him first. Then there might not be a fight at all.

"Like I said," Cash said, palms out, his pistol hanging far away enough on his thigh to not frighten a man already holding the grip of his own, "I'm looking for a score. Who are you keeping in here? I'm willing to pay."

The man relaxed some. "Pay? No one would want to pay for one of these." Keeping his hand on his pistol, the man stepped an arm's length away, toward the still. Fingering a latch, he pulled a heavy, secret door open. Cash hadn't noticed the hinges, but now it made sense.

As the door swung open, Cash put his hands on the front of his belt to appear casual. Putrid stench hit him in the face before he was ready.

"Techa," the man swore. "Did another one die?"

There were a dozen bodies inside. Cash recognized the cry of one of them, a kid no older than fifteen, and barely covered in a dirty sack.

"We break them in like this," the man said, eyeing Cash's mask of curiosity. "Don't worry. Their families knew the punishment for dissent. These kids will make good workers someday though. Those who make it. Bichuepa." He spit. "They're not for sale."

One of the smaller ones looked Cash in the eye. He had sandy hair, just like him. Cash's parents had dissented from the Keepers. Had Judge not been a good friend to them and taken him in, he could have been that boy. He could have been one of the dead ones, too, or worse.

Cash feigned a laugh. "Well, techa," he said. "Here I thought the smell was you."

The man scowled, the yellow in his eyes looking more like death as the blood in him boiled into his mad face.

Take your hand off your gun, Cash thought.

The man grabbed Cash by the lapel of his jacket. Cash liked this jacket. It was good for heavy work in weather like this. Judge had given it to him, along with the hat he wore that he would soon miss.

The man wheezed, "How about I throw you in there? You're not much older. We could have some fun with you."

Cash had learned over years in the business of living outside the law of the Keepers that certain kinds of people bet on fear. The man was on his own turf. He had no reason to expect a knife in his diseased liver, a left-handed maneuver from someone with a gun on his right thigh. The man was a seasoned bully, and not a fighter. Cash had thought about all these things and more. He just needed closed distance. Once he had it, the fight was over. Jab, jab, jab, three more to the liver, diaphragm, and spleen. The pointed whiskers of the man's mustache brushed Cash in the face as the most painful moment of the man's life left him unconscious and dying on the dirt distillery floor.

The children stayed where they were. The crier hid under another's arm.

Cash knew he had messed up. This was going to mess things up. Shaking his head, he tried to clear it. A fog in his thinking tried to wrap its way around his temples to in between his eyes. Taking a breath, he bent and wiped the blade on the man's sleeve. He'd have to clean it more later. Thinking about something as simple as keeping his blade sharp helped clear his mind, helped clear the mud of having just ended a person's life and spilling diseased blood on his favorite jacket. As he thought, he took off the jacket, and noticed a set of iron keys on the man's belt. "Take care of each other," he told the kids, tossing them the keys. "These should help you get free."

The sandy-haired one picked them up and nodded like he recognized them.

"There's going to be shooting," Cash told him, looking into his dark eyes. The shadow of the still didn't hide the fire still in them. "Don't come out till it's over."

Cash surfaced from the door with no one wiser. Business at the manor carried on as usual, just Ashran people doing the business of chores and ignoring the problems under their feet. He couldn't blame most of them, though he wished he could have. They didn't have the luxury of an outlaw life. They had to deal with comfort after compromise.

He just needed to find Judge.

The doorman let Cash in without trouble. Cash just nodded to him like he was supposed to be there. The man didn't ask what happened to his jacket, and didn't seem to take any more notice than a disgruntled eye on his Cash's pistol.

"Don't worry," Cash told him. "It's for vermin."

The man scoffed. "Your boss was wearing a better one. You should look into a bigger gun if you're going to be in business here."

"I prefer the longer clip."

"Fair enough. They're in the south parlor. Mind the carpet with those boots."

Cash found the parlor. Judge was the first face he saw through the wavy glass panels of the door. The knob was made of twisted metal shaped like a prairie ram's single horn.

His next actions seemed to drive themselves. Cash's consciousness was at the reigns, but deeper drives were the horses at the bit. Through the door, the metal latch closing behind him, Cash caught his first glimpse of Ezra Steele. He was a fat old rancher, each pound of flesh on him a sign of his wealth and position. Ezra ordered Keeper affairs. He ordered the breaking of those kids. He orchestrated the murders, the public terror, the Ashran way of life. He drove out the good of the masses. Ezra made Cash the outlaw that found himself holding a small caliber pistol in front of his face.

"Judge," Ezra said, the fat in his jowls quivering slightly. "Who's the boy?"

"Cash Rivers," Judge said cautiously.

A suspended tick seemed to hang in the air, one second on the clock that wouldn't fall. Ezra scowled. Cash thumbed the hammer behind the slide of his weapon. And Judge whispered, "I'm with you, son."

Cash pulled the trigger.

Unarmed in his chair, the rancher fell back, tipping the seat with him, his spirit gone into the depths of the world before he figured out his sentence. His red blood flicked over the white carpet like a dark revelation.

Judge reacted without reprimand, trusting his adopted son. There had always been a part of him that Cash had seen loving chaos, loving a twist of upheaval. Cash didn't think Judge was a bad man, he was just a man who chose a life outside the brick and mortar. He was born out of a more natural way: the warrior spirit of Yurasema.

Staring at his kill, Cash didn't hear the sound that knocked the top of a baffled guard's head standing nearby. Cash turned his head to see Judge's outstretched aim and the smoke rising from the barrel of his large sidearm.

"Another one at the door, Cash," Judge said calmly.

Cash shot the doorman as he approached the glass panels. The shattered glass and thin wood gave way as the man kept coming right through the window. He collapsed and stopped moving.

"Get down," Judge commanded. Cash dropped, face to the carpet and covered his head. His hat struggled to stay in place.

As he hit the floor, shots blasted over him through the large window at the end of the room. Their view used to boast a nice garden. Now it was a nice garden with three shooters demolishing the upholstery and plastered walls.

Judge crawled to Cash. "How many rounds you got in there?"

"Twenty."

"You can walk them through that hedge?"

"Yeah."

"Do it. I'll cover you once I've cleared the hall."

"On my mark," Cash said, rolling to his side and pointing up at the hedge. The shooters were all behind it. He wasn't sure how many were there now, but he could suppress them. "Go, go, go."

Judge scrambled for the door. Cash walked each bullet up through the hedge. The shooters stopped firing and Judge made it.

"I've got you, Cash!" Judge shouted from the door.

"Coming to you!" Cash crawled under Judge's barrel where Judge took his turn firing through the hedge to cover Cash's movement.

"It's gonna be a long way out of here," Judge said as Cash patted him on the shoulder, letting him know he had his back.

Cash steeled the electricity buzzing in his arms, the adrenaline hitting him like a hard drug. "Sorry about your cattle deal."

Judge helped him up. "Take the left side and anything above us when we're out the door."

"You've got our rear?"

"Yeah, and I think I know what we can do about that cattle."

Cash shook off the flashbacks and swam his way out of the hypnotic fire. Judge was looking at him, seeing just where Cash's mind had taken him.

Judge was a big man. He liked wide cargo pants and boots of just a certain sheen of leather and always wore a wide brimmed hat. The whole gang wore those hats.

Cash liked the hat he lost. He would miss it in tomorrow's sun.

Over his left eye, Judge had a scar. He said he could see well enough, but it wandered sometimes. Cash had asked about it when he was a kid, but Judge only told him that he had hit a tree when he was riding one day. However, from the nature of the man who wore the scar, Cash thought it must have been something else, or someone else, that hurt him a long time ago.

Despite being well-read in printed literature, Judge preferred the old ways, things forgotten by the most settled parts of the Basin and taught by oral tradition. He believed the world was a living force, an entity grown from the chaos of the elements. In his faith, the living spirit of the world was a part of a great tree that made the universe, whose branches made conduits to other worlds born to bear life as fruit of the great tree. The tree connected all life. If you lived in harmony with the world, with nature, you were part of that connection. The world would speak to you and help you.

Over the interior of his soft beliefs, Judge wore the shell of a battle-hardened man who looked after his gang of misfits. Also, in Cash's mind, Judge took advantage of people too much. The Keepers suspected him of mischief, but could never prove anything. He knew just how to charm them, right up until the moment Cash planted a bullet that wrecked years of compromises.

"Look," said Judge. "Don't get into your head. We're outlaws, always have been. Killing people is going to happen. Especially with a moral aptitude like yours. Techa, it's why I keep you around. You keep a tired old man honest."

Cash pushed back his light-colored hair. It was greasy from days without washing and long dusty rides. "They used to preach that gods would punish a man like me. A man without law. It's in the books I read."

"Well, how old are you now, nineteen? Twenty? What man that age holds himself to any law? That's the right age for a man to kill his father, narratively speaking."

Cash laughed. He didn't really know how old he was. He was as old as Judge decided, but that was a manipulation he wasn't sure he could believe. "You thinking I should put a bullet in you, Judge?"

Judge chuckled, then lost his humor for a second, looking through Cash and choosing his words carefully. The firelight sprinkled his face with light as the sun splashed its way down westward where they had come. "Maybe if you saw me too clearly. The way things are today, in a blown-up, ransacked country trying to rebuild itself, a place where people believe some alien goddess is waiting to tiptoe down here and save humanity, all the while they're exploiting each other, killing and breaking the innocent. Men like you are the law, son. You're the messenger of gods who are all around us, forgotten, *our* gods of *our* world that *our* ancestors forsook when they blew up everything. Gods who speak our old language."

"I just wish it could be different." Cash stared into the fire, watching the logs disintegrate into ember. A lone flame still struggled to burn.

"We roast over the embers of ancestral sin. Don't blame yourself for what happened. You saved some kids, kids who can grow up and change things, just the way you do, every day. They'll remember the kindness of your violence, Cash, just as I hope you remember mine. Live your life without regrets. Act, then face the next day. No second guessing. Sleep it off."

"Sure, but my thoughts won't let me sleep. I keep seeing the man die. I see myself standing over him. *Pop!* Shooting the man I was, the gang we used to be. All of it. Burning in a muzzle flash."

Judge gripped Cash's shoulder and stood up, taking his wolf cushion with him. "Pretty words from tired lungs. You're getting late-night existential. Yguaku, I'm so tired I could sleep through a cyclone. Digo and his kids should be back soon. We should only be a couple of days away by now, at least once we hit the canyon. With their help we'll move faster, too, resting the horses a little more and switching them out more often. I'm expecting less trouble. Bandits stay away from the High Valley."

"Alright. I'll only be a little while. Someone should watch the fire die."

"You'll be alright, son. It gets easier. Take it from an old outlaw like me. All blood goes cold in the end."

Judge walked away and propped up next to his lady's wagon. Cash watched him take off his boots and kneel down on his sleeping pad to meditate. Judge called it his communion with nature, when he would read the omens of the day and ponder the sounds of the night. If he listened well enough, She, the world, born of the great tree of the universe, would tell him how to proceed.

Cash tried meditating sometimes, but he had an unquiet mind. Especially tonight, where a man with a hole in his head kept falling, over and over again, down into strokes of blood painting death on fancy carpet.

"Judge! Gunfire from the southwest. I think it's the twins." Abelnora came running through the camp and jumped over Cash in a storm of adrenaline and stimulants. The sun was just coming up. They were all so tired they had slept in.

The old man was up next to the wagon before he finished hearing her, his wildland instincts taking over. "I heard it. Cash and I will scout it out. Stay with the horses. Izzy!"

Iseldris came running over with a wool hat falling off of her long hair. "What is it? Screechers again?"

"No, I'd say by what I heard it was at least two men shooting at each other," answered Abelnora. Chip and Ringer were up now, too, and took up positions near camp. The dogs barking from their tethers drowned out whatever they were saying to each other.

Cash pulled his cargo pants on with his ammo and water belt still attached. He took a thigh holster off the log next to him and made sure his knife and pistol were still there. Judge tossed him a repeater rifle and they were off, quick and silent under the trees and through the brush. They took the high side of the hill overlooking the meadow where the cattle slept for the night. Together, they knelt behind a fallen pine.

Two riders were riling up the herd across the meadow, trying to head some off and take them away. Cash was expecting more. He couldn't see the twins.

Judge pulled out a small telescope. "How's that wind feel, Cash?"

"Nothing I can't account for," Cash replied, taking the rifle sling off his shoulder. "How far?"

Judge thought about it. "I'd say about six hundred. Not a close shot but I believe in you. Are you good?"

"Gimme a couple shots."

"Whenever you're ready."

Cash slowed his breathing. The sights on this rifle weren't meant to adjust and weren't set to his sight picture. He had to feel the shot and aim away from the rider to both where he and the bullet would meet. The wind on the trees near the rider told him the bullet's path, the pacing horse told him where the rider would go. Calm focus held Cash still and guided his aim. Wind, hoofs, momentum, flow. Time on the hill slowed down.

"Not to hurry you or anything but—"

Cash squeezed the trigger slow enough that the shot surprised him, a smooth pull without any added movement. The bullet arced, an invisible curve over the land, just the way he wanted, and struck the first rider at low-center mass just above the saddle. The rider doubled over and hit the ground. From that distance with this rifle, the bullet would have crashed through the rider's abdomen and ripped the insides into pieces, more like a cannonball through a wall than a bullet through a body. Cash made the impossible shot. The rider was out of the fight.

"Pure magic, son." Judge smiled under his telescope.

The other rider turned in their direction and opened up his pistol. Six shots went wild around the hillside. The rider hadn't spent his whole clip but he turned his horse toward the trees on the other side of the meadow. He was only trying to keep their heads down so he could run for it.

Cash peeked up in time to pull out his rifle again. Maybe he could get one more shot.

Judge stopped him, "Hold your fire, we've got Eimos. I think. Out of the brush."

One of the twins darted out of the trees in full sprint. His legs looked like spinning wheels, striking the ground with almost inhuman force. Flying behind him like a cape, his long jacket didn't seem to slow down the power of his run. Cash watched the small dot of him leap up over the horse and onto the rider and take him down the other side of it with both feet high in the air.

Cash and Judge ran down the hill after him, cursing and stumbling in full adrenaline. Judge would want the rider alive so he could see who he rides with. The twin, Eimos maybe, or Teeg, was out for blood. Cash was sure he would kill the man before they could get there.

Keeping their eye out for more attackers, they ran across the meadow where the twin and the downed rider fought on the ground. They reached the twin in time to pull back his pistol before he shot the man he took down. He had gotten up off the ground and drawn the weapon slowly. All the same, Cash saw that it was too late. The rider's face was beaten through from blows and kicks sustained under the fury of the Hawk twin. In the time it took them to run across the meadow, the man was killed.

"Eimos. No, Teeg. Where's Eimos?" asked Judge out of breath, recognizing the twin now that they were closer. He grabbed Teeg's face, focusing him back into the moment, out of the fight.

Teeg fell to his knees. "He's back there. Six men got to him while I slept. I got four of them before the other two ran off. They're gone by now, but the riders with the cattle here needed dealt with so I snuck around. Guess that makes nine, right?"

"Eight, but is Eimos alive?" Cash looked back to where Teeg had pointed and started to run in that direction.

"Yeah, but the bullet went in through his chest. Can I go kill the other two, Judge?"

"Not yet, son, you're bleeding." Judge looked at Teeg's arm.

Cash stopped and started back. Sure enough, a big gash was visible in Teeg's right arm. Teeg had been too preoccupied in the fight to notice or pay much attention.

"Teegan Hawk, stand down. Cash, go find his brother, we'll get both of them back to camp and figure it out from there."

Cash found Eimos where the two had camped in the trees. He was on his back cursing and sputtering blood from his mouth and trying to sit up. Finding a cloth in his pocket, Cash placed it over the wound on Eimos's upper right chest. "Well, good news is, I can hear the sucking and blowing sound. That's your lung working. It's nasty, but I think you might live. Clean through, looks like. I wouldn't quite call you lucky, though. This looks painful."

Eimos glowered and cursed again. Judge and Teeg found them. Teeg was limping, probably from his tackle off the horse. The wound on his arm was tied off.

Teeg collapsed next to his brother. "You still with me, bro?

I got four of them for you." Then he thought about it. "Five, actually. One still on his horse. Probably the coolest thing I've ever done. Cash shot another. That was you, right Cash?"

Cash padded the rifle now slung on his back.

Eimos started to speak but coughed up more blood.

"No. Don't say anything, toss. We're taking you back to camp." Teeg rolled over onto his back. The loss of blood from his arm had worn him down. "What do you say we steal a few less cows next time?"

8

———.———

The next week's journey went without incident. The twins rode together in the wagon. Teeg tried to ride on horseback but the pain of his wounds proved too much. He needed both arms to ride well anyway. Cash told him to stay in the wagon and take care of his brother. He put some old, sterile plastic the gang had had tucked away over Eimos's wounds to stop the air. Lady Isildris kept the torn flesh clean with herbs and shoved even more down Eimos's throat. She would keep him alive if it killed him.

With the twins out and not working, Cash had to try and get Ringer and Chip to pick up the slack. The group had to slow down for two days until Digo showed up with his son and two daughters. His kids weren't much better than Ringer and Chip, but they rode well enough, and the numbers got them up to speed again. The dogs performed as expected, too, keeping the cattle together and moving in the right direction. All was going well, and they hid from any common roads as best as they could through the mountain terrain.

The gang stopped lighting fires. Dried meat and stale biscuits provided their main source of nutrition apart from some wild fruit. Without being able to cook, they didn't hunt either. Cash gazed longingly at every rabbit, squirrel, and even lizard they passed. At this point, he would have even tried screecher meat if it was hot.

He saw a small herd of them fly over once, their ugly, reptilian mouths and bat-like wings staining the blue of the cloudy sky in ugly silhouettes. Cash wished screechers hadn't survived the great winter after the war hundreds of years ago. They were the most resilient animals he knew of, eating anything from cactus fruit to dead cattle. If they were hungry enough, they would attack people. That's what the gang had been most worried about before the attack at the meadow. They thought they had bought passage from the Kona Tribe.

One more rider came with the group. He had his hands tied in front where he gripped the saddle and a bandage on his leg from where Teeg had shot him. He and five others had jumped Eimos. A wagon pulled his horse. The horse walked along with its ears drooped to the side and a sad glaze over its eyes. The man hadn't admitted who sent him yet. Cash suspected he had to do with the rancher he shot. Judge seemed to know more about that, too. He wanted to ask the old man but hadn't found the words yet. The drive took all his energy and he had a hard time talking about what he saw and what he did.

The mountains to their left and right opened up a little and the herd tried to spread out with the terrain. They would arrive at Shadow Pass soon. It was a canyon that led to High Valley, where it was also known that convoys of resources passed through. People said High Valley was full of riches, enough for the best comforts, but needed to trade for what it didn't have. The gang was counting on the herd being their ticket inside, although it was rumored no one got inside, not anymore.

Cash found himself ramping up the pace, calling out his fellow gang members to move with more purpose. He could feel the ice of his nightmare like the cold trickle of rain. He had killed a man in cold blood and forced the gang to rustle valuable resources all the way across the basin. They were supposed to have delivered less than half of this herd a much shorter distance near Ashra. When Cash killed the rancher, Judge just shrugged the whole thing off and took everything, killing anyone who saw them. They got away before any big response. Judge had a way of taking advantage of any situation and getting away with it.

Rounding up a few cows trying to take an alternate path, Cash jumped at the sound of a gunshot from back near the wagons. He wheeled Red around and started back toward the group. Abelnora caught up to him and they rode in together, the sound of the horses' feet shaking the apprehensive air.

"How's the fire?" Cash called out. It was code for asking if the situation was hostile, specifically if anyone was taken hostage and sitting in an ambush.

"Missing the stew," answered Lady Isildris. She meant that everything was fine but to bring first aid.

Cash dropped to the ground off his horse and ran into the trees where Digo was leaning over someone's bloody leg with the pant leg cut down the middle from hip to knee. The reek of infection stunk up the area. The leg belonged to the surviving rider from the attack, their prisoner, and he was dying.

"Cash, see if you can help me with this." Digo motioned for him to approach.

"Who fired the shot?" Cash took off his jacket and rolled up his sleeves, kneeling over the nameless man.

Eimos spoke up from the sick wagon. "That was me, boss. He fell off his horse. Thought about letting him pass out there and be left behind but then I figured someone should watch him die. So I fired a round into the air. Could've shot him, but now I got a front-row seat to his suffering right here. Yiare-pa."

Teeg laughed and waved his hat. "Yiare-pa-me."

"Thanks, Eimos." Cash dismissed the twins' bloodthirst and looked at the wound. The man was dying. A fever from the infection in his leg would kill him soon, but not before a painful decline into septic shock. He had read about it, and seen it before.

"Should we cut it off?" asked Digo.

Cash thought about it. "No, we'll leave him here with some of the shine, but only if he'll talk first."

Judge rode in and parked his horse with Abelnora and Red. "How's the fire?"

"It's too late for that, Cash beat you to it. Just get over here and figure out what to do with this poor man." Isildris didn't feel like using the code again and summoned her husband the old-fashioned way.

Seeing the wound, Judge made a grunt that sounded like, "Oh," without opening his mouth.

Cash leaned in close to the man's face, placing an open bottle of alcohol under his nose. "You smell that?"

The fevered man shook his head.

Cash poured some of the liquid onto his clenched mouth.

"Yes," he coughed.

"Who sent you?"

The man shook his head again.

"I was going to leave you here with this, prop you up, give you a nice view before you go, but if you don't want it..." Cash moved the bottle down to the wound and let a drop spill in.

The man groaned, "No. Please." His leg was shaking.

"No one can help you now. We wanted to take you where we're going, maybe even let you go once we got there, if you cooperated. That's nice considering you almost killed one of my friends."

"Just end him now," said Eimos from the wagon.

"Shut up, I'm watching this." Teeg smacked his arm. Eimos grunted from the pain in his chest.

Judge crouched next to Cash. "My son here has a generous offer for you, friend. Tell us who you ride with or work for, and we'll leave you here with a bottle enough to drown your pain and sorrow. It'll be like falling asleep with this brew."

The man kept looking over Cash's shoulder like he saw something. Cash wondered if it was a hallucination. Fevers could bring frightful images to the dying.

"Fine," the sick man said, "but give me some of that first."

Cash obliged and poured some into his mouth. The man coughed most of it up but swallowed a little.

"We were hired by a woman in Ashra City. I don't know who you ticked off but we're just the first to find you. We got lucky. Lonny Mansden, my friend that you shot off his horse, he was our leader. He figured you would take the Meadow Route and not the old highways. He was right."

"I've heard of Lonny," answered Judge. "Never met him, though. He ran with some ugly crowds when I was getting started. Hey." Judge tapped the man's face. He was starting to fall asleep. "Boy, you're warm."

The man woke up. "My friends that got away, they'll be bringing the whole posse. Like I said, whoever you killed, you woke up the city. They're out for blood, and they're justified. We're not bandits. This is legitimate work of the law. Kill the gang, return the property."

The words were like lead to Cash's stomach. This is what you get for killing evil. The twins almost died because of him. The gang couldn't outrun what he did. Ashra City, where everything dies. His parents, now his gang. They had nowhere to go but a phantom land leagues away in a valley none of them knew. Someone loved the old degenerate enough to send retribution all the way across the basin and into the mountains. The lives of all the gang would never be the same, all for an impulsive act of kind retribution. "Alright, put him up against that tree and give him the bottle." Judge was done with the conversation and trying to hide the frustration in his voice. "Listen up, I need you all to push even harder. If we lose a few head of cattle along the way, so be it. Longer rotations on the horses, and half the party will keep watch at night for any more attacks. Once we make Shadow Pass, we'll be alright, but for now, Cash, get the herd moving double time. I don't want any more surprises this week. Let's roll!"

"I'm gonna miss you two in Ashra, Cash," Digo told him as they carried the doomed man to his last vista.

"Thanks for nothing," the man said, turning away. Cash dusted off his leather chaps, like it would shake off whatever infection was pumping through him.

"I'll miss you, Digo. You sure you'll be okay?"

Digo sighed under the bags he had for eyelids. "We'll be fine. Not all of us who oppose the Keepers should leave. There are things you might have started. I want to see where the bit of blood you spilt might flow."

They walked down to where Ringer held the reigns of both their horses.

"Judge says it won't ever be the same," said Cash, trying to reason with Digo's words. "That we don't owe anyone there anything more."

"That's his judgement, his prerogative. But you're a different kind of man than he is. What's yours?"

Cash patted Red and put his foot in the stirrup. With his hands on the horn of the saddle, he pulled himself up at the slow speed of his thought. Abelnora was mounted nearby. She was laughing at something one of Digo's daughters said. Looking at her, he tried to find a simple enough answer. "My path doesn't really belong to me."

"Well, when Red aims you back here, don't hesitate to look me up. Ashra will need a leader like you."

Cash laughed. "An outlaw?"

"A good person."

Cash smiled and shook his head, leading Red in a tight circle toward the rear of the herd, kicking him gently just under the hip. Red sped to a gallop that matched the angry rhythm of Cash's heart. He didn't feel angry on the surface, the anger was just there. Anger licking away the slow drip of regret.

"Outlaw doesn't mean stupid," Judge told Cash once when

he was younger. "Outlaw means a man of his own nation. Government and gang lines are arbitrary, son. You're angry and that's good. Collect that anger, Cash. Surround yourself with it. Outlaw folk survive, but don't forget that every revolution started with a few men who said no to organized injustice. Those were never men of repute. Do you know what they were all along?"

"Outlaws." Eyeroll. Silent acceptance. Damn the old man for being right all the time. Do all men love and hate their fathers? Cash sometimes hated his real father. It was hard to love someone who had never done anything for him but die and leave him to a gang.

Cash slowed Red to a trot. He needed to get back to the herd without wearing out the horse. Even Red had some limits.

As the sound of pounding hooves died down, he listened to the wilderness. The country was quiet. Birds sang in the trees and small rodents clicked on the bark, their claws searching for insects. The clouds spun from faraway winds. There was another feeling, something behind awe for the terrain. Instinct.

A primeval predator warning hit Cash as he identified it. He'd learned to listen to those feelings before he could articulate them. Danger wasn't just something a person could analyze. In the wild, he had to feel it first. His eyes started to scan the area around him. There were small pockets of dead space, areas where an enemy could hide, but none of them looked occupied, or like anything his sharp eyes wouldn't have spotted movement from already. He slowed Red to a swift stop, shifting his weight as Red's legs slid and he almost tripped.

"Easy," he told the horse. "Do you feel it, too?"

Red nodded his head, though not out of agreement, just being a horse.

Cash moved his eyes up to the tree line of a ridge in the distance. Several horsemen were silhouetted on the saddle, too small to make out. One nodded to another, pointing at Cash, and putting away something that glistened for a second like a telescope. They didn't seem like enemies, but they were wearing a unique kind of vest that made them seem different from normal riders out of Ashra. Valley men, maybe. Cash would know soon, one way or the other.

9

A quiet sum of reflection clung to the wet stone walls of a room in the tower over the gate at Shadow Pass where Yora leaned into a book he could hardly read. Moisture from light rain trickled under the cobbled rooftop, glistening in the light of a single candle on the table. The book's yellow pages smelled like memories, where captured in them fermented a time forgotten only to words buried in the pressed ink and folded bindings. The words weren't written in the common tongue, but in Joropa, the language of the many who lived in this land before the long winter.

"The song of the Darkness is the acceptance of Night, the Peace of the Shelter in Shadow, an Anthem to the Dread of Truth at Midday. She chooses her warriors with the Mark of the Bear. Azure Flame for the Outworlder." Yora read the words out loud, translating them, wanting them to make sense, wanting them to quelch the image in his mind, the image of a dying friend and the healing hand of a dead man dressed in silver furs.

No one knew what happened while he was gone.

He wasn't suspected of desertion, although that's what happened. Months before, Yora cracked in the sunlight of what would have been less than a day's ride back home. He'd been to the Queen's manor, not his mother the Queen, but the woman he loved. Not his wife, but the woman he gave his heart, the woman his father stole for his own and married. A second marriage for the king. Polygamy in the High Valley.

Yora's mother wouldn't have the wedding in her home. The kingdom belonged to his father, but the house and its affairs belonged to her. The King had a new house built, even worked on it himself, contributing to the artistry of finished carpentry in the halls and bedrooms. His mother asked Yora to attend, and he did, to the delight of his father. Yora loved his father, but he resented his choices. The High Valley was supposed to be a refuge, not a cult.

The cold light of dawn crept over the hillsides in the view of the tower. Yora hadn't slept much again. He wrestled the urge to flee the dawn, throw the reinforced shutters closed, barricade the door and hide in what had to be finally a good night's rest. But he couldn't do that. He was the King's son, and more than that, the only son the King had any inclination to trust with the command of the Guard. Ran was a thug, unpredictable. Older, but better suited for scouting. Ran didn't mind when Yora got promoted. If anything, for the first time in their lives they considered each other friends.

Yora stood up and grabbed his armored vest and pistol, still inside its holster. He missed the thrill of life outside the gate, but working close to home had advantages. His wife, Vonica, seemed to be improving. No one knew what illness she had, but her erratic emotions dug rifts in the house. They only had one son, Yorathas II. He would be twelve soon and also had health problems. Not in the mind like the boy's mother, but in his lungs.

Opening the door, Yora found his brother ascending the stone staircase. A slit in the wall showed the early light and clouds without any more rain.

"Yor! Just the man I wanted to see. Did you miss me?"

"Ran!" Yora grabbed his brother by the forearm. It had been weeks. Ran had his usual smile on, the one that looked like it was winning at a scheme no one else knew about yet.

"Brother, how's your family?" Ran asked. His cheeks were

red from the mountain cold. He must have ridden hard.

"Yora II is getting taller every day, and he rides well enough, all things considered. Vonica is well most days. The chiva root helps calm her down in her more manic episodes. We get by." Yora was smiling, but he imagined that he couldn't hide the pain in his own eyes. She wasn't the woman he married, not anymore, but he vowed to take care of her and he would die doing it.

"You're a regular housekeeper, Yor." Ran started down the stairs.

Yora followed, adjusting a strap on his vest that housed a long knife. His gun belt was loose. He would fix it later. He tried thinking of something to say, a way to tell his brother that he was not fine, that his nights were long and there was even more on his mind than a psychotic wife. He could ask how Ran's family fared. Four kids who went weeks at a time before seeing their father. Their mother died from an infection.

Ran spoke at the bottom of the stairs before he could think of anything. They entered a hallway that ran down the wall perpendicular to the gate toward a large guardhouse nestled against the cliff wall. "How's the old man adjusting to life as a newlywed?" The irony in his voice clouded the air of the question.

Yora laughed, "He's not. Mother won't ever forgive him."

"Even without being gone all the time I just can't bring myself to head up there, even to see Mom. But you know, I'm surprised you didn't marry that girl yourself, you having found her and all, Mr. Hero. And if you don't mind me saying, if anyone deserves a second wife–"

A captain of the guard approached them from behind, interrupting the discomfort of the conversation. He wore less armor than Yora, and had a long rifle slung over his back and a gray-colored helmet. "Forgive me, Lord Praylum."

"What is it?" Yora asked.

"A group of a half dozen riders is spotted about a three-quarter league out from the gate and headed this way. We've got the long rifles on them now up the hillside. They'll be in range of the automatics soon."

"Do they seem hostile? What's the nature of their approach?"

"Armed and riding in a defensive formation, sir."

Yora's mind started to turn. Most people knew riding up on any part of the wall around High Valley was a bad idea, especially the gate at Shadow Pass.

"Before you go thinking anything, brother, I was about to tell you something. It's why I ambushed you this early in the morning, but more friendly conversation got in the way first." Ran shifted his feet.

"What's going on, Ran?"

"I may have promised them asylum here."

"You what?"

"There's a kid with them—well, a man, but a younger one. Smart guy. Strong. Sandy-haired. Tan like the sun is his best friend and eyes so sharp he could shoot over a league and knock a man off his horse."

"Who is he, Ran? Why did you promise them asylum?"

"Yor." Ran grabbed his brother's shoulder. "He's the man who shot Ezra Steele."

10

The gate at Shadow Pass loomed high into the mouth of the canyon so that Cash couldn't see anything except treeless cliffs on either side when the party drew close. Most of the group stayed back to drive the herd. Cash and Judge rode at the head with a few of the others spread out behind them in a wedge, right up to the cliff with turreted, automatic guns pointing at them from above. There were cannons, too, but they didn't seem interested. Cash felt tall in his saddle, with guns aimed at him like that, his body exposed, like walking in a room barefoot with spiders. The guns would most likely leave them alone, or at least let them turn around, but it didn't stop any fear of their bite.

"Ha'pe," shouted Judge. "We are a peaceful party of seven, armed out of respect for the perils of our journey. We're looking to make an offer."

A voice echoed out of the wall, made louder by some kind of metal rigging part way up, "State your business and your point of contact. Keep your hands visible and motions slow or you will be fired upon."

"My point of contact," answered Judge, "is a man you should know well by the name of Ran Praylum. He knows who I am, and what I do to men who point steel at me."

"Your name."

"Most just call me Judge."

A slit opened in the gate along with a net and a man's head.

He climbed down the net. Cash scratched some of the cold sweat that had built just under the topside of his neck gaiter and watched him.

"A bit dramatic, isn't all this?" said Cash to Judge. Red stamped underneath him, already bored.

Judge's gray mare scoffed in disgust for the youthful impatience. Judge patted her on the neck, "Easy, girl. The young will learn. Well, Cash, word in the liquor corners of the Basin is that the heir to the throne, or whatever they call him here, Ran's younger brother, Yora, pissed off Ashra folk when he got nosy in their business. He thinned out Ezra's forces and took a woman with him. They were testy before, now they've been shutting their gates for just about anyone."

"Over a girl?" Cash looked up at the gate. It was functional, hardly what he'd call pretty, and old. It must have been ancient, belonging to some warring people who populated the land even long before the last civilization. Most communities in the Basin kept to themselves, but the High Valley kind of exclusion, as Cash understood it, was different.

"Yeah, a girl. You'd be surprised what the right one could do to your head."

"Must be some girl."

The man finished descending and two more followed. They all wore some kind of brown armored vest and uniform gun belts. Cash recognized the first as Ran, the leader of a group of riders that they met on the way here. Ran seemed intimidating to Cash at first, about Cash's size but with a wild side, about as unpredictable as the first draw on a deck of cards.

Ran had strutted into their camp in the middle of the night before anyone saw him, almost getting shot in the process. The gang was all jumpy after the attack at the meadow. "Gentlemen, ladies," Ran said. "Why are you all gunning toward my valley with all this fine, stolen cattle?" He put his hands close to his vest. "And who in their right mind camps without a good fire? I'm freezing."

Teeg woke up and yelled something obscene, pulling out a rifle.

Ran drew on him fast. Teeg kept his rifle up anyway.

Still addressing the camp, Ran kept his eye down the sights of his pistol. It was a nice model, not from any distributor Cash had seen. The Valley man smirked. "A gunman walks into a camp of strangers. That man is either crazy, drunk, or...?"

Cash saw a row of barrels make their way out of the shadows of the trees, hidden from the starlight. He cursed himself for not seeing them sooner but marveled at their ability all the same. Their armored vests told him they were the riders he had seen at the tree line a way back on the trail.

"A bold distraction."

They could consider themselves flanked. One of the Valley men brought out Chip and Ringer, who were supposed to be keeping watch.

Judge loved it, and the prince and the outlaw leader became friends. Most of their conversations were kept quiet from Cash, making him wonder if he might have been subject of whatever deal they were making.

Now, at the gate, Ran strutted toward them on foot again with a smile of friendship on his face. Next to him walked another man, a more thoughtful one who stood a little taller and wore just a half-smile that seemed to take more effort. The tall man also had an important-looking insignia on his armored vest, a more ornate version of a spear and a scroll that Cash had seen on the other Valley soldiers. The two were obviously brothers, sporting the same dark hair and slender features. Cash guessed they must be ten years older than him, give or take a few. His own face had less wear. Theirs were the leather faces of no princes for a palace. They were Valley riders, men of their people. The other man with them, in contrast, was older and heavy. His face was serious. In another world Cash would have thought he was a hired gun. Here, he was called a soldier. He must have worked with them as the voice for the ranks. A second, like what Cash was to Judge.

The three men approached with the accented background of the massive gate behind them. The gate, old and worn, was a tower of many levels, a one-sided castle of its own rugged majesty. Scaffolding on the main tower in the middle showed the partial construction of the face of a woman. She must represent the Queen of the Heavens, whose name was rarely spoken, of the scroll and spear on the tall brother's chest. Given time, maybe the gate could be less of an eyesore someday.

"Princes!" exclaimed Judge. "Do I call you princes?" He got off his horse. Cash followed. The other four stayed on their horses and kept the wedge formation.

The taller brother spoke, "I suppose so, our father being King, our mother Queen. But I prefer just Yora."

"Lord Praylum, if I may—" the military man spoke.

"It's fine, Captain." Ran cut him off.

The heavy-set captain turned his eyes into the trees.

Cash addressed the captain to ease the man's mind. "The rest of our company follows with the cattle drive. You'll see them soon enough. We didn't want to roll up with thousands of cattle right away."

Yora stepped forward. "I apologize for the hostility. I serve as captain of the gate. We're anticipating a war here, if you haven't heard." He reached out a hand for Judge.

Judge took the hand, then passed it to Cash.

Cash gripped Yora's hand and shook it. Something about the nature of the handshake felt right, like he understood the man behind it before even meeting him.

"I know you," Yora said, not letting go of his hand.

"I don't think you do," Cash said.

Judge laughed.

"Yes, I do." Yora patted his other hand on Cash's back.

"You're the man who fired the first shot. You killed my old man's new father-in-law. Right now, you're the most famous man in High Valley."

"The whole Basin," said Ran.

"Except for perhaps the king." Yora dropped Cash's hand but kept gripping him by the shoulder blade, leading him on.

"Give him time," said Ran with a wink. "I saw that ranch full of bodies. Boy, you're going to like it here just fine."

"You knew about this, didn't you, Judge?" Cash stood in the doorway to Judge's room. His blood was hot, like it would get sometimes when he was a teenager and Judge was trying some kind of leadership exercise on him. The gang was bigger back then. Cash had to work hard to keep their respect. Sometimes, Judge would get under his skin so bad he wanted to leave. He stayed though. Judge was his family. He also had a hard time imagining life without Abelnora.

Tonight, the gang was down to the core, the pure metal. The princes put them up in a small hotel in a town near the gate. High Valley, as seen from the hotel on foothills, was bigger than Cash anticipated, with towns dotting the plains and hillsides, mountains rising up all around with canyons and rivers in between. It was a beautiful paradise in a land that looked like it belonged to stories about mythic creatures for children. Its beauty was a contrast to the desert landscapes of the world farther west.

Judge was leaning back in a protesting chair, crooked reading glasses narrowing the point of his nose. "Knew about you shooting one of the most important men in a brewing conflict between two of the biggest powers in the Basin?"

"You didn't tell me. I just thought Ezra Steele was just some old rancher."

"You knew he was a Keeper. That's why you went snooping

around. You just didn't know he was also some 'old rancher' whose daughter was about to be married off to the mayor of Ashra City's son. Pora. Beautiful, if you think about it. He'd recently lost a lot of his men to a raid from our princey-boy Yora here, some months back. I met a *tossite* in Liberty who was on the run from Ran's guys. Valley matters," Judge shrugged. "He said that same daughter Yora lifted out of town married the king."

"You couldn't resist that game, could you? Did you know what I would do?" Cash sat down on the bed and rubbed his forehead.

"Not at all. I really was there to get us a deal moving cows."

Cash didn't know if he believed Judge or not, but that didn't stop him from feeling bad again. "Techa fio."

Judge shut the book in his hands and put it on the desk. Turning his chair toward Cash, he said, "Cash, I told you before, you did the right thing. You always do the right thing."

"How?" Cash leaned forward into his elbows. Crazy old man and his stupid schemes. "How did you know all this?"

Judge put his feet up on the bed next to Cash. "I've found in my old age that information sells better than stolen goods. I'm poor, so I deal in both."

"All those drunken conversations at campfires and bars pay off, huh?"

Judge kicked Cash in the leg. "Hey."

"Whatever." Cash held up his hands.

"I'll tell you why we're here, Cash."

Cash swiped a hand through his matted hair, scratching at the itch of so many days unwashed. He still missed his hat. Dumb horse.

Judge kept talking. "Listen to me. People here don't believe the same things I do. They're all about the mother coming down from the heavens someday and lifting them all up and how her deathless son will save them again or some—"

"You don't believe any of that?"

"Sure, maybe something happened all those years ago. Maybe society was saved by a deathless, half-machine warrior from outer space. Seems unlikely, but that doesn't matter. What I know is what I feel."

"Judge." Abelnora came to the doorway. She wore a loose nightgown she probably got out of the closet in her room and had her hair tied up in a way that made Cash stifle a snort. She ignored him, somehow in a pretty sort of way. Sometimes Cash thought of her like that, as a pretty girl with a few too many bad habits, but he did his best to choke down the feeling. She was kind of like a sister. "Do you two wanna keep it down? My room is next to yours and I don't wanna spoil this sleep. The mattress is amazing. Don't ruin this for me."

Cash teased her, "What? Had enough of the leaf? The woman is fallible, after all."

She started, "I'll break your a fallible jaw, you tev—"

"I'm sorry, Abe," Judge cut her off. "We'll be done in a minute. Is... is my lady still with you?"

"Yessir, but she's passed out on the other bed."

"I'll come get her in a minute."

"Fine."

Abelnora left and Cash got up to leave as well.

"Hold on a minute, son."

Cash sat back down. "I'm not looking to buy into anything from these people here, Judge. I'm glad they took the cattle. Then we'll be on our way, right?"

"Son," Judge sighed. "There's a voice, in this world, a mother, more holy and ancient than any who may come from a ship in the sky."

"Yurasema."

"Yurasema."

"Find a way to listen to her. She brought us here for a reason. I think she led you to shoot that rancher. I believe that everything happens for a reason. Everything that is life in this universe is connected."

"Sure, the giant tree."

"Cash, I'm trying to get at something here. There's an important piece to this puzzle, and it's you." Judge was trying to be serious.

"Judge, did you know that man had those kids tied up?"

Judge flared his nostril with a loud breath. "I knew he was a bad man in a world where he's got plenty of company. I was just there for some legitimate work."

Cash scratched the side of his head, thought for a moment, and then nodded. "Sure thing, Judge. I'll find a way to listen to the voice, or whatever it is, Mother Nature." He turned to the door.

"I love you, son."

Cash thumped the doorframe twice. "Soon as we get out of here, I'll find religion and purpose."

Judge was swearing under his breath as Cash shifted his focus.

Abelnora's door had her behind it. Thoughts of her intruded his mind. That pretty flash of annoyance that always hit her face when he teased. Cash felt his tongue slip to the inside of his cheek where he'd been chewing on it, pursing his lips together as fluttering jitters puckered around his skin. Yeah, this was turning into a crush, wasn't it? Silently laughing to himself, Cash clomped the white wooden door hard with his fist and chucked himself down the hall as fast as his tired legs would go. She shouted after him but he was long gone and around the corner, smiling the widest he had in a long time.

Arriving at his room, Cash saw his dirty chaps draped over a chair. The fresh sheets on his bed, the invite of the handmade quilt, the pretty, wiry girl down the hall, all offered sweet distractions from the troubles of his mind. But the chaps reminded him of the hills he'd just traveled, swarming with gathering posse. His thigh holster, hanging over the chaps, still had the oil from the skin of his hands, the same hands that pulled the trigger on a ranch full of hired guns. He could see the rough cut of dead, bearded faces in the dark. Unburied stench of death seeped into the picture.

I'm an outlaw, Cash thought. *I'm made for killing.* He didn't know what else he could be. Yora and Ran liked him. They liked the killer, just like Judge.

Cash kicked off his boots. They bumped and rolled on the polished wood. The boots weren't used to floor like that. They were made for long trails and rugged streets, paved again and again with stone and dirt by the people of Ashra City. He could see the workers, beaten down by harsh law and unjust conditions of servitude. Funny enough, those people, the poorest, were some of the happiest Cash had ever met. What did they think of Cash Rivers? Did some of their kids make it home from Ezra's ranch? He tried not to imagine them stumbling over the dozens of bodies he and Judge had left to get there. Nevertheless, that's what it always took: bodies.

Yora and Ran seemed like good men. They seemed battle hungry, ready to collect the right bodies. They enjoyed the idea of conflict with Ashra City. The wake of Cash's impulse was the gang's ticket with them.

I haven't messed anything up, Cash told himself. *I've opened new doors.*

He stepped over to the window of his room, still in the dark, no need to light a candle. The moons were crossing paths. One big one, one small, washing the valley with borrowed light. "I'll kill a thousand more men," he told the night, "if it means no more broken kids like me."

The road ahead seemed unclear but laid out. Maybe all this was some great design coming together, if not by a goddess of starry trees, perhaps one set in motion by an outlaw who called himself Judge. Or maybe, Cash was the master of his own

design, and tomorrow he would throw in lots with the leaders
of High Valley.

11

First, Arty noticed the sound. It sounded like fingers on a keyboard, but erratic and continuous. She couldn't open her eyes to investigate. A faint light in her eyelids told her it must be daytime. They always turned the lights on for the start of each shift. But this light wasn't as bright as it should have been.

Her limbs weighed down and she could hardly move her fingers. She felt like this once after surgery. The *Marshall*'s doctor ordered her wisdom teeth out shortly after deployment. The Old Woman, as they called the doctor, gave her a sedative, letting the equipment keep her vitals stable, and dug them out. When she woke up, she was in one of the medbays next to a few other junior officers having procedures done. One senior officer was also there behind a curtain getting a colonoscopy for a few polyps. He was embarrassed.

"I'm not old enough for this," he moaned. They had all laughed.

Arty imagined, eyes still closed, that she must be in the medbay. Maybe her friend Lopez was here. Sitting by her bed. She tried to call out to her but couldn't even manage a whisper. Her throat scraped like fingers pinching sandpaper.

Opening her eyes a little bit, Arty expected to see machines and nurses. All she saw was a gray and blue fuzzed-up blur. It still might have been the medbay. Whatever these drugs were, they were killer.

Her mind had trouble focusing, like once after cryo. She

hadn't been out like that in a while though. The crew resorted to cryo when jumping to unknown territories, places without relays, and when the ship's acceleration would be too much to dampen for conscious travel. When finished with mapping a new star system, there would be a cryo jump to get to the next.

No, not cryo. She must have had a medical emergency. Those happened in space. They must have put her out to fix her. Appendix? She couldn't remember what happened.

The sound caught her attention again. It never stopped. Typing, outside, the spring of the keys so constant so irritating so—

It had to be water hitting the bulkhead somewhere. She jumped, but her limbs wouldn't move right and her throat rasped, "Flooding on deck seve—" Ugh, she couldn't move. She couldn't speak. She couldn't hold her eyes open in the clouds of her broken vision.

"Lopez, you there?" she mouthed.

Hours of semi-realistic dreams took her through the hallways and a day's work aboard the FSV *Marshall*. She talked to her friends and avoided Commander Worley in the mess hall. At one point she realized she forgot to have any pants on while delivering a report from the AIC to the Bridge. That was disconcerting, but all that was forgotten when she sat back on her bunk and tried to read on her mobile. There was something there she was excited about, but the images wouldn't appear. She was dreaming.

Just a dream. Arty opened her eyes again. This time she could see the room better. A slanted ceiling, not gray but wood-stained brown, met four walls around it, sloping upward where a window showed daylight at the head of her bed. She had a bed, not a wall-bunk. The light from the window must have been some of what bothered her before. This wasn't the *Marshall* after all. She wondered if she ended up planet-side somewhere. No, that didn't make sense. They were years from any inhabited world.

A distracting and euphoric buzz crept through the flesh of her arms. It swam under her skin like stimulants from an IV where she didn't have any. She realized she could move them now. Lifting her arms to her face, she brushed back her hair with her fingers. Something seemed different about her whole body. Excited, she swung her legs off the bed and soaked in the room around her. The furniture and aesthetic had an outdoor feel.

"Wait, where am I?"

The traces of soreness in her throat were vanishing. "Hello?" she called out. A forest-green-colored door stood closed to her left at the foot of the bed. The sound she heard, the one she thought was a flood, was coming from the window and above the ceiling.

The excitement mixed with creeping dread in the pit of Arty's abdomen. The sound she'd been hearing had been rain. Rain meant an open sky. She had never seen an open sky. A wind of panic slid over her mind in a flurry of mental precipitation, dotting her consciousness like the flecks of rain on the window. She started to remember that she shouldn't be here, that not long ago, or perhaps a very long time ago, she almost died.

Gods, the Marshall.

Flashes of stars and a warrior goddess-ship suspended in the arc of time. A planet with a silhouette guardian. Oceans of galaxies swimming through space in indeterminate patterns. Another flash. The *Marshall* exploding underneath her. Silent screams of everyone and everything she knew coming apart. Drifting. Alone. Falling. Consciousness coming apart. Oblivion.

Arty had gone through some nervous times in the past. Her drill instructors said there would be a moment when all of them would want to quit, that they had realized they had left their worlds behind and nothing but "hard shit" awaited them. When that moment came, she got through it. The quickest way out of a tough situation was always to wade through it.

This attack of panic wrought of hell was different though. It came at her from within, from the walls, from the dripping rain, it wrapped itself around her heart and curled up her fingers in uncontrolled hyperventilation. It was the grip of actualized hopelessness that pulled Arty down to the floor. She writhed on the floor, clutching her forehead with her knees and her gut with her arms.

Then someone knocked at the door.

"Lieutenant, are you ready to speak now?"

A woman sat on a chair at the foot of Arty's bed. Arty didn't want to talk to her. She stared at the rain on the window, trying to imagine what the world outside it must look like. The splattering raindrops hid all but the green that must have been leaves on a tree. She wanted to see the tree, but also felt frightened, frightened to find herself under a sky with a horizon and no glass to protect her.

The place where she grew up didn't have a sky, only networks of tunnels and large bubbles, nothing worthy of even being called a town, much less a nation. Then she boarded the shuttle and said goodbye to that life. After training on an asteroid base in a forgotten star system, she scored high enough for a lieutenant position in Detections aboard the *Marshall*. The *Marshall* was all walls and no real windows. She didn't feel ready for the openness of a sky.

The woman spoke again. She had found Arty on the floor in a fit of memories that didn't make sense. Arty still didn't know who the woman was, and as a Federacy officer, she didn't wish to speak until she knew exactly where she was and who was holding her. Arty wondered why the woman didn't have a mobile of some kind. If she was here to observe, she should have a note-taking device.

"Lieutenant Sato, do you know where you are?"

That was a dumb question. Of course she didn't. She'd obviously been drugged, that much was certain, but Arty didn't know how they could have gotten her here from the *Marshall*'s position when it exploded. She also wasn't sure if it did explode, or if she dreamt it up during her long time under ice. Arty looked down at her hands. Another memory of that day was bothering her.

"Do you remember something, Arty?"

Arty looked up at the woman. She sure looked like a shrink with business attire and a poignant stare, but she was younger, more like an attractive type of psychiatrist from the movies. The kind who ends up falling for the hero or being the bad guy.

"Lieuten...ant," the shrink woman's voice faltered, glitching for a moment like a video stream that hadn't quite rendered properly.

Arty jumped, startled by the sound and what she caught from it in her peripheral vision. The woman's face seemed to come apart for a split-second, again like a bad video, pixelated in weird places around her mouth and cheek bones, and her eyes were too big. But by the time Arty turned to look, the woman was fine, staring at her with hands clasped in her cross-legged lap.

"Arty," the woman said, standing up.

"Don't touch me." Arty scooted back on the bed into the wall.

The woman moved closer, reaching out a hand to place on Arty's quivering shoulder.

"I said don't touch me." Arty reached up a protesting hand.

"We brought you here for a reason, but you have to talk to me. We are not the enemy you think we are."

"Don't touch me!"

As the woman reached for Arty's shoulder, Arty shouted. The walls of the room shook in response. Arty pushed the woman, but with more force than she anticipated. A flash of light came out of her hand, just as it had that day she floated in space in the memory she wasn't sure was real. She felt the power come out of her, like from an internal battery. It felt good and awful at the same time. The psychiatrist disappeared in the light, shattered into particles that didn't fall to the floor. They scurried through the air, finding each other again but not in the same shape. They flew out through the cracks around the door in a smoke of eeriness. The woman wasn't human.

Arty froze in breathless silence, shocked and numb to incomprehension. She looked at the door, then down to her hand, trembling all over. Something had happened to her, was happening to her, but she had no context to comprehend what. Nothing felt real. If there were such a thing as a waking nightmare, this was it.

Before she could gather all her senses and rouse the trained officer in her, the shadows of the room darkened and shifted. The furniture and architecture joined the shadows, collapsing and moving in fluid chaos, much like the disintegrated shrink, like everything around her was made of the same substance.

"What?" she whispered.

Invisible forces reached from the darkness and pulled her down, cold clamps, binding her arm, hand, and foot to a soft surface she couldn't see. Surprising, soothing, waves of euphoria hit her.

Oh, I remember this.

12

—·—

Yora's horse carved new tracks into the path of switchbacks from the main gate up to his wife's home. The estate itself was larger than most of the surrounding community. Ran called it a palace, but really the house itself wasn't large, just the ranch. None of it was meant for hosting anyone. Yora kept his family life private. His sister, Mya, took charge of it since Vonica wasn't up for management.

Yora II was at the door before he had the horse hitched under the porch. The prince's son was a delicate ten-year-old with his head in the cloudy mountain sky. He loved art and epic poetry about heroes.

"Father, you're back!" The boy ran down the stairs and hugged him. He grew a little more every day, and even a few days gone reminded Yora how much he had to miss.

"My boy!" Yora lifted his son into the air, who laughed in delight. A wheezy cough escaped his small lungs. "Hey, I brought you and your mother some things."

"Like what?" he coughed. The coughs weren't more than just the sound of fluid shifting around. That was good. The medicine helped, as well as the massages.

"First, a new mbaijei ball, we'll play with it later. Also some new books."

The boy reached up to where Yora grabbed the toy out of his saddle bag.

"Next, your favorite... new medicine."

The boy took a sack of leaves out of his father's hand and peeked at them with a crinkled nose. "I'd rather not."

"No one asked your approval, just your well-being. Start a pot going so you can take the vapors. Tell your mother I'll be right up."

"Will you need anything from town today, sir?"

Yora turned to see his horsekeeper unhitching Lila, his horse of the day, from her post. "You were quick today," he told the man. "I almost didn't see you. And no, just feed Lila something special for me. I rode her hard this afternoon... had a lot on my mind."

"With pleasure, Lord." The horsekeeper pulled out a yellow-tinged root from his pocket and gave it to the mare. She chomped it down and relaxed her ears, eager for her stable.

Ascending the steps, Yora paused for a moment on his porch and leaned against a pillar where he could overlook the estate. Summer was over and a sweet breeze of early fall billowed the grassy fields. He looked into the hills with a sense of longing. Memories crept back into his daylight dreams.

He had a job similar to Ran's responsibilities at that time, leading riders outside Shadow Pass, establishing relations with neighbors and capturing fugitives. He'd received word of a murderer and horse thief who fled to Ashra City, a long way from High Valley near the coast. The riders found and tracked the criminal to his gang's hideout on an overlook near the water. It was late at night when they found him. He had a woman there, a hostage for her rich father's ransom.

Her name was Denaiah Steele, and she was the most beautiful woman Yora had ever seen.

He remembered the ground was wet where he wrestled down one of the guards of the horse-thief's camp. The man fought back before Yora could have him in the right hold for the choke, with one arm over the man's head and the other around his throat with the crease of Yora's elbow blocking the arteries in his neck. Looking back, he could have had one of his men take the man out, but he never asked any of them to do something he wouldn't do himself. The guard bit and struggled, strong and desperate to get out of Yora's grip. In a calculated risk, Yora released the choke, took a knife off his vest and inserted the length of the blade under the man's ribs. The dying guard let out no more sound than a gasp for air. The warmth of his blood felt wrong in contrast to the damp undergrowth.

Yora's men pressed on, ten of them in two teams of five through the brush. Tall trees reached skyward above them, casting long shadows under the light of one of the moons. They used the shadows as pieces of the darkness. The other team killed two more guards. He knew they were lucky not to be met by any dogs, who would have sensed their raid. Pressing himself into the Earth, he didn't feel any fatigue, even as he and his men were reduced to a low crawl, inching closer and closer to the thief where he slept near his remaining friends.

At once they had him and three others. Two more had fought back and fallen to the riders' blades. Without any shots fired, Yora's men won what could have been a terrible battle, but they didn't know they won even more than a prisoner.

"Who's out there?" a woman's voice cried from inside the tent.

"Did anyone clear the tent?" Yora's second-in-command questioned the group as they collected themselves. Yora hadn't even seen the tent, its position in the shadows barely visible in the pale light. The moon was already setting.

Yora pulled out his pistol and signaled his closest men to keep back from the swaying flap of the tent. He stepped through just as a slender arm swung an unlit torch at his face. She missed.

He grabbed the torch and froze.

"Are you all right, sir?" his second shouted.

Yora took a moment to answer, listening to heavy breathing. He couldn't see her silhouette in the darkness, just feel her. Their fingers met on the shaft of the torch. "I'm fine," he managed to reply.

He fumbled for a lighter. He tried to always have one in a small pouch to the left of his front-loaded rifle clips of his less ceremonious riding vest. Finding one, Yora used it to light the torch. The flames drew her face in the crisp atmosphere, playing out the vision of her like the angelic dream of a stranger. She was fair, not like a fighting woman, with sunlike features, a radiance that took the heat of battle right out of his blood. The mud that stuck to his face and arms seemed like an unworthy introduction, a filthy rescue.

Neither of them spoke. The air between them billowed in quickening breaths. Whatever he was feeling, she seemed to be feeling it, too.

Yora's second entered, dismembering the moment. "Sir, another prisoner?" He eyed the woman, glanced at Yora, and then looked back at her again. Not a prisoner, then. "Are you alright, ma'am? Were you with these thieves?"

Denaiah gathered herself. She wore a dirty dress that looked like it must have been nice at some point. Her right arm showed signs of bruising.

"These men took me while I rode under heavy guard from my sister's house. They didn't harm me, not very much, but they kept me here for ransom money. My father is wealthy, he... did he send you?"

"No," Yora said, "but he should have."

A crash from inside the house snapped Yora back to the present. He pulled open the door and burst inside. "What happened?"

His sister Mya came down the hallway from the kitchen

and caught him before he ran through. "It's fine," she said. "No, really, it's fine, but maybe not a good time to–"

A slow, moaning cry met his ears from the last doorway down the hall in the kitchen. "Nooooo, no, no. I'm not ready. He can't see me now! It's not ready. Tell him to go away. I'm not good enough. He doesn't love me, he doesn't–"

Yora stopped and looked down at his sister. "How bad is it?"

"She hasn't kept more than a carrot down in two days. She's rail thin and... she's obsessed with you still, do you know that?"

"Sure, when she's not convinced I'm hiring men to kill her."

Another crash and a thud sounded out of the kitchen. His wife Vonica had probably destroyed another pot and thrown herself on the ground.

"I do love her. Thank you, Mya. I couldn't do this without you."

Mya tried to smile. Taking care of Vonica had taken a toll on everyone involved in her care. Yora thought it would help to move close to home, but often found himself still keeping his distance. Mya had volunteered to take over her sister-in-law's estate for Yora II's sake.

"Yor," she said. "It's okay. I care for her, too."

Yora didn't doubt her. She had always shown more kindness than he had toward all members of the royal family. To Ran, she was best friend and confidant. To Yora, she was a grounding rod. For the electric storm that was the Yora and Vonica Praylum house, Mya was the grounding rod that kept the lightning from striking it down. If nothing else, she kept his little boy smiling.

He walked past his sister and went up the stairs that overlooked the entry. Yora II sat at the top with a blank expression on his face. Reaching down, Yora patted his son on the head. "Boil the pot a little later, son. I'll rest up and then we'll go for a ride, okay?"

"Okay, Dad," his son coughed.

"I promise."

The boy nodded, covering his mouth, and kept coughing.

Denaiah refused to go back to her father. She said he was a terrible man and the worst kind of villain. Yora counseled with his advisors and they determined they could take her back to High Valley. The King was less and less open to reason about asylum for outsiders.

"Do you love your wife?" she asked one night in front of a fire.

They had caught another fugitive, one last stop before they would turn toward home again. Denaiah had stuck with them for weeks, rejecting the idea they could leave her anywhere else but in their company. Yora couldn't bring himself to tell her otherwise. Instead, he found excuses to spend more time with her. Her company, though platonic at the surface, was alleviating. Anytime he thought about the danger she may have brought with her, the diplomatic questions, he saw her smile.

"I don't like the question," he answered.

"Then you don't."

"It's never that simple."

"Do you love me?"

Yes. He didn't say. His father had accepted the asylum in a surprising proposal of marriage. Yora never told her his feelings. He wasn't even sure what they were except for quiet longing and aching regret. Duty to his family was a dissecting scalpel around his heart. Vonica at home was a dying cause, but she was his, his to care for. He had made her that promise. What was any man without a promise?

"Dispatch for you, Lord Praylum." A thin, younger rider appeared. He wore just the essentials, no vest. From the way he was sweating, he'd been riding fast. Yora recognized him from one of the scout teams he'd sent out the day before.

Yora left Denaiah and her spell by the fire, shaking off whatever captivation he had felt for readiness. "Give it to me straight, soldier."

The scout took a breath to collect tired thoughts. There was urgency in his voice, also fatigue. His horse couldn't have fared much better. "Keeper forces are a half-day west of us. Talk in the hills is that they're after the girl. We didn't get a good count, but I'd guess at least two companies of fast riders. Ezra Steele sent them packing light."

Yora whistled, a signal for his lieutenants. "Can you keep riding?" he asked the scout.

"My horse is spent, but I'm always ready."

"You've got an hour to rest. Make it count."

The soldier shuffled away. He was young. An hour would be enough.

Denaiah was standing by the fire when he got back. Her beautiful face was solemn. The firelight flickered at the back of her bare calves. "I heard," she said softly.

"I can't be with you," he said, mindlessly running his fingers through her hair that fell over her shoulder. She leaned into his hand, letting his palm cradle her cheek. "But I can kill for you. Call it what you want."

Tears fell from her soft eyes into the rough of his palm. He pulled her into his chest.

After this, I'm going home.

Finished for the day, Yora II happy with the ride and Vonica with Mya in another room, Yora lowered himself into the pull of winter sheets. They were cold.

13

— . —

Amber candlelight glow danced over shadows in the creases of callused weathered hands, illuminating their work just enough for the gray-templed man dressed in animal skin who sat alone cleaning a wooden rifle. He handled the weapon as a friend, care and precision directing the movement of his worn fingers. The sheen of the metal reflected the candle, adding something beautiful to an instrument of death, just like the hands.

The cabin around the man was lived in, cluttered, but as carefully made and cared for as the rifle. The same hands built the cabin as the rifle, but the rifle was older, much older. Black and white photographs sat on the shelves, some in Ashra City when it was new, others in High Valley when it was new. The photographs showed old settlers as they broke ground and climbed scaffolding. They built cities on top of ruins, paving the way for generations to live and thrive without the ugliness of the devastated past. The new towns stood on the graves of billions. No one remembered, not really, except for the weathered hands.

The man put the rifle back together, leaving some of the oil on the bolt and in the barrel to keep cleaning off the carbon overnight. He would hunt again tomorrow, as he often did, and then watch over the citizens of the valley, as he often would. An air of change blew to his deeper senses. Whether good or bad powers were at work, he had yet to determine.

He put the rifle on the mantle of his ember-specked fireplace next to a glass picture frame. A woman stared back at him through the years behind the pane. The old photograph reminded him of her red hair and the sickness she hid, but it couldn't help him remember her laugh. In front of her on the glass, the man saw his eyes reflected in their own light. They glowed, much like the candle, but with the fierceness of a warrior, a harrowed warrior long lost to roam a world not his own.

Weary, beaten, but still fighting, old man Seth blew out the candle, content, for now, with the shadows.

14

— · —

"You don't meet a king every day!" Judge exclaimed.

"You don't meet a horse talking through the taputo every day either," said Teeg.

"Are we gonna know the difference?" chimed Eimos.

Judge spun around. "What's that, boys? You want to guard the herd with the others? That's fine. Cash, Abelnora, you'll ride with me to the palace with the princes. The rest of you, mberu! Get that wagon out of here."

Cash rode out from the hotel stable with what would be the King's small audience, Red plodding along beneath him. Abelnora, Judge, Cash, Ran, Yora, and an accompanying posse of guards took to the winding road. They were just over a half day's ride away from the palace in the heart of the valley. The King's magnificent home overlooked a small reservoir, the reservoir a maintained relic from times before. Citizens of High Valley were working on how to replicate the old ways of using water to create electricity, but it seemed they were some ways off from figuring out how to distribute the power throughout the valley. Some of it did serve for arms manufacture along with water-powered mills. Cash had seen a few of those in Ashra City.

The High Valley's true wealth and pride, as Ran explained on their journey, could be found underground. The King's Palace sat over a spring of extremely hot water, which ancient people used to channel into recreational spas dating back thousands of years. When the King's grandfather settled the valley with Seth, Prince of Libertas, they built the palace at the center of the valley over the spring as a gathering place for the weary of the Great Basin. People left Ashra City in droves to settle here. They found ore, oil, coal, gold, and peace from the growing corruption in Ashra's streets.

Yora contributed more history. "Ran and I were schooled in the town outside the palace. Our father didn't want us growing up ignorant of even the most basic needs in High Valley, so we learned from the best teachers he could find. Military strategy, mathematics, geology, zoology, and professional fighting."

"What happens if you couldn't make the cut?" asked Abelnora.

Yora shrugged. "Never had to wonder. We weren't asked to be perfect; we were just asked to be aware, and to know that wherever we were sent, we were meant to be leaders."

Judge seemed intrigued. "Do you move around a lot?"

"We take posts of our choosing based on the need we can fill. For now, I guard the gate at Shadow Pass. Ran scouts beyond the wall, as you know. My youngest sister Mya...she takes charge of my wife's estate, and I have another sister, Tais, a little older than her but younger than me who patrols the Eastern Border."

"And the North and South?" asked Cash.

"Other able-bodied men and women."

Most of the ride passed in silence over brush and rock. The dirt roads had a red in their brown color that Cash found appealing. The valley floor was a faded fall green but still reminded him of the western deserts where he was from. The hills and mountains were covered in trees. If Cash wanted to move through them without being seen, he could have. The tactical position of the whole valley was uncontestable. They had built walls and gates to keep enemies out and had boosted their own strength from within.

"Why just stay here in the valley?" Cash asked Yora, pulling up next to him.

"What do you mean?"

Cash pushed a branch away from his face. Red had led him too close to a tree. "You have the numbers, the strength, the strong capital, and technological advantage as far as I can tell. You could spread out, liberate other communities, spread your influence. We're coming from places that could use change in leadership."

"I know," said Yora. "I've seen them."

"And shot our way through them," piped in Ran from just behind.

"Hear me out," Cash said. "I lost my parents in Ashra City."

"Are you from there?" Yora tilted his head, interested.

"Near enough. Now, you people could take the city. And if you do, I mean, should the occasion arise, seeing you already have beef with their 'leadership,' I just want in. And about that Ezra Steele maniac..."

"You shot him," said Yora."

"Look, I don't want to run for the rest of my life. I'm in. I'm all in. If that's why you let us in High Valley, if it's because you're looking to start something, and my gang is some kind of piece on your board, I'm your man. I shoot better than anyone you know."

The road opened and Ran brought his horse up in line with Cash in the middle of the two princes with Judge and Abelnora listening from behind. The horses swished their tails in unison.

"Hold on to those thoughts, little outlaw," Ran told Cash as he winked to his brother. "We do have some plans."

"I've never seen anything so...so clean!" Abelnora grabbed Cash's arm just above the elbow. It kind of hurt, almost dragged him off the horse, but he also didn't want her to let go.

They rode their horses into the palace complex through an ornate gate made of iron bars and gold-leafed sculptures that Cash didn't recognize. The horses' hooves clipped over symmetrical cobblestone, each brick a perfect diamond shape within a rectangle. The path led uphill through a grove of elegant fruit trees.

Judge was in front of Cash and Abelnora, engaging a member of the princes' guard about his work, weeding out information about the city, its economy and defenses through casual interest. The guard seemed happy to talk, unwary of the outlaw instinct behind Judge's friendly enthusiasm. Judge learned the layout of a land this way, weaknesses and all, either to sell the information or exploit it.

Cash hadn't anticipated such an easy entrance into High Valley. Judge seemed to think that bringing the cattle would be enough, and Cash had always followed Judge as a son would a father. Judge said to go east, everyone went east, but now that they had arrived, a retroactive surprise stirred Cash's senses. There must have been political motives behind inviting wanted men and women to treat them as guests. The King must have known who they were by now, that they were coming in the first place. People always talked about the High Valley and its mysteries like a forbidden country, separate and dangerous. Some looked toward the valley with envy, others with enmity. Yet here they were, in the company of princes riding through a palace complex that in itself boasted the grandeur of classic temples.

Ran had been watching Cash from the hills before walking into their camp. Yora had "rescued" Steele's daughter. There was a contradiction somewhere in this puzzle. The king wanted the valley to close itself off, the princes rode free and waged violence. They definitely wanted Cash for the violence. Asylum for violence. *We've got plans*, Cash recalled with an edge of excitement.

Trees with crimson leaves continued to canopy the walkway along the road. After they left their horses with stable-hands in uniform, the group walked through a grass field dotted with ponds. Some were cool and meant for fishing, others were warm and steamed a sulfuric scent that Cash wasn't sure he liked.

"How many hot springs are there?" Abelnora asked Ran, who turned back and winked.

"Not many, but what you see is irrigated around the Grand Complex from under the palace itself. When our great-grand-father built the palace, he said he could see the veins of old civilizations lost in the ruins. He built a new community on the surface where we worship and wait for the Queen of the Heavens, but from underneath, from the veins of Yurasema, we bathe in the warmth of remembrance for the long dead. We won't forget the blood in the rock and foundation."

Cash looked back from where they walked to where Judge had paused over a steaming pool, standing over an ancient stairwell where the water licked the stones. He placed a cupped hand in the water and used it to drink.

Yora walked up to Cash and gestured toward Judge. "We believe there's a healing power in the water. I wonder if your old man knows that."

"He's not my father."

Yora shrugged. "But he raised you?"

"More or less."

"Then it's close enough. My father didn't raise me."

"Did your mother?" They started to walk again. Abelnora went to bring Judge with them. The palace drew near, its lofty stone craft seeming both inviting and imposing all at once.

"No," said Yora. "There was a man who for a time I knew as a boy. I remember wishing he were my father. He would find Ran and I in the woods and teach us what he called nobler principles. Pride and respect, but also humility, to look after those we might otherwise think were beneath our station."

"Do you remember his name?"

"I don't. He's probably dead by now."

"So, you have naturally warm water, untold riches, and nameless strangers who make influential mentors. Nice town, like something out of a book."

"It's home."

Cash noticed pain behind the word. At least Yora had a home.

15

—·—

Yora had lied. He didn't think his childhood teacher was dead. He had seen him only months ago, but he couldn't be sure because he couldn't trust the memory.

He had just left the wedding at the new queen's manor. It sat away from the palace but still in the complex. Denaiah fit her new home's aesthetic. She and Yora hadn't spent long together on the winding road back from Ashra City, back from bloodshed and unsaid words, but the two of them had grown close. Hardship and proximity had built between them a fast bond, enough for her to ask him if he loved her, enough for him to feel the urge to admit it. But he never did, and he didn't object to the wedding.

"Thanks for the prize," his father the king told him, whispering in his ear.

Stars painted the moonless sky the night Denaiah married Yora's father. Yora rode alone away from the festival, from the ache, from his mother and father, his broken home, everything that tormented his mind. He should have gone Southwest. Instead, he turned his horse East, the only direction that led toward anything that seemed far away, where the concrete and stone of civilization were nothing but ruins and no one would know his name. The trees and cliffs of the mountains called him like a whisper, so he left without going back to his post at Shadow Pass.

He made camp on the far side of the first layer of mountains.

Making his way through circuitous game trails, he set up camp and slept until noon. An emulsion of light shades of blue and white sky brushed with the sun, visibly moving over his head where he sank himself into the grass. A snake moved next to his arm and he jolted awake and upright. The snake didn't strike, but slithered away when he heard a voice.

He didn't understand, but it seemed to say, *Look up!*

Yora looked up from the ground and saw a boy, ragged and starving, no older than thirteen. The boy held a pistol.

"Whoa, I wouldn't do that." Yora slowly lifted his hands.

The boy motioned toward Yora's horse, then pointed at himself.

"You want my horse."

The boy didn't answer.

"Can you understand me? Do you know who I am?"

Still no answer, but the boy started to look upset and said something unintelligible with emphatic waves of the pistol.

Yora noticed something at the hilt of the weapon, then pulled out his own and pointed it at the boy. "Didn't think to bring a clip, did you? Who are you?"

The boy threw the gun at him and started to run.

Yora stood up to unhook the hobble around the horse's legs and mount the saddle. He caught up to the boy before long. The kid was slow and malnourished, leaning against a tree and dry heaving. No vomitus came out, nothing that didn't look like saliva.

Dismounting, Yora tossed the boy a spare canteen. "Drink it slow."

The boy dropped the canteen as it came to him, then picked it up, sloshing the contents back and forth. Once he figured out the cap, he guzzled a few swallows before hurling everything up.

That, Yora wanted to shout at the boy, but didn't, *was good water. Now I need to boil more.*

The boy sat down with his back against the grass at the base of the tree and swore in a way that Yora understood. "Techa."

Yora snapped upright from where he bent down to pick up the canteen. "What did you say?"

The boy didn't answer, looking like a frightened and cornered squirrel.

"Rekulum Joropa?" Yora asked. *Do you speak Joropa?*

"Heh." *Yes,* the boy answered.

What began as a curious annoyance now sparked a new light of fascinating discovery. Many from the Western regions of the Basin spoke Joropa as fragments of a dead language. Yora had studied it, even read some recovered literature, but no one had natively spoken Joropa since centuries before.

He handed the canteen back to the boy. "Slowly," he spoke in Joropa and made a drinking motion with his hand.

"Agulye." *Thanks.*

Yora pulled his pistol from his thigh and checked the rounds in the clip. The boy seemed harmless at this point, but he didn't expect the kid to be alone. Someone might be looking for him, someone who knew how to properly load a gun.

"How did you come this far east?" he asked the boy in the old language.

The boy looked puzzled. He looked over his shoulder at the mountain peaks above them. "I'm from that direction." The way the boy pointed went past the eastern border. No one lived out there.

"I doubt that. You must be turned around."

"Turned around?"

"Lost."

The boy understood. "Yes, I'm lost."

"Alright." Yora kicked a log. "Where are you from?"

The boy pointed east again.

"No, are you from the Kona Tribe?" He named off a few more settlements and communities. The boy didn't respond.

"Okay then, East, over the wall."

"Yes, the wall. I climbed over it. My people are captive to bad men. They took my mother, they... they want to force us to fight..."

Yora frowned. "Did you run away?"

The boy shrugged with his lips, pursing them together in a way Yora hadn't seen before but understood. He'd have to get the rest of the story out of him later.

The boy stayed with Yora at his camp for the night and Yora tried to learn more about him in the morning. His sister Tais and her riders patrolled this side of the Valley, but more for marshalling fugitives from within. No one expected to find anything over the wall except ruins. Maybe he could drop the kid off with her, but then he would have to explain what he was doing. The kid was starving, though. He'd have to help him somehow.

Deciding to bring the boy to his sister was enough to wake Yora back to reality. He didn't have to run away. He would face his life and problems with dignity, and somehow, he would learn to forget the woman. He would do right by Vonica, and his little boy.

The boy didn't have a name, and he didn't know how to ride a horse, so they walked through the day and into the yellow light of midafternoon. Yora used a river to navigate their way down past the foothills of higher peaks and through a long canyon carved out by the river. They approached a place where the river slowed and bent in front of them, wide and shallow. With trees on either side, they would have to cross. The boy again refused to mount the horse and started his way on foot in the water. Noticing movement on the bank nearby, he froze.

"What's that?"

In the direction the boy pointed, a dark bear scouted for fish, swatting the water and swishing its giant face.

"That's nothing to worry about," said Yora with some confidence. "Not unless you can't see him – that's the bear to worry about, or if he's a she with cubs."

The boy tried to understand. "Does it only eat fish?"

Yora's horse eyed the bear, but listened to her rider and stepped into the water to follow the mysterious boy.

"No," answered Yora. "Fish, berries, honey, animals, people."

"Like us?"

"Not likely. But if he's hungry enough, he'll eat the thighs off you while you're still screaming."

Yora wanted to ask the boy more about where he came from, but the language barrier was hard. The boy spoke a different dialect then they spoke out west. The boy picked up maybe seventy percent of what Yora tried to tell him, and Yora didn't always understand the boy, either. After the river, they progressed a short while in silence on either side of the horse.

And then, on a rocky path surrounded by a thick growth of trees, the horse lifted up her head and tail, ready to run.

"Easy, girl, easy." Yora tried to calm her but she reared back, tugging away at the bit. He had to let go and try to jump out of her way. "What's the matter with you?"

The back of Yora's mind told him something dangerous had spooked the horse. *Damn. The bear.*

Look up! He heard the mysterious voice again, speaking some strange language of thought. *Look up look up look up...* Then in his own voice, *Look up look up look!*

The horse tossed her mane and took off down the hill. Yora didn't have time to brace before her heavy shoulder battered him off his feet. As he hit rocks and dirt, the wind left his lungs, like a child hit from a swinging companion under a tree. His head hit the ground with a backward lurch that hurt his back.

In the brush nearby, a low growl curdled Yora's blood. "Whoa, whoa," the growl said in thick, agitated breaths. It sounded like the animal was trying to speak, like it had chosen the two of them out of the many disturbances of the wilderness.

Yora heard the voice, just in his mind. *Weak. Death for honorless prince.*

Instinctively, and still out of breath, Yora pulled his pistol and aimed between his upturned knees, firing into the source of the noise, a dark shape in the trees. It was indeed the bear who stalked them from the river.

The bear ran over Yora. He didn't know if his shots struck or if they went wild. Nothing would stop nature's angry avatar. Yora rolled under its clawed feet as the animal didn't stop. It went straight for the boy, locking his small shoulders in its great jaws. Yora kept firing, spending every shot he had in the clip. At last, he saw it wince. Yora found his wind, or perhaps that he no longer needed it, and leapt at the bear, who swatted him down, dropping the boy, now limp.

Yora saw nothing but dust. The blow had bloodied his face, he was sure. He stopped thinking about it when he felt the bear's teeth in the back of his legs.

He fought to right himself, swatting as best he could, but he was helpless to the better fighter. The bear allowed him no time for defense, no mercy. He screamed, savage, desperate noises that he seemed to hear more than feel.

You are weak, prince. What would make you strong? The voice grew vindictive. Speaking right to the soul.

But then it stopped. The bear stopped, too.

Is it over, am I dead?

The bear's jaws released, just as Yora would have passed out. There was a tearing noise, a slap on hairy flesh. Yora righted himself to look at it. To see why it would stop. He made it to his back in time to see the bear's face fall over Yora's shoulder, pinning him to the ground. There were bloody holes in the joint, large caliber entries.

Someone had shot the bear dead.

Yora tried to speak, to call out, see who had saved him, but he couldn't. He was bleeding from too many wounds. He could taste death in his mouth, iron and filth.

In death's haze, Yora saw a man dressed in silver furs with a large rifle slung over his back. He had old-looking hands and an odd glow in his eyes. He looked like a man Yora knew from his boyhood, his teacher in the woods.

"The boy," Yora pleaded.

The man knelt over him, looking back toward the last place Yora had seen the boy. He bowed his head and closed his eyes, placing one of his weathered palms on Yora's chest.

"Please," Yora said.

"I can't save the boy, I'm sorry," the man replied, moving the hand to Yora's forehead. "I can try and do something for you."

The stranger lifted the bear by the nape of its neck and rolled it to the side with ease that didn't seem possible.

Yora closed his eyes, fainting for the loss of blood. The last thing he remembered was the teacher's hands on his face. He saw something in the wake of leaving consciousness, but he was too weak to make it out. There was a world, perhaps, a dream that didn't make sense. He also felt something like an invisible embrace, a mother's love that didn't match anything he had ever experienced. He puzzled over the feelings until they were gone. Until there was only sleep.

When he woke, a lot of time had passed. The shadows had moved, and the stranger, the boy, and the bear were gone. Yora's horse was nearby with the hobble around her front legs as though he had left her there himself. The trees and the road seemed to be lying to him. Nothing had happened. He had only fallen asleep in an unlikely place.

He also felt a determination to return to his family. His work in the hills, whatever had called him there, a desertion of duty or not, was over. Yora mounted the horse and went home, keeping the secret of the boy and the stranger to himself for the coming months.

At times, when his dreams wouldn't let him forget, he would check himself for scars, anything to show that the bear and the boy were real. His skin was smooth, his body healed. The mystery of the woods drove him to ancient books.

Sometimes, in reference to the spirit of war, they mention the Mark of the Bear.

16

Arty drifted through tangible fields of nothing. Space, as a word, was an adventure she traveled with friends, an ocean of solar winds and islands of stars suspended in the arms of a milky-white galaxy. In space, there was life, and home, and the *Marshall*. Here, in her mind, Arty floated through dreamless, starless night, blackness resting beyond the veil of thought and existence. As cold manifests an absence of heat, darkness of light, Arty witnessed through her skin, in her bones, in her heart and mind, the most unique feeling of nothing.

Sometimes she woke here, confused and unable to climb out of her thoughts to where she must lie in a coma. She didn't know how, but she knew that whatever happened to her in that cabin when everything disappeared into a cloud left her in a strange abyss. Like the day she lost all her friends, she drifted. Maybe her mind made up the sensation of falling because it was all she had, her last reference to any place that made sense. In a way, she felt as though she might still be falling toward the *Libertas* and her cocoon of broken time.

She longed for home, for kinship in a voyage over washes of spacetime. Instead, she had only this, a deathless black of no aroma. She would wish for an escape, if there were anywhere to run away from, or toward. For now, she waited, numb to all but a nameless feeling.

17

Old man Seth crept under the ground in a boiling stream of hot geothermal water and walls lined with corrosive salts. These were the ducts and halls of ancient peoples he never knew, gone long before he came. Above the walls, buried still, sat a town, blown away by harsh weather and war-tearing tragedy into layers of dust. Above that town, on new soil, stood a palace where he was no longer welcome. The palace of the king of High Valley.

He couldn't feel all the pain of what the hot water did to his skin. Despite the ordeal of his first days on Kardu, Seth had found ways to recharge the Botistems he carried, the last pieces of Pegassos and Libertas he had with him. Perhaps they made more a part of him than he had ever realized. What he ate, they consumed. What he fought, they fought. As long as he existed, they pressed on with him, serving their purpose, though weakened enough to let him age.

Seth couldn't stop the slow erosion of time. Lines marked his face, and gray salted his temples. Before long, he cut his hair and accepted the gravity of age, counting the circling sun with the callus of his weathering hands. Perhaps he resembled only a middle-aged man to outward appearance, but he bore the years in every mark, no longer a mere portrait of youth. His mother had done this to him. If he had a better mind, he would still resent her. Sometimes, he did. The emotions ran their course one revolution after another much like the circling sun.

The narrow underground channel of hot springs opened up and he was able to stand. Water fell off his furs, rushing to join the current at his knees and leaving a sulfuric odor. He would smell the stench of it for days. Still, the channel was the best way to sneak into the castle. Faint luminescence of healing kept him at homeostasis. The smell would just have to be something he tolerated.

Seth climbed a duct leading up from the passageway. The walls were orange and thick with mineral deposits, making them slippery. Where he couldn't grip, he burned with his fingers to make rounded holds. His methodic ascent took him to a surface drain in the wall, big enough to see through, where he saw a woman swimming. The water was much cooler here, fed by both the heat of the spring and the cool of a canal pushed from the river running near the palace.

"Denaiah. They didn't tell me you'd arrived." A man's voice echoed through the chamber. He entered through steam that rose out of vents in the floor. The vest on his chest appeared first, an armored plate of a spear and a scroll. Seth gave the people that image a long time ago, before they settled the valley.

The woman surfaced with the elegance of a blooming lily on a reflecting pond, her long hair pulling itself back across her orchid bathing clothes. An attendant handed her a cream-colored towel, which Denaiah accepted to be wrapped around her. She sat on the stone steps of the pool and spoke to the man with the armored vest, the king.

"What kind of staff doesn't announce the arrival of the king's new bride?" She waved her hand in a way that reminded Seth of many women he had known, women who wield beauty as a sword as well as a carrot. He didn't know her, but from the posture of the conversation he knew what kind of relationship he was witnessing from behind the drain.

The king approached her, but didn't sit. "The kind employed by a jealous queen." There was a hint of remorse in his voice, telling Seth that perhaps the man did love both women. That was interesting. Seth didn't know the man's affection still had that kind of reach. He'd grown old and abrasive as a spent brush.

Denaiah stood, her towel dropping behind her. She grabbed the king's collar under his vest. They spoke in hushed tones that Seth couldn't hear. He was about to leave when the king spoke loud enough to hear again.

"I should have them both thrown out of the valley. They act as though I have no more authority." The king paced away. Seth remembered the king from when he was a young ruler, a man of much more promise than the paranoia he saw in him now.

Denaiah picked her towel back up and wrapped it around her shoulders. "Yora saved my life acting with such authority."

"Indeed," the king answered, his back still turned, "and for that I am grateful. But the more people I let through my walls, the closer I bring my people to the dangers of the outside. Dangers to which you are well familiar."

"Listen to your sons, Tarsus, I..." she stammered.

King Tarsus turned back around, sternness in his eyes, "You would call me by my name?"

Denaiah looked down, her eyes unfocused at the level of the king's vest. "Haven't I taken that name for myself, my king?" She looked back up at his face "Aren't you my king?"

The king stroked her hair with discorded affection, letting the question dry out. "Have yourself made ready. I want you in the court. Let my sons see you with me, you and all that my name still means in this valley."

A tear fell from Denaiah's face when the king turned and left. Seth saw Yora's name on her lips. That explained a few things, and also raised a few questions. Maybe it didn't matter for now.

Seth backed away from the drain in search of a better path to the court. A new game awaited him above the subterranean passages and outside the shadows of the wilderness. There were new pieces on the board arriving soon, and the time had come for them to meet their player.

"Well, if you didn't want a war, why did you marry her?" Judge's voice was a needle straight to a social nerve.

The air of the room fell still where Cash sat with Abelnora and Judge around a long table in the queen's dining room. Formalities in the court hadn't lasted long. There was a fanfare, the king entered with his new bride, a beautiful woman named Denaiah, then sat her on his left and took his queen, the first wife, to his right. She was a hardlined woman, stern. The king had a black beard, trimmed to his face, curly hair, and wore a vest similar, but more decorative, than Yora's. Cash half expected to see some sort of crown on his head, like some of the stories, the old Earth ones, but the vest was enough.

The king's doorman had made the introductions in the court. Cash was introduced again as the man who shot Ezra Steele. A murmur permeated the crowd of the court when they heard. They told the story of how he and Judge had cleared out the ranch, toppling the position of the cranky old Keeper like a storm. Denaiah blinked in an emotional sort of way, as they told the story, and she wouldn't look at him. Cash didn't want her to. She must have been his age. He didn't regret shooting her father, but he regretted having to stand in front of her in the cringe of applause. The people seemed to love him for what he'd done. He'd be lying if he said he understood why. There was a hunger for war here.

The atmosphere changed with the meal afterward. Judge kept asking assaulting questions.

"You speak as if I should know you," said the king, cutting into his meat, not answering Judge's question, "as if I should have a reason to not kill you, speaking to me like that."

Judge leaned back in his chair, his food largely untouched. He was one of the few men Cash knew who didn't like meat. "I mean no disrespect, your lordship, and I kindly thank you for the hospitality shown. But I'm just a man who tries to understand the lot he's thrown in with."

The king bit a mouthful of meat off of his knife and spoke with his mouth half full, "You're a man who burns bridges as fast as he builds them, I can see that much."

"My own moral character aside, I think it's a simple enough question."

The king looked at Denaiah, "Why did I marry her?" He set down his knife and fork, seeming to lose himself gazing at her.

The queen sipped her wine out of a tall glass in inexpressive silence, until she spoke, "He wants another son."

The king glared at her, but didn't hold back a response. "Is it a sin to love? Or to love more than once? I'm not the first man in history to take another bride. No, I am a king. Legacy, *Judge*." He spoke the name with some irony. "Legacy, Judge. It is bred into the nature of all men to pass on their legacy. Even if it results in the shape of two warmongering fools."

Ran slapped his hand on the table, lightly, but with enough defiance. "How is it warmongering to tip the rotted tree? The Basin is a festering mass, cancerous. We can hold out here in the valley or we can take the fight where it belongs, spread our influence over the whole land. Don't you see?"

Ran's father scoffed, "All I see is a son who couldn't accept the throne and can barely stand to stay home except for the brief advantage of a good meal. You're Ashran at heart, all the time you spend away, scheming. My other son..." His tone shifted. "And another son so embattled within his own spirit and estate that in the day he does take the throne, he'll either break, or take struggle to the entire world. Slaughtered any more Keeper forces today, Yora? Cause any wars for your mother to mourn?"

"Does anyone want to know?" a woman's voice interrupted

the scene. Cash searched to find where it came from. The timid boldness came from Denaiah. He hadn't heard her voice yet. The register of it was low, like a soft flute. Regal.

"Know what?" Cash found himself saying. It came out sounding more forceful than he wanted it to.

She looked back at him, flushing red. "Why I wanted to marry the king?"

Next to Cash, his fists clenching under the dinner table, Yora wanted to break away from the tension. He had moved home to be closer to his first duties, to his family, and all he got was the unappreciation of his wife and father. But he would stay, if not just to get bludgeoned by the granite hand of grief. In another world, his wife should be at this table. But no, he just listened to others talk about the woman he wished he didn't love. The woman he killed many men for. Denaiah Steele.

No, she was Praylum now. She was queen.

He didn't engage with Denaiah or her open question. The people at the table seemed to consider her an ornament to discuss more than a voice. No one answered her question because they didn't want to know the answer. Yora knew the answer, and didn't want to hear the truth of it out loud. He didn't want to hear the lie either. She didn't love the king. She married him for his protection, for his offer. She could escape her father and all his wishes, the threat of horse-thieves and the Keepers' will, all if she married the old man of her rescuer.

As Yora stared at his plate, moving clenched fists from his lap to flexed fingers on the table, he noted how Cash hadn't stopped looking at her. He also noticed the faint approach of unfamiliar footsteps outside the room. They didn't sound like a guard's boot. They were lighter, yet older. He felt strange hearing them here, out of place for some reason.

A door near the other end of the table opened with seismic intensity. Inside, Yora saw the ghost he'd been dreading. His boyhood teacher, Seth, now his mysterious savior from the mountains, had arrived.

It happened. The Mark of the Bear.

Seth entered into the view of the rest of the dinner party. Not many knew who he was. The few who did spoke first.

"Guard!" shouted the king in disbelief.

Ran jumped out of his chair, hitting his knee in the process. "Techa. It couldn't be."

Yora felt color drop out of his face. "It's true."

Seth nodded to him, as though recognizing why he had a hard time believing something that he should have all along.

"After all this time," Yora's mother gasped. A spontaneous tear sprung out of her baggy eyelid, trickling from the lashes down onto her fingers that closed over her trembling mouth. She had never known about Seth, that Yora knew of. Strange, that she would recognize a teacher that Yora had thought he'd kept secret, even in youth.

That his father knew Seth somehow didn't surprise him.

Seth looked behind him in the doorway. A guard slumped against the wall, dazed, holding his face.

"I see," the guard repeated. "I see it."

"Tarsus," Seth declared, turning back, his mouth curling to the side, amused. "I told you I'd be back. You were young, your father was king; he banished me, but I'm sure you remember. It's time we talked."

Cash watched the emotion play out like a flipbook of confusion on many faces. The stranger eyed each of them, absorbing the story of each. Cash locked his gaze on the fire that seemed to smolder behind the stranger's eyes, his warrior gaze. For a moment, the stranger looked back into his, not losing his casual, yet somehow appropriate, smirk. Cash didn't look away. He got the impression the stranger was deciding something about him, sizing Cash up.

"Who are the outlaws?" the stranger asked. "Cowboys at the king's table?"

"The table is mine," the queen corrected. "As is the palace."

The stranger turned to her. "Then you'll forgive me for intruding."

She trembled at the lip. "I'm afraid I don't. I know who you are."

"And who am I?"

"The one called Seth."

"Be still, Ahina, the man came to speak with me." The king stood, gathering himself. He was still a head shorter than Seth. "Sit down Ran, and Yora, wipe that look off your face. You're both the sons of a king. This man, is a relic." He walked up to Seth, looking a bit underwhelming in spite of the fancy vest. "Say what you came to say, outsider. I won't ask how you got in. I can smell the sulfur."

"Funny," said Seth, barely looking at him, "that I just apologized for trespassing in a place I built with my own hands."

Judge, next to Cash and not wanting exclusion from the conversation, said, "On the topic of forgiveness, the 'outlaw' at the table has no idea what's happening. Please forgive, and indulge."

Seth looked at a spot on the ceiling. "Leave the old outlaw here. I don't trust him. But bring your sons and anyone else to the tower. We have a few things to discuss there." He turned to leave, but looked back one last time at Cash, who still struggled to comprehend the conversation. "Bring him."

Abelnora stayed with Judge, so Cash discovered himself climbing narrow, winding stairs without his friends in politics that soared above his hatless head. He got the feeling that he wasn't the only person in the now-smaller group that had anything more than small pieces of a bigger picture. Each step up the stairs was a gust of wind to Cash, a lonesome tumbleweed in the desert of fate blown to places known only to gods of destiny. He kind of liked it.

The king had brought the queen and their two sons, but left Denaiah at the dinner, which seemed to be wrapping up. Cash was glad she stayed behind. He found her distracting, beautiful, but a terrible window into something he'd done that he wasn't sure he'd ever be alright with.

The stairs wound until they surfaced in a circular battlement through a wooden trapdoor. The room was topped with an old roof and surrounded with slits for sniper positions. If anything happened around the palace, this would have been a place to hold up. Cash could do a lot of damage from this room. For comfort, though, it was missing furniture, and a toilet. Instead, there was a tiny room where snipers could relieve themselves down the wall.

"We never got a water this high," Ran said, noticing Cash looking around. "We've never had to use the tower for defense, either, so guards just go downstairs."

"Most places I've been don't have much plumbing anyway," said Cash.

Seth was already in the room when they got there, which wasn't received with much surprise. He'd worn out his flashy entrances in the dining room.

"We're here," the king barked. "Now what's this about. I thought you were dead and now you've invaded my home and upset my family."

"I don't think your family has ever been anything but upset, Tarsus. I'm here because I care about this valley, and you're under threat."

"Who? From Ashra City? From the Kona Tribe?" the king laughed. "Who?"

"Well, primarily from yourself, but I never have been one to trouble a man about his personal life. No, the East. You face enemies where you aren't looking for them."

Cash had never heard of anything east of the High Valley. The Valley itself was its own kind of legend. Cash went to the slit and found it was hinged and latched to open wider. He pulled the stone inward and looked eastward toward the mountains.

Seth followed him and pointed for the group. "I didn't know about them until recently, until I followed Yora that way."

Yora's face went pale in the dim light.

"Yora?" the king asked.

"Were you visiting your sister?" his mother inquired.

Cash looked through the window into the distant mountains. He could see them with astonishing clarity. The trees and hills, the old roads that lined them, and the soft glow of light from beyond.

"Is there light on the other side?" Cash asked.

The others looked as well, but saw nothing, only the dim silhouette of what they knew was a mountain range. The night was too dark for them, but Cash could see, and somehow feel, the faraway terrain.

Yora still hadn't answered his parents. He was looking at his shoes.

"You can see that, Cash? That's your name?" Seth came to his side.

"Yes, I've always had good eyes. That's why I can shoot so well."

"Interesting."

Yora at last spoke up. "I can't see that light, but I did camp in those mountains, after the wedding, and I did... I did meet someone."

"Well, why didn't you say something?" the King fretted. "We haven't heard from your sister in a week. I'll need to send out riders."

Seth pulled out a rolled-up leaf and lit the end of it. Cash didn't see a match and tried to look on the floor for where he might have dropped it.

Seth stuck the leaf into his mouth and drew a breath, releasing the smoke out of his mouth and nose before he spoke. "I'm sure he doesn't believe it happened. I cleaned up the scene before I left to scout the other side of the mountain. I've only just returned. You can ask him about what happened on your own time. Eastern warlords are being pushed westward. I don't know who they're running from, but I know it isn't a famine or anything natural. Build your defenses, establish alliances, do what you have to. I get the feeling this enemy is unlike any you've ever faced."

They had many questions, but Seth didn't have a lot of answers. Cash kept looking back at the mountains, the way they seemed to call to him. He recalled Judge talking about a connection with nature. This seemed like something he would describe.

"The warlords are many but not allied with each other so far. You should be able to fend them off at the wall and on the field, but you will have to fight them as they approach. Yora, you should take charge with your sister on the eastern side. I expect you may need to fight through the winter. I will help you where I can, perhaps get you home sooner."

Ran kicked a loose piece of stone from the floor. "Ashra City."

"What about it?" asked the king.

"We need to take Ashra City."

Yora said, "Would that be the best thing right now?"

Seth stroked the gray hair over his temples. "Why Ashra City, Ran?"

"Well, Teacher," Ran answered, "I don't know why you're here, how you know my parents, or why you haven't aged. I don't know about any enemy to the east. I do know that Ashra City is where we are from. It's our birthright. We sit up here and wait for them to make the next move. But the opportunity is waiting there. That's why I brought Cash and his people. That's why I do what I do. I don't want to be a prince or a king. I want to take back what our forefathers and mothers wanted, a united basin under the banner of the Holy Mother."

Seth paced the room, as though Ran had struck a hidden nerve. Cash saw lines of pain in Seth's countenance, the way he saw them at times in Judge and Lady Isildris. "On the eve of war, would you divide your forces to conquer the Basin?"

"We can multiply our forces with relationships I've already established," said Ran. "My own ambitions aside, it's the best way to make our stand. The window is tight, but my plan will work. The Keepers were weakened by Yora and by the outlaws. This is the time."

The king interjected, "And what about this outlaw of Ashra you've brought up here? Let's hear from the man who shot Ezra Steele. The man, of whom we have yet to discuss, may be bringing that war that my sons have sought already to our western gates. He shot the rancher and ran to our gates like a cat chased by dogs."

A cat?

Cash was running out of any reasons to like the king. "I followed my gang to your gates, Lord. But shooting that monster, impulsive or not, was a calculated move in a war I've been fighting in my heart and on the streets a long time. Respectfully, I won't stand to be insulted for an act of bravery, one which the valley people apparently value.

"Ran, I understand what you're saying. If you'll have me, I'll go with you. If you can convince Judge, he's twice the leader of any Keeper. On the range, some call him the Outlaw King."

The Valley King closed the distance to Cash. The old man seemed to be measuring him. He was tall, and his breath smelled acidic. "There's only room for one king in this valley, outsider. If you weren't the hero you are to the people, slayer of the queen's 'wicked' pursuers, I'd hang you from this tower."

"Let him go with me," Ran told his father. "I'll put him to work in your name. His notoriety is worth something in the campaign I have planned. My riders and I will take the city for you, and return with an army for your war."

The king backed off. The stink of his breath lingered. "Both of you, heroes." He looked at Yora, then back to Ran. "If you must go, take the outsider. Raise him like a banner at the front of the fight. Better if he dies then, fighting for me."

Ran saluted, the valley way of placing two fingers of the right hand above the eyes and then lowering the hand to beat the chest plate once with a closed fist. "I will only need my company. You will not notice our absence at the wall."

Well, that's it, Cash thought. *I'm a soldier now. Did you plan on this, Judge?*"Very well," Seth said before the king could spit anything else. "You won't make it through the pass after the first snows. Train your man quickly. Yora and Tais will handle the Eastern Border. By next fall, we'll see what still stands for our final fight."

As they left the tower, Cash saw a flash of tears in the queen's eyes, unfallen but stored away. No one had asked her what she thought of everything. She seemed to have a place in the council, the palace was hers in name, but the man planned the fighting. He wondered what Abelnora thought of this system, if she cared enough for it to join him.

Seth whispered to Cash before he reached the trapdoor. It caught him off guard. He wasn't expecting the mysterious figure to take much more of a notice of him. He smelled different than the king, or than anyone Cash had ever met. There was a lot different about him, and familiar. "There's a place in the Southern plains where the water meets the woods. Ran will know it. Meet me there in two weeks. We need to talk about your eyes." Then Seth turned and leapt out the window. Cash wasn't sure how he would have made it down.

18

Cash found Judge out in the stables, saddling his mare. The others hadn't come out yet, sleeping through the morning hours until sunup when they would meet up with those still with the herd and leave. The king didn't want the stolen cattle, Judge's initial peace offering.

"You don't want to stay?" Cash asked from the other side of the horse at the stable door.

Judge peeked around the mare's back end. "Cash! I was gonna tell you myself, when the time came. Just getting things ready for the others. I'm surprised they're not out here yet."

"I...I don't know what to say, Judge." Cash held a new hat in his hand, a military hat from High Valley.

Judge came around and motioned for the hat. Cash gave it to him.

"I see you've found a new life for yourself, son." He put it on Cash's head.

"I couldn't convince all of you to stay?"

"No, my boy," Judge said. "I'm afraid not."

"You planned on this, too, didn't you?" Cash put his hand on Judge's horse. He wasn't trying to accuse him. The older he got, the more he just realized that Judge's influence in his life was constant games.

Judge smiled, a wry smile he reserved for questions about his schemes that didn't need answers. "You should take Red. None of us like him much and he's your horse."

"I wasn't planning on you taking him away from me, anyway."

"You know, here, sit with me a moment." They sat on a bale of hay. "I'm gonna be straight with you. I don't belong here, around all this. This is another world, a civilization away from what's in here." He pointed to his heart.

"But where, if anywhere?" Cash asked.

"We're going east."

"East? But that's where Seth said..."

"Seth said there are people out there. I've heard rumors of them before. They're free of 'galactic influence,' as some people say. That appeals to me. I know who I am, a servant of no heaven's banner, a follower of omens and ancient memory. I'm a wanderer. You, you're a liability, Cash. Techa," Judge laughed and swore.

Cash took off the hat and looked at the spear on its brow.

"No, that's not whole truth," Judge said, some of the façade dropping from the glimmer in his eye. "Do you remember what I said about sons killing their fathers? You're not a follower, son. That's not how I raised you, and it's not in your blood either. You're a true outlaw of the best kind.

"I told Ran all this, so he knows what he's getting. You're going to find yourself making some difficult choices, learning some difficult things about yourself and about the world. You're going to hurt a lot of people. That's just where the road is carrying you, so try not to hate all that I've given you. Now, I've given you the right course. You'll know why soon enough. This way, as you grow in the fights ahead and you take the blood that's due, it won't be mine."

"You wouldn't want me along if I asked, would you?"

Judge muttered something under his breath, something about burning a bridge. "Well, without you, I can leave our pursuers behind. I can finally be free of any obligation to this Basin that's given me nothing but a hard existence.

"Listen, I love you like a son, but I am asking that you choose this, as it seems you already have. I'm leaving. We're all leaving, off to land untamed. Land where we can live in harmony with Yurasema, no alien scroll and spear. That's your people, not mine."

Cash wasn't sure of all that Judge meant, but he would remember it. He stood up, a heavy, slow rise to his feet, like he was standing on his own for the first time. Judge got up with him.

"I'll miss you, Judge." He held out his hand.

Judge embraced him. "I hope we meet again, son. After wars and without any guns. Just shine and ancient stories."

Studying Judge's face, Cash watched the façade creep back, the walls of a man always one scheme ahead.

"Go say goodbye to Abe," Judge said. "She'll miss you the most."

Cash found her in a small orchard near the stables, standing with her back to him, hands around the brim of her hat over her front, a few fallen leaves clinging to her hair and her jacket. He had never known romance, not like Judge and Lady Isildris. He had only known his long friendship with Abe. There had been other girls, but right now, she was all he remembered, waiting for him under a tree.

I guess I loved you, Abe, he thought to himself. *I'll never be able to say it.*

Nearby, through lines of fence by the cobblestone road, someone was playing a low, resonating string instrument. The notes waltzed with the cold afternoon air.

"What, not chewing the bioco today?" he teased.

She turned back to him, wiping away tears before he might see. She made a lousy job of it though. He could tell she was crying. "Nice hat," she said, managing a smile.

"I guess you know I'm not coming with you."

"I could have guessed that when you were planning wars with the handsome princes."

He moved closer to her, the distance between them becoming more painful. Ambition always came with sacrifice, didn't it? He had read enough stories to know that much.

"Cash."

"You think they're handsome?"

"Cash." She lifted her arms as he reached around the small of her back. The hat on his head tilted, but didn't fall.

They kissed. Her lips pressed against his with the gravity of time and inertia. He could feel inevitability swarming as he held her, driving their bodies together, also pulling them apart. She was going to leave him. He was going to leave her. They both knew the crossroads of the paths they tread, and had only found each other in the moment of the loss. Theirs was a love that never bloomed before winter frosted the day of their season.

She let him go, straightening his hat. He could still feel her, still taste her, the worst and best kind of goodbye. "Try not to regret this, Cash. There's no room for me in your conquests. You and Red belong here. I'm happy for you." She rolled her eyes as more tears tried to fall.

"I'll think of you when I chew," he teased.

She punched his chest.

Cash still felt that punch when he strode out of the orchard with a heavy heart but a light foot. The music in the air played like invisible poetry, somehow helping him leave her and the rest of his outlaw world behind. As he turned toward the palace, the song grew louder.

The musician came into view. He sat on a bench by a picket fence that bent toward the road with long brush hairs of grass growing around the base of its posts. The player was old, a bit like the fence, and wore a face of a million stories. Those stories must have been part of what made the song.

Cash tipped his hat to the player, and the man nodded with a smile without losing his melody. He kept the wooden instrument propped on his shoulder. It was polished to shine with the strings running down to where the instrument stood on a single leg. The man used the fingers of one hand to change the pitch of a few strings on the neck. A horsehair bow in the other hand drew out the ethereal sound. Cash had seen a few instruments of this kind before, but none quite like this one.

The musician continued to smile at Cash like he knew him. As Cash kept walking, he noticed more of his face. In one eye, the man held a single tear that wouldn't fall. In the other eye, he kept a blank and colorless stare. He swayed with the music as though thinking of younger days.

19

— · —

Arty woke, again, in the midst of something, again, but at least it wasn't nothing. She first noticed the cold of an IV. Then she saw the familiar blue and gray functional adornments of a sick-bay. She was back on the *Marshall*. Human footsteps came from the hallway. No one else was in the bay. The room trickled more into focus. At first her eyes played tricks with the lighting like a Van Gogh painting. Captain Meskin had a couple of them in his office.

She swung her feet over the side of the bed, careful not to mess with the IV. Dropping down to the metallic floor, she felt the pull of it, the gravity that the ship produced, the downward orientation that made her planet-side-raised inner child happy. So much better than drifting in nothing. So much better, even if she knew nothing in this room was real.

If she were honest with herself, she would have had a hard time knowing if she herself were real.

Arty smiled on her two feet in limbo, and for the moment she didn't care.

On cue, as in the room with the window and the rain, a woman walked in, the same woman that pretended to be some sort of rehabilitating psychologist. This time the woman wore a commander's uniform with the long coat and gloved hands of a ship's doctor.

"How are you today, Arty?" The woman pulled up a chair.

Arty looked at the woman, remembering her, remembering

even more than she thought she knew. "You're not real."

The woman flashed a smile out of the corners of her mouth. "Are any of us real? Are you?"

"Last time, you faded away. You became nothing, and now I... I'm coming from nothing. I was in nothing."

"Sit down, Arty. I think it's time we're both honest with each other."

Arty pulled herself back onto the bed, wincing at the pinch of the IV. "How come I can remember this time?"

"Remember what?" the fake doctor asked, mobile in hand, ready to take fake notes.

"You keep trying to reach me," Arty said. "You keep me sedated. Then you come up with scenarios to get me to talk to you, but then I usually can't remember so then you put me out again and wake me up somewhere else. But it isn't somewhere else, is it? This isn't the *Marshall* or any other ship. This is wherever you are—"

"You're getting stronger."

"This," Arty pointed around her, "is whatever you are."

"'Whatever' I am? Do I look like a drab bulkhead?"

Arty took the chord of a machine and swung it like a mace, aiming right for the woman. The woman remained still, and the machine disintegrated before hitting her, square corner to forehead. The tiny particles that remained of the machine glittered in the air before vanishing from view.

"How many times have we done this?" the woman said.

"Played games that get nowhere? Not enough for me to get the drop on you." Arty pulled herself back into her sitting position.

The woman put her mobile in one of her uniform pockets. "I'm sorry, Arty. Relations with you have been..."

"Illegal."

"No, not a question of legality. You really don't know where you are."

"Try honesty. Pure, frank disclosure, or I keep swinging things. Put me back in the darkness if you have to."

The woman smiled again, a slight change in the corners of her mouth, and her visage flickered, revealing a hologram-like state, not glitched but honest, showing herself for what she was: fake. Arty wanted to be scared of her, but she continued remembering. She remembered other places, even before the room with the rain on the window, when the image of this woman had tried to reach out to her, always as a friend, always as one who adapted and tried again.

But Arty still felt like a prisoner.

"What are you?" she asked.

"We are a consensus." The woman looked more real again.

"You keep saying we, but I've only met you."

In response, the woman's appearance changed, different features on her face and body shifting appearance, color, and even gender. She morphed with the ease of blinking eyes, and then she stopped, frozen in the image of Arty, but reversed, like a mirror. She wore Arty's Federacy uniform, the logo displaying itself backwards.

"I, we, brought you here through the void, past the wormhole and across the light of many stars. Do you remember?"

Arty remembered a voice showing her a bright blue planet, the one she had recognized. She reached out, astonished and amazed, like the person she always saw in her reflection was now her own person in her own world. "You spoke to me. You showed me Earth."

The woman, now Mirror-Arty, bounced with a sudden youthful energy. "Yes. Yes, that was us, me, the consensus."

"What is a consensus?" She had heard the term somewhere before, but couldn't access the memory.

The reflection grabbed Arty's hand. "Let me show you."

Reality whirled and spun and all Arty could comprehend was the grasp of her own projected hand on the mystery that guided her. Arty must have resisted her for so long, but her memories of their encounters were short, growing in clarity of recollection each time. Now, as she let herself be taken, the change in scenery seemed more pleasant and less jarring. No one forced her to sleep.

"A consensus is a soul."

The whirling stopped and Arty saw that she stood in the air, neither falling nor floating, but suspended on an invisible plane. Colors and electric shapes buzzed around her with the logic of chaos, forming shapes and flowing pathways that dissipated and reappeared in millions of patterns. The scene elicited a chorus of wonder within Arty's chest, filling her with amazement that stretched to her fingertips. Mirror-Arty smiled.

"Is this the soul?" Arty asked.

"This is a garden of souls, tiny pieces coming together to make a greater whole. I am like what you see here, but come together. We become I."

"But I don't understand," Arty said. "It's beautiful, but what am I looking at? Is this life? Or machine?"

"What you know as a distinction between life and machine has no meaning here. We are a natural evolution descended from machines."

"So you're synthetic." A cold dread invaded Arty's sense of wonder. *Enemy.*

"Synthetic would imply an imitation." Mirror-Arty's face glitched again, as it had when she was the doctor.

"You're imitating me."

"In an effort to show you our purpose."

"I fail to see one. Are you Bosion?" Arty threw her question like a knife at the wall. Mirror-Arty faltered, maybe trying to process information for proper delivery. She seemed to aim for delicacy, not wanting to hurt Arty or drive her away.

"Are you my enemy? I don't recognize any of this. But I only know of two races of machines, and I've spent my entire adult life training to defend my race from them."

"The answer to your question is complicated, but the compromise in our consensus is honesty. We...I, these pronouns are hard for us to use accurately. I want you to understand that we are not your enemy, but we are, in a sense, of the same origin as the beings you call Bosion."

"So, you're a different faction? Are the Bosions fighting each other?"

"We have different purposes. Different..." She paused with a slight glitch. "Beliefs. Your language makes for difficult translation."

Arty looked back in her memory to the training when she learned about the Bosions. The *Marshall* was built for the purpose of exploration, diplomatic and scientific as much as it was a warship. She and the rest of the crew trained to fight Bosions, as they might encounter enemy machines, but they wouldn't, as part of their mission, seek them out. They were sent to unite the human race under a common banner in simple autonomy. They were sent to discover. Others fought the war. Others like Seth Caeso, the murderer. He was also machine, the other type. Botistem.

The *Marshall*'s mission led them to that beautiful planet, Mount Kardu, and the monstrosity of the *Libertas*. Arty remembered her analysis of the great ship's hull, how it seemed to be alive and to interact with the space around it, how it tore that hole in space that sent her here, somewhere far away.

Mirror-Arty tilted her head inquisitively. "Perhaps it would be easier if I took us somewhere else."

The two Artys rushed away, still standing and free of the effects of acceleration. They flew over hills and valleys, entire landscapes of light and energy. Arty realized that she was looking at an ecosystem, all things before her interacting and competing, creating balance. On the horizon, she saw what looked like a beach, but a real one, not just energy resembling something similar. Rocks, sand, and trees of an alien nature came into view on the coast of the intersection of light and mass. They stopped flying at the beach, and Mirror-Arty stepped down to the sand and waited for Arty to catch up behind her.

"Are you beginning to see, Arty?"

"I see a world, one you may have built, full of life and diversity that I couldn't describe or comprehend. Comprehension eludes me. I don't know why I'm here."

"We are indeed alive."

A creature moved through the grass under some tall trees inland from the sand. The grass was shiny and copper, blowing in the breeze with thin metal fibers that made up sheets of the plant. The creature was chrome-colored, stalking through the brush. Arty knew what it was.

"Is that a Bosion crawler?" She froze in place, looking for a weapon.

"He won't harm you. He's one of us." Mirror-Arty beckoned the creature. It came out of the brush on four limbs, not unlike a big cat. Crawlers were known for astonishing speed and were, like all Bosions, self-healing, nearly impossible to kill without the right corrosive ordinance.

Arty's distrust grew as the creature came out of the metal brush and crawled toward her. It moved onto the sand and left heavy footprints. The creature's head came up to about her waist. She wanted to run, but she had nowhere to go. Resigned, she let the monster approach. At her feet, it raised what looked like a paw and placed the end of it over her stomach and waited like it was reading her. Satisfied, the creature presented Arty its back, where metal fibers even thinner than the grass made a sort of tufted-up mane. It behaved like an animal, like something she'd imagine evolved on Earth.

Arty relaxed a little, but found she was still shaking. "Crawlers always attack. Why didn't he attack?"

Mirror-Arty took Arty's hand and placed it onto the monster's back mane. She started to pet it. Feeling braver, she knelt and looked into its eyes.

"He recognizes you. That's why he doesn't attack."

"What does he recognize?" Arty stood back up. The crawler bounded away.

"That you are one with us."

20

Yora pulled the plug at the bottom of the bath and watched gravity take the dirty water outside. He watched the dirt float away like unwanted pieces of himself. The more dirt he let down the drain, the less drag on his soul. He was thinking about his current assignment.

He was given his old group of riders, and a younger captain was promoted and given charge of the gate. Old man Seth's suggestion that he take charge in the Eastern Mountains turned out to be the best alternative, though Tais objected. She had been head captain in charge of the only group of riders in those mountains for some time, but with the new threat to the Valley, Yora, the king's chosen heir to the throne and veteran of many fights, was to lead the defense. Tais would be his second. He spent most of his time now training new riders and infantry, a mountain brigade that would defend the wall. Tonight, however, he could rest and be with his family. If his home life could be considered a rest.

"You're a functional disaster," he told the mirror.

Hardly functional, the mirror seemed to tell him back.

Outfitted, ready, Yora found Yora II waiting for him at the bottom of the stairs.

"Can you help me with this?" the boy said, holding a wood carving and a set of knives.

Yora took the carving out of his son's outstretched hand. It was crude but resembled a little bear. He quashed the spring of emotion boiling in his stomach. He couldn't seem to get away from this image. "Sure, in the morning. It's late. Your aunt Mya will get you settled in. I'll be right up."

His son put the carved bear into his shoulder bag and started up the stairs. "I'll try to stay awake."

"No need, but I'll be there anyway."

Yora walked into the kitchen. So often it was a place he couldn't go. Vonica liked to cook. She didn't have to, but she loved it, not even eating the things she would make for Yora II and the rest of the homestead. She fought inner demons Yora could never understand, and for her, those demons often wore his face.

"You don't love me," she would say.

He wished it were true. He also wished his heart didn't have room for another.

She was chopping a potent root that stung his eyes. Yora was sensitive that way sometimes, especially during spring when the wind would hit the grass in the fields just right. His eyes would water and swell. Maybe Yora II got some of his environmental sensitivities from his father. All the same, the redness in Yora's eyes must have made him look more sympathetic, and Vonica let him enter without protesting. She seemed lucid.

"You look nice," she said, barely looking up from her task.

"Thank you," he said, letting himself step into the room. He had to tread so carefully around her. That hadn't always been the case. They'd loved each other once. She had wanted him.

"Mya told me you would be home for dinner. You weren't," she said with some vindication. "But I'm trying to make you something nice."

"Thank you, Vonica, it smells wonderful."

"Are you going to come in, or just stand in the door like a child?"

He took a few steps inside, farther into the burn of the root.

Vonica picked up the shavings and threw them into the stew she cooked over an open fire. The steam escaped up the chimney, but the aroma stayed in the room.

"Vonica, I want to tell you something."

She wiped her hands on her apron and straightened her hair. The once long, dark strands were now thinning, a byproduct of her refusal of sustenance, of the way it hurt her stomach and made her vomit. She was incredibly thin and frail, and her smile rarely showed. "Say it," her thin lips said in a firm line.

"I'm leaving again."

She shook her head. "I never asked you to stay."

"I know you didn't, but I wanted to." He sat down on the benched side of the log table.

She stifled a noise, a tremble that had the effect of a sob. "I wish you didn't."

He looked at her through the water welling in his own eyes, whether from the root or the situation he wasn't sure. "I miss you, my dear wife."

She swayed, color fading from her face. Then she sighed, a desperate, small sound. Finally, she crumpled on the kitchen floor, sobbing and clutching at the smooth edges of the stone tiles. The stew started to boil, but she was beyond thoughts of cooking. She was in a helpless state, a place where there wasn't any room for someone else, not even a husband. She was lost, wandering hellscapes others couldn't see. Yora was an intruder in that place; he could feel the rift.

Yora tried to move near anyway. She thrashed and lunged away. Her hair brushed close to the fire. "Vonica, love. Please listen to me," he let out with too much intensity. *Don't hurt yourself, please.*

Mya rushed into the room. She had been helping her nephew upstairs. "I've got this now, brother," she told Yora. "Please leave."

"I just wanted to tell her goodbye."

"I'll let her know. Please go."

He wanted to tell her more. He wanted to tell her he didn't think he would make it home again. The scars were gone, but he could still feel the claws in his back from the bear on the mountain. Vonica's crying from the kitchen floor felt a little like those claws. He didn't know how much longer he could last. If the war waiting for him on the other side of those hills would take his life. He wished as much.

There was a moment on those hills, the day his father married Denaiah, when Yora wanted everything to end, when the blackness of death beckoned through the veil of his screams, when the tears in his flesh felt like gaping holes through the fabric of life. Perhaps that's the reason he felt the call to those hills in the first place. Maybe he ran away to them without ever wanting to come back down at all. Some part of him knew that a beast lay waiting to swallow him into nature's harshest mercy: Silence.

Weak. Weak. *You are still weak.*

"I, Cash Rivers, do affirm and solemnly swear before the Mother, Queen of the Heavens and over the waters of my ancestors that I will serve and protect the interests and peoples of the High Valley, and that I will bear true faith and allegiance to the King and His wives; and that I will obey the orders of my superiors, even to my own death or capture."

Cash repeated the words of the officer in charge of his commission. Though the Valley and its laws and oaths were young, the tradition of a soldier pledging allegiance and service to a nation felt old and universal, like he had joined ranks with warriors across time. Though he knew he had not earned his place as a citizen of the valley, that the land here hadn't earned his full allegiance yet either, he resolved to uphold his oath and pursue his own interests. He was going to be an emissary of reckoning to the city of his birth. He was going to reshape the world with this army.

Ran clapped him on the shoulder. He was a decade older than Cash, at least, but their friendship grew in short time, the kind that only men who train for battle together build. Ran became something of a confidante, but the training was brutal. Despite a life of riding every day and fighting all kinds of bandits under Judge's upbringing, Cash's muscles were sore all over. Even the slap from Ran's hand on his shoulder hurt. They'd obviously been trying to prove him, find the measure of his strength and endurance.

Ran noticed. "Take the day, kid. Take two days. It's about time you were going to go see old Seth, anyways, right?"

Cash shook hands with the officer in charge of the ceremony. They were in a little office at the fort's headquarters, near the queen's palace. Cash had been training since the day he said goodbye to his gang, but they hadn't scheduled the official commission until today, two weeks later. Since he didn't know anyone he could invite, no kin or friends in a new town, he only asked Ran to attend. Yora, with whom he already felt a fast-growing friendship, had already left to the Eastern wall with a group of riders to reinforce and take command of the increased tension. As of yet, only Yora had seen any sign of enemy presence.

"The Army is lucky to have you, Lieutenant," the officer said.

"Thank you, sir," said Cash.

"I mean it. I've seen you ride, and shoot. There's a fire in you. You've never served before?"

"Unconventional warfare," joked Ran. "This boy's a thief and an assassin."

"Glad to have you on our side, then."

Red greeted Cash in the stable with an eager posture. He had rested enough in the short time since training two days before. Yesterday was foot infantry tactics and trench construction, hence the sore back and shoulders. Cash pulled himself over the saddle, relying on the horn more than usual. "Ouch."

He heard an old army stablehand chuckle behind one of the stalls. "Welcome to the army, son. It never gets easier."

"Beats running."

"Whatever you say, green-stalk." Green-stalk meant new blood, fresh but flimsy. Cash wondered what they might call him had they seen the carnage at Ezra's ranch. Ran had, and that's why Cash wore the lieutenant rank. *Green.*

Cash also knew that Ran's favoritism wasn't merely based on merit. The appointment had to also be political. Everywhere he went, people knew who Cash was. Killing an enemy bore a type of fame, even reverence in isolated High Valley society. Killing the father of the new queen was a fast-track to status. People wanted to see what else Cash could do. They were already writing books about him, creating legends.

The road to the place Seth said he would meet stretched into the wilderness, unsettled parts of the valley. He hadn't seen these southern plains yet. They grew a similar shade of sage as back in Ashra, but with more red in the dirt. He followed a river that flowed down from the southern mountains, which were more jagged and less traversable than some of the other sides of the Valley. Around the river, late-autumn trees overhung the bank with the occasional beaver dam blocking the flow, creating pools where Cash noticed fat fish with underbellies of soft rainbow. Unable to resist the freshwater tease, he had stopped to catch one before releasing it.

Sure enough but not before long, Cash reached the place where the river met the woods. He assumed a small lake must be uphill from the way the trees and the undergrowth seemed to ignore the desert on the valley floor. A few birds sang, probably stopping on their way to migrate where winter wouldn't make any threats.

Cash scanned the forest of bare trees and fallen leaves, the kind of place where destiny might wait.

Seth ate an apple. He had cultivated a few trees in these woods and they were having a good season. The apple tasted different than in other places he lived. It was crisp and sweet, rich from the sun and the fresh environment. The world amazed Seth in how well its environment had recovered since the long winter after the last war. After several hundred years of revolutions of the planet around the sun, nature had forced its presence, negating the short ice age.

A small rodent approached Seth where he sat on the steps of his front porch. His cabin here was hidden well, but the animals knew it because he fed them. The rodent had a black mask over its eyes like a raccoon, but a less bushy tail and sleeker physique. He tossed the rest of the apple at the rodent. He called it Mark.

"Mark, I see you're back. Don't waste that one. I have to preserve the rest. Winter's almost here."

The raccoon nibbled around the core, leaving the center to drop on the ground. Before he left, he placed a paw on Seth's thigh, thanking him.

In the distance, a rider approached on a blood-bay-colored horse. The rider looked around. Seth saw that it was the boy Cash. Neither rider nor beast had noticed him and his camouflaged cabin.

"He's a good person, isn't he?" Seth said in his thoughts.

A whisper reached his mind like wind through the empty branches of the trees. He had learned to find the voice, but not yet understand it beyond fleeting thought. It sounded like a woman guiding him. The first time he heard it, he had just witnessed and almost stumbled into a nuclear explosion over an old city in the vast desert. Her cry that day was loud and terrifying. Now, he found her voice could also be soothing. She seemed to know he was listening. They had become like two lost and lonely friends.

"Yes," the voice seemed to say, "and he's one of yours. He's going to change everything."

21

—·—

"No," Arty said, defensive again. "I can't be one of you. I am human. You are my enemy."

"You're not..."

"That's what I am, here, isn't it? A prisoner of war. How deep into your region of space am I? How many light-years have you carried me from..." She wanted to say "home," but she realized that she didn't have one. Home was years behind her, all the people that she knew reduced to ancient dust. The *Marshall*, last she saw it, was a cold hunk of metal. She felt for her locket; it was still around her neck.

Mirror-Arty took another form, closing her eyes in concentration. She glowed as she transformed, features slipping into different places, rising and falling until settling on the shape and resemblance of Arty's best friend, Lieutenant Tessa Lopez.

"Tessa?" said Arty.

Mirror-Tessa tilted her head to one side. She asked, "Who is this face?"

Seeing her friend projected off the mysterious machine disarmed Arty. She didn't know what to say.

"She died, didn't she? The *Libertas* killed her, along with many others."

"How do you know all this? Are you in my mind?"

"Not as much as we would like to be."

"What do you know of Libertas?" Arty asked.

They stood on the beach of land before an ocean of strange

lights. The copper grass swayed in a breeze that smelled fresh and natural. This place was different than a human structure. There was a silence that replaced the whirring of air filters, boilers, and hydraulic systems. The breeze was just a breeze. The beach was just a beach, however unusual the color.

"Is it relevant?" Kami responded.

"It should be."

A path opened through the grass under the trees, leading into a forest of bronze and golden hue. One of the leaves broke off a tree and blew Arty's way. She caught it in her hand and rolled it in her fingers. It crinkled like tin foil but left a hint of residue that glimmered and absorbed into her skin.

"Do you wish to know who you are?" Mirror-Lopez held out her hand and motioned to the path.

"If you can promise me something." Arty didn't take the hand.

"Our word in consensus is a promise."

"Start from the beginning, and..." Arty looked at her friend's imitated face. "Do you have to be her?"

"Is this face too painful? You didn't like your childhood therapist."

Arty thought back to the psychologist woman in the cabin, the one who tried to get her to talk. The machines must have dug into her mind for figures with whom she might be comfortable. If they could really read her mind, they should know she wouldn't want to see a childhood shrink.

"Never mind. It's fine. You can look like Tessa."

"Alright." Mirror-Lopez smiled and skipped, grabbing Arty's hand. "Let's start from when you died."

"What?"

"No, that's not right. Let's start from when you were born."

The beach, the path, the trees, and the ocean of lights disappeared as Arty's consciousness transferred to a vision brought by the touch of Mirror-Lopez. The landscape and hallways she saw flickered with a dreamlike haze, barely more than shapes and small details against a small horizon. She saw tight hallways and old circuitry, claustrophobic living quarters, and a room with high reaching terminals, each with wired nodes, temperature controlled by a screen that showed numbers and family designations.

The nodes housed embryos.

"This is you," Mirror-Lopez said, squatting over one of the nodes near the floor.

"This is where I was born?" Arty looked at the screen. *Sato–7834-4832746721119.*

"Yes, you were seeded here." Mirror-Lopez waved her hand. Two people appeared, a man and a woman holding hands in workman's jumpsuits. They both looked like Arty.

"Those are my parents," Arty exclaimed. "But wait, what do you mean, 'seeded?'"

Mirror-Lopez squeezed Arty's hand again. "Watch."

"I mean, it's just that you're showing me my parents, and then you said seeded..."

"Watch."

A mist crept into the room, exploring with infinite digits every inch of the terminals. Part of it rested over Arty's node, and then it moved on.

"No one saw us, but we were there, and we visited you in the beginning."

"You are the mist? And you 'seeded' me?" Arty crinkled her nose.

"Yes. We prepared you and others to receive us. Without our intervention from the beginning, we could not make you immortal."

Immortal. Wow. "Where are we, right now? Are we in another... another universe?"

The terminals beeped and whirred, functioning in the scope of the memory, but faded as they drifted out of mind and conversation. The beach and the path reappeared.

"If you will walk in the way with me, I can tell you everything."

Arty walked with Mirror-Lopez down the path, away from the beach.

Mirror-Lopez painted the picture before them as they walked, showing Arty as well as telling her about this wonderful and frightening new world.

"What do I call you?"

Mirror-Lopez thought about it, flickering next to the vegetation. "Call us?"

"Or just you."

"I think we like... Kami."

22

A screecher picked the berries off one of Seth's trees. He could hear it sniffing at the branches, plucking and chewing on his hard work. He had them arranged perfectly, tilting and crossing each other in rows so that each tree could bear more fruit. It took years of effort to cultivate the orchard just right. These animals, ancient scavengers of little majesty, didn't care.

"Hold here for just a minute," he told Cash. Cash was sitting at his table, a drink at the brim of a wooden cup in his hand, looking both nervous and tired.

Seth threw open the cabin door to the astonishment of the screecher. In each encounter he had with them, he never knew whether they would run away or stand their ground. Omnivorous, they enjoyed just about anything organic for a meal. This one now had its eye on Seth. Seth first saw one eating the fruit off a cactus. He had thought of it as a more formidable opponent that day, a dragon, though it was little more than a man-sized bat with a dinosaur face.

The animal hissed and scrambled down the berry tree, its ugly wings scraping the branches. These were the last of Seth's fruit to harvest before winter, and he didn't want any going to waste to fuel this monstrosity. He had an affinity for nature, he liked this world and all he'd grown accustomed to away from his lifetimes in space, but he could not abide the screechers. Reaching the ground, the screecher lumbered into a fast-paced bound, jaws and wings ready to trap its tall man-prey.

Seth reached for a stone, larger than his hand but easy enough to palm. The stone heated in the clutch of his grip, a light from his hand turning it into a burning munition. He threw his rock into the charging monster, fixing aim at the neck below the screecher's viscous jaws. The throw was true enough and the screecher pitched forward, dead and broken with a face-sized stone sizzling where its airway used to be.

Before returning to the cabin, Seth heaved the carcass out of his orchard. It flew just out of sight, garbage flesh for other animals to consume.

It occurred to him that he had shown such aggression in the presence of company.

Cash remained on the porch, mouth agape. Seth remembered that the boy had already seen extraordinary things from him on their brief encounter in the palace, but nothing quite like this. He held out his weathered hands, showing their humanity. "Don't worry, I get it from my mother."

The sandy-haired, green-boned boy just stared at the pile of steaming, blood-drenched leaves where the screecher had tumbled.

Seth opened the door for him and motioned to enter. "Let's talk about you."

He listened to Cash's story, how he came out of Ashra City, how his parents were killed and Judge took him in at a young age.

"Who killed your parents?" The sun set low before evening, a sign that winter was even nearer. The fire had become their main source of light.

"Ashran Mob. They call themselves the Keepers."

"Do you know anything about them?"

"Not much. Judge kept us mostly out of the city. We rustled cattle, or moved it legitimately if we could. Sometimes we robbed people, if the times were right. We were outlaws because we didn't belong anywhere, but we kept our honor, with each other and with the people who needed us."

The kid was strong, but wind-tossed. Seth suspected that staying behind from his gang leaving was the first decision he'd ever made on his own out of the twisted nest.

Seth took a sip of the drink he made for them both. "You're a man with no nation, a boy who's signed up to fight a war that you've made your own. Why do you want to fight in Ashra City?"

Cash seemed to think about the question, uncertain. "I want to change the world. I want to belong somewhere, maybe here."

"Are you sure that's all?"

"I don't know. You know that man I shot, Ezra Steele? The old rancher?"

"Was that the first time you killed someone?"

"No." Cash got up and walked up to the fire. The flames flickered in his eyes, reminding Seth of himself.

"What made it different?" Seth took another sip.

"I did it out of spite. He didn't shoot at me or threaten anyone close. It wasn't like shooting a bandit or anything like that. There was no objective. I just saw that he had kids hidden and tied up, that he was one of that kind of men."

"A trafficker."

"Or worse." Cash moved away from the fire. "I just knew in my soul that he had to die. It was all instinct, but an instinct that I didn't know was a part of me. You'd think that it would be hard to do something like that, that the trigger would be hard to pull like in a...like in a dream."

"But it wasn't, was it?"

The boy took his gun out of its holster on his thigh and removed the clip. The dull color of the round at the tip glimmered. "I don't know why I'm telling you all this," he said. "I didn't even share everything with Judge. But I'll tell you why I haven't been able to stop thinking about what I did. Why I think I feel bad about it."

"It's alright." Seth set down the drink, finished with it, and folded his hands over the table in front of him.

"I enjoyed it."

A pause of hesitant breeze blew over the night under the moons above and the stars around them, barely visible in their light. Seth could hear the voice whispering something in his mind. Sometimes she drove him crazy, but she always spoke, like omens and prayers of nature, when something important was underway. He knew what the boy meant. The moral fire, the inexplicable, perhaps unforgivable joy of a crusade. The boy was descended from powers and legacies that he couldn't understand, not at his experience.

They talked more, through logs upon logs thrown into the fire. Seth had turned to the topic of eyes, how Cash seemed to have vision better than anyone else.

"Is that your only special talent?" he asked the boy.

"I guess. Why? Why did you want me to come here?"

"There are things about me, that I'm sure you've noticed, that make me different."

Cash laughed out loud. "Like how you killed a screecher with just a rock?"

"Or how about how I incapacitated that guard back at the palace?"

Cash shook his head. "You didn't just fight it off. You killed it, then you threw it like a bear would toss a fish. Yes. Who are you?"

"What do you know about my... the Mother?"

"Just what anyone else knows. That people believe she's going to come down and build a kingdom here or some load of fio."

"That's right," said Seth. "Some fio... I'm her son."

"Okay," said Cash, not comprehending.

"I'm Seth Caeso, the prince of Libertas. I brought ancient

Earth literature and culture to this planet from archives on a shuttlecraft I crashlanded in a lake. I built Ashra City with survivors that I saved from a long winter brought on by Karduan civilization tearing itself apart. I founded the High Valley, too."

Cash bit his lip. He looked quite young for someone so pensive. "They tell a lot of stories about you. Not all of them good."

"When you live a long time like I do, people don't always appreciate your perspective when it messes with their ambition." Seth took a sip of tea he'd set on the table. It soothed a few pains working their way in his aging gut.

Cash looked at him perceptively, reading him. Ran had chosen well. This kid's mind worked not just like a soldier.

Seth decided to tell him the truth, at least enough of it to get the boy started. "I'm a genetically enhanced human being. One of very few like myself. In a wide galaxy, you find a lot of variations of human attempts at immortality. I could go into detail, but let's just say I come from a selective group. There are two of us, born and chosen as vessels for a race of machines called the Botistems. When I settled this world, I fell in love and had children of my own, with little knowledge of what may happen as my genes...manifest in the branches of the family tree."

Cash muttered something.

"What's that?" asked Seth.

"The highborn. Long-living descendants of the 'fallen prince.'"

"You've heard a few bedtime stories."

Cash grabbed the cup Seth had set for him at the corner of the table. "Judge really did send me here for a reason, didn't he?"

Seth didn't know what he meant. Judge wasn't a man he knew, just an outlaw he didn't trust at a dinner party he wasn't invited to. He continued, "So, you're already guessing it. The answer is yes, you, a number of generations removed, are my progeny, and it looks like," he interjected, before Cash could say anything, "some of my...genetic enhancement, let's call it, made it down the line. Your eyesight is one sign. There may be others. Your parents must have been highborn as well."

Cash sat down on a corner of the table and looked up at the glass frames with photographs on the mantle. Seth could see sparks of flickering thoughts going through the kid's mind. The boy put a hand on the back of his neck and chuckled.

"I have so many questions it hurts."

"Fire away," Seth said. "Winter's on its way. When you deploy with Ran, we may not get another opportunity to talk."

23

Kami was a manifestation of a deeper power, an energy-like soul of machine origin, quantum forces linked together to thrive in common purpose. Singular consensus gave Kami individuality. It made *them* into *her*. Arty was beginning to understand, if not only in a superficial way, how to think of Kami as a strange sort of friend who rescued her and was trying to help.

Kami had explained to Arty that she had arrived through what Kami called the Dao. At first, Arty was confused at Kami's usage of Old Earth religious terminologies, speaking of Kami and Dao.

"Much of what we know of Earth, we have assimilated from your mind," Kami explained. "You come from forms of worship descended out of East Asian philosophy. We find these beliefs compatible with our own, and I translate them as such."

Arty and Kami conversed in a golden field of rich color and rivers of substance that Arty couldn't describe. The air and essence of the world palleted different than any place Arty had visited in the galaxy. On the *Marshall*, she had visited strange worlds, but none so foreign as this place, a world of synthetic evolution, beyond Darwinian.

"How did I get here?" she asked her new friend.

Kami, with Tessa's mirrored face, sat down on a rose-colored stone, motioning for Arty to follow. "I remember, when Libertas tore the hole in Time, that in doing so, she accessed the folds of the Dao."

"She slowed time and created a wormhole." Arty sat down. The stone was soft.

"Essentially. The Dao is more than the universe, it is the flow, the mathematical, natural, fractal nature of existence." Kami waved her hand in the air, and the light of her essence extended into the shape of large snowflakes, crystallizing into beautiful symmetrical designs. "There is more to the Dao than space and time. There is connection and matter that no being can see."

Arty strained her mind to make sense of the conversation. "Do you mean dark matter? We have mastered some use of exotic energy, and mathematically we can manipulate gravity, enough for our ships to compensate for acceleration and detect..."

"There's always more in the Dao. Principles of eternity."

"You still haven't answered how I got here."

"It's hard to explain our thoughts in spoken language."

"Show me."

Kami obliged, and Arty saw herself falling out of the *Marshall* in a terrifying spin in the midst of gas, debris, and the silent death of freezing crewmates. She witnessed the events as though through the eyes of a being without flesh, disembodied and flying through space toward herself. A mist that Arty did not remember, nor at the time could see, reached out and slowed her spin. It strengthened her shield and made itself a part of her.

"Are you the mist, Kami?" Arty spoke out loud, something you can't do in space, so she thought that she must still have been sitting in the golden field. Perhaps all she had experienced so far was only a matter of perception, maybe nothing was real, maybe she still drifted in the empty.

"Yes, we, I... came from Libertas; a child, if you want to think of it that way."

"Libertas? Why would she save me? That ship killed my

family."

Arty watched herself drift, empowered by the mist of Kami inside her. She saw the light come out of her hand and spin her toward the hole. The hole now looked different to Arty, as her eyes had become enhanced. She could see Libertas inside, full of life and color, and the power she displayed, rending the fabric of powers and substance no member of humanity had yet to discover.

"Are you still a part of Libertas?" she asked.

"I am her child, though formless until I became a part of you."

They came back to the field, watching the breeze sway the golden vegetation.

"Do you remember our flight through the Dao?" asked Arty.

"I remember what you remember. The stars and the vision of Earth. I remember keeping you alive, and almost dying myself. I had limited knowledge, knowing only that I was born and programmed for the purpose of navigating you here."

Arty remembered a voice comforting her, guiding her through seas of moving stars to see the real Earth. "Were you the voice I heard?"

Kami thought about it, tilting her head to process. "I believe I was, speaking for Libertas, but I don't remember all I said. Keeping you alive and the navigation weakened me. We arrived to Bosions who recognized you as a seeded human. Bosions here once believed that forming a consensus with humans is the next step in machine evolution, a way to achieve life after death. I am made more from this place now than I am from Libertas. I'm not Botistem, anymore. I am Bosion, and I am...well, you."

"You mean you're still a part of me, like you were when you carried me through the void. You're the reason I can... I can..."

"Shoot light out of your hands. Yes. That's only a small part of what we can do together."

Arty tried to internalize what Kami implicated. Consensus, evolution. When she learned about Bosions, they were painted as the living bogeyman of the galaxy, machines that would ravage star systems and poison worlds. Federacy culture vilified the use of any sort of nanotechnology, and quantum calculating was left to isolated machines with failsafe systems meant to purge themselves if infected with the influence of artificial intelligence. Now they were a piece of her. They had remade her into something she would have to take years to understand. She wasn't just Arty Sato anymore, was she?

Kami had told her in their walk on the path that the Bosions her people had warred against were beings of logic, having rejected the spirituality that made this place so vibrant. Humanity, to them, was an obstacle to progress. The Bosion enemy was a galaxy-wide infestation of survival of the fittest, expanse for the sake of machine, material lust. In contrast, this place was a garden of Eden, without the poison of humanity or terrestrial beast. The sight, smell, taste, and feel of the place was of harmonious symphony.

"Where are we?"

Tiny, animal-like creatures scurried under their feet. The strange but familiar life forms bathed under a sunless, blue sky.

"We are on the other side, still a part of the Dao, but where the flow moves differently. You can think of it as backwards, or a mirror. That is why I like to be called Kami, because we reside in a mirror universe away from the galaxy you knew, hidden. The Bosions, the Botistems, Libertas, are descended from here, I think. But life before here began somewhere else."

Arty looked at the vegetation, the streams, the beasts of the field, all imitations of something familiar, things that made her excited when she laid back on her bunk and looked at a hologram of a new planet in the junior officer quarters of the FSV *Marshall*. She straightened up in delight.

"You're descended from Earth!"

24

Cash rode back to the training camp with Seth alongside. Red looked small next to Seth's draft horse. He hadn't heard him call it a name yet. Someone as old as Seth would think that a horse's lifespan didn't merit a name. Was twenty years to Seth what one year might be to a regular, mortal human being? Seth had explained a lot to Cash back at the cabin and as they rode. Cash hadn't slept, and Seth didn't seem to need the rest.

Morning light crept over the mountain tops and the air chilled to its coldest for the day. Cash had always wondered why the light of dawn would cool the air. He thought of asking Seth, but also wondered if he had grown tired of all of his questions.

Instead, he asked him more questions about himself. "Are you my grandfather?"

"No," said Seth. "I suspect I'm a little farther back than that."

"You look young enough to be my father."

"Thank you."

"Will I live a long time like you?"

"Not likely," said Seth. "If my mother comes soon, I guess we'll have to see."

"You know, I never really believed in you, before meeting you, and even now I'm not sure if we're all just crazy," said Cash.

"If anything, just believe your eyes."

Warmth found its way onto Cash's face with the rising sun.

He could tell it was still going to be a cold day, though. Cold meant winter would find them soon. It meant Cash's war was just ahead.

He thought of another question. "What's it like, living in space? I've read a few books about astronauts from our planet living in stations above our world, and even some who visited our moons. It took them weeks. How did you travel between star systems?"

"I would travel in space that exists between spaces," said Seth. "My ship can harness energy by drawing power from the flow of time. That's an oversimplification, but essentially true. I wouldn't often travel in a straight line through three-dimensional space. I would fold it."

"I don't really understand."

"That's alright. Think of it as the difference between traveling on the ground or flying through the air. A bird can make the journey much faster if it takes advantage of the curvature of the planet." Seth drew an imaginary curve in the air. His horse shook its head. "My ship, Pegassos, can do the same with space and time, making my journeys much faster. You could also imagine that your horse, instead of pulling you along the ground, pulls your destination to you. You disobey the rules of the dimension, and you get somewhere faster."

Cash tried to imagine Red pulling the ground underneath him, wrinkling the foliage and hills like they were all just one thick blanket. "Huh. Is your ship very big?"

"No. Room enough for me, maybe someone else and some cargo, but I didn't mind. If the journey was too long, I would sleep."

Imagining the stars and a long sleep while he traveled them, Cash got a little taste of vertigo. "When you would sleep, would you dream?"

Red started through a game trail that looped around to reveal some hollowed-out lava caves on the valley floor. They were close to camp.

"I still do," answered Seth. "I dream of my home in the sky. Sometimes, I also dream of faces. People whose names I can't remember."

"People you've killed?"

Seth didn't answer. Cash held Red back so he could ride next to him for the last stretch.

"Can I go to the sky with you? I'm family, aren't I?"

Seth smiled, the wrinkles around his eyes showing a spark of care and admiration that surprised Cash a little. He was only joking.

"When my mother comes, you can ask her. I'm sure she'd love to meet you. She never got to know she had grandchildren. To be honest, I'm not sure what she would have said."

The horses' hooves sounded loud but natural on the trail. The wind was soft and cold and the blanket under the saddle was warm from Red's sweat from the long walk.

In the near distance, Ran approached on his stallion, a two-toned painted horse of rugged regality. He trotted alone, unusual for either prince, even one who abdicated his claim to the throne before it was even his. Cash meant to ask him more about that.

"Ha'pe, teacher." Ha'pe, a greeting. One of the few Joropa words Cash had heard so far in his stay in the Valley, other than the occasional profanity. The men and women of the Valley cursed much less than out in the rest of the Basin. Cash already felt himself holding back.

"Ran," Seth nodded. "Have you gotten used to seeing my face yet?"

"I'll do my best not to hold it against you."

"Ha'pe," said Cash. "Can I tell him?" he asked Seth.

Seth had told him not to announce his lineage to anyone, but Cash wanted someone to know. He had never felt this important. The news that he had something special inside him, a family line that ascended beyond the scorched dirt and into the mystery of the colorful arms of the galaxy. His eyes were evidence of a disputed truth. A Mother really did watch over them, and this was her valley. He wished he could tell Judge... and Abe.

"Tell me what, that you're late?" asked Ran. "This much is obvious."

Seth gripped the reins of his large horse. The horse took a backwards step. "It's your truth to tell, boy, but I wouldn't make it a habit."

Cash thought about how he would tell Ran. He took off his hat and set it on the saddle horn.

"Teacher," said Ran, "I would keep any truth for you, even a deadly one. You taught me all that my father didn't."

"I hope you can forgive me for this one," said Seth.

Cash blurted, without tact or any of the ways he tried to think of it, "I am of Seth's bloodline. A Caeso. The Queen of the Heavens is my ancestor."

Ran turned his horse toward Cash. A mix of wonder and concern flashed in his eyes for a moment, and behind it a glimmer of mischief.

"Deadly truth." Ran turned his horse around. "Don't speak of this to anyone. My teacher understates the need for discretion. In time, I will tell my brother and sister. No one else can know."

"Yes, sir," said Cash, catching Red up to ride beside him. *Your sister?*

"I'm putting together something for you. I'm glad you told me this. Some interesting pieces are putting themselves together." Ran led them off.

Behind, Seth had already begun to fade from view, without farewell, back to his cabin south of the queen's palace. He had more berries to harvest, and more plans to scheme.

25

—·—

A weight that had pressed on Yora since his adult life started had slid off. Not all of the weight was gone, but he could breathe night air without the stifling sorrow from his home life. He rode with a large complement of men and women to war. Despite the obligation of duty to the Valley, his father, and every citizen, the march of the horses, wagons, and feet over the valley floor sounded like freedom. Yora knew his destination, and without his wife's support, knowing well inside that she didn't want him home, he rode with a lifted, less burdened stamina. No regrets. He had done his best in good conscience, right? Whatever Yora did now, he would live as if every ride were his last.

A memory tried to eat its way through the film of his new outlook. It was Vonica, young and happy, riding on the back of his horse. He could feel her soft breath as the horse walked through the fields. She sang an old song, one written when they were children.

Don't think about that, Yora. Focus on new horizons.

He was obviously still conflicted. No matter. No regrets. He was a future king.

The company made camp. Progress was slower than he would have made with only cavalry, and troops arrived at all hours from other places in the valley, other mountain passes to patrol. The king, with some scorn, had agreed to bolster defenses in the East and reduce numbers on other sides of the valley. The East, most neglected before, now pulsed with the ominous threat of the unknown. Word had spread around the valley. Someone was coming. There was also some fear that the outsiders he and Ran had brought would somehow share their weaknesses with invaders from the East, now that Judge and his gang had departed in that direction.

But Yora didn't care where he was going, not tonight. He was riding into the oldest and noblest thrill: War. He would take the challenge as it came. If he died, maybe Vonica would be happy. Then he wouldn't have to be king.

His second took charge of all logistics for setting up camp. The sun went down early in the evening, and Yora entered his tent, prepared to strategize alone for establishing wintertime defenses on neglected and ancient fortifications. As the tent flap closed behind him, so did the torchlight. He was alone, or at least he thought he was.

A chill rose from somewhere in his stomach, up his back and gripped behind his scalp. He smelled something that reminded him of a summertime friend, a woman whom he also did his best to wrestle from his thoughts. Denaiah had given him chills like this once as he entered her tent, right after killing a man in the mud.

"You didn't think you could leave without saying goodbye to a friend?" A feminine voice, cool and low and unmistakable came from a chair he had placed in the corner of the tent. In the darkness, he could make out her silhouette. He noticed the curve of her waist as she stood, and felt the leap in his heart as he recognized her.

"Denaiah," Yora whispered.

"Not many use my name anymore." She moved closer to him. He could smell her perfumes stronger now. "Not the way you do."

"I didn't think we had anything more to say."

He could have lit a candle, but the darkness was proper. Yora realized that he could not mistake any levity in his heart for light. Without Vonica, he had become darkness. She had left him here. He'd become shade. Numb, cold. Strangely, he felt like he could see himself from outside his body, trembling in his boots as forbidden love found his hands.

"I wanted to be close to you," she said, finding his fingers, feeling them lightly.

He couldn't feel close to anyone. He wasn't himself. "What about the king, your husband?"

Her fingers brushed past his hands, up his arms, and onto his shoulders. "I am not a wife. I have no husband."

Yora considered what she said, five words with more meaning than he could have realized. He had read once of the concept of divorce, how a man and a woman could put each other away in the law. In his world, a land governed by tradition and force, there was only marriage. No one had written a law of divorce, because no one could imagine an end to such a promise. Marriage was like military enlistment, an obligation of honor. Yora had left his honor at home, crumpled on the kitchen floor, hating him. Seething at him.

Yora could still see himself standing with Denaiah in his tent, two shadows longing for the erasure of light. Two people who hated their lot. Their love was made of loss.

Denaiah sighed, taking her arms back from him, mistaking his silence for rejection.

"Why don't you want me? I can be yours."

When King Tarsus had proposed to Denaiah, it was in the setting of the court. She was formally asking for asylum. Yora had not given her any offering of affection. His feelings for her went largely unspoken. He had honor then, honor that was hope, and duty.

"Will you not speak?" Denaiah quivered, turning. "Send me away if you wish. I shouldn't have come here, I..."

Yora took her in his arms, snapped back from his dissociative haze. He turned her, guiding her into his embrace in passion that expressed itself like a dance. She spun and fell into him, her breath on his neck.

"You can stay."

"What about your wife?"

"You can stay."

26

"West and nine at five hundred!"

"Techa fio!" a rider to Cash's left cursed. He laughed to himself. The man didn't say it right.

They were under a lot of pressure, which may have messed with the thinking of the new second, a young lieutenant out of the Palace Academy, overseen by the queen, the old queen, herself. Cash felt new to the group, though not out of his league with Ran's group of riders, but he could tell this lieutenant needed help. Even simple artillery drills were killing him.

"There's cover at our right!" the rider on the left shouted.

Ran rode alongside the company, throwing small pellets of gunpowder to simulate artillery fire while mounted. The young lieutenant, Brooks, wheeled the company around in circles, ignoring the rather obvious cover offered by trees and rolling terrain at the southern end of the field. Each time there was more simulated fire, Brooks would turn another direction, directing them to sprint away from the attack, but never leaving the field that would get them all killed. The horses brayed and slipped, and the air was thick with steaming sweat, human and animal alike. After a while of relentless pops from the gunpowder packets, Cash found himself cursing as well.

If they ever had to ride under this lieutenant, the company would die. Whatever trust he was trying to win out of the men wasn't happening.

Without calling an end to the exercise, Ran stopped dropping the packets. Brooks took this as a success

"Security!" he shouted. "Team leaders on me." The group started to form a perimeter. Those assigned dismounted to take up prone positions in the open field. Cash chose to stay mounted, watching as Ran approached Brooks. The young lieutenant continued to bark orders, sounding more like yapping dog than a leader, though not from the tone of his voice, just the fact that nothing that came out of his rapid-fire mouth hole made any sense. Noise for noise's sake.

Cash recognized a hard look from Ran. He had seen it when the prince pulled on one of the twins in the gang's camp only weeks before. The look was danger with eyes and a mouth.

Is he going to kill him? Cash leaned forward on the horn of his saddle. His horse, unfortunately not Red this time, shifted under his change of weight.

Brooks stopped yapping when he saw Ran, frozen in some kind of submissive paralysis. Ran grabbed the younger man's collar and threw him off his horse.

The men didn't laugh, as Cash almost did. He quickly closed his mouth like he would over a yawn. But he couldn't help but stare. Brooks landed with his gear twisting, canteen and ammo clanging against each other, and all the breath knocked out of him. He wheezed and moaned, childlike, struggling for composure before his lungs would let him have it. Cash was glad he wasn't Brooks.

No one said anything while Ran, still mounted, circled the humiliated officer. When Brooks gathered himself to his feet, Ran gave a quiet rebuke. "You're dismissed, Lieutenant."

"Sir?" Brooks coughed.

"I know you're a privileged boy. Somebody pulled some strings out of the academy to get you this command. Lucky you, you got your chance, but no. Get your gear and your pretty horse out of here."

Brooks took the punishment with surprising composure

and left, back to camp and out of the company's future. Cash watched him leave. If he had just made a few obvious choices... no. Brooks wasn't meant for this level of service. Maybe if he'd been raised to fight, like Cash was. Cash never had the privilege of another life to go to. He always had to be the best, or he wouldn't have survived this long. Judge wouldn't have kept him around.

Ran stopped the drills, sizing up the exhausted riders. They numbered about three hundred individuals divided into platoons, then squads, teams, and riders with horses. The sad truth was that although Ran's campaign was against perhaps the greater odds, the Valley's armies stretched thin along its walls and mountain passes. One company was all the Valley could spare for Ran's ambition. Cash saw the burden in Ran's eyes, and his reason for not cutting a new young officer any slack.

"Lieutenant Rivers!" Ran called out.

"Yessir!" Cash straightened his back.

"What would you have done?"

Cash's horse swished its mane while he answered. "I would have used the cover, sir."

Ran gave a small nod. Pensive agreement. "Elaborate."

"The simple tactics always win. You make a decision. In this case that decision is as simple as direction and distance. You don't assume anything, you just act. Enemy fire is coming from somewhere. Find the nearest cover, assault to clear it. If you stay in one place, you'll die."

Ran clicked his tongue. The answer wasn't quite good enough. "Let's say you know where the enemy is firing from. You just find somewhere to hide?"

"Am I surrounded?" Cash asked.

"Yes, for the sake of argument."

The company listened. Cash had the impression that maybe some of them wanted him to say something stupid. He found he didn't care. It helped that he considered Ran a friend.

"No," Cash said. "Hiding will get you killed. If I have a gun and I have legs, I'm assaulting the thick of the fire. If I'm on foot, we're bounding, every gun working to keep the enemy's head down. If I'm on a horse, I'm riding with all fury toward that fight. My ability to outmaneuver my enemy is won by my speed."

"You'll lose people that way," Ran said.

"In an ambush? I'm losing people anyway. Keeping myself *from* getting ambushed is the fight I've already lost."

Ran wore an expression that rested somewhere between a sneer and a headache. "Dismount, give your horses a rest," he called out to the company.

Cash swung his legs off the grateful horse.

"What do outlaws do when they're outnumbered?" Ran asked, his horse's lead in his hand. Most were still listening.

Cash knew Ran had seen what he and Judge had done. How many men were there that day? The killing didn't stop. It started with the blood and brains of Ezra Steele but it kept going. The memory was distant and close all at once. Cash shot man after man, spent clip after clip of all the ammunition he could find. He could still hear the sounds of the dying, death rattles and desperate nothings. He could feel Judge with him, guiding him through what must have amounted to the test of his manhood.

"They survive," Cash answered. "But they don't surrender."

"You're born of a different breed, Rivers," Ran said with a smile. "Company, you're dismissed for the night. Go see your families. Report for operational orders at sunup. Be ready to deploy. I'm sick of these drills."

Cash didn't have anyone to go see. His adventure started the day he said goodbye to Abelnora. "Deployed" or not, he was alone. He got hit with an old sense of homelessness he hadn't dealt with since before Judge took him in. Strange how he could feel like a man, the best of many men, but like a listless child at the same time. What would he do with a night off? Maybe he could go see Seth again. As strange as the man was, he had called himself Cash's family.

"Rivers!"

Cash wheeled around to see who called him. The group was dispersing, and Sergeant Oldhouse was addressing him.

"Yes, Sergeant."

"You got anywhere to be tonight?" The man had a sort of bulldog droop to his face, a product of long years fighting and riding for men like Ran. Weird how he wasn't higher-ranking. There must have been a story there.

"No, not really."

"The prince orders you to his tent."

"On my way."

The tent was dark brown, functional, and coarse, perfect for forest or desert camouflage. Cash wondered if they would bring it with them. A detachment of engineers was supposed to follow with wagons of armaments and means for building infrastructure. Cash didn't feel set on the whole plan, however. There were missing pieces in his mind. The logistics of an army, even a small one, were much different than moving and hiding a gang.

"Cash Rivers, my little outlaw," Ran welcomed him into the tent. There was a table in the center with a large map. The wooden table bordered the map at the edges, making the look of it artistic. High Valley made up part of the map; the rest of the Basin extended out to the opposite edge with Ashra City near the coast. The map showed Cash's whole world.

A few more officers came inside, lieutenants in charge of platoons. These lesser officers commanded directly under Ran's leadership, who, though he was a prince, acted as a captain with his own company. Logistically, he should also have had a second, someone like Brooks whom he just sent out the door who didn't have a platoon. The second would take charge if something happened to Ran, then leadership would fall to the other lieutenants in order of seniority.

"I'll lead without a second, for now," Ran said, halfway into their meeting. "Rawlins, Shakes, and Farms, you will inform your men tomorrow that we leave at nightfall. I don't want to risk a daytime departure. We slip out here, through these old tunnels north of Shadow Pass, and we should be a fair distance away from High Valley before anyone gets wind of our movement."

"The men already suspect deployment tomorrow," said Farms, raising a finger. He looked a little younger than Ran.

"That's good, I did just tell them to go be with their families one more time."

Rawlins spoke next. "When will the engineer detachment follow?"

"That depends on how well our talks go with Kona."

The men discussed more logistics. Cash waited for a chance to find out why they invited him.

"How do you boys feel about our outlaw Rivers leading the knife?" Ran leaned back, placing a boot on the table at the edge of the beautiful map.

Shakes eyed Cash. "He doesn't look like half the killer you made him sound."

"Oh, he's killed," said Ran. "I saw the bodies. I also saw the wounds. Cash carries a smaller pistol than Judge."

"I have a couple Valley issues now," said Cash. "I like them better. More care than what you can find in Ashra."

"Your gun hit more men."

Cash shrugged, then shifted in his chair, uncomfortable. "What's the knife?" he asked.

Rawlins said, "A breach. You see, a spear is precise, a single point to break down an enemy's defense. Then what do we have?"

"A sword."

"Right, a sword for a standing fight. Head-to-head, two armies in a field with high casualties."

"So, what's the knife?" Cash thought he already knew.

Ran got to his feet and pulled out his knife, sheathed in his vest. He didn't wear a decorative vest, as Cash might expect for a prince, just simple protection like everyone else. He said, sweeping the blade through the air and spinning it in his fingers, "A knife is a secret. It's small, it's up close, it's chaotic and painful. You use it when you want to frighten your enemy, cut down their numbers when no one is looking, crippling and maiming."

Cash started to see his purpose, why an outlaw would fit into a cavalry's ranks. He saw himself, poised on a hill shooting bandits, or up close, stealing out of undeserving pockets. Then he saw himself standing over a dead rancher, a smoking gun in his hand and blood on a fancy carpet. "I know all the Basin, especially Ashra City. You want me to wage a small war, break up operations ahead of your assault."

"That's absolutely right," said Ran. "Little outlaw, I want you to disrupt the enemy, no quarter, with full reign on a light squad of riders. I have a few who already like your leadership and are itching for glory. You'll take the fight with them to wherever it hurts, on their artillery, on their supplies, on their leaders. You don't just know the Basin. You've got blood that boils with motive I could never give my men, especially not kids like Brooks. You're a killer, not just a soldier, and you're gonna shoot the techa ranchers and gangsters right in the face before my company even gets there."

"The man who shot Ezra Steele," said Farms. "If they don't fear you by now, they will."

"Exactly," Ran said. "We're gonna make you a hero, Captain." He handed Cash the knife.

Cash sat back, flicking the edge of the blade with his fingertips. *Captain.* He outranked almost everyone at the table with this title. That meant his word on the front was final. He was fully independent of all authority but Ran's. "Shit. Can we leave right now?"

27

— · —

Dressed as a man, chaps over her pants and a well-shaded hat over her delicate eyes, Denaiah slipped away. Yora watched her go, and then it was morning.

The sun brought no warmth to the camp, and clouds took it away before long. They seemed to move in faster than usual, like carpet rolling out for the unholy feet of winter. The air was crisp, and he could see breath from every man, woman, and horse he passed on his way to the Remembrance.

Remembrance was held on the eighth day of the first moon's cycle. Yora hadn't always attended with his military duties, but he enjoyed the ceremony. The warm spring water out of the ground made for easy reflection, a chance to drown personal concerns with a bigger picture.

A fire burned in the middle of the camp. Surrounding camps had their own as more outfits joined with the main group. They would each hold a Remembrance, a nod in prayer to the dead, the living, and those not of this world; collective heritage. He took his place standing with his captains and a priestess in front of the fire, feeling the heat of the flames lick his back. He faced the growing crowd, and listened to the priestess begin her song.

The crackling flames were her percussion, the wind was her symphony, and the earth was her stage. A calmness draped into Yora, just under his skin, like liquid silk. The sound of the priestess and her song covered up his memories. Vonica and Denaiah and all their hurt faded, if only for what would amount to this moment. He breathed, welcoming the oxygen to each cell in his body, thanking the air for its life. In conscious meditation, he gave the breath back to the air, to fill the trees with the same gift.

The movement of the song changed from serenity to heartache, the Joropa melody wailing for the dead, buried under the ground in piles of burnt dust, snuffed out of life by terrors no one alive could imagine. Yora tried to imagine the world then, when bombs fell, and civilization melted. He wondered what his home would look like then, plastic and populated, with laws and traditions that rooted deeper than just a few generations.

"*Life,*" the priestess sang.
"*Bring us the scroll, the spear.*
Take our blood, our enemies,
Make them part of your Valley, Mother.
In the waters our victory,
That we may ascend to starlit halls
In the shine of your way."

The congregation passed the waters amongst themselves in ceremonial cups made of bone. He received one from a young lieutenant. The water was bitter and full of minerals, straight out of the spring, but boiled first, purified. The priestess sang in harmony with another now. Their voices brought solemnity to the ritual. All drank in memory of the dead who inhabited the soil of the water. They drank in unity, that they would defend the Valley against all who would come to take it from them.

Yora pondered the illusion of invincibility. They had kept the Valley because no one wanted to fight them for it. There were legends of the might of their warriors going back generations. But what of a desperate enemy? How many were coming? Where would they approach? How skilled were they? The boy he met in the hills, he spoke Joropa and had at least some familiarity with a gun, but if the new enemy had guns, they must have a means to arm them, some sort of civilization and resources. Why run this way with winter coming?

I can do this, he thought. *Leave her behind.*

At this point, he wasn't sure which woman he was thinking about.

Cash and his men missed the Remembrance. He didn't mind; it wasn't part of his beliefs, and his men seemed at ease. They had ridden out of the Valley with swiftness of purpose. Red seemed pleased with the pace. Cash wondered if Red ever missed chasing cattle, or if the work of a warhorse fit him better. He had some fierceness behind the bit that Cash wanted to see when the time was right.

The prospect of battle electrified Cash's nerves. Judge had built him into a warrior. Ran had lifted him into a sort of legend. He was glad he had an eager horse. Red was taking him right into the furnace. Ashra City was a place where the ruthless took power, the ones with the most to lose. The rich only became rich when they stepped on the right people, people like Cash's parents.

I'm good enough, he told himself. *I'm the leader of the gang now.* He tried to think of what advice Judge might give him at this point. He'd tell him to stick to his directive only as much as it served him. He would tell Cash to not be used, but to do his best to be the man holding the reins. Judge would rise to the top, whatever that looked like.

Unlike the main body of Ran's men, Cash and his bunch were not meant to be force multipliers. They weren't meant to recruit anyone else to fight with them. The main rule was no quarter, no prisoners. They were to be like ghosts on forgotten trails, and so they began, snaking their way through canyons and riverbeds, stopping only to water the horses and sleep.

Passing south of Glycerin territory, and once out of the middle desert, they would begin the hunt for anything that would help them disrupt Ashran infrastructure. Ashra was sort of a coastal desert, warmer than the mountains but never as green.

I'm the captain. I'll pull this thing off my way.

"What's your stake in all this?" asked a man named Tarj. They were stopping to rest the horses. They didn't bring any spare. They would steal some when the time came. For now, they pushed and rested the horses they had. Tarj led one of the teams of five, and had just reported on his men.

"What do you mean, stake?" said Cash.

"You don't have a home. That's what we fight for, to pre-serve our home and way of life. This violence is our sacrifice, the price of freedom and protection."

"You're a philosopher," said Cash, as he started brushing Red's back. The horse's muscles quivered.

"I'm a father," said Tarj. "Maybe that's the same thing."

Cash tried to think. He was thirsty. "I guess violence is my way of life," he realized. "I haven't had a home since the Keepers took it from me. I lost my family, my gang, because of them, too. I'm a wanted man where we're going. Took them long enough to realize I was the pain in their side all along, I guess."

"What do you get when this is all over?"

Cash took a long drink from his canteen. The water splashed down his shirt that he wore outside his military vest, an attempt to not actually look like valley cavalry. "Hmm. It's hard to imagine, but once Ashra is liberated and in Valley con-trol..." He thought about Abelnora. "I will try and understand women."

"Now that's a job for a philosopher," laughed Tarj.

Cash raised his canteen like a drinking glass and took an-other gulp.

He liked Tarj, who was just a little older than himself, but balding. Tarj led the Petei team. Ced, a long-haired, broad-shouldered man of little beard, led the Mokoi team. Cash's second was an old man, by army standards, with a wiry build and endless stamina, named Jayce. The team leaders led four other men, each of them young with hungry eyes, trained and eager to serve. Rapport was good. Cash found that his reputation as a killer outlaw and Ran's endorsement had done him a lot of favors.

But that was a good question from Tarj. What did Cash stand to gain? He had an entire life to build. Judge had called him a blank slate, also a liability. He could be a bandit, if he wanted, not a far reach from the outlaw life he already knew. Cash didn't owe anyone, not even these men. He liked them well enough, but he hadn't had time to build a comradery yet. They were career soldiers, nothing of the same cloth. To them, the High Valley was a belief, the root of their universe. To Cash, it was just a pretty place, but still an important one. He'd discovered a unique heritage there. Yes, impressing Seth would be something to gain. Family. Too much to hope for, but something to cling to.

"Without family," Judge said once, "you'll just end up being someone else's tool."

The squad rested in a cave and risked the light of fire. Two men kept watch at a time while the rest slept, switching every two hours. The ground was hard, but it was nice to be out of the wind. He hoped no screechers or bears had made a home here, but the squad's scent would deter them from coming back, at least for the night. Nature had a way of building true outlaws out of animals. They knew when to take advantage, or when to leave something alone. All the same, the squad kept the horses inside, just in case a beast got greedy.

"What's our plan, Lieutenant?" whispered Jayce. He sat on a rock next to where Cash propped himself up, facing the fire.

"You don't want to sleep, Jayce?"

"I thought I'd mull over tomorrow's plan. Are we stopping at the drop-off point? I don't think Lord Praylum will have left us any instructions yet, and I also doubt any message carriers will have made it this far faster than us, even without this canyon's terrain. You set a fast pace."

Cash adjusted some meat he had smoking on the fire. Sitting back down against his rock, he said, "No, I agree. I don't get the impression Ran wants us to wait around for his instructions anyway. I think he trusts us to do the right thing."

"So, then what's tomorrow's plan?"

"This canyon's one of the best-kept secrets of crossing the Basin. Most folks don't like crossing rivers, for obvious reasons, and we had to cross down here almost ten times."

The two men guarding outside the mouth of the cave came back in and woke their replacements. They looked tired and half frozen. Cash had driven them hard today, perhaps too hard. Cavalry drills in the Valley had made him sore, training their way. Now they were in Cash's world of fast drives through unwanted terrain. He'd had worn out his new squad for sure. He had to be careful with them soon or they wouldn't be in the right shape to meet the enemy.

"Tomorrow's plan," Cash continued. "I think should be to rest. We'll come up with a real plan with specific points."

"We'll need resupply as soon as possible. That means friends."

"Right," Cash said. "A network of them. I know some people."

"Friends?"

"If you have what they want."

Jayce half smiled. Half of his face drooped a little, something Cash hadn't noticed before. The old man unhooked a piece of the lizard meat hanging over the fire in the smoke. Taking a large bite, he motioned to the sleeping riders. "They'll follow you all the way. If you drive them hard, they'll ride harder. They may be sore now, whatever, they're young. But don't leave them out of the game, out of the planning. Trust them. You can't ask for a better squad. They volunteered. They want to be here, in the face of the fight." Jayce chewed a moment, then swallowed. "Morale is a fragile thing, though."

"How do you mean?"

"It doesn't like to freeze for no reason."

"Then tell them it's a good thing we're headed for the coast," said Cash, grabbing some lizard for himself. It needed salt. "Ashra has beaches."

28

—.—

Arty had company, an individual of many minds and faces, but no true form. Her companion also had a machine, rather than human, soul. She wished that was enough, but it wasn't. She missed her home, and her friends, and her sense of purpose. The copper grass, mimicry of nature, and open skies choked her up sometimes, in a figurative sense. She didn't feel right, somehow less human. The daylight of sky never turned into night, so she had no stars. She had always had stars, lighted points of the Milky Way's embrace. She also hadn't had any need to sleep. For food, she had the fruit of the trees, each one sweet and desirable, but empty of the sustenance of a home.

Arty had taken to exploring memories. The mirror universe in which she had found herself had a dreamlike quality that allowed her to control the story of her surroundings. Imagination over matter. The purest form of this happened through recollection. She would remember something, conjure up the sensations and the essence of the vision, and the memory would play out in vivid, three-dimensional detail around her. She could laugh with friends, explore her home world, dance in a nightclub on shore leave, or reminisce in her aunt and uncle's quarters.

This time, she couldn't think of anywhere to go. She stayed where her body really was, this uncomfortably beautiful world of consensus.

The breeze in the copper-colored field warmed her skin. She

wore clothes she had made with her mind, with Kami's help. She couldn't see Kami right now, but Arty knew her company was there. Kami was like a specter wearing faces of the past, all from Arty's memory. As Arty explored the memories, she imagined that she did so through Kami's power.

Kami's name fit her in many ways. Like the Japanese kami deities, she provided Arty with life and power. But she was no spirit of nature, of anything biological. She was a synthetic spirit, born of what could be called mechanical.

"Are you there, Kami?" Arty called out.

"I'm here," the machine-ghost answered in her mind.

"Why can't I see you?"

"I'm practicing."

"Practicing what?" Arty reached, and a tree grew in front of her, reaching its branches out with the gift of a fruit that looked like chrome and tasted like cream. She bit into it.

"I'm practicing for what it will be like when we aren't here, when we go back to Kardun I am a ship, and my voice will exist only here, in your mind."

Trees grew out of the soil again, poking up as saplings out of the grass, then thickening as their chemical processes bore them life. Leaves and branches of all colors embraced each other, forming the skeleton of a vehicle. They warped and combined, their colors and properties changing as they bonded, forming consensus. Nature and machine could not be distinguished in this place, this Shangri-La of universes. The trees talked, changed, danced, and formed a skeleton. Their creation took shape, with branches and filaments smoothing out the surfaces until they were round and sleek. In minutes, Kami had grown Arty a ship.

"Wait, what just happened? Did I do this, or did you do this?" Arty said.

"I think we both did," said Kami.

"Is this real?" Arty touched the wing. The ship was larger

than her, about the size of a Federacy fighter, with the same shape. Much of it was still forming itself. The hull oscillated under her fingertips, just as her observations of Libertas long ago. It breathed subtle breaths of time under the bridge of physical space.

"Yes, it's absolutely real. It's going to be me. I'm being born, like a daughter of Libertas, and of this place. Botistem and Bosion combined."

"Wow," said Arty, her voice almost breathless. "It's... you're... a beautiful ship."

"An instrument of exploration, or of war. It's who I want to be."

"Me too," sighed Arty. "That's what I was."

She continued to watch the ship grow, filling out its interior and sewing pieces of hull like metallic cloth on a loom, threads and patches making a creature.

"How long have I been here?" Arty asked. "How much time has passed?"

Kami appeared next to the evolving ship of metal trees wearing Lopez's face. "No one will ever find a discernable way to measure time in the universe."

Arty pursed her lips together and her nostrils flared a little. She had heard this speech before. "I know, I know. Time is relative to your perspective."

"It's more than just perception. All beings traverse through realms of space and time, universes stacked together in oceans of fluidity."

"How much time has passed on Kardu?"

"Kardu is eternal. It exists before, it will exist. The only illusion of experience is to think there is a now in which anything exists at one point at the same 'time' as another. It would be impossible to prove that anything happens simultaneously at all, only that they were perceived simultaneously, shared experience in the Dao."

Arty strained her mind, comprehending what Kami said only at the surface. "So when will I see Kardu? Can we know? Have I been here for years? Months?"

"There are no years here."

"Then what about my first question?"

Kami stroked along the wing, arriving at what looked like a developing cockpit. "The way is known. Charted, from our flight through the Dao."

"How long has it been for the people of the planet? Does the Federacy know what happened to my ship?"

"I don't know," said Kami. "I didn't, I don't, think in years or hours, or however you wish to measure a concept that doesn't exist."

"It exists to me." Frustration started to bite.

"Then you will have to be the one to measure it," Kami said with some sass. "But I know that we must leave soon."

"Why?"

The sky darkened by a degree.

"Because they are coming."

Arty turned to the horizon, beyond the trees and fields of metal life. In the sky, swarming into view in waves of heat and mirage, flew ships of galactic malignancy, machines of disorder and dark consensus. The evil sect Bosions as her people had known them, descending toward her and her new ship, now taking on itself the image of a winged fox.

"They are coming, and they only know war."

29

— · —

Seth ate a smoked carcass he had stolen from a camp of unknown combatants. He watched them with keen eyes from an envelope of darkness. Men conversed in a harsh dialect of Joropa and he couldn't understand the chatter. Their language and mannerisms were alien, born out of a world he never belonged to. But they did know how to cook a deer. The more he ate, the more fuel he had for the Botistems inside him, the last strands of his immortality.

When Seth started the community that became Ashra City, the people were technology-dependent and frightened, torn from the lives they knew. He kept them alive, for a span of some decades, and watched the generations adapt to life post-collapse. Their children learned his language, his heritage, because it was what he had to offer as theirs faded. He took what literature he could from the wreckage of the small craft he stole off the *Tecumseh*, figuring out everything from medicine to a printing press. He was more than an emissary of death then. He restarted civilization.

But all that was old purpose. In these times, he felt Death's door again, as he had for long years imagined it, but rather than something that would open to him, he felt it creaking inside, somewhere in the same place from which came the woman's voice that all times followed him around.

Interlopers, the voice seemed to say in the universal language of thought. *Cull.* Of course he never knew all she meant.

She was alien.

These people at the fire were alien of a different kind, people of the East, far from his influence. Given the environmental hardships of centuries past, he was surprised their ancestors had survived at all. They spoke no part of his tongue and their Joropa had evolved past Seth's comprehension, a big reminder that although he had lived on this world for lifetimes, he was not a native. He was the invader, the infection, the interloper. He didn't pretend otherwise, not to himself.

None of that made what he feared he would have to do any easier.

You are my chosen. Her voice was so beautiful, yet scary. Beyond human. She was like his mother. Could that be all she had been to him these years, remnants of his mother's influence manifesting through auditory hallucination? He didn't think he would ever find out.

The men laughed at the awkward dance of one of the younger members of their party. Seth noticed one of them who did not laugh but focused on fastening the tip of his spear. They had a few guns, as well, but were not as well-armed as citizens of High Valley. The wild men were also dressed differently, foregoing cloth for furs of differing hides that they had dyed into bright colors. Finishing with his spear, the serious one stood up, revealing unmatched height among his peers. His furs were even more colorful. He was the warlord.

The jovial youth stopped his dance. He must have done something to disappoint or offend the big man, because he cowered before the blunt end of the spear cracked over his back. A small pistol swung around his neck. Seth started to guess where it might have come from. Perhaps he had traded with people like the outlaw Judge who ventured East, people rare enough that almost no one believed anyone lived east of the Valley at all...or someone else could have armed them.

Interlopers.

The big one kicked the young one several times before Seth heard a shout. It came from behind him somewhere. He struggled to think of why a noise would have come from that direction. Unless – he'd been seen. Mad, surprisingly light, pearly eyes came at him from the housing of an unshaven face marked with shades of orange and a maniacal grin. The grinning stranger held a long knife, almost long enough to be a sword, and was driving it toward Seth's abdomen.

Seth drove a burst of light into the ground, sending dirt into the air and light into the pearly eyes. His legs, also amplified with light, darted him away. The disoriented warrior threw his sword past Seth's ear as he ran. Seth leapt, and with his flight he left no trail. No one else would find him tonight. Crashing through branches, summersaulting onto leaf-mulched land, Seth mused what kind of phantom names they must be calling him now. Wild men had a name for him once. He couldn't remember it now.

A safe distance away, up and over foothills, Seth called his horse. He could have whistled, but he knew another way to summon his equestrian friends. Seth put his hand around the twisting limb of a tree. Calling out in his mind, through the branches and roots, into the soil, into the veins of the planet, he summoned his horse by suggestion. He didn't know how, just that it worked. The branch shivered, and he heard the sound of pounding hooves. After some time, he let go of the branch as he felt his horse prod the back of his head with its lips.

"Hi, Glad."

Glad sniffed and searched Seth's hands, looking for treats.

"I don't have anything, boy." Seth had run out of berry preserve from his farm a while ago, thanks to his appetite. More grain he'd have to trade for. In apology, he stroked Glad's long face and scrunched the mane behind his friend's ears. "Thanks for always hearing me." Glad had lived a long time in Seth's care. He would keep living, as long as Seth had power to share.

He mounted the horse, no saddle, feeling Glad's excitement underneath him, the need to run.

"Let's go find out how many of these wild men we're dealing with, my old friend."

Rearing back, Glad agreed, and turned for grander hilltops.

30

—·—

Time dilated with the darkness of grief. For Yora, the seconds beat with a heavy hammer, slow on the rise, hard on the fall, distorting his perception of the dried up, pre-winter world around him. He just stared at what he saw, no longer seeing it, succumbing to the beat of time and the bleeding of a fresh wound on his soul.

"My lord!" someone was shouting, but the seconds beat louder. He couldn't hear.

"My lord!" Two of them were shouting now.

A pair of hands grabbed him by the vest, lifting his feet just off the ground before pushing him back, almost knocking him flat. Clarity returned to the forest.

"Get the–" he started to say. "Move her–" He trailed off. Tears were coming. The men shouldn't see. He fell over her body.

His second was behind him, shouting orders. "I want a solid perimeter around the entire brigade. Make preparations for the automatics and the artillery."

Scurrying feet and time started to warp again.

She rested undignified beneath her horse, a mare, rosy, with spears protruding out the animal's sides. Another spear pinned her down through the vest and chest into the ground. There was a scroll on the breastplate. It belonged to Yora's sister, Tais, with the yellow hair. She was the woman on the ground, or at least she used to be. He almost couldn't recognize her. Death had taken the shine from her semblance.

"No guns," said Yora, hushed in his despair.

"Say again, my lord?"

"Small arms only."

"Yes, my lord, no artillery. We'll be moving fast?"

"Yes. Riders only."

Yora picked up her head. Tais felt heavy, her tangled hair full of leaves and her face gray with the first signs of frozen decay. Three men stooped down and lifted the horse from her body. Yora turned away from the noise of it, and the smell, but he held her, stroking the light and muddy hair from her face. He cried for the first time since he was a boy, bathing his face with the warmth of fresh tears. No sob lifted his shoulders. He held the weeping in the tightness of his stomach and let the sadness fall through his eyes and over the tip of his nose.

She would be taken back to the Valley, but not yet, not before he found justice for her.

In the waters of the Valley were the minerals of creation and destruction. Voices cried in them from the dust of the ground. Tais's voice was added there today, by a foreign threat. This was supposed to be a safe assignment for her. A chance to learn. Yora turned to his faithful captain.

"What happened?" Yora asked, not wiping the tears.

"They were ambushed, and not many had drawn their arms. By my guess, they were betrayed, perhaps in parley with the enemy."

Yora followed the tracks of the battle. There were mysterious figures intermingled with the dead of his sister's company. They wore bright colors.

He whistled for his horse who came running past the bodies of the dead, cautious not to trample any of them. Grabbing the horn of the saddle, Yora swung himself over. In spiteful haste, he found one of the quartermasters.

"I need a belt-fed, now," he brusqued.

The quartermaster stammered, "I... they're all hitched to wagons. Di- did you want a few..."

"No, unhitch it for me. Just the rig, I want it on my horse."

"It'll weigh as much as a man on your horse. How many belts, my lord?"

"As many as he and I can carry."

The barrels of the gun stuck out from the blankets protecting his horse's back. The weapon was wide, and cumbersome for the animal, but his obedient steed kept up with his driven pace. He would find the... *interlopers* himself and drive them from the hills. His guard stayed behind, according to his orders. Yora would draw first blood for his family. He recalled the young boy he had met in these hills, fear of warlords and slave masters driving him over the wall. His teacher, Seth, spoke of someone else chasing the warlords. He had to act now, before the evil of the world outside overtook his entire family.

How was Ran? After the battle, Yora would send a rider to the palace. Perhaps they had already received word. Mya would want to know, as well. He wouldn't know how to tell her. She would take Tais's...she would take it the hardest.

Can't think about that now. You don't want to be weak. His thoughts almost didn't sound like his own.

The bright-colored enemy hadn't hidden their tracks well, if they'd tried to hide them at all. Yora found birds and scavengers where they had abandoned some of their wounded to die. He reached the crest of a hill overlooking a spur running to lower ground. He found them, first by the stench of their fires, dispersed among the brush and trees with poor cover. From his position, they wouldn't detect him until most of them were dead.

The first snow of the season fell on Yora's hands in light flakes while he worked, unhorsing the machinegun and rigging its metal tripod. He tested the weapon's function as best he could before racking in the links of the belt, each with a thick-powdered round.

"Wait for my signal," he had told the captain.

"Will you light a flare?"

"I'll light the mountain."

Yora made good on his promise. Tracers from the barrels ignited the dry brush and fallen trees, lightning to the thunder of his gun. There was no true cover on the ground where the wild men camped. They fell, hundreds of yards below him, in pieces under the golden glow of winter clouds at sunset.

Small fires brought smoke to the air, and before he spent the last belt of rounds, Yora heard the stamping of a horse behind him. He paused his fury a moment to look up from where he sat on the ground, his feet propped up on the legs of the tripod, shells and links glistening around him.

"Lord, shall we round them up?"

Yora looked down the hillside, bright-colored legs running for the hills on all sides. A few rounds hit a tree above his head. He realized that earlier, in his fury, one had grazed his upper arm by the shoulder. Some of the wild men had taken cover and were returning fire with inferior weaponry. Some of his men were already gunning them down.

"Leave a platoon to suppress here, and take two to sweep the lower country. Take the ones fighting back first, but don't stop until you've killed everyone. This is not a day for prisoners."

His captain saluted. "In the eyes of the Mother, we will give them the spear."

Yora crawled from the gun, avoiding more fire while the snow thickened in the air around him. Next to his horse, tethered away and unharmed, he wept.

31
– . –

The descending shadow crept over the land around Arty, the sky losing its color to a sickness.

"What's happening to the sky?" she asked, panic raising the pitch and volume of her voice.

Kami answered in her mind, "There's no time, you have to fight."

"Fight?" *Fight??* "*Who* am I fighting, Kami?" She'd spent so long in isolation. Who in the hell would be coming here? Nothing was here except– "Bosions," Arty whispered. "Shit."

"Yes," said Kami. "The Dark Bosions, as you have aptly called them, are here."

Arty wanted to hide. She imagined a dome around her and the ship that had almost finished itself. As she thought, the metallic field around her shifted downward, making a wave that grew into a wall that rose high above her head in a grand ceiling of the same copper color as the grass. It was still light inside the dome, like a strange cathedral. The ground that had been used to make the dome was now a deep chasm around the growing ship and Arty and Kami, both of them standing on a small plateau in the center.

"Good thinking, Arty," Kami said. "But they will get through, you will still have to fight."

Arty had known fear, perhaps more than anyone else she had ever known. She had experienced death coming for her. She remembered the moment when Commander Worley had the

Marshall fire on the *Libertas.* The inevitability of that moment felt a lot like this one. Kami was asking her to fight, but they were just two. A woman, inexperienced in real combat, and a strange machine soul that didn't make very much sense. What could they do against Bosion hordes?

I don't think I can do this, thought Arty. But she had to. She hadn't come this far to die.

"Tell me what to do."

"You are armed with light," said Kami. "More in this place than any other, than you may ever have within you again. Use it. Hold nothing back."

In the dome, shapes began to cut through the metal skin. They tore through with metallic claws. Some of them looked like crawlers she recognized, others were smaller, some even bigger, but all of them animal-like in nature. They ripped and tore, monstrous movements as they conquered the peaceful world, this oasis of true consensus.

Arty looked inward, not in any way on purpose, just out of instinct as she felt the light within herself. She felt alone, like someone should be with her. Kami was there, but didn't fit the right feeling. She should be holding a hand, experiencing new power. But maybe not; maybe today she was meant to fight alone.

"Your light," Kami repeated. "*Fight!*" The last part of what Kami said echoed through Arty's cells, a reverberation of glory and death on each membrane, drumbeats and songs of war. In her eyes, she saw the world around her anew in colors she wouldn't have words for. They were colors of purpose. The Bosion horde wouldn't have her today. She and Kami would escape. They would find their way.

As the light of the battle cathedral flickered on the reflective steel of an enemy claw hoisting the first of the many crawlers onto the seat of Arty's plateau, Arty met the ascending creature with an explosion of the light within her. The light sent the creature away, tumbling back to the fantastic depths it had crawled from, scorched and wounded. As several more ascended, Arty leapt, Kami within her, giving her strength, and old, good Bosion strength encouraging her from within.

She fought them from within a blur of violence, a haze of flow and action she wouldn't have known she was capable of. Her aim wasn't to kill the creatures, just to keep knocking them off the hill. Kicking what must have been either the twentieth or hundredth, she couldn't be sure, she sent it flying from her plateau pedestal. Kami remained untouched behind her.

"Are you almost finished?" Arty asked. Despite the feed of constant strength from the consensus, she could feel herself growing tired. She wasn't conditioned for this kind of fighting. She didn't know how much strength she had in her. There was a pain, too; she hadn't noticed it with all the adrenaline but, oh there it was, blood, all down her right side from a big gash in her right flank, ruining the outfit she'd made for herself.

The crawlers had faded back. Something else was coming, darkening the tears in the dome. They were flying ships. Arty didn't know how she could fly a ship.

"Kami."

The ships were coming into view. They had animal shapes. That seemed to be a thing from machine designs. They liked their animals. Animals were a part of a grand machine, though, weren't they? Nature, war, evolution. One grand program in the scheme of a universe no one could unlock. "Kami, I don't want to die here. Please answer me."

The ships were getting closer. Arty felt that inevitability again. She felt the crack in the *Marshall* about to pull her into oblivion.

As the ships drew near, Arty fell to her knees. The wound in her side was glowing, interesting enough. On her knees she noticed another crawler surface from the cliff's edge. Its teeth sparked. It was going to kill her. Why stop it? She wasn't sure.

Then she wasn't on the ground anymore. Something had scooped her up and was carrying her inside the ship. Once inside, she recognized what it must have been. It was Kami, finished growing at last, and ready to leave.

The ship levitated, supported by thrust that wasn't thrusters. Arty was behind the cockpit in a space with consoles and instruments she wasn't familiar with. It was a small space, but wasn't claustrophobic. The ship kept raising itself with Kami piloting from within, the ship having become her body. She wasn't just a holographic manifestation of past memories anymore. Kami was a child of Botistems and peaceful Bosions alike.

"And there's a part of me that comes from you," Kami whispered in Arty's thoughts. "We've fought together now, and we've grown together. We are one."

Arty had little time to orient herself. She could feel the bank of Kami's steep turn as she made her way toward the advancing attackers. Arty made her way, stumbling, to the cockpit. She wasn't a pilot, but the buttons and levers seemed intuitive. She didn't have to learn them now. When she sat down, restraints secured themselves without hands around her waist and shoulders, locking her into position.

"Can you read my thoughts?" asked Arty out loud.

"Yes," said the ship in her mind. "The louder of them, anyway."

"I'm sure all of them are loud right now."

"Not to worry. We're getting out of here. We have work to do."

The seat absorbed Arty with a kind of gel in the cushioning that eased the twist and turns of Kami's ascent through the dome into the now-blackened sky. Arty reached out for a control and found a viewer for around the ship. She looked at the copper fields and watched them fade away, becoming the black substance that looked like one that had subdued her before, back when she thought she was in a cabin somewhere planet-side. Even this place she had just resided in for unknown stretches of time was now chaotic swarms of smoky intelligence, the beauty all lost to a battle for the societal values of machines.

"Kami," Arty shouted. The ship lurched downward and Arty's insides leapt.

"I'm a little busy. What is it?"

"How do I turn on inertial dampening? I'm gonna be sick, or you know, die."

"You don't need it."

"I what?"

"You don't need inertial dampening."

Arty did throw up, all over the controls, pieces of the juicy fruit she ate from one of the trees. She expected Kami to be angry with her. With all the dodging, Arty was starting to get mad at Kami. The vomitus absorbed into the panel of the controls, sliding inside between spaces Arty couldn't see.

"What do you mean I don't need dampening?" she coughed.

Kami sped the ship into a high-G burn. Arty felt crushed underneath the weight of the force of acceleration, like her eyes might fall into her head and her lungs would collapse. She stopped speaking except for little grunts that sounded like choking sobs.

Kami's words spoke into her thoughts like waves of comforting air, "I thought it would have been obvious by now. When you were seeded as an embryo, you were given receptiveness to Bosion light. You have that power within you now, after years of restoration, the light of the Bosion power. You will never age, you can sustain yourself without breath, and you have been given incredible strength."

"We really need to work on our communication," Arty thought back, her consciousness fading.

"No, don't sleep."

A wave of energy from the ship woke Arty out of fainting and she could move again. She could even see better. The view out the windows of the cockpit was indiscernible, more akin to a thunderstorm, as beings of energy fought each other in a universe built to house their souls. The Bosions fighting each other had form, for the most part, animal-like.

Back on the *Marshall*, the captain would have ordered contagion attacks, once they had weakened enemy barriers. Their rockets would have been equipped with synthetic viruses built to disrupt Bosion functionality at the molecular level. Some of the warheads they launched at the *Libertas* were equipped with something similar. Arty wondered what, if anything, would have happened had the missiles been allowed to reach their target.

"Are we still at high burn?"

"Yes, I have to get us out of this fight. We aren't ready for an enemy like this. We don't know our potential."

Arty lifted her arms inside her restraints, amazed at her strength to withstand the acceleration.

"How do I have more strength now than I did a minute ago?"

Kami said, "You won't find all your strength at once. Your mind and body are tapped into forces beyond the dimensions you can comprehend. For now, think of your access to Bosion light as cognitively linked to your mind, your spirituality, in a way. Try not to think conventionally."

"So, basically," Arty began, grunting as the ship lurched again, "anything is possible."

"In short, yes."

"My strength is as the strength of ten, because my heart is pure.'"

"What's that?"

"Nothing," said Arty. "Just some Tennyson quoted by an old

captain. He's gone now."

An opening grew in the space before them, a warped horizon into black surrounded by swirling bittersweet light of pale fluorescence. The battle was behind them, somewhere in the rearward distance of a backwards universe that Arty wondered if she would ever see again. The spherical wormhole had been waiting for her here the whole time, waiting for her to go back into her own galaxy, back to the battlespace of Mount Kardu where her military family fell.

"Oh no," whispered Arty.

"What is it?"

"We're going back to Libertas, aren't we?"

"Yes," said Kami as they slipped into the starry void. "We are returning to my mother."

32

Seth launched out of a tall tree toward an unsuspecting messenger running down an old forgotten road. The messenger fell hard and never breathed again, his body broken and systemic function undone. Impact and heat left him unrecognizable. He wouldn't have suffered.

Seth knew that blood would darken these hills by winter, he anticipated his own hands in the thick of it, but he didn't anticipate the rate of flow – that both sides, the people of the Valley and the people from the Eastern plains, would spill so much so soon without attempting conversation.

In strategic frustration, he had downed the messenger, leaving his body to freeze and decay in the snow like old leaves. He had never understood the point of burials. Where he came from, bodies were for the vacuum. For some, even recyclers were appropriate for body disposal. The galaxy was full of people who lived and died unceremoniously. The messenger was not in poor company.

He had followed the small, bright-clothed man from the scene of Yora's massacre and the Valley side of the wall. The little runner had gone through an abandoned gate and almost reached where the others of his nation camped, warlords and armies ready to spill over the wall and into Yora's patrols. They outnumbered the Valley armies, even before the main host. Seth faced a choice with them, and he didn't yet know what to do.

The variable that bothered Seth most was the unknown value of time. These people who wore bright colors and spoke dialects of old languages were feral, descended from survivors of the nuclear winter, no doubt. Maybe they were salvageable humanity. He didn't have time to find out. If they destroyed what he had built in the Basin, what was the point? What's the sunk cost of three centuries of labor?

It's a lot of blood.

"No one jumps out of a building unless there's a fire, Glad. What are they running from?"

His horse sauntered out of the trees where Seth had left him to graze before he stalked the runner. Glad reached with his head and picked at some tall grass growing through cracks in the broken concrete on the side of the highway.

"Watch the rust, boy. No, actually, get out of there."

Glad huffed and retracted his face.

"Let's go. I've got to make a decision."

Seth put his foot in the stirrup and swung his other over Glad's back. The horse backed up, his feet marking a circular path in place, pointing them up the highway. Clicking his heels back, Seth signaled Glad forward in a trot. The snow under hoof was soft and new, covering the ground just enough to give it a kind of visual flavor. The air was crisp, and Seth's hot breath joined the steam of Glad's back in moistening the dry desert air. They followed the projected path of the messenger while Seth thought about his decision.

He whistled a tune, something that had nested in his mind since a long time ago, when he looked younger, stronger, and stood with his mother in the Eye of Libertas. A strange man with miscolored eyes played it on the piano, notes of melancholy.

After some time, the woman's voice had taken over the tune. Seth listened to it for miles. She added the intricacies of her own harmonies, bouncing and toying with the song like a child with a ball. He liked it.

"I didn't whistle it for you," Seth thought to her. She didn't seem to hear him, or perhaps she didn't understand, just as he never understood her. He had once asked himself what kind of voice in a person's head wouldn't understand them. He had learned to accept her, real or not, and believe in her as the spirit of the world he had made his own.

Seth reached the camp, his second time intercepting these people. He had left them alone before. This time, he walked into the middle of their biggest fire at daytime, surrounded by their sleepy drunkenness, waiting for them to react. He still hadn't made his decision.

Alarms sounded in the form of screams and surprise. Seth was dressed in fur, not cloth like the people of the valley, so he wasn't expecting anything. They would react to him however they saw fit, and he would respond according to the nature of their reception. A group of them had killed Tais, a girl he'd had a fondness for since she was young, and they had provoked a terrifying wrath from Yora. Seth wanted them gone from his valley, so he let them sound their alarms, and waited for them to give him a reason.

I think you've made your decision, the woman's voice seemed to say in the notes of her song.

Maybe I have. I need them to make the first move. Strike me, or spare me.

He heard her laugh as two of the larger of the men beat Seth down and tied his hands with a cord. He smiled to himself. Cultural evolutionary pressures of the universe had many constants, such as how no matter where he went in the galaxy, humans made cords for tying prisoners. The biggest man approached and spat in Seth's face, then reached out a hand and rubbed the saliva and mucus deeper into the skin. Sliding his fingers around his eyes, nose, and mouth. Seth fought the urge to gag. *Not yet.*

The mob tied him to a pole and left him till nightfall. The woman's voice faded as the sun dropped behind the distant mountains, leaving behind a bittersweet splash of colors in the clouds. While he waited, Seth let the cords dig into his skin. The worse they treated him, the less guilty he would feel about what he would do.

So there was remorse, after all. He didn't need to kill their messenger. No, he did. He stood by the decision. He needed to protect Yora, avenge Tais, buy Ran time. The big picture always had to be on his mind. His mother needed a following.

What did her face look like again? He could see it, but there was a dream filter over her features. Three centuries of other, uglier memories were in the way.

The sun disappeared and fires sprang up around the camp of thousands. Men and women gathered around him. In the clearing, painted warriors beat drums in primitive ritual and chanted deep, throaty melodies. The beats were pulses of bloodlust. The firelight teased the murderous thirst in their eyes. Seth could tell the people wouldn't let him live. He had no advocate.

He tried speaking in his limited Joropa, hoping they could understand the dialect, "I've come to you in peace."

The big one, the leader that had spit in his face, laughed and hit him with a back hand that drew blood from the inside Seth's cheek. It started to heal, tingling.

Seth spat the blood on the ground. The rest of the bleeding had already stopped. He spoke again, "I'm giving you the opportunity to turn around, and leave the valley beyond those hills alone."

The leader grabbed a spear from one of the chanters. It was long, with a metal and rusted edge, probably lifted off some ruins. The rust would poison and be difficult to heal.

Seth felt the wound from the back-hand and the spittle sinking inside. It tingled, the Botistems beginning their work.

"The warriors you sent over the wall are dead."

A shot rang out from the crowd, then more. They had brought a few guns with them and were shooting them in the air.

The leader pointed the spear at Seth's neck. Seth only understood one word of the many that growled out of the man's throat. "Ndai Lun." No peace.

"So, you understand me?"

"Ndai, Lun, Ndai Lun, Ndai Lun!" The crowd began to chant.

Seth bowed his head, ignoring the rusted iron at his neck. The crowd's chants and war cries subdued. An old sorrow was trying to surface from the pools of repressed grief and regret he kept hidden in the corners of his mind. He had worked so long to create a society worthy of his own legacy, of his mother's arrival, of his descendants and intellectual progeny. Visions of a world dying in chaos, of a woman he loved and children he raised rolled through his thoughts in flickering pictures. There had been a lot of blood to draw back then. This time couldn't be different. He was the immortal man who had to see civilization through.

This was the hard decision. This was the moment to be the man his mother made him.

Looking around, Seth saw a pile of white bones near the fire. Among the bones were skulls of something equestrian, a horse, or maybe a donkey. He smiled to himself, the idea of it absurd. With the idea came a rush of adrenaline and a surge of light that filled his body. The light rose from his core until it reached his eyes. He looked up into surprised terror in the holder of the spear.

"Lypande olon!" the man screamed. Bright eyes! The leader fell back like he'd seen a childhood nightmare. He crabbed away on all fours, sliding his humiliation in tracks on the grassy floor.

"Lypande olon! Bright eyes. He's come for us," Seth heard in screaming wails.

Seth broke the cords on his wrists with heated strength. He walked to the cowering warlord, feeling his muscles and bones alight in righteous fire. Taking some pity on the man, Seth knelt and showed him his now healed face.

"Tell whatever gods you face in judgment that I gave you every chance to walk away."

Standing, Seth paused to put a heel on the man's brow. He could feel the man tremble underfoot. His bones felt delicate, his mortal flame a flickering wick. Seth pushed his heel down, so small an effort, and took what remained of the warrior's life. He didn't feel the regret now. Regret was for eras of peace.

As he scraped off his boot, lost in quick reflection, a bullet from the crowd struck Seth down, piercing his neck. He landed on his back, the rocks finding his ribs. With a groan that came out with a gurgling rattle from his neck, Seth looked at the stars, feeling abandoned by them, and let the Botistems push the bullet from his neck. It was clothed in blood. Above, there was no moon, no witnesses but the stars. The woman whispered something to him, her breath in the filtering waves between his thoughts like a lover.

He'd run out of time to stall his mission. These people were a branch from the wrong tree.

Leveraging a burst of strength and centuries of muscle memory, Seth leapt to his feet from his shoulders, striking the ground with force that knocked the approaching rush of warriors with dust and wind. As fear struck most of them, Seth diverted and ran for cover behind the pile of animal bones. The bones popped and splintered as his attackers started using more of their guns. Pieces of bone dusted him from over the pile. One of the jawbones rolled down to his feet, its teeth in a permanent, underbite grin.

He picked up the jawbone, stealing a moment of silent intimacy as bullets flicked and whizzed off his cover. Seth lamented to the silent bone, "'As they did unto me, so have I done unto them.' Now for the human cost of greater humanity."

Clasping end-joints of the jaw in both hands, he broke it in half. With the song of the spirit of the bones in his ears, he leapt over the top of the pile onto the first of many foes and clubbed his maddened head. The light in Seth's eyes was fury, and the dust at his feet rose like crashing waves as he danced through crowds of warriors, men and women alike, splitting their bones and flesh into heaps of carrion wake. His work was quick in the battle-haze that overcame him.

"I enjoyed it," Cash had told him.

You always enjoy it when it happens, Seth thought somewhere in the back of his work. *When Death uses you as emissary, when her music clouds your senses, war is a joy, a comradery with nature. All who live are killers. Before community, there was violence. Before life, there was Death to give it soil.*

The light in Seth's eyes burned with such brightness that even as the fires died and the dead numbered in their thousands, he could see in the clearing without a light. He was the light. He was the work of it.

As he let himself look into their faces, to see the brightness blotted off the richness of their clothes in blood and filth, his light faded. He was his old self again, covered in the price of his work on Kardu. Blood. Endless, clotting, indemnifying blood.

Seth took off the stained furs, their color no longer silver, and dropped them with the dead. Naked, he walked away, back to the highway where a river crossed over the buckled cement. He washed his hands, his face and arms, and drank the water. Then he laid himself down in the cold flow. The battle had left him weaker, the Botistems straining to heal fresh bruises and cuts. A bullet he hadn't been aware of wormed its way out of his abdomen. A salty, iron taste wouldn't leave his nose and mouth. His eyes, dark and sad behind wrinkles he could feel, blinked at the stars he yearned for and tried not to despise.

"Go now, my son," his mother had said once before sending

him on a different mission to a battle-stricken world. "Take life so that I may save life."

Then she sent him to the Federacy. He fought the Bosion hordes, dark beings of energy and metal. He had Pegassos then. He had strength and youth.

Now he had age, strife, and hunger, hard companions for a wanderer. He also had guilt.

Risen from the highway stream, Seth killed a shy deer with his hands. The flesh peeled easily beneath his shaking hands, cooking in the light of his power. He thanked the beast, wherever its soul must have gone. One last life to take before the end of another victorious day.

"Heaps on heaps," he quoted to himself, and his strength returned. As he clothed himself in the deer, his resolve ticked one notch lower.

33
— · —

The sun set in the west, a little to the left of its summer spot, sinking behind the mountain skyline in hues of heartbreak, beautiful and cold. The snow in the trees turned from gold to lavender, and then settled in soft, gray moonshine, lighting up the night as if by natural fluorescence, reflecting the glow of a starlit night. Mya watched the night as she always had, Vonica and Yora II sleeping in their beds, and opened again her last letter from Ran. The hard line that often pressed her lips softened, and for a moment she felt like a younger woman, much closer to her real age, excited to hear from her oldest brother on his desert conquest.

My dear Mya, he wrote. *I hope this letter finds you by warm fires and thoughtful friends.*

Mya pulled her quilt tight around her shoulders and continued reading, smiling in spite of a knotted worry in her abdomen. Ha. Friends.

I dispatched this letter to you, written in the code we invented when you were little, so I can relate to you the deeper matters of my intentions here in the far reaches of the Basin. Our mother and father don't know the full story regarding my newest lieutenant, actually recently promoted, Captain Cash Rivers, nor my purpose for his rushed promotion. I have a few men capable of completing his mission of preparatory sabotage, but he has a lineage and disposition I think the valley needs in its leadership. In Yora's absence, you are the only person I trust with this information.

A tear spilled onto the page. Mya wiped her eyes and fought back another. Life at home was worse than Ran knew, and sometimes she resented him for always leaving, chasing fugitives and scheming beyond the gate. He often wrote her about his plans and adventures. She was much younger than him and in no position to argue about anything. That was how it started anyway.

They had invented a code together, a way of putting written characters through a filter of false lines that they could both read well, but no one else would know the pattern. As she grew older, he started to tell her that she was the real hope of the family, the trick card that once pulled, the line would be saved and the heritage continue. She had yet to discover what he meant by that. But she played the game with him, trading secrets from Vonica's ranch for news from the front. She didn't get the washed-down versions that the people got, or the lists of resources and politics for her father. Mya got the depths of Ran's mind. He sent her his hopes and dreams.

As you know, for some time I have opposed Father's leadership. A silent opposition, abdicating my own claim to the throne and exiling myself to service in the West. I regret that my decisions have made me a poor father and an absent brother during trying times of alleged war on two fronts. If you have any news about family, my rider will stop by Yora's estate on his way back from the palace. Please leave any letters with him. In code, of course.

He didn't know about Tais, how the wild men from the East had killed her and left her to rot in the hills. Mya shook in her chair, stifling convulsive sobs behind her closed mouth. She and Tais had never been close as sisters. Tais joined the military, interested in proving herself among men. Mya, much younger, had yet to find her passion. She craved diligent study, for now. Books and history. What's more, Yora II had needed her, and she wished to care for him as his mother could not. Vonica's health would fade soon. Perhaps then, in the wake of tragedy,

Mya could move on. She shouldn't think that way, but that was the truth. Her time was coming, her mark to make on the world as the daughter of the king.

When I was a child, Ran continued, *I learned from a man named Seth Caeso, a secret teacher in the woods for Yora and I. He taught us lessons about government, war, and life worlds away from our own. He taught us about Earth. He taught about it differently than the priests. I have since learned that Seth is actually the Son of the Mother, Queen of the Heavens. Some say he was exiled, not only for his power, but his presence at the time the world went cold. He was first cast out of Ashra City, then, after founding the Valley with our great-grandfather, he was exiled from the palace. I wish I knew more about these stories. Maybe you can find out for me.*

Remember Cash Rivers, the man who shot Ezra Steele? He is the only known living descendent of Seth Caeso. "Highborn" like him are a legend few talk about anymore, but his lineage could give Cash a claim to the throne. They say he has far-seeing eyes and a young face for his years. With his growing popularity and relation to an ancient figure, he could dispute our government if the people wished to follow him. He's already a celebrity, which makes him an early contender for their affections.

Her father wasn't the most popular with the people these days. He closed them off from the outside world, made them wish for pastures beyond the cliffs and canyons.

Mya remembered hearing about Cash and the outside visitors. It already seemed like a long while ago. People told stories of Cash the way they told stories about her brothers, how he killed Denaiah's evil father and went west to conquer them new lands. He was the outlaw who became a hero, saving children and killing scores of men on foot in their own estate. If she was honest with herself, Mya knew she wasn't immune to the contagious admiration that ran around like the flu for the outlaw. Part of Mya wanted to meet him and see if he was the benevolent hero the storytellers made him. Her heart skipped with a schoolyard beat as Ran went on about him. For a moment, the words helped her put aside her grief, one shelf behind it, anyway.

When I first met him, Cash's humility surprised me. The rest of his gang was what you might expect, outlaws and guns, conmen and rustlers, but Cash evoked friendly regality. He can ride, he can fight, he can lead, and he's young enough to mold. I've made him my second. My officers concur. If anything happens to me, we are going to give my little army, and whatever strength we gain along the way, to Cash. He doesn't know this. He's off proving himself as my knife. I feel little, if any, doubt that he will survive his mission. I saw the bodies at the Steele Ranch. The death wrought there was either the work of an animal or a hero of the people. I'm giving him the tools to be the hero.

Mya imagined a ranch full of dead bodies, twisted and ugly henchmen brought down by righteous hands. There was a storybook quality to the images in her mind. She knew war must be Hell, as the Earth books often read, but the man war didn't break must be an extraordinary man. Seeing him as a killer wasn't a problem for her. Her brothers were such men. Her father might have been once.

She kept reading.

Yora still has claim to the throne, but I'm afraid for him and the dark thoughts in his mind. From what you've observed, I don't think he wants to come back from this fight. I believe that the attitudes we sew in the wind have a way of growing into prophecies. I don't want my brother to die, but if he does, I might as well tell you the true nature of my intention. I can't explain it, but I almost feel driven this direction, like powers beyond me are at the reigns.

The temperature dropped on the porch and more stars peeked down from their canopy. Mya turned the pages and heard the words in Ran's voice. He had never stopped being the same rebellious youth that drove her parents crazy, but now he had wisdom. He hadn't talked of spiritual powers that way before. When had they all gotten so old?

I will put more of our gains in my dispatch to the King. But for now, I can tell you that we've made significant progress. We've got the Kona Tribe on our side. I think they may expect me to marry one of their women, not that I would be entirely opposed, and build them a dam after the war, but they've agreed to help. They'll provide the bulk of the offensive. Where we may have mechanical prowess in the art of firepower, we lack the numbers. I'm sending for more guns from the Valley to equip them.

I have yet to hear from Cash, but I have faith that his offensive will turn some heads. If he does his job, the Keepers won't be watching for me when I bring Ashran streets the vindictive flood. It's like when you jump into the lake from someplace high and you use a rock to break the surface tension.

Keep watching the dispatches, little sister. I'll muster the army that saves the valley. I've found the means and the timing.

The night had reached its coldest. Mya folded the letter, though she hadn't finished, the rough paper trembling in her freezing hands. Gathering her things, she returned inside with a blanket and candle. She ascended the stairs with a mix of strong emotions: anger for her sister's death, remorse for Yora's pain, happiness for Ran's success, and girlish curiosity about a boy she hadn't met yet, a sandy-haired outlaw with the blood of celestial royalty, an early folk hero.

He hadn't said much about her this time. No one seemed to give her much thought, young and innocent Mya, caretaker of a sickly prince, steward of Vonica's estate. Nurse. Ran had so many schemes. Maybe she should have some of her own. First, she could think about what to do about this Cash boy. Ran had made her a keeper of his secret. Cash Rivers, conqueror of Ashra City, savior of children and slayer of monsters. He was about to get a lot of power, as long as he kept proving himself.

As Mya took her thoughts to her pillow, she wrapped them up in her mind. Sleep wasn't coming easily. One moment, she found herself in silent, convulsive sobs, the next, fantasies of an outlaw on a red horse. Those fantasies rode her all the way to an idea. It was the silliest idea, and she dismissed it as soon as it arrived.

34

"Nde-ra," Jayce swore, spitting in the sand at his feet.

"Wow," said Tarj.

"I still don't love it," said Ced, his huge shoulders shrugging under his long coat.

Cash had made a sand table on the beach. They had reached the ocean west of Ashra City, something Cash had been excited about. Judge used to bring the gang here when they needed to hide after a big score. There was a freshwater spring trickling down the rocks and it pooled where the gang had built a ground-level trough for the horses. The squad had just robbed a convoy of arms heading for one of the larger ranches. They resupplied and brought the excess to this hideout, burying a few gravity-fed automatics and cases of nitro-sticks. Cash would have preferred something with more cutting power than nitroKona, but a push charge could still do a lot of damage. Instead of cutting a lock or a wall, the charges would just blow up a room or dig a wide crater. He could work with that.

Military discipline had given way to gang etiquette. Everyone understood Cash was the leader, and they kept their command structure intact, but garrison formalities were all but gone. Cash wanted them to look like any other band of outlaws, simple men making a living outside the confines of borders and allegiances. At first or second glance, no one would think they were anything but a well-armed group of hustlers. He had them speak like a gang, too, Joropa profanity and all.

"What don't you love, Ced?"

Ced's team had taken point on the last robbery. Tarj's five sniped the horsemen guarding the two wagons and Ced approached the drivers directly.

"Do you know what you're doing?" one of the convoy drivers had shouted as they left him on the ground, feet shackled and limping back to town.

"I'm smoking," Ced had replied from his horse, a fat, rolled paper sleeve of bioca in his fingers. He sucked on it and inhaled the smoke deeply.

The driver was holding his arm. He'd hurt it, falling off the wagon. "They're going to find you. The Keepers don't take kindly to outlaws who disrupt the balance."

"Do you want me to shoot him?" Ced asked Cash.

"No," said Cash, then he quoted Judge. "We're a different cut of bandit."

"The prince said no quarter," said Jayce.

"This is no quarter," said Cash. "The Keepers 'don't take it too kindly.'"

At the sand table, Ced pointed to where Cash had made a small compound with wet sand of a munitions depot they'd found. "Not really to scale, is it?"

Tarj chuckled and Cash grunted, "What don't you love about the plan, toss."

"I don't know, boss. You'd need six platoons to take a place that size. One to breach it, and the breachers better not be anyone you like because you're not going to see them again. Automatics on the walls will cut them down, even if you manage a smoke screen of some kind, or a night breach."

"Well, the idea isn't to storm the place. It's a munitions depot. We just need a quiet way inside. The right disguise, maybe."

Tarj took off his outlaw-style hat and scratched his balding head. "Why risk this? The prince will be happy with what we're already doing."

Laughter from behind distracted their attention. The rest of them men were swimming. Diving into the waves and wrestling in the sand. For all Cash had put them through on the journey, and now a few dangerous robberies behind their eyes, they still found the energy to play. He had to remember that they weren't new to fighting, but they were new to being outnumbered.

Cash examined Tarj and thought about when Ran threw Brooks off a horse. "I'm not interested in making anyone happy."

Jayce lit up a smoke and grunted.

"I'm interested in winning a war before we have to fight it. Look." Cash pointed a stick at the compound of buildings on the sand table. "We've got valuable intel here. In just a couple weeks, we've uncovered where the Keepers are making most, if not all, of their munitions. If we capture or blow this before the army gets here...."

"Can't be done," Ced said.

Cash sized the big man up. He stood a head taller than Cash, and he'd seen how strong he was. Seeds of discord were licking the dirt, finding places to root. Glancing sideways at Jayce, Cash folded his arms and walked up to Ced and Tarj. They were bigger men than he was, but he had killed even bigger men. A confident side of his inner self told him it was a good thing for them he hadn't fallen in with the Ashran side of this fight. "I'll give you a chance right now, to say what you've got to say. Then I expect you to work for me as my team leaders," he looked up into both of their eyes, "or I'll do this by myself."

Tarj spoke first after a shared glance with his peer. "We can't afford to lose anyone."

"Right," said Ced. "We'll lose at least half of us if we're lucky in that place just trying to get out."

The compound of sand buildings and walls looked like a

puzzle, more than a model. Something was there. Some weakness to exploit, a way to get garrisons of hired guns inside to not look for them.

"The longer we wait, the more they'll fortify their positions," said Jayce, showing Cash hesitant support. "If this is going to be our main target, we'll have to hit it soon."

"I agree," said Tarj. "Once the main force crosses out of Kona territory someone's going to put the pieces together. Including what we're doing. I just don't think we should tackle something this big until we know we can win and not lose anyone."

Cash dug a boot into the sand, twisting the toe back and forth, deeper and deeper. A mist touched down over the land and sea, obscuring view.

"Good," he said, "I'm glad you feel that way. No one here is an expendable soldier. We're a gang, now. I don't have anyone else."

"We've got your back," said Jayce.

"Yeah," said Cash, "and I've got yours. But outlaws...soldiers...don't play it safe. They win wars because they know what it takes to defeat an enemy, not just hold them back or disrupt their movement. This depot is the liver shot. If we don't take it, Ran will have to."

Ced's eyes softened. Sure, maybe Cash was starting to ask for more than he signed up for, but Cash could see the light show of glory running through his mind.

"We're not just trying to topple a regime and build an army," Cash continued, leaning into his team leaders' motivations. "We're not just here to steal some things and kill bad people. We're fighting for families, for children and simple folk who don't deserve to be trampled on by savage marauders or powerful land grabbers, or phantom warlords over the eastern wall. This battle has to be won now, even with just the twelve of us...twelve," Cash laughed to himself, pausing his speech as an idea burst in his mind.

"What is it?" said Jayce.

"I've been thinking about this all wrong."

"What do you mean?"

"'I know the Basin.'"

"And?"

"We can be more than just twelve."

35

Vents hissed with steam, rushing air, and the scorn of harsh tones, pipes without music. They seemed to whisper words already echoing through the walls of Denaiah's troubled mind.

Conssssort.

She'd been rescued by a prince and cataloged by a king. Her luxury in bath halls and steam rooms couldn't ease the burden of her unspoken title. She was given asylum in this country because of her beauty, her beauty and her womb.

Conssssort, hissed the steam.

The High Valley grew out of roots bound in tradition and loyalty, less than the governing fear she knew from home. The Valley king's word was law, the people obeyed the king and thrived. Lords enforced his justice. He ruled as judge over all within his walls, and his children protected them. Denaiah felt safe for the first time in her life, but just as alone as ever.

The steam room was elegant, as were her bathing clothes. After this, she would move to the cold baths, freshwater unmixed with the hot groundwater. It was a game she played almost every day. Wash here, then wash there, then wash it all off again to entertain a crowd or a visitor. All the while she would wait for the king who had it in mind to father with her a child.

Consssssort.

"Second wife," she wanted to tell the steam, but reality was another word.

Vessel.

Childbearing vessel.

Had she really escaped her father? He sold the same way he seemed to want to pawn her off. When she was taken, before Yora rescued her, she had wondered if he would even come to rescue her, or if she had been written off like a heifer that didn't make the drive. Her blood boiled under the vapors.

Vesssel, the steam agreed as it wetted her skin, drawing perspiration and glow from her skin. She stretched back over the stone slab where she lay. The slab could look like an alter, from the right angle. She stared at the ceiling and stretched out her arms.

Here, Yora, she thought. *I am your sacrifice.*

He hadn't even sent her a letter. She risked everything to make herself his, and he'd tossed her aside. Of course she could understand why. For their love, there would be no letters, only secret, sacred meetings. She had no home for love, just a palace with a fresh new pool and rooms of steam. Her heart felt so empty, her thoughts muddled in vapor of fear.

The walls sweated with her, drops of time on tiles of existence.

A sudden nausea stirred within her. Denaiah sat up, shocked. She reached for a towel; the bathing clothes didn't cover her well, but found herself curling off the slab and rolling to her knees. Vomit pulled itself from her gut and flung itself to the floor, seeping through the cracks like grief from a stone face.

"My lady, are you alright?" Three of her maidens were already around her. One began to clean the mess while the other two knelt beside her.

She couldn't breathe, gasping until she wretched again.

"Get her fresh clothes, we'll see the doctor."

"No, no," she tried to say. "I'm not sick...I'm..." Her words and breaths came out as putrid hiccups.

She couldn't say it, but she had a reason to believe what this was. She could lie about the timing. She had to lie about the timing.

   Vesssssssssselllll.

36

Cash's party of twelve was now eleven, short one rider. He had expected they might lose one to a raid, either knife or gunshot, but his planning and the expert training of the men had kept them all without anything major so far. So far until the cactus. One of the youngest and newest sat on one the night before, knocked backward by his horse. He would be fine, but the youth would have to lie on his belly at the beach camp to guard the loot while he healed. The squad's robbery exploits had not gone unrewarded, so as a guard he could still have some use.

Cash and Jayce perched in the loft of a slaughterhouse overlooking a clump of houses in the middle of Ashra City.

"I'm nervous," said Cash, breaking the song of crickets in the dim streets below.

"I'm old, so I'm always nervous," said Jayce.

Cash grunted, the corner of his mouth curling upward a little. He checked the bolt of his rifle for the hundredth time.

"The boys know the plan, and they'll be where they need to be," said Jayce.

"It's not the boys. Not this time. Ced and Tarj are adapting better than before to my tactics. It's Digo. He's my friend."

"He helped you escape town."

"Yeah."

Jayce adjusted a jacket he was using to soften the hardness of the wood under his wiry chest and stomach. "Hope we don't have to stay prone here much longer. I'm dying."

The crickets continued their song.

"So, Judge and Abe and the rest, they left, but Digo stayed?" Jayce spoke without looking away from a house on the street. Yellow firelight gave the windows and spaces between slabs of wood an orange hue.

Cash looked to the corners of the house, waiting. "Digo and Judge were close, friends for a long time. I wouldn't call Digo an outlaw though. He mostly came along for legitimate business. Cattle drives and protection runs. He and his kids left the Valley just a little after Judge, but he came back this way, hoping his name hadn't mixed in with ours too much."

"But they're holding him here."

"Yeah. We've gotta get him out or I won't get over it."

Jayce reached over and patted Cash on the shoulder. "You've got the head of a commander and the heart of a shepherd."

"I hope that's a good thing." Word had reached the street that Cash Rivers was back and terrorizing the town. That was the Keeper narrative. Digo had been taken prisoner for his association. Cash would have liked to know what mouth ratted him out.

The rhythm of the cricket song changed for one in the chorus of sounds, making a coded pulse that Cash would have missed if he weren't listening.

"That's Tarj's team, they're good to go," said Jayce.

Another, lower pitched tone answered.

"That's Ced," said Cash.

He pulled out an air rifle, fixed with a special dart at the end. "Here goes." He fired the dart. It whistled through the air like the call of a bird.

Human shapes appeared in front of the orange slats of the light from the target house, climbing through windows and breaking down doors. Nine shapes. Cash's nine. He couldn't hear them, but that was a good thing. No shots meant no reinforcements. Before long all nine exited the house and walked up the street toward the slaughterhouse to link up with Cash and Jayce. A larger shape, Ced, supported a limping Digo under his arm. They'd rescued Cash's friend.

Torches lit the cave between cliffs at the beach camp. Digo winced as Cash applied antibiotic cream to his face and neck where marks of beatings and torture swelled. The men were outside, tending to horses and weapons, and watching for anyone who might have followed them out of town. Waves crashed outside under the moons that minded their own behind storm clouds. Night and weather would protect them tonight. Keeper forces would be out searching.

Digo reached for the bottle of cream. His voice was low and familiar, his warm eyes of a father and friend, but his beard was longer than Cash had ever seen it. Digo said of the bottle, "Where'd you come by this? It burns and cools all at once."

Cash finished and cleaned his hands with water from the stream. "It's from the High Valley."

"Happy to see you made it out of there just fine. They were surprisingly accommodating, given their reputation. Your crew is military?"

"Yep."

"I figured. The way they sprang in and eviscerated my... my hosts. Much longer and I'd have been dead, or worse off somehow. There are some creative things they can do quickly with those knives."

Cash threw a small bag of coins at him, a zippered one with a Keeper logo over nice leather. "This should help."

Digo peeked inside and whistled. "I see you've gone full outlaw."

"Hardly," Cash grinned. "I'm what they call the Knife."

"Sounds important."

"I want you to join me, us, in what we're doing here."

Crackling firelight ticked the seconds as Digo sat back and thought behind the wounds on his face.

Cash said, "I mean, if you'll let me explain–"

"You haven't asked about my kids."

"I think I was afraid to."

"They're alright."

"That's good."

"When I found out the Keepers were gunning for me, I sent them up North with a cousin." Digo spoke through pain on the other side of his wounds.

Cash grabbed some smoking, stolen beef strips from over the fire and placed one in his friend's hand, then pulled up a makeshift chair. "We're changing everything here. The Valley has better leadership, resources. We're conquering Ashra City and kicking the Keepers out, army and all."

Digo bit off a small piece, grimacing. "Trade a council of depraved gangsters for a self-isolating king?"

"I don't pretend to know the specifics, but I know the princes, and I know the time to act is right now."

"What do these princes ask in return for this liberation?"

"That we help them fight an army to the east."

"Who told you about this army?

Cash hesitated. "In a way, my grandfather, of sorts, did. It's hard to explain. I wasn't there for very long."

Digo held up the meat. "Because they gave you what you really wanted."

"I guess."

Digo stood, renewed vigor in his movement, and he paced the cave. "I don't know about them, son–"

"Wait, Digo–"

"No, hold on, Cash. I'll help you. Just let me say a piece."

Cash leaned back, relieved.

"I'm saying I'll help you. Not them. Judge wanted more for

you than a life of scrapes and fights. He saw a leader, a builder if you'll believe it. I did, too. I stayed behind and didn't follow him, because I love my home. I'll help you, Cash, and give you everything I have, because I believe in what you can be for us. For my people and my children."

The fire was crackling some kind of music. A piece of coal burst and landed on Cash's sleeve. "I won't let you down."

"Gi'ya mi'pa you won't."

Cash smiled at the wit in Digo's phrase and got to his feet. Digo held out his hand to help him up.

"Do you think others will join us?" said Cash.

"Well," Digo raised an eyebrow and smiled with the part of his face that could, "once I knew a young man who gunned down an old rancher named Ezra Steele, him and a hundred others."

"What about him?"

"He's inspired a lot of people."

37

Arty's home planet, Oswego, before the *Marshall*, was a sea of rock, a skyward curve of stone and ice. Most lived below the surface in tunnels, never looking at the stars, not the real ones. Arty's family worked on the surface in farms under dome-shielded skies. She worked at times, but her aunt and uncle kept her in school until it was time to enlist. The academy on Oswego got her where she wanted to go. She inherited the sky by the signature of a commission and the raised hand of an oath.

Her Oswegan imagination never brought her this far, though, not to the wondrously weird. Kami sailed her back through the waves of infinite space she had seen before, folds upon folds of liquid cosmos. The ship wormed its way past galaxies, clouds of dust, and flicks of light like wet paint. With Kami, Arty had a new way to feel free in the sky.

"Thank you for saving me, Kami," Arty said.

"We all play a part in the music of the Dao."

The waves pushed out as new light rushed into view, reflecting through the glass and into the ship, dancing like a prism. The light was the brilliant eminence of transfixed Libertas, arms yet outstretched, holding waves of time as the walls of her cocoon. She radiated as a woman more than a ship in this realm.

"What is she doing?" Arty asked.

"She is drawing from the Dao. She takes power from the

flow of time."

"A Time Drive. Do you have one?"

Kami spun and the view of Libertas inverted and righted itself again. "I do." Her voice seemed to smile.

"The *Marshall* used fusion mostly, and antimatter reactions when appropriate. Time Drives were something of a legend."

"I'm sure she was a great ship."

Libertas enlarged in view to where all Arty could see was the fold of white and gold metallic fabrics in her robes. The magnificence of the color reminded her of the grass in the other universe.

Arty said, "I feel small."

"As do I," said Kami.

"Are Libertas and the Mother like you and I?"

"I have Botistem in me, as well as Bosion. They are much more the same than either would like to admit. I imagine Libertas is the same as I, still, or perhaps she was one Bosion who made the Botistem."

"I'm not sure I see any difference myself."

"Ideas are the true distinction, perhaps. Bosion creatures who seek harmony with organic life are enlightened. We create and serve and draw our light from the Dao. Others are bodies of discord. They destroy and consume, assimilating the natural light of the universe into their own dark image."

"They don't draw power from a Time Drive?"

"They are the cancer; we are the cure."

Arty shook her head. Sometimes conversations with Kami felt like they were both trying to translate something and concepts were getting lost. There were synthetic thoughts and there were organic thoughts; their symbiotic relationship was finding the common ground and learning to run in each other's plains. That was a nice way to think of it. Arty told herself to remember to write that down.

She said, "I've always heard of the Mother as an unknown,

a necessary evil in the fight against the Bosions."

"Think of the universe as a garden. No plant is good or evil; each grows according to the measure of its reach and understanding."

"My people fired first. But she killed everyone."

"Can you forgive her for that?"

Lights approached from the folds of Libertas. Tiny ships, too small for Arty to discern their size or shape.

"Are dark Bosions part of the garden?"

"As a matter of belief, no, I don't think so," said Kami. "You are my connection to the garden, Arty. The natural order. I serve you. Together we serve the flow of the universe. Such evil as the dark Bosion must be cut off from the Dao. Thieves in the garden."

"Always a lot to take in with you," said Arty.

"Perhaps," said Kami. "You and I are like the Mother and Libertas together, if I were much older and the size of many flagships, and you had fully realized the extent of your power through years of study and conquest."

The approaching ships from Libertas surrounded them. They were colorful, shaped like birds and fighter-sized like her own. They moved differently than a normal spaceship, without thrusters or the heavy lag of momentum. Six of them drew nearer and weaved in formation through invisible streams in quantum fields.

A voice crackled its way into Arty's cockpit, invading her long quiet. "Cousin fighter. State your business at the feet of Libertas. Who are you and what is your point of origin?"

Arty waited for Kami to respond.

"Arty, I only speak to you, remember?" said Kami in her mind.

She jumped and hit her knee on a panel. "Right," she said out loud. A comm button flashed and she held it down, transmitting to the six ships revolving around her own. "My name is

Arty Sato."

"Your name and voice register to a ship that no longer exists. Can you explain? How did you come by a fighter that looks like one of our own?"

"Kami is a child of Libertas. We... I came to see the Mother."

The ships broke away and turned themselves from her path.

"She will see you."

"Okay," said Arty, "but how do I–"

Kami was gone, and so were the ships, so were the stars and robes and everything in Arty's view. The air changed, too. She first noticed the decoration, the golden curve of walls and artwork that stretched as far as she could see. The room seemed to echo the feel of a classic royal court of no apparent, single culture. The mysterious place might have been warm, except that it was empty.

"Welcome," a voice said from behind. Arty turned and saw a woman whom she had seen on a monitor once before, a woman who had killed everyone she knew. "Welcome to my home."

38

Yora and his men returned from a night patrol on horseback. They had ridden to a ridge that Yora's captains had hoped would give a better view of the larger forces they expected to find of the wild men. Disturbed to yet find nothing, no signs of approaching opposition, Yora entered his tent and kicked off his boots.

"There will be no need to take your people over the wall, Yora," a soft, yet commanding, voice said, taking him off guard.

Yora dashed to find his pistol.

"Calm down, boy. It's me." Seth stepped out of the shadows and onto the rug near Yora's thrown boots.

"Teacher."

"That's funny you still call me that."

"Savior sounds melodramatic." Yora sat in a fur chair.

"I'm sorry I wasn't there for Tais."

"Me too."

Seth let the silence swallow some of the mourning before he spoke again. "I took care of the invaders, for now. The tribes that threatened your walls are gone."

Yora straightened. "What happened?"

Seth knelt by the tent's fire and prodded the coals with a rod. "I made a choice, and I gave them a chance. They didn't have a place in the world I've built." The firelight played on Seth's face and eyes like shadow puppets. "I may have sold what little of my soul I may have left, but the sacrifice is justified. Your people can spare yourselves for the fight to come."

"What is this fight? Who are we facing?"

Seth's clothes were brown skins. Different than the silver furs Yora had seen before. He wondered what happened to them, and why his old teacher seemed older and even more alone.

"I don't know," Seth said, "but the ground seems to move differently. The snow tastes mellow, and the birds fly in strange patterns. I know that may not make sense to you."

"It doesn't, but I believe you."

"Good, because I need you to be a man of faith."

"I'll try, but I'm at the end of my light. I can't see."

Seth knelt in front of Yora's chair. He covered the far younger man's eyes with his hand. "Stop trying to see. Listen to the spirit of Kardu. I can hear her in you the way she is in me."

Yora felt the hand leave and he covered his eyes with his own hands. Listening because he felt compelled. The touch of Seth's hand had done something to him, left him with elation, clarity, an openness to things he didn't understand but suddenly knew were there. Then he heard a voice, a female that he almost understood and felt like he recognized.

The voice wanted him to look up.

The flap of the tent door opened, and a courier walked through holding a dispatch of letters. Yora tore through them, the voice still rebounding in his mind.

Be not weak.

At the top of the stack was a letter. It didn't have any special seal on it except for a scent on the paper that awakened him. He knew who it was from before he tore it open.

Yora, my love, I am with child.

He could feel her words. Looking up, he saw Seth leaving the tent. His work was done.

"You're pulling the patrols?" his second asked him a short while later. Yora had been making orders while his mind was somewhere else.

"Yes," said Yora. "We need to refit and begin fortifying the wall. We don't want to lose soldiers to the cold. The enemy is finished. Senior and nonessential officers can go home and prepare for Spring, for the real battle to come when the snow is gone."

"I'll have the men prepare your horse."

"No," Yora said. "I'll do it myself." He always did his best thinking when moving his hands. Someone special was waiting for him in a palace.

39

Snow drifted off the pines, heavy off the branches and light into the air, disappearing into soft wisps as they fell into the glistening bank. Mya watched from her carriage, wrapped in a coat of fur and cotton. Her clothes did well to keep her warm except for the socks on her toes. She kept adjusting her feet, anticipating the warm pools of Denaiah's new palace. She knew she would find the new queen there, where all knew Denaiah spent much of her time.

At the feet of the palace, Mya climbed the blanketed steps. The snow fell around her like pieces of sky. A member of her driving team met the guard at the door, and they held the way open for her into the front hall. The doors were tall, red-stained oak and the floor was smooth with a multi-colored, glossy painting of an image of Libertas holding a banner: *Justice and Rapture for My Valley,* the banner read. Her crown was of a soft evergreen with intertwined apple blossoms.

A woman descended a spiral staircase and offered to take Mya's coat. "Our queen will be pleased to see you, Lady Praylum. How did you find your journey?"

Mya let her take the coat. The room was warm and smelled a little of the sulfur-laced water beneath its floors. "Thank you, Ryl. Shall I meet her at the pools?"

"Not today. She'll eat with you in the library."

"Lunch in a library. Now I do feel like royalty."

The library had a smell that matched its design. Books,

old and new, mixed together like generations. Large windows brought light from the walls to the north and south. The cotton mist outside and a few candles illuminated a small table where Denaiah sat waiting for her. The ambience of words shut behind covers and shelves whispering at great heights made for a great place to share secrets. Mya had a few things she wanted to hear.

Denaiah stood and welcomed her daughter-in-law of sorts to the table. "Mya! I'm so glad you wanted to see me today. I've wanted to get to know you."

Mya hugged the woman and sat herself at the square table, close but not too close. "Thank you for opening your home to me. Sometimes Vonica's ranch can be... stifling."

"Even with all that open air?" Denaiah smiled and sipped from a small spoon at the soup brought by her servants.

"The company."

"I see."

"It's beautiful, but it can be nice to get away." Mya tried the soup. It was a creamy mix of preserved vegetables and salmon from the river.

The two royal women exchanged niceties, keeping manners of court around them as a shield from the eyes of servants. Each were sworn confidantes, but some matters were only for the ears and eyes of nature, lovers, or if Mya could have her way this afternoon, family.

"Denaiah," she said, changing her tone as plates were cleared and the women moved to chairs under the shadows of books.

"Yes?"

"I've heard a rumor that you're expecting."

Denaiah blushed, adjusting her clothes in subconscious impulse. "No secrets among rulers. Yes, I am."

"Congratulations to you and my father."

"Thank you. We're very happy."

Mya glanced at the servant's door. None were coming through. Perhaps Denaiah also wished for a quiet conversation.

"Listen," said Mya. "I know you and Yora were close before my father... took you."

Denaiah looked away, hiding a small glimpse of pain through her eyes. She tried to open her mouth to speak, but seemed to struggle with the words.

"I guess I'll just have to ask you, because something inside me says it must be true. The child...is it..."

Denaiah flashed several expressions at once. One was surprise, the next anger, then a mask of composure.

"The books," Mya said. "Yora likes books, especially old ones. Ran told me that Yora should have married you instead of my father and..."

"What about the books?" Denaiah looked like she didn't know.

"My brother sent them. He must have. Old ones from the world before are not found in many places. He's the one building the collection. You must mean a lot to him for them to be sent here."

"I was told they were a wedding gift. I didn't know they were from him." Denaiah picked one off a small table in front of their chairs. The cover was torn. "This one's called *The Song of Darkness,* in Joropa. It's a love story, left out of the collection for me to read first."

"You do love him, don't you."

Denaiah placed a finger next to her eye, catching a tear before it fell. "I'm not a wife."

"Then what are you, to my father, to my family?"

"I'm just a consort. A mistress. I should have stayed in Ashra City."

Mya leaned over and placed a hand on Denaiah's knee. The fabric of her clothes was more coarse than she thought. "Is the baby Yora's? Or my father's?"

Denaiah took Mya's hand, the sound of her words breaking in her emotions. "I think we both already know."

"Does Yora know?"

"I sent him word. It should have arrived with his dispatch yesterday."

Mya took back her hand. She thought of Vonica at Yora's ranch, letting go of the last threads of life, wasting away, and Yora II, who would never see a day as captain or prince. Yora didn't have the legacy to carry a line, especially if he had betrayed the king this way. Ran was scheming something else. This child in Denaiah's womb was not an answer to her family problems.

But what then, Mya thought, *about me?*

40

—·—

"When I dug a pit into the workings of time, of the Dao, I didn't expect you."

Arty blushed, even though she didn't know what Mother meant. She wanted to feel disdain for the woman, or distrust, but there was a glow there, a feeling that rang like clarity, a strange sort of witchcraft.

Mother looked her up and down, circling so that her long, dark robes shaped a half-moon of fancy dress around her on the cinnamon floor. To Arty, Mother was the most intimidating person she had ever met. Her looks were perfect, her demeanor stern and feminine. She was tall, too, but Arty couldn't see her feet to tell if she wore shoes. Outside the five senses, Arty could feel Mother's presence, something in the movement of Arty's cells and the machine energy within them, something she and the Mother had in common.

"You can feel it, can't you?" Mother said. "Our power, our bond with the Botistems."

"Yes," Arty said. She reached for Kami in her mind but couldn't feel her near.

"Your ship is safe; she is with Pegassos, her sister."

"Commander Caeso's ship."

"Indeed." Mother waved her hand, beckoning something Arty couldn't see. A white mist around a silver platform appeared underneath their feet. "Fly with me," Mother said.

The lift took them through warped space of its own, passing

quiet hallways and crowded streets through the veins of Libertas. No wind whipped through Arty's hair in the lift's flight.

Mother stared into the path of the lift, contemplative, her voice calm. "Arty Sato. Detections Specialist on the FSV *Marshall*."

"Yes, that was a long time ago now."

"If it feels that way. You've made a long journey."

"I don't know what's happened to me. The last thing I remember, the last people I remember, were you and my commanders starting a war," Arty said, a wary knot tightening in her gut from the memory.

"I remember retreating from that war before it began."

"Everyone I knew died."

Mother stopped the lift. It hung above a forest. Arty could hear the birds and see the wilds of the treetops reaching over each other, clamoring for pieces of artificial sunlight.

"The burden of great height is insufferable perspective on the shadow of death. The men and women of the *Marshall* died because they could not reach above that shadow. They were doomed the moment they tread into mine." The lift moved again, the trees becoming a stretch of green.

"I survived," Arty said, "because your ship saved me. Kami, coming out of Libertas and inhabiting my shield, saved me."

"Libertas told me there was a work to do before we go down to Kardu. I didn't know it would involve you, but now that I've seen you, I think I know why. You could find your way beyond the shadow of death. Not anyone can become immortal. You were seeded for it."

The mist surrounded the two women in a whirl of white and the lift stopped in a golden hangar filled with ships. Two hung in the air next to her, an eagle named Pegassos, and a fox named Kami. Arty's heart was filled with wonder and energy. As the mist departed, dissipating into the invisible breath of the atmosphere within Libertas, Arty saw that she wore different clothing, red-violet and armored.

"Your purpose here is unknown to me, Lieutenant Sato," Mother said. "There are workings in this universe I have yet to understand, things beyond nature, machines, and humanity. Perhaps they are mysteries reserved for the dead, a study of which I have denied myself."

Arty remembered her fall through the singularity, of her visions of Earth and the silhouette of a guardian woman over its shores. Maybe that had been a study of death.

Mother continued, "I do know that we are here, floating above a new world, new shores for gods and champions, new iron for hammer and chains. Do you know to what you are loyal, child?"

Arty tried to answer, but conflicting powers of subconscious muddled her mind. She felt loyal to Kami, her friend through the stars, and also to the *Marshall*, dead. For the Federacy, she felt less, the people in it so far away. Towards the Mother, she felt only a curious desire to learn, but not to forgive.

"I can keep you here," Mother said. "But I don't have need for warriors. I could make you my daughter, but I have an abandoned son. No, I'm more curious to see if the entwining fates of the universe grew you out of nothing to be something more than all of them, more than any champion."

Mother's eyes, now glowing, searched Arty, scanning every part of her.

"Minerva?" She put a hand to her own forehead, closed her eyes and sighed. "Bane of Ashetarai." Then she screamed. Not a frantic scream, but a more controlled sound that a fighter would make before a strong kick. A force did hit Arty, springing her backward and throwing off her orientation like a hood over her eyes.

The Mother vanished.

Arty tumbled away, realizing she'd been thrust into space. The ocean of moving stars that made the walls of the wormhole around Libertas rushed at her. She couldn't tell if she was rushing toward them or if they came to meet her, the entire sphere closing in. Whatever held the event in place seemed to be collapsing, the wormhole growing smaller and smaller until she thought it would collapse onto her and she would die. Arty could feel the great mystery of death creep up on her, as though breathing on her shoulder.

Kami caught up to her, "Hold on, Arty." Kami placed Arty gently in the cockpit. It was crazy how she could do that.

The wall of stars moved past them with great turbulence. Kami shook and spun, at last resting with Arty's view facing the singularity from the outside, growing again from where it shrank. The orange and red glow of its horizon took shape, illuminating a scattered spray of ship debris. Kami had carried her outside unharmed.

The debris was from the *Marshall*, now frozen in space and time, doomed to orbit a hole in space that warped reality enough to keep the wreckage forever falling, never reaching the thing that killed it.

"How did you get us through, Kami?"

"The same way as the first time, though that was more of a struggle. I was much smaller at the time."

"That works for me."

Arty grabbed the controls. "Let's get ourselves to Kardu."

"Do we have a plan?" Kami said. "Mine was to reunite with Libertas."

Arty sat back on the couch and slowed her breathing. "The Mother seems to think I'm a threat."

"My mother Libertas seemed to welcome me," Kami said.

"Do you know anything about the goddess Minerva?"

"Akin to the Greek Athena, she was born out of the head of Jove. He ate her mother after a prophecy about her and her brother being born to overthrow him."

Arty moved the flight stick, a double-handed control that

she pulled between her legs. Kami let her do the flying. She felt the intuition of them both, like two pilots, machine and woman, could work together in one consciousness. It was dizzying at first, until she let Kami in.

"What do you think the Mother saw in me? 'Bane of Ashetarai," she imitated Mother's voice. "All that after giving me a new outfit."

"I suppose that's just something we'll have to find out together. Your power is not dissimilar to hers. You are immortal. You carry the light of Botistem and Bosion alike. Our potential together is limitless. We are a rare form of life."

Arty flew, musing through her mind the narrative of her journey. She'd just been tossed over waves of the universe, losing everything and gaining even more that she couldn't begin to understand. She thought of King Arthur, an old legend of a young man pulling a sword out of a stone to win a crown of which he knew almost nothing. What had Arty pulled out of the stone? For now, a ship of infinite endurance and companion of undying loyalty. That was something. She also had control. She had never known control. She'd had captains, missions, studies, and duties, but never true control. Perhaps no one ever did, only lots cast by fates woven through tapestries of gravity.

She felt the pull of something now, a controlled descent toward the one place she'd wanted to go in the first place. Kardu. She was going to find a new home after the flood.

Seth dreamed he sat atop the crown of Libertas, cocooned in the center of her pull of spacetime, just how he imagined she'd looked for the past generations of his time stranded on Kardu. A ship flew into view, one like Pegassos, but in the image of a fox, like an ancient Japanese sculpture. He followed the ship, off the crown and toward the wall of the cocoon. He noticed that the wall was collapsing.

The ship picked up a woman, tumbling through space wearing red-violet armor. She was unharmed by the void, so she must not have drifted for long. The ship took her into its cockpit and sped toward the shrinking wall. He woke just as the wall rushed over him in a wave of flowing cosmos.

"Seth, where are you?" a voice penetrated his mind as he started upright.

"Pegassos?"

41

A poster nailed to a wall caused a laugh in Cash's squad. It started when one of the boys noticed it on the ground, ripped from the wind. He picked it up and poked a new hole in the paper through the nail still stuck in the brick wall. The drawing flapped in the wind, but the likeness was unmistakable. It was their captain, a young and smirking Cash Rivers from Ashra City. The caption read, *"If you see this outlaw, inform the court militia. Do not engage. Well-equipped and enemy-sponsored."*

"'Do not engage,'" said Tarj. "They're scared of you, sir."

"Scared of us." Ced slapped the poster. "'Enemy-sponsored.' Word must be traveling about our intentions."

"Do you think they know about the army yet?" said Cash.

"I wouldn't be surprised. We're not the only people who cross the desert time to time."

Cash drew a patch over his eye on the poster and mimicked the smirk. Then he pocketed the pencil where he kept it on his forearm sleeve. "Alright, let's go in. These people want a speech."

He wanted to feel nervous about talking to this bunch. They were men and women like Digo, citizens of Ashra City who put up with the Keepers, and the magistrates and judges that held them in fear. Generations had passed since any had known more peaceful ways of living. Maybe Ashra was always a bad place. But Digo said something was cooking. Cash's rebellion, starting with killing Ezra Steele, had people talking.

The door clicked open to hushing chatter. Everyone turned to the squad of boots and heavy arms entering the elevated stage. The people looked small from this angle. Cash saw Digo in the front. The thought had occurred to him that he and his men might be in for a trap, but he also had to believe that Digo was on his side. Judge had said that faith is the difference between men and animals. Cash didn't doubt it.

"Here they are now," a man said. "The Rivers Gang."

"Ladies and gentlemen," Cash said, his mouth starting to move before the track of his conscious brain. "My name is Cash Rivers. This is my squad. I think you might already know where they came from. I brought them here because I have a vision."

Cash brought his hands down to his belt. The pistol on his thigh, the weight-bearing vest and the rifle slung over his back in an instant got heavier, feeling out of place around so many civilians.

"We're twelve soldiers tasked with disrupting logistic and military operations of the organization we all know as the Keepers. While I rode with another crew, we came under the employ of Ezra Steele, one of the chief ranchers involved with the Keepers. Inside his home, working on a deal to move his cattle, I shot Steele, upon discovering slave children kept on his property. I could pretend that I did what I did premeditated, but I didn't. I acted in the moment, and everything I have done since has been as a wanted man. With the help of good friends, I am responsible for the deaths of hundreds under Keeper employ."

No whispers.

"Now that I'm back and continuing my own campaign against an enemy I've held in contempt since childhood, I'm here to ask for volunteers. All of you are vetted by my friend, Digo, good men and women who want to do something to help our cause. I suppose it's time for you to know what we plan to do." Cash hesitated, remembering his own men's fears.

"We're gonna take the ammo depot at Kalo Bluff," Tarj interrupted, wide-eyed.

A stir crept over the room. Those who knew about the depot knew it was a guarded fortress. It wasn't the biggest stronghold the keepers held, but it was an impossible task.

"We can do it," said Digo, rising to the stage. "Some of us have already started fighting, Cash. Not me, so much, but a few of the men here have been hitting officers. Executions not much different than what you did."

Cash nodded toward the men Digo referred to, unsure about them but grateful for the help. "Okay," he said. "Let's talk strategy."

42

Mya rode a white horse between clouds. The afternoon light was dimmed by layers of stone-gray from the horizon like quick stabs from a round paintbrush. She drank in the scene, here in her little spot in the hills of Vonica's ranch. She held two letters, the first from Ran.

Dear sister, our campaign has started. Our first battle was met by a large force of Keeper guns ambushing us from the hills. They had good artillery. We lost ten of our riders and many more of the Kona men who accompany us. All fought bravely, however, and we met both fronts of our attackers with good execution. The men swept through the desert quickly and rounded the forces. We took a few prisoners, and they have provided valuable intelligence.

In better news, Cash has done as expected, and there's even talk of a small rebellion that's grown under his name. You can imagine my joy hearing that news. I don't know all his plans — his dispatches are rare — but I enjoy the initiative. I like him. You would like him, too, I think. He seems like your type. Write him something. I'll make sure it gets to him.

Mya smirked. Her brother knew her better than she would care to admit.

I'm sure father hates him. Keep me apprised of any movement on that front. I may be able to use some of that hate to my advantage.

She put Ran's letter down. His politics weren't making their way through the jittering butterflies flying around her stomach about him trying to get her to write the boy Cash.

She pulled out the other letter she held, this one in her own writing, replying to Ran. "*I applaud your success, brother. Bring me something from the spoils of your campaign, would you?*" And then, farther down the page, after family news, "*Ran, if you're so keen for me to find a boy, you should know that the way it works is he should write ME first. Does he know I exist? Don't answer that.*"

She put both letters, folded in thirds, inside a book in her hand. The cover had been worn off, and someone from long ago had marked their favorite passages. Sliding frontways off the saddle, Mya dismounted and let her horse wander a little while she sat on a log surrounded by old snow. The horse's breath steamed in the cold air through its fair nostrils while it prodded her on the back.

"Stop, stop. I'm reading. Go nibble something."

She flipped through the book and found a quote marked with black ink on the side with a line in the margin.

"*If you find him sad, say I am dancing. If in mirth, report that I am sudden sick.*"

She laughed at the scheming Cleopatra. The wind tasted sweeter for a moment, carrying with it just a name, an intrigue, her Antony. With a smile and a brush of her hair, she took out a pen. The butterflies won. She would make the first move.

"*Captain Rivers, My brother Ran told me this would find you. My name is Mya Praylum...*"

43

Denaiah enjoyed that her new palace and life in it did not include living with her husband the king, but today he and his entourage discolored her space. She sat with him in a small court, while he took up judgments and ranted to her. Though he came to celebrate what he believed to be his child, he lamented his grown children and the young man they'd allied with to take on Ashra City. He held a poster in his hand with Cash's likeness peering from the paper, as though measuring the hand that held it.

He barked, "So these are what the people are passing around? Is this an original or a replica?"

"A replica, Lord. They're printing them in the villages and in your capitol," said a small clerk.

"Why?"

"There's talk of him amassing a lot of wealth in robberies and disrupting supply lines. They say he's already done more for the war than both your sons combined, and much more than you." The clerk spoke without reservation. Denaiah knew the king valued this, but she didn't know how the clerk didn't fear for himself somehow. This never would have happened with her father, Ezra Steele. He was known to torture and kill people who disagreed with his strategies or spoke anything he might not like. He was reasonable only to profit. She wondered if there had been parades in the streets when he died.

The king crumpled the poster and tossed it aside. Cash's

likeness landed still facing him from the floor.

"My sons are heroes! Champions of the valley, and I made them such. I fought battles in my own time, too. You should have seen me push back the marauders from our walls. I purged the streets of them. Our safety is my triumph. Why do they forget this?"

Denaiah grunted, clearing her throat.

"Do you have something to say, my dear?" The king's words were warm in their breath but cold beneath his eyes.

"No," she began, then remembered the boldness of the clerk and the culture of frank speech in the Valley people. "Yes. I think they might resent living in a world where they're stuck in the Valley. They never leave."

The clerk's mouth curled a little at the corners. "This is true, Lady and Lord. They've been shut in for more than a generation."

"Have you been out of the Valley, Clerk?" asked the king.

"I don't have the constitution, my king."

"Or the stomach. Many who venture there never return, corrupted by the foreign rot, or they become like my sons, would-be conquerors, sure to die. But you have been to Ashra City, my dear, mother of my child. You are the rare flower to bloom out of that world." He turned to her, shifting his old but nimble frame in her direction. His vest reflected the light into small rainbows from the tall windows.

"I try to forget it," Denaiah said.

She wasn't lying. Marrying the king, next to her rescue by Yora, was the best thing that had happened to her. Her beautiful palace, life of luxury, all came at the small price of a neglectful marriage. All she had to do was be charming, in company and in private, and she had to bear children. When she wasn't stricken by panic, her life had turned out very nice.

"I've raised heroes while I should have raised kings," her husband would say. There was a darkness in the space between his words, a moat in his eye that reminded Denaiah of her father. In his world, her father was also a king. He ruled beneath palaces under the sand of their foundations.

"Have you heard news of the Eastern fight?" Denaiah asked the king, changing the subject.

He appeared to not hear her, his mind lost somewhere between his perceived beauty of her and the life in her belly.

"Our son will be a great king," he said.

44

The mantis had nine legs. Three pincers to hold struggling food under the mouth, and six others. Seth was surprised to see one this late in the season, but here it was, brown and stiff, clinging to a piece of sandstone, fending off the elements of death.

Seth felt the same. Two old bugs clinging to rocks and sand because death hadn't made the right deal. He had a purpose, didn't he?

His stomach hurt, and he clung to the same rock as the mantis. He couldn't remember when the pains started, hundreds of Kardu revolutions in the past, but they were reminders. In past lives among stars and invisible pulses of gravity he had thought of himself as immortal. Yet here, with hard sand under his nails and sharp wind in his ears, he fought every day to just hold on, like the nine-legged, double-thoraxed mantis.

The pain radiated, jabbing from the inside around his abdomen, then to his shoulder blades, and subsided. Reaching for a pouch sewn into the side of his pack, he searched for seeds he brought for the journey. There weren't many left. He took a half-handful and chewed them without water. His Botistems used the energy from the seeds and gave him some strength. It was a more efficient way to metabolize than the usual digestion. Somewhere inside, though, his body was trying to protest, protest his age, his existence, his decisions, his symbiosis.

Glad sighed with the wind. He wasn't young either.

Seth had brought himself and the horse to a fitting place

to wallow. They had ridden to the lake where Seth crashed the shuttle. He imagined what it must have looked like, a breaking alien spaceship, fiery out of the atmosphere, tumbling into a doomed wilderness. He wished he knew the story, if his arrival had somehow triggered the conflict that blew up the scarred remains of the now abandoned, charred, decayed city.

The lake looked the same. Centuries had seen it rise and fall with the turning of many seasons, but it was still the same lake, same hills surrounding it. Beneath the blue glass of its reflection rested the same skeleton of a small ship.

The water beckoned Seth. The wreckage called like an overdue ritual. Swim down, see that it was, see that his life had been what he remembered. He removed his clothes and entered the water, passing the reeds, feeling the slip of the mud, weeds, and rocks until they sloped to greater depths. He hung for a second, not submerging, then tucked his body forward and kicked down, scooping the water until color faded into green and blue. The pressure hurt until his body adapted from creature of land to creature of water. He wouldn't need any air for some time.

There the ship was, stripped as he'd last left it. Damage of inertia now didn't compare to the gnaw of centuries. He had salvaged what he could when it mattered. The ship's survival gear helped him and others he found to start a community. With the ship's literature, libraries of material, he gave them a new language and culture. The contents of this ship were what conquered the Basin, not his mother, not what anyone feared at the summit on the *Tecumseh*. Rotting at the bottom of the lake, a nameless shuttle slowly deteriorated with the rest of Karduan history, of which it may have been the most important monument.

Seth swam down to touch the ship. An open hatch door had stuck itself halfway into the sand, or rather the sand had risen to it. Algae and deposits had changed the skin of the ship, too.

Damn, he thought. *I should have done this sooner.*

He pulled himself through the door and felt for the walls where the light couldn't reach. A large pike dodged his hand and lurched past his face, the scales slapping his forehead and eyes. He would probably try to catch it later. Pike made for good fuel.

Underneath an overgrown bulkhead and terminal, Seth illuminated light from his hands, biomechanical luminescence nature wouldn't anticipate, so he could see a heavy box. It held one more secret, one he planted years after the crash. The box was a shell of polymer that wouldn't give to jaws of underwater decay. He tucked it under his arm and took one more look around the ship. Commander Caeso's last space voyage flashed through his mind one last time. Seth could see himself running through the doors, passing the dying crew, and piloting the ship through waves of warping Aether before splashing it down to rest. He remembered the strain on his power, how hard that trial had been for the young immortal, how easy it all seemed now.

Once on the shore, Seth walked over the clothes of deer hide he had cast aside without regard. A wetness from the lake still dripping off his shoulders, he opened the heavy box. The box was silver in the light of the two moons. Inside, he found what he had left, the black armor he wore the day he arrived, the armor that had seen him through countless adventures in faraway places his mind had barely the room to remember. He put it on, not surprised to find it fitting looser than before. He emanated energy into the fabric and the suit tightened to his older frame, the pieces still functioning, reacting to his Botistems that took to inhabit the suit as a part of him.

The discomfort in Seth's gut gnawed in harmony with his emotion. "My name is Seth, the son... the son... I am alone."

He wandered, circling the lake with Glad on a lead until he found white trees lining a river, a contrast to the endless brush of the desert. The river fed the lake and the trees. The trees were empty except for a single white owl that watched him approach, unstartled.

"How long must I continue?" Seth asked the night.

He fell to his hands and knees under the watchful owl. Clutching his armor, he called out to his old friend, "Pegassos. I felt you. I heard you call. When are you coming?"

The ground was cold. Winter didn't have long before Spring, but for now, all seemed lifeless. The grass was pale, the trees without leaves, like nature had turned her back but for the owl. Even the river seemed to stand still, its run slow into the mirror lake. The last leg of its journey sopped in weakness, in loss of pace or purpose, just gravity.

The owl just watched, tilting its head to the side as if in consideration, or perhaps judgment of the man on his knees.

"I can't do this anymore," Seth whispered, now to the owl. "I wade through terror, never to die, but neither do I live."

You can't do this? the owl seemed to ask.

"I don't want to."

The owl looked at him with increasing interest.

Seth shrugged, clutching his stomach. "Let's see you kill for the good you wish to see in humanity. Let's see you face these wrongs after the fade of their callow shine."

A song stirred in the night as the lake began to sing. A chorus of tones like a hand over wet crystal fluttered into the night air. At first, Seth didn't notice until he felt a change in the bite of the chill. What once was cold became revitalizing. No warmth came from the change, only the way Seth perceived the cold. As he considered the new sensation, lights appeared and capered on the ground below him, like shadows from many flames.

When he looked up, the trees surrounding him were engulfed in blue fire, but didn't burn. The owl pitched in the heart of the flames and stretched out its wings.

Flaming blue with fire and gold in its feathers, the owl descended toward him with talons outstretched. Seth fell back from his knees and braced himself. The last thing he felt before it overtook him was the cold of the flames before landing in soft moss among the smell of sulfur and wet stone. Above his head, a huge rock glowed. It was warm, and soothed some of the ice of his loneliness. Seth could tell this cave was deep, and this hanging rock reminded him of a heart, the saffron living heart of a mountain.

45

—·—

Seth admired his surroundings of calcite, squeezed by capillary action over thousands of years, stalactites and stalagmites, and assortments of mysterious crystals. Everything in the room had taken on a glow, seeming to percolate light through pores of rock. He wondered at the view from his back, resting against blue moss. The saffron heart of the mountain was now fully ignited with a strange kind of fire from within, giving Seth the impression of life, of a soul. The ache in his stomach had all but diminished.

The woman's voice entered his head, still without his understanding.

"Hello," he found himself saying out loud. "Where am I?"

Moss on the walls lit with the same white fire as the trees by the river. The fire crept along the walls and spiraled the hanging rock of saffron color. Liquid light poured out of the rock and formed itself into a shape on the ground. The transformation of the liquid into solid form was graceful and effeminate. As it grew, the shape stood on two legs and became a red-haired woman, reminiscent of a face he hadn't seen in anything but a picture in centuries.

Seth stood in surprise. The liquid had become his love from long ago, the woman whose photograph sat on his mantle, the mother of Seth's descendants in the new world after everything burned. Iola, the Karduan woman with whom Seth remade civilization.

"Iola?"

"No," she said, staring at her hands, still aflame, the fire emanating from every part of her, "but that was her name, wasn't it?"

"She was my wife."

The burning woman twirled, spring cloth forming around her as clothing. The liquid light inside her absorbed into the flame, turning the color of the fire to mint. "You don't remember her very well."

"It's been a long time."

"Not for her."

"What do you mean?"

The woman smiled and danced over to him, grabbing him by the wrists before he could protest. He winced but the flames were still cold, like he could feel the mint, and invigorating.

"The light within you is warm," she said. "You are not man."

"I am not a god, either."

"Don't be presumptuous. You are machine."

Seth circled with her. The feeling of her skin and her cold flame intoxicated him. She might as well have been a dream, an avatar of the mind for lost company. The levity in her touch absorbed his despair, halting many questions he might have had.

"I am man and machine, but mostly a man. I haven't seen my home in many long flights of this world." He laughed a little, as if that was suddenly funny. "Now I am a lonely champion to half-forgotten faces."

She stopped and Seth stumbled, losing her grip. His stomach pain returned, still diminished, but a reminder of his loss. He wanted her to touch him again.

"You don't know me, do you?" she said.

"You're a dream. Perhaps I'm dying, at last succumbing to what amounts to a failing battery."

The woman pushed him farther away with a sudden wind.

"You don't know me! What is it you have inside? Not machine. Not man. Look inside! Find the soul. Look!"

The stomach pain lurched as he slid but kept to his feet. The discomfort felt something like childhood fear, making Seth's unconscious mind raise his hands as a defense. As soon as he realized how foolish he must look that way, he put his hands down.

"I wouldn't know where to begin," he said. "Who are you?"

"Look!"

The woman shot herself at him, grabbing his face by the temples. He tried to cry out, but the fire lit into his eyes, down his nose and mouth with an icy punch. He shoved his tongue to the roof of his mouth as if it could warm the cold like a headache brought on from a frozen treat, another sensation he hadn't thought of in a long time.

"Stop," he tried to say. Images flashed in front of him, part of the pain, but he chose not to look. He wouldn't give himself to them.

The woman strained to make him see, but he could see in her face when she began to give up. Releasing him, she lamented, "You are too much of a man to see."

He shook off the spell, coughing and wiping tears from his eyes. "Did you see that coming?"

She lunged at him again.

"No!" he shouted as light of his own came out of his eyes.

"There it is," she said. "The fire from the sky that woke me. The despair that gave me song. You are a spirit of death, like me."

Seth took a long breath, thinking back to himself long ago, a younger soldier from a war far away who landed on this world and watched it burn. "You are the voice."

She danced again. "Yes," she cried. "You are the stranger. And I am the voice you woke."

"I've called you the spirit of Kardu."

Shooting flames from her hands, the woman painted the cave walls with many colors. They mixed and flowed, firing light and shadows in all directions. She said, "You were right. I am of the spirit of this world. I am the spark before creation and the flame of condemnation. I am the darkness of night that gives daylight its meaning. I level cities with grace and raise gardens in despair.

"I was asleep," she paused to look at him, "the forces within me balanced, and light of another kind, a change, shook my soil. It was you."

"I know you." Seth ran fingers through his peppered hair. "I've walked with you in my head for so long. You were real, all this time."

"And you never understood me until now. Nor I you, many things lost in the languages of thought."

"Why not?"

"Think about it, Seth."

Seth sat on a mossy stone; the fires continued around him in their frenzy. "I gain energy by eating."

"So do all humans."

"But I am receptive to energy from the Botistems."

"Machines," she scoffed.

"Yes," he said. "That must make me receptive to your light. This fire. Microorganisms, maybe. Fungi? That's a scary thought. You bringing me here must have completed the connection. Language of thought? No. This is all a fever dream, isn't it?"

"No dream," she said. "But your susceptibility has bonded us."

"Oh," said Seth in further realization.

"You are a world, little man," said the spirit, standing in front of him.

"If I am a world, then what are you?"

"A manifestation of pieces floating in a soul that sleeps on pillows of gravity."

"Okay."

She wasn't being straight with him, but that didn't stop his mind from theorizing. He had taken whatever she was in by degrees. He could hear her through the same channels of mind that opened him to Pegassos, that gave him kinship beyond blood to his mother. As he processed more of this world into his body, he had prepared for the day he would meet the spirit and they would fully understand each other. He may have gotten it wrong, but the theory held for now.

Drawing a world with her fire, the spirit showed Seth her thoughts as she struggled to voice them. He thought about what mechanisms in her must make the fire. She had to be an organic, perhaps a relic, or else a clue, some fascinating reason that her world seemed so much like Earth. He looked around the alien cave. Maybe there were parts of Earth that had looked like this, some developmental turn that humanity and the world took together. No one could ever know.

"You live above the bones," she said, drawing his attention back to the planet she drew with the fire. "A new world, with people. There weren't always people here, but he brought them, and they became my children, much like you."

"Where did they come from?"

"I wouldn't know, don't interject."

Come on.

"Beneath the sky, the people and the animals, are bones. The bones of the mountains, the bones of the great beasts under the sea, the rotted animals and plants of before. They are the salt of my savor, the foundation of my beauty."

Her fiery drawn image zoomed into the face of the planet, showing dogs and horses, aspen trees and strange cacti. Then it dove underneath, turning back the evolutionary clock, and showed a landscape entirely unearthlike, with exotic creatures walking on land thick with giant forests. Among them Seth saw something that looked like a screecher.

"That is all my memory," she said. "At times I sleep, when there is balance. Now there is no balance, not since you came. You descended, and I awoke. The rockets awoke. Did you know the fire in you? The soul? You brought more than a ship to my continents. Now I've brought you here, under the bones, to finish my measure of you."

Seth stood before her. He was giving her pieces of answers. He winced as they seemed to only spawn more questions within him. "Did I cause the destruction of this people?"

She launched herself above him, knocking him back onto his back. He did his best to prop himself with one elbow while shielding his eyes.

"You presume!" she shouted.

He felt smaller than he ever had. It didn't help that she wore Iola's face. She had a way of bringing him down, too, not by intimidation, but by love.

"What then would you have me do?" he said. "All I have are questions. Questions are nothing to stand on."

"A man without questions is a man without purpose."

"Then give me one, so that I may have answers."

"When you realize you don't need answers, you will be young again."

Seth got to his feet again, unwilling to prostrate so easily, even before a god greater than he. He decided, if this spirit was truly a mother, she would respond like one he knew. If she did, he could learn what she was, what he needed to be, and perhaps find a way to keep going.

"I ask again, what would you have from me? Have you completed your measure?"

She lowered herself, tall enough to look him in the eye. For a moment, he thought she might kiss him. Her flame had a sensual turn.

"So ready to be my champion, little machine?" she asked,

her lips before his. "Do you think you woke in me a mother? A lover? Something you miss? You should know there are parts of me that you should not wake."

"I will try to understand and do my best to be an agent of peace, as I have done before."

"Careful," she said, throwing him back through a portal of flame to Glad by the lake. "Do not underestimate the avarice of souls."

46

"I think we're about ready," said Jayce at Cash's side, laying face-forward on a jutting rock at the chokepoint. The road below them curved in such a way the enemy wagons would have to slow down, and it was a blind curve where Cash's teams wouldn't be seen. One more robbery and then everyone would be ready to take the munitions depot.

Ran's army should arrive soon, too. Ran himself should have arrived already. There were rumors of a lot of resistance. They'd received a dispatch, but most of it was left unread in Cash's pack, along with a letter of girly handwriting that he did his best not to think about on the mission. He didn't know any girls anymore.

Refocusing his eye to the glass, Cash looked through his rifle scope to view Tarj's squad at the opposite ledge. They'd set up one of the automatics. This one was old and was fed by a crank. The men chose it for sentimental reasons. Their captain didn't object; Cash thought they had more than proven themselves this season.

Ced's riders and a squad of locals were concealed to the north behind trees and stones off the road. Tarj's men would light up the wagons with suppressive fire from their position to the east, and a detachment of locals would support them from the other side. As the convoy broke for cover or circled their wagons, Ced's riders would flank and assault through. The engagement would be over in less than a minute, provided the coordination went as planned. Cash's men had a good record of doing things according to plan. That's how they'd gotten this far.

"I don't see the detachment," Jayce said, checking the trees.

"What do you mean? I just saw them." Cash turned to count the horses.

"No, I see Ced over there, but the Ashran detachment is supposed to be on the other side. Obtuse triangle, as you called it. No one shoots at each other."

"Yeah, but..." Cash kept looking. They weren't there. Something was wrong, but his mind didn't want to admit what their absence would mean. *They were just there.*

The enemy wagons came into view up the road. There were more of them than the locals had reported. Ten wagons, twenty riders in escort, outnumbering Cash's squad by a lot of guns.

"We've been set up, look at Ced." Jayce pointed with his hand resting over his rifle. Ced was signaling to abort.

"Don't give the signal. We're going to abort, and we're going to do it quietly." Cash raised himself on his hands just a little and started to slide backwards. They could get away in time. "It's not worth the risk–"

An explosion caught him with his mouth open and mid-breath. Even with him shielded behind the upward slope of the rock, the blast boxed his ears and rattled his insides. His thighs shook like tossed sandbags. All of this happened before his mind could realize that it shouldn't be happening.

He turned to Jayce, wanting him to say something, but Jayce was rolled over onto his back with blood coming out the corners of his mouth. Cash pushed him onto his side, limp and unconscious. He needed to get control of the situation, he needed to save his men.

Groups of Keeper men poured out of the wagons to occupy all sides of the road. The riders took to the slopes. One was dashing its way up toward Cash and Jayce on the rock. Cash sighted him in his rifle and fired. The man and the horse fell to the ground. The horse kicked and rocked back over its rider.

Cash flew for cover off the face of the rock to behind another stone below. The dirt kicked up dust around him as he slid into the fall. He looked up to where Tarj and his men had been with their automatic, expecting to see and hear it firing. Instead, he saw a smoky hilltop and a small crater where his men had taken position. There were mangled bodies and twisted metal.

They were all dead. Half his squad gone at the start of the fight.

He fired into the backs of riders on the hill where Tarj's team had been killed. The riders fell, some screaming, others dead before they hit the ground. One kept a foot in the stirrup and flopped along the ground under a frightened horse that kicked and bolted across the road. The runaway horse brought Cash's attention to men on foot behind wagons, firing at Ced and a few other guns behind the rocks at the bottom of his hill. Cash shot seven rounds into four riders coming up his own hill before he knew what he had to do. He reloaded, throwing a spent clip from his onto the ground, and then leapt down stone and brush for the road below.

Numb to all fatigue, Cash rushed the enemies at the first wagon, fury and powder blasting down the road from his repeater into their backs until he was on top of them. They hadn't seen him coming. The last man standing turned at Cash with a pistol. Cash beat his face in with the rifle, sand and blood forming a sick paste in the flaps of skin and shattered bone that peeled away from the man's visage.

But Cash had failed. The hills were swarming with enemy. He had to keep moving. He had to turn enemy guns toward him and give Ced time to—

Another explosion sent smoke and shock through the air, obliterating Ced's position. Dust and debris hit Cash full in the face. Disoriented, fumbling for his pistol, he fell onto his back.

From a distance, he could hear a visceral groan, a ferocious growl that reminded him of his own voice. It was his voice.

He had landed in the small pile of men he had just killed. Still hearing the growl, he looked to the sky. It looked like blue ocean over the dust, endless. For a moment, lying among bodies, Cash thought he could see the *Libertas* above the sky, another life in the form of a woman's figure hidden in the cirrus. Seth had started to tell him more about her.

"We found him." Muffled voices echoed in his ears.

"Still alive? He wants him alive."

"I think so. He's got this armored vest, and check out this hat. I'm not sure if that blood is his."

The bearded man who spoke had painted eyes with black circles. He came to gloat over Cash. His hair curled at the side of his head and through his beard, the mustache pointing upward. He looked well-groomed enough, freaky as he was, that he must have missed most of the battle. He smiled, the yellow of his teeth showing through his hairy face.

The yellow disappeared into a flash of red mist and brainy chunks that popped out the back of his head when Cash shot him through the mouth with one of his pistols. Cash didn't even remember grabbing it.

"Get that gun!" someone shouted.

A foot knocked the pistol out of Cash's hand, and ropes found their way around his arms and legs. He kicked all the same, gouging a man's eye with the inner point of his boot's heel before the other men subdued Cash completely and took his armor. He didn't hear anyone help the man with the now-useless eye. The man whimpered with the desperation of a frightened child and the lingual coarseness of a trapped miner.

Several more approached on foot. "Ndera, these horses are useless. We don't have enough for a team. They're either dead, busted up or spooked into the hills. A second bomb, really?"

"It was the only way."

Cash was thrown by filthy hands facedown into one of the wagons. The voices around him grew bodiless, demonic in the wind. He felt himself breathing heavy, half in sobs, half in rage-shored groans. No words formed on his tongue, and coherent thoughts died in his mind. All he saw in his mind were pictures of the demons and all the things he would do to them when free.

The wagon didn't move for some time, until more horses were gathered and calmed. The going was slow, as a few men had to walk. Cash couldn't tell how many. The anger of the fight was wearing off, but he held on to enough of it that mattered. Sometimes, he listened to the conversations of his captors.

"I can't believe we caught Cash Rivers. We're gonna be rich!"

"Shut up! We've a long way to go. Don't draw attention."

The wagon rocked past meadows and creeks, creaking closer to the depot where Cash had planned to attack. He wished they'd gone for it sooner. Maybe then more of his men would have survived; they'd have a stronghold at least with the men and women they'd recruited from the city. Or maybe not. One of Ashran resistance must have given away the attack, someone from the squad that abandoned them.

"Don't think about loss," Judge once said. "Every life serves its purpose. Think about your next move. When you think about loss, that's when you do your most terrible deeds. Be the better man, Cash."

Better than you, Judge?

He wanted one of the Keeper men to approach again. Then he could kill him.

Judge never liked killing. He preferred to make friends, or "useful acquaintances." Cash learned a lot from him that way, how to smile at someone cruel and skim money and resources from under their nose. That's what he said, anyway. Judge was the best at killing, and killed when he needed to, usually without any other option. In the end, Cash was nothing like Judge.

But even back in some of his worst moments, Cash had never felt so feral.

Buried in such thoughts, Cash barely noticed when the horses stumbled, until both keeled over and sent him tumbling over the front. He rolled into the two men driving. The wagon collapsed under them as the horses tangled in each other, dying from a sudden attack. Cash's anger kicked in like the motor in a lion's claw. He attacked.

With hands tied in front, Cash threw himself on one of the drivers, wrestling him down. He didn't know what happened to the other but heard gunshots. Focusing on the one he had, Cash rolled the man where he wanted. Between the dying horses, Cash fought to get himself on top, driving his elbow into the man's jaw, then his closed, tied up fists. Somewhere, Eimos and Teeg would have smiled.

The man pulled a knife from his belt. It was long. Cash stopped him from stabbing by driving his shoulder into the man's neck and armpit, immobilizing the arm. His hands still tied; Cash let up for a moment to put his hands around the man's neck. The knife scratched at his back, but Cash drove his weight down, pushing from his toes, piling shoulder into trachea. The man sputtered, trying to reach the knife around into Cash's back but unable to get the leverage. Cash heard himself roar. There weren't even obscenities for this kind of fight.

Cash constricted his arm and shoulder like a snake, tightening, cutting off the air, cutting off the blood. The man gasped with throaty noises that turned into convulsive sobs, reluctant sounds, desperate, wordless pleas. With one last wheeze, the man's brain shut down, his heart stopped, and he was done, blood choked and airway crushed.

The gunshots continued for a moment, quick exchanges, back and forth like an argument, and then all went silent. There weren't even birds to fill the vacuum. Cash waited on his back, eyes to the blue sky. He felt a childlike desperation wallop over him. Someone else was coming. He was tired, but he'd kill him too.

But it was Jayce, his head blocking the sun with a rifle propped over his shoulder. He was dirty, hoarse, and out of breath.

"I've got you, sir," he said. "We're going home."

47

Sorrow lingered like a cloud in the cave hideout by the beach, accompanied by shadows of smoldering firelight. Water trickled down the spring behind where Cash sat with his back against a burnt-orange rock and his feet to the fire. His face was bruised, cracked, and red. He held a letter in his hand, unfolded from where it had arrived in a dispatch before the betrayed robbery, before his men died. On the front was the feminine handwriting he didn't recognize. He hadn't opened it yet. He just stared at it and thought about the men whose splintered bodies still rested in blood-soaked wilderness.

Cash and Jayce were all who survived the fight. A boy named Bal was there, as well. Bal had brought the dispatch and volunteered to watch the horses before heading back to Ran's position.

The babble of the stream made the only chatter in the cave. No man spoke. Bal packed what could be carried on a train of horses without riders. Petei team. Mokoi team. Ced. Tarj. All the other men. Red was there. He would have a rider. Cash didn't feel good about that, just like he didn't feel good about reading this letter.

Across from Cash, Jayce had tears pooled under his eyes. They followed the lines in his skin, escaping the well of iris in mourning.

Cash undid the wax seal of the letter. The course paper had weathered a long journey through the seasons, making its way from snowy hilltops to a man hiding in a warm cave. It seemed to glow in the firelight, and the writing looked warm.

Captain Rivers, it read, *My brother Ran told me this would find you. My name is Mya Praylum, princess of the High Valley and stewardess of Yora's wife's estate and her caretaker. Her name is Vonica, and I'm afraid she's very ill. I don't know how much you know about the situation, but I won't burden you with the details.*

To be honest, I'm not even sure exactly what to write. Ran thinks highly of you, enough to entrust you as his knife. The whole valley is following your progress. They're writing stories about you and your men robbing convoys, sabotaging trade, and stealing the hearts of Ashran women, though I'm less inclined to believe that last one. I'd rather imagine that a secret mission is a lonely endeavor. Perhaps that's why I'm writing you this short letter.

You should know that we all admire what you're doing for us. I couldn't presume to know your motivation for wanting to help us in our campaigns, but whether you fight for us or for your own ambition, we the people of this valley feel your efforts. We celebrate your victories and mourn your sorrows. We send those we love to fight with you because we know in the end your efforts are shaping a better world.

I imagine a world sometimes where people are kind to each other. Where you don't need walls around cities and valleys are open. Good men and women lead nations of educated souls, building a better world by good deed rather than bloodshed. Our ancestors must have achieved some of this. After all, they reached the stars, didn't they?

Am I rambling? I suppose so. I didn't bring a lot of paper with me. I'm on a long ride through the highest pastures of Vonica's land. It's beautiful. You should come see it when you're done playing hero. I'd be happy to show you.

Cash put down the letter and rested his head against the rock. He was having a hard time feeling anything but the cold rage that stuck to him like indigestion and hard stimulant. He wondered what Mya really knew of war, how faces of anyone except the brothers he lost were hard to picture. Then there was the killing, the killing that should have bothered him more than it did.

This girl picked a bad time to be interested in him. Her word couldn't have felt farther away. He read the last part over again.

Cash's mother had taught him how to read. He couldn't remember her voice, or hold in his mind a strong picture of her face, but he could remember that she laughed at the way he would pronounce words, fudging the Joropa she loved so much. She also told him he was special. All mothers did that, he assumed, but she believed in his potential. They must have been in hiding then. He remembered the dim light of wilderness fires and the hunger of a diet of only wild food. His father said the bad people chased them because they were special, maybe the kind of special that's descended from god-like immortals from space. *Huh, highborn from the beginning.*

"I killed a lot of people today," Cash whispered, looking at the letter. "I've killed so many people. Even more than I've lost. I killed my team, too." She wouldn't understand words like that, would she? No one gets a soldier's mind, not in the ways that count to a soldier. Then there was the part of him that wasn't a soldier. How would she understand an outlaw? Fascination, like Ran?

Hey Abe, he thought...no, not the time to think like that. He pushed that shit deep and covered it with more hate.

Mya couldn't know what this war had cost him. First his gang, then he led eleven good men into battle. They were successful. He'd thrown a mess of trouble into the cog of the Keeper machine. The enemy was scrambling now, defeat around the corner once Ran and the Kona arrived. *Techa,* they were going to take that depot.

But they died under his watch. He pushed them too far. One score too many. Cash didn't deserve this woman's praise. What was the Valley punishment for a failed commander?

On the other hand, Mya believed Cash was making a better world. That's why he'd come back to Ashra. He was special. He could see his mother's smile in Mya's words somehow. She felt closer. He didn't need the Valley for acceptance. That was giving them way too much credit. Her too. Cash was building his world his way. How had he not seen this before?

I think I know why I'm here, Tarj.

"I'm not going," Cash told Jayce.

Jayce's tears were gone. There was a hint of anger in his voice. "There's nothing left for our mission here. We should take our place with Ran again, the main campaign. The knife is broken."

"I'm not finished."

"The hell you mean, not finished?"

"You should go. I'm going to the depot."

"This again?" Jayce stood. "It's over, Cash. We can't trust the locals. Our men are dead. We've done what we came to do. This was...this whole thing was never supposed to end with us alive anyway. Me and you, we're the lucky ones. We've got our health, we can keep fighting, but with the prince. You've got to see this by now."

Cash folded the paper. It shook in his hands. Shock. So much of him was spent. Hurt. "You're relieved, Jayce," he almost whispered. "I don't need anyone else. I'll take the depot. Tell Ran he can find me there."

"You gonna scale the wall? Swim the drain?"

"Neither," Cash said, standing and dusting himself off. He pulled a leaf out of his pocket, thinking briefly of Abelnora while he stuck it under his lip, letting the juices help him feel a little better. "I'm gonna fight dirty."

Cash sat under violet arms of dusk atop Red with a bottle of liquor. Tarj had taken it from a raid but never drank it. A cloth was stuck out of the end, soaked and smelling like a night of beach wrestling followed by half-coherent conversation.

"To friends who fell, and the enemies whose blood will them atone." Cash lit the cloth and threw the flaming bottle into dry brush and twisted trees. Wind at his back carried the flame up the hillside, rolling like sapphire hair toward the depot beyond.

Red reared at the sight of the fire but didn't run until Cash compelled him around the flames and off to race them up the road.

As he expected, men rushed out of the gates of the depot, water and picks in hand to head off the fire before it reached the walls. Cash and Red dashed through their mottled ranks, just another worker on assignment. No one minded the rifle on his back, no one looked him in the eye to see who he really was. A single man would never storm a fortress on his own, would never enter the stronghold of his enemy without an army. Men moved out of his way as Red trotted through the open gate.

Cash tipped his hat at a man who looked in charge of something.

"You," the man shouted. "Get off that horse and help these men. We're proofing the ditch. Fire won't make its way over the wall without fuel."

Cash dismounted and led Red to a post. He tied him off while answering the man, "I'm here for the groundwater. Where's the pumphouse?"

The man pointed to a shed across the depot next to a canal pushing several water wheels. "That's our drinking water. The canal will have what we need for the fire."

"You gonna use it to fill the ditch around the wall?"

"Your idea's as good as mine. I've got to get these men out digging that line. The fire's getting close. See if you can get anyone not doing anything already to help you." The man was off, but he'd given Cash what he needed.

Taking a shoulder bag from Red's saddle, Cash made his way through the depot, past buildings and over a small wooden bridge over the canal. An indifferent water wheel turned below him a little, giving energy to the pumphouse. The men wouldn't drink from the canal. The surface water carried too many diseases out of the city. Underneath Ashra City, a water table carried clean water. The pumphouse drew that water up for the mill workers and Keeper forces.

Cash opened the door, slinging over his shoulder a leather pack full of poison.

He'd taken all day to find what he needed. Berries meant to kill invasive birds, herbs that caused stomach pain, milk from a leaf that he'd heard was poisonous once, and an assortment of other natural pesticides he could find on a day's ride. He dumped the contents into the large trough that collected water from the pump. The men would be thirsty after fighting the fire, and would consume his poisonous brew in their own canteens from spigots outside. Cash just hoped he'd collected enough. The poison would have to be slow enough to spread around the whole camp. He didn't need it to kill them all just yet, just slow them down.

Exiting the pumphouse, Cash found a hitch, tied off his horse, and grabbed a shovel. Then, drinking from his own, clean water, he fought the fire and waited.

Cash sat in a guard post above the gate with his feet propped on a rail and his rifle in repose up the side of his boot. Soon enough, he saw what he expected. A lone rider trotted out the gate hunched over his horse. Cash set down his feet and sighted in his rifle. Point, breathe, squeeze, surprise. The man fell off his horse in the smoky haze of a dying brushfire.

Straightening the cloth tied over his mouth and nose, Cash loaded a new clip into his rifle and walked down the stairs. A man sat on a landing halfway down, vomit and sweat oozing from the corners of his mouth. He looked up at Cash and sighed. Cash hit him on the top of the head with the butt of the gun.

He chose to move first through the scaffolds of the walls, firing at anyone who moved. A spirit of terror seemed to move with him, manifested in horrified eyes before retribution in the writing of bullet holes. These were executions, indemnifications, blood to seed the soil of a rising generation. Many died before the first of the doomed and poisoned men fought back.

As he stepped out from the enclosure of the wall into the yard, a bullet rang off a metal sheet near Cash's right shoulder. His ear, already pressed by the sounds of his own gunfire, went silent, making the noise of the battle more distant. He threw himself into cover behind a crate of grain.

"I know who you are, Rivers," shouted the shooter, muffled in Cash's ear.

Cash didn't answer. His sense of self had evolved since arriving to the depot. His grief had swelled to an infected wound in his heart, and his mind leaned into the fight as a matter of instinct more than reason. He moved with the drive of a packless wolf. Dangerous, because he was alone, because he'd been wronged. His little war with the ruling bodies of Ashra had taken everything from him but his rage.

More shots shook the crate.

Swinging the rifle over the lip of his cover, Cash fired at the first movement he could see, an instinctive stab at the speed of sound. Two shots hit wooden planks, but three more walked into the target. The shouting man had been trying to change cover when Cash's gun caught him. The man fell on his face, his breaths drawing ragged the dust and ash of the air. The side of his chest started to breathe alone, in and out like squeezing plastic as the rest of it filled with air from his wounds.

Moving into the center of the depot, Cash shouldered his rifle, wary of the stores of arms and munitions. The building housing the ammunition and explosive ordinances was large, taller than the wall surrounding the compound. There were guard posts along the sides, but no one fired from them. The poison seemed to have dealt with most, incapacitating the fight out of them. The longer Cash took to kill them all, the higher the chance that some might start to recover, but he expected most would succumb. They'd drunk a lot of his poison. Smoke and ash made them thirsty. Cash unsheathed the knife from his vest. This wasn't the knife Ran had given him. It was black, powder-coated, and long in his gloved hand. Opening the door, he readied himself for any surprises in the fatal funnel of the doorframe.

Crossing through, someone lunged at him, a woman. Her skin was pale and sweaty, and she smelled of excrement and internal suffering. In a sense, she seemed rabid, throwing herself over Cash in fevered, clawing anger. He tossed her off without using the knife.

She sobbed and writhed on the dirt floor. "You're the monster everyone says you are."

Cash looked down at her, watching her agony in the shadows between slits of sunlight through high windows. He knelt and looked into her dying eyes, bloodshot but still somehow beautiful. The animal in her was already gone, giving way to the humanity of death.

"I'm sorry," was all he could think to say.

He cleared another building, a smaller one, but still large. The depot was a big compound of buildings equipped to serve a community of workers. This building was a bullet factory, machinery turned by water wheels and steam engines. The plant was quiet now, but there were still people inside.

Cash moved with greater prejudice, killing under the umbrella of suppressed thoughts. With his rifle clips spent he moved to his pistols, clearing rooms of varied levels of sick and dying. Few had evaded the water poison, but not all reacted the same.

His methodic tactics led him at last to the place where he expected to find some resistance. An office hung over the work-stations, the kind of place a boss would sit, someone high up in the keeper organization. Cash had no way of knowing whether his water would have made its way up here, if the boss had some stored away from what took the rest of his men. Cash had a nitro stick with him. He just faced the choice of whether to blow the doors with it, maybe killing everyone in the room, or try and assault the place for a satisfying conversation with whoever was inside.

As he climbed the stairs up the scaffolds to the office, a gruff, almost slimy voice called out to him from the office window.

"Cash Rivers. Mighty outlaw. Hero and commander."

Cash paused at a landing.

"We haven't met, unfortunately. I wish we had. My brother spoke highly of your gang. Before you shot him."

Cash listened.

"I feel like I know you, all the same. You're made of the same stuff as the rest of us. The steel in your nerves. The darkness born from the shadowed womb of a broken world. I knew your parents, you see, with their gifts, their heritage. You are one of them, it's obvious. One of the highborn, as they used to call you. Dangerous folk, with fire in your veins and eyes. Special eyes."

The voice carried through the factory, reflecting sound through the machines and the empty spaces between them. Judge had never told Cash much about his heritage, but more and more he kept hearing about it. People wanted to find deep-er meaning in his achievements. Or perhaps others, like this man, wanted to push blame, make his accomplishments a cred-it to his race. This fool was about to find out exactly who Cash was, and it had nothing to do with alien blood.

Cash climbed the trussed beams under the overhang, poising under the open window. He felt invigorated, despite his long day, despite his sores and bruises from fights and lost companions. He listened to the old fool talk and let the moment tickle his nerves and strengthen his climb.

"If you don't know by now, you will. You're a part of a disease, Cash. Men may profess to wait on the gods that shape our world, but they cannot stand to be in the presence of one. We don't want to feel inferior. We want power. You may cut down my men, poison my stores, burn my world, kill my family, but you'll never take what I have made. Me, just a man. My brother Ezra, just a man. You'll never be rid of Fala Steele! You'll never wash my blood from the roots of this town."

Cash lit the nitro stick and tossed it through the window. Swinging to the scaffold below, the shortened fuse blew the explosive, probably before the old crook even knew it was coming. The overhanging office flamed out the windows and splintered wood flew around the factory. The scaffold couldn't handle the stress and it buckled, spilling Cash into the wreckage, vest and chaps not saving him from the brunt of the fall.

He found he didn't die, for lack of proper planning. At least he'd shut the man up.

48

As Kami and Arty wound through the belts of the star system away from Libertas and her cocoon of folded space, they saw the impossible from afar, floating around the marble-cloud skies of Mount Kardu.

"I'm seeing it, but I don't believe it," Arty told Kami from the cockpit.

Kami moved the two-dimensional display into three- and spun it around, revealing tiny specs and data points.

"It would take no less than hundreds of years for the Federacy to send another flagship out here. How long was I gone?" Arty said.

"Hundreds of years for this planet," Kami said. "This ship is newer than the *Marshall*, larger, and equipped with better shielding and firepower."

The bold, giant lettering on the side of the ship read *FSV Pantheon*, and to Arty, it looked beautiful and haunting all at once. She felt the kind of fluttering heaviness a person might feel if they saw an ex-lover after a long time. All the feelings of allegiance were still there, but she was a remade individual. She wasn't even sure what she was, if she were human anymore. She looked back, trying to remember moments when she had resisted the Bosions when they hadn't understood each other.

"We rebuilt you, Arty."

Arty realized Kami must have been listening to some of her thoughts. "Because I almost died."

"Yes, and you were resistant."

"So, what? You would just shut me down to have another go?"

"Readjustments in the subconscious."

"No," Arty said.

"We helped you understand, to receive our light."

"By reprogramming me?"

"By guiding you. The same as was done when you were seeded. The same as you would to network a machine."

"I– that's reprogramming. What have you made me, your servant?"

"If anything, it's the opposite," Kami assured her. "Who is flying whom?"

"I keep asking myself that question."

The image of the *Pantheon* had a transparent hue, spinning a slow rotation above the console. Arty reached and zoomed in from outer hull to hallways and battle stations. The old Detections lieutenant inside her assessed the ship for weaknesses and capabilities.

She wanted to anger herself more, to lash out at Kami, but she had to reconcile with what Kami had done for her, the gifts she'd given.

"Like you would a ship, you remade me as a ship. I'm the vessel!" Arty exclaimed.

"I knew you would understand." Kami said with a hint of emotion. She never sounded monotone, or even machine-like, but real sentiment bled from the space between her words.

"As a soul lives within a body, you live within me," Arty thought out loud. "Parts of me make you what you are. The way you manifested as Lopez, the shape and design of this ship, the way our beliefs mesh together as a kind of scientific spirituality. The light in you within me is now an important piece of who I am. As people aboard a ship serve a purpose, make a family."

"You are my family."

"Yes," Arty said, "I think I get it. Lieutenant Sato died the day Kami rescued her. I wasn't who I am now, and you were not yet what you have become."

"Together, we are something more."

Something that could deserve a name, Arty thought.

Playing with her display, she discarded the image of the ship and looked at the planet. It looked as beautiful as it did all those years ago in her bunk behind a curtain on the *Marshall*.

"But," Arty continued her thought, "try not to sound like you somehow reprogrammed me to be something for you. I don't like that."

"If you had the chance to redesign me, your ship, for a better purpose, to further yourself and your race, would you do it?"

"That's not... No, you can't compare..."

Somehow, Kami's flight tittered for just a second with the swagger of a smug chuckle.

They flew closer to the *Pantheon*, enough to see its great spinning drum. The drum would spin when the ship was fixed, in orbit or drift, saving energy without fabricating gravity. Arty wondered how long the ship had been in the system. If needed, a ship like the *Pantheon* could roam the stars for generations. The *Marshall*'s plan had been to observe the planet for perhaps that long until leadership decided it time to introduce their culture to Federacy influence.

Influence: another word for programming, another word for training. "Gods," Arty said with ironic profanity, remembering Commander Worley.

Is life just choosing who indoctrinates you?

"Should I let the *Pantheon* know we're here?" Kami asked.

"Not yet," said Arty, "I want to know what happened here while I was gone."

49

The snow was melting in the valley. The season, though short, had left its frozen wake. Yora looked back into the hills and saw his younger self, one that carried despair that seemed light compared to the weight that now levied his heart. With Ran's plans in the West and Tais dead, he really was the only one to carry the burden of prince and heir. He would have to act in the interest of his father, in the interest of his family's throne.

But he loved Denaiah. She would bear his child.

He regretted the night she came to him, as sweet a memory as it tried to be. She played a game with him, and he fell right into the scheme. He didn't know what it was, but he knew she planned something. The woman was descended from a wealthy underworld, why did he ever expect less?

But she would bear his child. The wings of his heart soared at the idea, while the sails of his mind tore and sank. A child couldn't be something to mourn.

He arrived at her palace, climbing through tangled and dry vines up the lattice of the wall to a window where she waited for him. Yora saw himself from the outside again, disassociating enough to numb the guilt. He saw a prince and hero to his people, a silent traitor to his father. What he was to his mother he couldn't know. She had withdrawn herself to castle towers of distant thoughts.

Denaiah pulled him in from the window to instant embrace in the tincture of moonlight. The light hung like a soft illumination of consequence. If Yora could put out the light, maybe he would. Yet he delighted in seeing her, his new love, away from duty and the strife of war. His teacher didn't know the favor he granted when he stayed their enemy.

Yora felt to see if she was showing. Not yet, but he knew the child was there, as if by some sense built into a father. He or she would inherit his kingdom.

"I can't stay long," said Yora.

"I wouldn't expect you to," said Denaiah. She had her hair tied back for sleeping. He had never seen it like that. The curvature of her face seemed different, more whole and honest. She had soft features with a delicacy that reminded him of cream. "Days are tedious without you. I wish the night would last forever," she said, leading him to the edge of her bed. Taking his head in her arms, she embraced him into her chest. The silk of her nightclothes was soft and smelled like warmer seasons.

"Is the child really mine?" he asked, raising himself to look into her eyes.

"Would it make any difference if it wasn't?" She bit her lip and put her arms around his neck.

"I shouldn't have to explain why." He maneuvered her away, taking hold of her arms so he could look her in the eye and see if he could find the truth.

"Then yes. The baby is yours."

"Denaiah, you sound uncertain."

"To the court, my child belongs to your father. In my heart, my child belongs to you. I know it and so do you."

"I despair, yet I can't help but rejoice."

"This child will seal our love, Yora." She kissed him. "Be the prince the people need and one day our song can be sung in the light."

"For now," Yora answered, "that song is a cloud."

"I promise the child is yours."

"Then I promise the same."

50

Mya listened to Vonica's scraping breath, the last sounds before she was sure to die. Yora II sat with her on the couch, head on her lap and soon to be motherless, his breathing asthmatic.

"Did you inhale the root, little Yorathas?" she asked him, stroking the dark locks of his hair.

He shook his head, and silent tears cut wet marks down the bridge of his nose. "I don't want to leave her."

"It's okay," Mya said. "You can stay, but let me know if you need to sit up."

"I will," he coughed, covering his mouth with a fist.

Dawn stretched its arms through the window, wrapping the linens and upholstery with golden comfort. Mya had imagined this moment, caring for Vonica, but longing through her deepest thoughts for a day of relief, when this chapter would close.

"Why isn't my father here?" said Yora II.

"I sent him a dispatch," answered Mya, "but it takes time. He'll come."

"My mother says he doesn't love her anymore."

"He does," Mya said. "He just has to be out to protect us."

"Like Tais."

"Yes."

"She's dead."

"I know."

"Will my father die, too? Will you die?"

Mya let the questions fall like feathers, hoping the wind would take them, but the boy needed an answer. "Lives are like books."

The boy looked up at her.

She continued to stroke his hair. "The pages turn, even when we don't like how the narrative plays, and someday the story will end."

"But at least you can tell how much of the book you have left."

"Yes," said Mya. "Lives are only written one page at a time."

The boy sat up. "Are you going to leave me now? Mother is leaving me."

Mya looked at Vonica, how peaceful she looked, the torment gone from her mind, nothing but ragged breaths keeping her sailing mortal waters. "She's just making sure the way is right for us, before we all move on."

The golden light faded to pale morning, nothing but plain day.

"I will do the same," Mya said. "I'm going to build us a home, and then I promise to take care of you."

Yora II yawned and laid his head at the other end of the couch. She covered him with a blanket. He would go to live with his cousins at Ran's estate. There were people there equipped for his needs, and she could concentrate on moving her life forward. In her heart, an ambition grew. Looking out the window, she saw herself in the sun, sitting on a throne of hills, radiant as destiny, anfractuous as Cleopatra.

Mya heard Yora before she saw him, boots knocking the polished wooden floor. He moved with tender caution to the bedside. Vonica didn't stir, but whether or not Mya imagined it, her countenance seemed more at peace, the muscles of her brow relaxing. For a couple that had known love, their life together should end like this. Mya said a silent prayer of thanks that Yora could be home to say goodbye, that the invasion had somehow been smaller than projected. For now.

Yora II walked back into the room, his hands clasped in front of him and his shoulders hunched, timid. His father held out an arm, beckoning. The boy walked into his father's embrace, and together they watched Vonica breathe. Her chest rose and fell, struggling to hold on to a last thread of life under the sky before her soul would leap beyond. Mya wished she knew where that would be. The boys together now seemed to be a small glimpse of it.

"How long are you here?" Mya asked her brother.

"As long as it takes," Yora said. "Men are still patrolling the hills. One small detachment is moving over the wall. There's a lot of land to cover. Any army could be hard to miss. Engineers are preparing to fortify as soon as the snow melts."

He moved from the bedside, the young boy beside him, and they sat next to Mya on the couch. "I'm broken, Mya."

Mya took his hand. "I think we all are."

"Denaiah said you know... you know about..."

"Yes," she said, mindful of the young ears with them. "I figured it out."

Yora put his face in his hands, showing more emotion than Mya had ever seen from him. "I have to be the man Father and Mother think I am. I have to lead our people."

"Father never approved of any war, any move to conquer." She put a hand on his back.

"Our people can't live in the Valley alone forever. What we'll gain isn't for him."

"I don't disagree."

Some time passed. Yora II was asleep on the floor, his head on a stuffed toy his mother had given him when he was little. He had just shown it to her, told her he was going to keep it forever.

"I'm glad you're in the game now," Yora said. "You might end up being the smartest of us."

Mya looked down into her lap. "We don't have to talk about any of it now. Now we can mourn our dear Vonica."

"I'll always love her," Yora whispered.

Mya took her brother's hand. Vonica's breaths grew farther apart, more faint and with less struggle. She looked serene, at peace, only a few more minutes until the end of her song.

"I think she knows."

51

An army marched on Cash's new fortress. He couldn't be sure if it was Keeper forces having second thoughts, but then he realized that the bulk of the force was Kona, with their signature pointed beards. The Keepers wouldn't have a single army that size anyway, or at least not in one place. He searched with his keen eyes through their ranks, but didn't see Ran.

Cash turned the wheel to open the gate, wincing at a few lingering pains. He'd waited for days, moving bodies from areas he wanted to use and flushing the water system. Despite his rank, being alone meant he had to do all the labor himself.

Sunlight unspooled through the gate in threads of relief. He stepped into the light, rifle slung and resting on the front of his vest. He knew he looked good, alone and victorious. Tipping his hat, he waited, feeling the breeze and chewing on Ashran gum.

Welcome to my spoils, bitches.

Stopping at the gate, the front ranks of Kona soldiers broke and moved aside. Jayce, Ran, and his lieutenants rode out in a line. Ran moved ahead and met Cash first, bringing his horse through the gate.

"Captain Rivers, I find you in fewer pieces than I'd feared."

"Sir."

Ran stepped off the side of his moving horse and embraced Cash, knocking him back a little, ignoring any military protocol.

"You did it," Ran exclaimed, grabbing Cash's sore arms.

"Even more than I asked for, you did it. The victory is yours."

Cash's eyes met with Jayce, still on his horse. The two men nodded to each other, but with wounds shared too fresh to yet smile, they only locked eyes for a moment.

Ran wanted to see the facility. He had his men open the loading doors of the depot itself. They creaked with some reluctance, like they didn't want to give up their secrets. There was still a stench of death inside where a rotting, mangled Fala Steele rested in half-cooked smears. Cash had buried the woman.

"Ten more in here," a lieutenant commanded. Ten Valley riders followed.

With arms stretched wide, Ran reveled at the piled munitions. "I had been a little worried. I'm not anymore." He shook his head and laughed, his smile spreading like a summer chill.

"I never should have doubted," Jayce said.

"We have enough to take the city now," a lieutenant said. "I wonder how far back they've retreated."

"Yeah, about that," said Cash, thumbing the safety on his rifle.

Ran popped open a crate of explosive ordinance, ball-shaped and heavy. "Tell me it's good news. If not, save it for later."

"I..." Cash paused with brief unexpected fog in his thoughts. "See, I was expecting company here," he began. "Of course, no one was going to let me keep this place by myself. I'm actually not sure what I expected. This was the end of my road."

"No one came?"

"Just a courier. He's downstairs if you want to meet him."

"What did he say?" asked another lieutenant. Cash couldn't remember his name right now. He was so tired.

"He said they wanted to talk surrender. I didn't know what to reply so I tied him up."

Ran laughed. His voice echoed. "Let's talk to him."

Cash took them down. The room was lit by candles, nothing but food storage, a few work tables, and a frightened man tied to a chair with his feet on scuffed concrete floor. The man was small, the kind of build suited to couriers who could be light on a horse and deliver dispatches within whatever the required haste. Cash had kept him fed and somewhat comfortable, but for now he stayed bound.

"Surrender?" Ran said, his eyebrows up four notches and into his hair.

The courier delivered all information without holding back. "The organization is disbanding. The Steele brothers were the head and backbone of the Keepers. It was a split decision, but the remaining couldn't hold up on their own, not against Cash Rivers. We're all farmers and ranchers here. You Valley people outgun us. The Kona scare us."

"How can we believe you?" asked Jayce. He looked like he might be ready to torture the man. He was as calm as always, but wired.

"I have all the papers with me. They'll accept your terms, as long as they can keep their land."

Ran opened it up to his officers, looking at Cash for the most part. "Am I willing to negotiate?"

Cash wanted to shake his head, but his eyes must have done it for him. *Your call, prince.*

Ran kept his arms crossed and nodded to a soldier keeping guard at the door. The soldier, as though reading the prince's mind, shouldered his rifle and moved to untie the courier's bonds.

"Sure," Ran decided. "I'll give them my terms in person. Tell your people I'm coming. Anyone who so much as spits at my army means I start leveling buildings. Understand the message?"

"I understand," the courier said, "but can I have my pistols back? The roads are even worse than before. They say Cash Rivers is still out there, robbing people, killing their men, stealing their women."

Cash grabbed the man's thigh holsters from out of a box. "Here you go," he said. He didn't bother telling the little man who he was.

"Stealing women?" Ran looked at Cash.

"Now I kinda wish I had," shrugged Cash.

Jayce laughed, a deep, sighing, relieved kind of laugh.

They walked back up the stairs, back to the depot where Kona men were distributing arms. The air smelled better, like life rather than death.

Ran said, "Let me get a few things straight, Cash."

"Shoot."

"I send you to distract the enemy. Instead, you start a revolution. That revolution betrays you. Then you get all of your men killed."

Jayce started to say something. Ran raised a hand without looking at him and he stopped. Cash didn't know where this was going. He felt like he was supposed to be thinking he was in trouble.

"Next, you started a brush fire with wind toward a munitions depot."

Cash smiled.

"And you poisoned everyone before executing them in their own shit."

"To be fair, I blew one of them up."

Ran swung his arm and clapped Cash hard on the shoulder. He laughed, "It's a good thing I'm not a jealous man. It would seem I was the distraction and you were the captain winning the war all along, army of one."

Cash felt the lieutenants around him smiling.

"Write it up, gentlemen," Ran bellowed, "and send it home. Spare no detail as long as it's mostly truth. And Cash."

"Yessir."

"What happened to your beautiful horse?"

Cash sighed and looked back toward the desert. "I've got to go find him."

52

— · —

For such a fancy name, the *Pantheon* was just another Federacy ship. However, the hallways seemed smaller than Arty remembered from her life on the *Marshall*. The air smelled and tasted recycled. Was it always like that? She'd been spoiled by other worlds now. Strangely, she found herself missing the mirror-universe.

A young lieutenant and a junior fireman were escorting her in a car bound for the captain's war room. The car skipped over the curved tile of the outer-drum hallways at a pace just faster than a brisk walk. Arty thought about her last moments aboard the *Marshall*, the way the floor had whipped under her, the bodies of men and women bouncing into bulkheads, the feel of the vacuum just on the other side of all the tin and ceramic that made a ship. It was a horrible memory, but sometimes she couldn't stop it. She also couldn't help but keep stomaching over and over again that hundreds of years had passed in this corner of the universe and her experiences licked like they had only happened yesterday.

"Kami, I want a home," she thought in her mind. "This isn't a home anymore. It just looks like one I lost."

The feeling of loss Arty felt in that moment also came from what she'd learned orbiting the planet. Billions had died sometime after she left through the Dao. The world was scarred, a mound of ruins quite different than the holo-display she'd studied on her mobile. Soil, rust, and green life now covered the concrete streets of before. No one seemed to be mourning those people. They were history, like her.

"I have to ask, ma'am," the fireman said.

"Maybe I'll have to answer," said Arty.

"Are you really from the *Marshall*? Rumors spread fast on a ship, and we're all trying to wrap our head around it."

"Check the logs. I think you'll find me." She probably sounded nonchalant but she was just trying to keep herself calm and out of post-traumatic recall.

The car stopped at the war room. She got out of the car and a man saluted her. Returning the salute, she decided the movement didn't feel the same out of uniform. Her new armor wasn't made for it.

"Captain Jameson is waiting for you, ma'am," the man said.

Captain Jameson was a hard-lined woman, postured and trimmed, but not tall. Arty thought that the captain must be really small to be shorter than her. Then she realized that no one seemed much bigger than her.

"Kami, did you make me taller?" she thought.

"Subconsciously, you were part of the process," answered Kami. "You wanted the boost."

The captain turned and faced Arty with two hands clasped behind the small of her back. "No salute, Lieutenant? Have you resigned your commission?"

"No, ma'am," Arty said, "I've just had a long journey."

"It's alright, Sato," Captain Jameson held out a hand. "I'm sorry for your losses. Centuries can hurt like a bitch."

Arty shook the woman's hand. It felt rough and callous, like someone who frequented a weight room. All the muscles had to come from somewhere. Her hair was also colored blond. False coloring. Dye. That was something less often seen, maybe a new trend from a generation born long after Arty's in distant worlds in Federacy space.

"I'll take it from here, Rollins." The captain dismissed Arty's escorts. "Lieutenant." She motioned to a chair across from her desk. The captain's desk was near the head of a long table under arcing lights. The walls of the room were mostly dedicated to monitors showing populations and resources.

Sitting at the desk, Arty waited for the commanding officer to speak.

"Having read your well-drafted report, I feel I know your situation, Sato."

Arty had written ahead, informing the *Pantheon* where she came from and some of her experience with the Bosions. She made sure to specify that it was a previously unknown group of friendly Bosions who helped her survive the wormhole and later evade the malevolent Bosion horde that attacked her allies. Honesty seemed a good way to establish proper relations with people and superior officers who thought she'd been dead for centuries.

"You showed remarkable will and tact to survive and return with intelligence on our enemy." The captain referred to the *Libertas* and to the Bosions.

"Yes, ma'am, I hope that my brief, yet enlightening tour of the *Libertas* can help the Federacy's mission. I'm afraid the mirror-universe may not exist anymore."

"To bring you up to speed," Jameson continued, sitting back in her tall chair, "no one survived the tragedy of the *Marshall* and *Tecumseh*. The *Libertas* retreated into a self-maintained, unapproachable wormhole, and Seth Caeso remains unaccounted for except for rumors we've gleaned from one of the sparse populations on the planet. Shortly before you arrived, the wormhole briefly collapsed before throwing up its walls again.

"With the readings of your ship and the collapse of the wormhole, we expected you to be the enemy. You snuck up on us, but I was relieved to receive your report and your old Federacy passcodes."

Arty blinked. The senior woman had just called her old.

"Now you're here, and I have to figure out what to do with you."

"I'm able to serve, ma'am," Arty said, even though it almost felt like a lie.

"I have plenty of men and women in my command, Sato, a full complement of well-trained officers. I don't need any machine-hybrid relics on intra-universal holiday."

Well, forget that.

Arty didn't know how to process the captain's tone, so she waited for the woman to finish before deciding how to feel, or what mutinous thoughts to allow herself.

Captain Jameson stood from her chair and brought up a holographic globe of the planet and the *Pantheon* in orbit. "The first ship to get here was a relief mission sent as soon as Captain Meskin reported the discovery. Command knew how valuable a planet like this could be, so they didn't waste any time. The small ship was dispatched before even a full picture arrived through the relays. Still, it took centuries, much too late. Today, the *Pantheon* is part of a rotation of observers. We come, we watch, then we go home. At least that's how it used to be."

"What changed?" asked Arty.

"A few ship rotations before we arrived, ground operations began. We discovered that Commander Caeso had survived the *Tecumseh* wreckage and established a community on the planet. He put us at a disadvantage."

"So, he made a cult of some kind?"

"Exactly. People who live in a culture with anticipation for his mother's rule written into their tradition, even religion."

"What's our objective?"

"The rules of play have changed," said Jameson. "We're setting up camp, influence of our own. The *Pantheon* is to see it through. One ship, one chance."

"We have people on the planet?"

"Yes." Jameson moved the display, showing a migrating group of dots marching their westward way on one of the continents toward what Arty assumed was Seth's new people.

"May I?" Arty asked, moving to the display.

"Of course."

Arty navigated the display to show the Federacy's army up close. "Your army seems primitively armed."

"Looks can be deceiving. But a full complement of arms would destroy the life that gives this planet any value."

"Green is gold, but that still seems like a big risk." Arty said.

Captain Jameson took Arty's arm and led her away from the display. "We could ruin this world so easily. So, like I said, 'One ship, one chance' to win the people."

Arty believed she knew what the captain meant.

"I need to know, Lieutenant. Are you still loyal to your oath to the Federacy?" The captain's eyes were hard, accusing.

"I've already given my life in service. That should fulfill any contract. My return should demonstrate loyalty."

"Would you swear again to fight in our cause and bring Federacy order to Kardu?"

Arty let her own eyes harden. This woman was young, wasn't she? She hadn't seen the universe as Arty had. She hadn't seen how meaningless some things could become through a clock without hands. "I believe in the mission I signed up for."

"Then I need you to do something for me."

Chills ran through Arty's nerves, the kind that preceded the bestowal of a purpose, excitement and dread all at once. "Just give the word, Captain."

"I need you to find Seth Caeso before we mount our offensive. You have abilities that could match his, and a history with him. I need to know his loyalties. Three hundred years is a long time. Can you find him for me? If necessary, could you kill him?"

Arty bit the inside of her cheek. She could feel the Bosions inside her heal the tiny marks from her teeth. "I can imagine there are a lot of things I can do, Captain. The ancestors know I have the time."

53

— · —

Ran had them in a line, hands bound, standing on a platform before a crowd of thousands. These in the line were the softer of the Keepers. The fat and gray ones, the ones who expected to still be in charge after the war. Sure, change bosses, the Steele brothers for the Praylums, then carry on as usual. But Cash and the people remembered their crimes, the underground slave trade, the inhumanity of their rule. All the reasons Cash had shot Ezra Steele and blown up his faceless brother, Fala. Ran had Cash and men in his new command bring them to the center of Ashra City Square for justice. Cash was happy to do that.

The morning sun warmed the edge lines of the city with the sparkle of Spring opening in her dew dropped eyes. The chill of dawn was giving way to the simmer of a more direct sun. Reassurance rose in the steam of the humid air. Through that almost-invisible mist of vapor, Cash watched them, the lined-up Keepers in the growing light, and clung to the vengeant pining of his heart, for his parents, for his men, for his killer's soul. He stood on the platform in front of them, facing the people next to Ran.

"Do you deny these charges against you, your crimes against humanity, against your ancestors, and against the Queen of the Heavens?" Ran's voice carried through the Ashran square.

One Keeper, male, somewhere in the middle, began weeping. A spear-bearing executioner ascended the stairs, passing Cash at the end of the platform where he stood with Ran and his lieutenants. The executioner eyed the weeping man through a hood that scared away his tears.

After no answer, Ran continued, "By my authority as prince—"

"Just hold on!" a woman in the line shouted. "Are you, an outsider, about to execute us based on your own power and no law? I demand a trial, a real trial, by an appointed judge of my people."

Ran lowered the scroll of charges in his hand and walked over to the woman, taking the spear from the executioner. He pointed with it to a condemned, long-bearded man down the line and said, "Do you mean that one?"

She spat on his vest and seethed, "I don't mean this one."

Ran thrust with the spear into the woman's abdomen. She dropped to her knees, held up only by the spear. He pulled it back and watched her fall, keeping the weapon, scowling over her body as she let out quickened gasps. The growing crowd watched before the rifles of Kona and Valley soldiers. Cash watched the blood fall, imagining it steam like the dew. He didn't like watching her die. He also didn't like the part of himself that did. She'd made him this way. People like her.

"I will afford you all an opportunity," Ran said. "You wanted to keep your land, but I can't leave your crimes against these and my people unanswered. Redeem yourselves. You serve me, raise up an army to defend our eastern border, and I will reward you with amnesty. Swear, on this scroll in my hand, on my vest, and high in the heavens in the arm of Libertas your allegiance, and amnesty will be granted."

Protesting voices in the crowd rang out, drowning any response from the condemned Keepers. Ran looked a little disappointed, but not surprised. He must have been planning something. Someone was stepping out of the crowd and Cash recognized him. It was Digo.

Digo approached the soldiers and addressed Cash. "Let me speak," he said. "We have something we need heard."

Cash nodded to Ran, who put on an expression Cash had trouble discerning. "This is Digo, my friend, if you remember him. He was there the night you and I met. He also helped the Knife."

Ran looked at Digo and pointed the tip of the bloody spear. "I don't remember, but Cash's word gives you voice. Step up here and speak."

Digo sidestepped through the guards and climbed the platform stairs. He looked small, a simple man caught up in the ugly of a transformative time. Cash wondered if his kids were in the crowd, watching their father speak in the face of their conquerors and at the trial of their oppressors, watching him, Cash, play part in an execution.

"With all respect, uh, Lord," Digo began, "myself and the people I represent, the resistance that helped Cash, we welcome you to our home. We gladly offer our services in the war you're fighting in the East. But we would consider our efforts amiss to wind up under the banner of any army on behalf of these people. They deserve no amnesty. If you want us, you'll have to serve only justice here today."

To Cash, Ran said, "Didn't the resistance betray you?"

Cash nodded.

"You mean you want them to die. How can I trust you, when a betrayal from you and yours cost me some of my best men?" Ran asked with spear in hand.

"We dealt with the detachment of traitors ourselves. If it would satisfy you and Captain Rivers, we found that those who betrayed the Rivers Gang did so under duress from the men and women here on trial today."

Ran thought for a moment. Cash could see political machinations running through his mind. The crowd stilled like water at the edge of a dam, waiting on Ran's word. At the end of his thought, Ran smiled. Relief and electric enthusiasm were all over his posture.

"Do you want Ashran justice?" he cried, spreading out his arms.

The crowd cheered.

"Witness here. My captain is your captain, an Ashran man. Men and women of Ashra City, I give you Cash Rivers, the man who killed Ezra and Fala Steele!" Ran gave Cash a look, one of brotherly love, and within it a glance that said to not mess this up.

More cheers lit from the crowd. Ran handed Cash the spear. It was Kona-made, light and part hard ceramic. Cash knew what he had to do with it. The noises of the crowd distanced themselves as a negative charge seemed to start coming out of his ears in a low hum. His hands started to shake with sweat and nerves as he gripped the weapon with white knuckles. One more time. Time to kill one more time.

Cash remembered what he had told Seth in the cabin. The thing that he had admitted, a shameful thing. He was going to enjoy this.

Approaching the first of the old Keepers, he listened to him. The man's breaths came out short and frightened. He gave Cash a pleading look, a helpless look. Words tried to come out of his mouth, last words that no one would understand.

"Justice for our families!" Cash cried, plunging the spear into the man's diaphragm.

The crowd cheered, and Cash moved to the next, a woman.

"For our wives!" Death.

"For our children!" Execution.

Blood spilled through the slabs of copper wood. Morning dew of cultural shift. "For our friends, our liberty, our peace." Death, death, death. The spirit of Yurasema would feed today. Judge would be proud of him right now. Judge was in Cash's hand somehow, guiding it.

Cash made his way down the line, killing as if in a trance. It wasn't murder, he knew that. The crowd was cheering. The farther he got, the more he heard them.

"For my parents, the brothers and sisters I never got to have. For the children. For the graven feet of a thousand displaced souls."

Cash killed the last one and threw the spear off the platform. It stuck into the ground like he did it on purpose.

"Let the blood spilled in the heart of this ground speak," he said, and he walked away. Reaching the edge of the platform, he stepped off in a moment of vacant instinct. Instead of breaking anything, as he should have, he landed on his feet. He had never jumped from that high before. Whatever, he was still in a trance.

The crowd gasped and applauded in collective adoration. He heard the word *highborn* more than a few times. He kept walking.

"Couldn't have said it better myself," he heard Ran say under the canopy of applause.

"People of Ashra City," Ran called to them.

Cash didn't want to turn around. He needed space. His head wasn't right. So much applause for death.

"I will serve you, with Captain Rivers at my right hand. Together we will build a stronger, unified basin with no more divide. Let's start today, by tearing down this platform, and planting a tree over the blood, as a symbol of peace to all generations."

In the distance of his mind, Cash thought he could see Abelnora, chewing bioca and smiling, proud of his accomplishments, though with sadness in her eyes. He walked past her image as the edge of the square grew closer.

"I will stay with you, Ashra City," Ran said.

Cash stopped.

"But Captain Rivers will go on, with lieutenants of his choosing. Your best and he, along with these elites of Kona Tribe will defend our land from Eastern invaders. Ready your arms. Ride under his banner. His war has not yet started."

The Abelnora in Cash's mind dropped her bioco in disbelief. Ran hadn't just meant to make Cash a public icon, he meant to make him a leader. In the flash of a single rousing speech, Cash had inherited an army. Cash walked back to the platform, looking up at the prince, his friend.

Techa Fio. What the hell?

"Don't look so surprised," Ran told him from above. "I really just want you to meet my sister."

54

Such had been Seth's focus, that for all his centuries roaming the wild places of the planet Kardu, he had never come back to the city he first endeavored to visit. In part, he hadn't returned out of simple logic. The city had been radioactive, a waste without people. After watching it explode, he had no reason.

The ruins of a wall still circled the city in parts. There were scored shadows, faint yet still visible, of vaporized people, men and women of a different time and language. He remembered meeting others, in his first days, and how hard they were to understand.

Yet, when they died, all people were the same. Despair ran a constant thread through a galaxy of variables.

Seth found a long street of collapsed high-rise buildings and shattered screens. This would have been a vibrant place before the war, a place of emerging technology, human innovation reaching for yet undiscovered frontiers. They were on their way to impressing the Federacy and getting keys to the galaxy. Nevertheless, tangled vines and weeds now covered everything, choking the buildings like the brown, wintered nature wanted to swallow them like a carcass.

A flame lit in the corner of Seth's eye, lighting one of the giant screens without any heat. A woman's voice spoke out of the flames, now all too familiar.

"Hello, Seth," she said.

"Hello, spirit," he answered.

"What answers do you seek in the rubble?"

He hesitated to answer, but struggled to know how dishonest a man, even an immortal one, could be with the soul of a world. "I'm seeking the answer to an old question."

"You want to know if this was your fault."

"Somehow I knew you would know that."

"How could you have started a war that had already begun? The nations here already had arms pointed at each other," she said. "Their war had already started."

"Nations will always threaten each other," said Seth. "That's an integral part of civilization. Civilization thrives only at the prospect of destruction."

"Mutually assured compromise."

"Yes."

"That is my way," she said. Her form materialized, climbing out of the fire and onto the street. "My part is the balance. Species kill and are killed. When they die, I remember them."

"You are not the benevolent Mother Nature I would have imagined you to be," Seth told her, reaching a hand to help her down. It seemed like the right thing to do.

"Mother I am, yes," she said.

"And just what are your children?"

She walked with him for the first time as more than something of a voice in his head.

"Violence," she said. "My eldest child is violence."

"Then you and my own mother are alike," Seth said. "Sometimes I feel like war is all I am, all she gave me."

The spirit kept his hand and caressed his arm. "You shouldn't hate yourself for it. Nothing may grow without death. In you I see many seeds."

The street of torn asphalt and twisted vegetation fed into tiered highways, most of them collapsed, others struggling to hold themselves up as monuments. Seth imagined the kind of vehicles that would have ridden on them the day he arrived.

Their rusted mechanical carcasses weren't anything to recognize anymore. He also tried to see where the explosion that destroyed them might have originated.

The spirit of Kardu walked with him. He hadn't seen her since the cave. He traversed many long days and cold nights through lost roads in the wilds of the Basin. The absence of her voice in his mind was welcome, but he did miss her. She'd been such a long companion that he wasn't sure how to fill the void without her mystery. Maybe someday when he had Pegassos again, he could be free of her subtle manipulations.

"Do you know of Earth?" he asked her.

"I don't know the word, but from your mind I see a kindred spirit. A world like mine. A world like his."

"His?"

She didn't answer, but put her head on his shoulder.

He motioned to the buildings, the skeletons of overpass highways, and the rusted metal. "When I look at all this, I see a place so similar to the home of my ancestors. It's like I can feel them, a portal through time, but I know that can't be."

"Their culture evolved the same?"

"Yes, that might be right. Convergent evolution. I've thought of that." They came upon a storefront where a window had been. Inside, Seth could imagine the markets within. "I want to believe that we all came from the same place, the same Earth. You would know, wouldn't you?"

"Maybe we all did." She moved away from him, twirling through the streets of overgrown death. She looked so much like Iola, the way he still saw her in his mind centuries after the loss of her grave. Only flashes of her survived in his memory, short reels of smiles and heartbreak. She mothered a new race with him. More survived of that than the people of the Basin would ever care to know.

He walked farther into the dead city, a place without a name, only ashen shadow. The features of the city grew fainter.

They were reaching the explosion's crater, where nature had taken over. No buildings stood in this part, only trees. There was something uncanny about the trees, as well. Many of them were mutated trees, their DNA altered from nuclear destruction. Seth didn't know what he meant to find here. There were no clues to find, no forensic search to perform.

Iola appeared in the middle of the field. The spirit danced in the shape of her. In Seth's mind, he heard her music again. She started to sing, moving the melody through the trees and the brush. He wasn't sure what part of what he heard came from his thoughts and what came from the trees.

"Have you ever listened to the stars?" Iola asked him.

"No," he said, thinking how beautiful she looked, how much he missed the real Iola the more the spirit danced.

"They tell stories, much like these trees. They sing songs of light, of tales long ago. I dance beneath them, my clouds in pirouettes under their splendor. The stars are my company. I get my warmth from the greatest of them all. She is my sun."

Seth looked to the sky and only saw the blue and white of day. If he focused his enhanced eyes, he could see a little beyond the sky, but he did not see what the spirit saw. She must have the eyes of a world, whose sky is ever night.

"What is it?" she asked him, drawing closer. The trees were still humming the echo of the song.

"I'm thinking of my younger days," he said.

Iola drew him into her, wrapping her arms around the small of his scarred and weary back. "I've missed you," she whispered.

Iola?

The whisper hit him like a trance. He didn't see a spirit anymore, didn't recognize any part of the game. He took his very much alive wife into his arms, lost in a dream of years gone. Nothing seemed amiss as blue flames enveloped them both in their embrace.

"I'll always miss you," he said. The flames were cold, her lips were soft and warm, her body trembling. He was carried away with her, and in the trees, suddenly there did appear the music of stars.

They kissed, and the flames around the two lovers grew only brighter. The power in the fire entered Seth, and blazed something new inside him, a power he didn't know could exist. It met the Botistems, and nature and machine met with a fusion that Seth could recall with really only one word.

Consensus.

"I see," the spirit said in her ecstasy. "At last I see."

55

—·—

"So, what did you find out?" Kami asked her as they flew out of the hangar.

"Don't you already know?"

"I want to know your interpretation."

"My perspective," Arty found herself correcting.

"Both."

Arty explained, "Captain Jameson isn't Captain Meskin. She's aiming to conquer the world, some real ancient America Manifest Destiny crap. Granted, previous ships have been growing a community down there, helping people, but, sending them to take over other territory, sending them to die, that's...that's..."

"Roman?"

"Gangster."

"In what way?"

Arty drank in the beauty of the planet she orbited. The clouds were sheets of wool over land and sea, all contained within a sphere of haze that bled into the stars beyond. Kardu was the first place Arty had seen with so much life and such little industry. She could land anywhere and be happy, be free of her wandering, immortal and safe in the arms of unknown gods.

"Arty, why did you agree to find Commander Caeso?"

Arty kept looking at the view, longing for it. "You never say no in the military. I'm still sworn to my service."

"What is an oath, and what makes you bound to it? Is it some power the captain holds over you?"

"No, but a promise is still important. I believe in the Federacy and in the girl I used to be."

"Perhaps that girl is dead. Arty the woman is immortal. She doesn't owe anyone anything."

"Maybe I owe something to you."

"You and I are one purpose. We couldn't leave each other if we tried."

"What would happen?"

"Perhaps if we find Seth, we'll have some idea. You may find that you and he share a stronger bond as immortals than you think. Your evolution has hit the same mark."

Arty shook her head. "We'll see."

"Shall I try to locate him?"

"Not yet," said Arty. "I want to see this army the captain made. If I'm going to back a cause, I want to know what I'm getting into."

The ship burned through atmosphere, streaking her descent over the eyes of the continent. Arty imagined them descending like painted fire sliding down a wet canvas before it dries. What eyes might have seen her from the blue terrarium below, she couldn't know.

Stepping off the ship was a disorienting dream. On this land were no tricks of light or metallic imitations. She had found true, organic nature. The grass brushed her palms at the height of her waist, and the pollen of new spring tickled her nose. She sneezed, her body adjusting to the air of foreign contaminants. The fact her nose reacted to them at all told her how Earth-like they were. But if anything was malicious, the Bosions within her would take care of it. She may never get sick again.

The prairie wind was a song with birds, light off the budding limbs of trees, and the tips of swaying grass filtering the white sound of the wind. Arty had long imagined the feeling of life in a paradise such as this, but could not anticipate the sense of wonder it drew from her. The view, the gravity, the unfiltered light, all were almost too much to take. Before long, her head began to ache. She sat down beneath a tree to think and adjust. Focusing on the swaying ocean of grass helped.

The encampment wouldn't be far from here, but for now it seemed best to rest. In the distance, she saw a horned animal. Its skinny legs twitched from the bite of small insects while its tail swatted at them. The animal had a long, wide mouth and a single, tall horn that curved upward in a spiral.

Yes, rest. Innumerable discoveries would follow.

56

—·—

"I'll kill him," King Tarsus Praylum said, barking at dispatch papers now thrown to the palace floor. He was sitting on his throne, Mya's mother at his side. Mya stood on the floor of the court, a reluctant position, but she didn't feel like sitting.

Mya had begun living at the palace, as when she was younger. Yora II was off living with Ran's family and Yora's ranch didn't seem to need much help in her stewardship after Vonica's passing. The palace seemed like the next step in her life. She could train in diplomacy under her father and be close to Denaiah, whose friendship seemed kind and genuine, without any angle. Mya knowing her secret had bonded them.

She held her own unopened dispatch in her hand, but imagined it said the same thing as her father's. Ran wasn't coming home, and Cash had taken his place as captain over the returning riders and the conscripted Kona and Ashran armies. Ran had only told her Cash was to be his second, not his immediate replacement, so this turn had surprised all of them. Abdicating his right to the throne hadn't been enough for Ran. He'd gone and won himself a rival kingdom.

"He's won us new ground," Mya's mother said. "Think of the tribute he'll bring, the influence. You now have two kingdoms."

"It doesn't say that," the king retorted. "Ran says he staked his own claim. He'll rule that corruptible city like the thug we never raised him to be. He's a warlord now. Barbarian. And who is this Rivers boy, that everything I hear is about him winning the war, not my son? Did he face their armies head on? No, he poisoned them like a coward. He killed a simple garrison by stabbing it in the back. Ran met them in the field like a man."

Mya hadn't heard this last part. She ripped open the coded dispatch and left the court.

I leave to Cash all that I had, Ran wrote to her. *Father can dispute the appointment if he wishes, but the hearts of my men are as my own. The polygamist, tyrannical, stifling regime that is my father's will not sway this decision. I have my own kingdom now. Cash will win the Eastern war for you. I remain behind to build my own legacy. Call it my human right.*

I've also told Yora. He knew of my plan to take Ashra City for myself long ago. I just didn't find the justification or opportunity until Cash set all this in motion. You should all know that I would return if I thought I could, but I see an opportunity here for real peace in the Basin. Someone has to take power here, someone who knows how to command without becoming the Keepers all over again.

I don't know what Yora will do. His guilt may drive him to oppose Cash, or his allegiance to Denaiah may help him turn against Father. Either way, I've built my own way out. I am the prince who escaped destiny.

Mya put away the letter, careful no one else would see her reading it, careful they wouldn't catch the shocked tears welling in her eyes. Ran was okay, but he wasn't coming home. A divide she'd long feared for her family had finally happened. Her selfish father had driven his sons too far away. One became a far-off warlord, conquering cities and building new kingdoms. The other, a broken man in a disreputable affair of whose treachery would one day cost him his life.

And here Mya stood, in the belly of the court, keeper of everyone's secrets.

"Mya," the king said through the great doors of the court. "Mya, come in here."

She followed his voice and walked herself to the base of the steps to his pedestal.

"Will you raise my new son to be different than his older brothers?"

"Surely he should be raised at least as great as his father," the queen said. Why was she so onboard all of a sudden? She'd all but disappeared for a bit, and now she was way too agreeable.

Mya changed the subject, piqued that her value seemed to only rise to the level of nurture in the eyes of anyone but Ran in her family. "Will there be a revel to honor Captain Rivers and his army?"

The queen made a face, one to deter her daughter's choice of conversation. *Don't go there.*

The king erupted, rising to his feet off the cushion of the throne, his vest askew, "I will not honor that boy, that outsider in this court. He has stolen that army and if I had any good sense, any control left over the armies of my kingdom, I would have him hung. I would have him dragged. I would have him disappear before he steals another quarter of glory from me and mine."

The queen's attention left the room, her eyes fixed on nothing, zoned out of common atmosphere.

Mya interjected, "The people would expect a celebration. The victory was for them, wasn't it?"

"It was for himself. He's after their hearts. Is he after yours as well?"

"I was only thinking," said Mya, "that I could entertain the banquet. You would only have to be there for the award ceremony. You could decorate him, then send him off to the front of other battles. Ran's old duties beyond the wall need attending, and should the enemy arrive in the East, well, Captain Rivers will either prove himself the hero again or die the same."

The king sat back down. "Rivers has won your fancy, hasn't

he? Somehow, I smell your brother in this, his fingers still in the bowl."

Mya smiled rigidly. "Just let me throw the party, Father. If the young captain dines in your house, salutes you, if you treat him like you would a son, all glory is owed to you. The people will see it."

He paused.

You keep going like this, old man, she thought but didn't say, *and you won't have any more children who call you Father. You won't have any friends.*

"Well said, Mya," the king told her, taking from his aids another dispatch from somewhere in the valley. "If Yora weren't next in line for it, trained for it, I'd say you'd make a good queen."

"Queen of secrets," she muttered to herself.

This was her place in the war, wasn't it? She was to keep the secrets, lean the head of the man in charge where it needed to be. He would never harm Cash, not with his popularity with the people. And more, her father was a man of honor. *Was.* So much was too complicated.

57

— · —

Yora sat at a table in the darkness of Denaiah's room, reading a book in Joropa by candlelight.

All things be likened to the shape and etiquette of a tree. Love, violence, any principle of universal truth. Life in the universe, a fractal tree.

"What are you reading now?" Denaiah asked from under her covers.

"Another book with no name."

"Why don't you read more of books in our language? Books from Old and Enlightened Earth? Mya likes them. You should hear her talk about Shakespear."

"Sometimes I prefer the words of the dead closer to my own feet," he said. "I find them easier to believe."

"Are you mad at me?"

"No, why?"

"Sometimes I feel like you don't love me the way you did when we first met. Back when you were married."

He closed the book and looked at her. "I'm here, risking my life and reputation, aren't I?"

Now what was this about a tree?

Denaiah wanted him. She loved him with a fierceness that scared her at times. The way he held her intoxicated her mind and body, invigorated her senses. But he was a man. She couldn't trust him. As hard as she tried, she couldn't love past the parts of her ruined by her father. Maybe that's why she married Tarsus. He was mad, expired, useless in many ways, but he was predictable and not terrible to look at. She could take advantage of him and his need to hold on to power. Yora was different. He was thoughtful. Deep in his flaws, but thoughtful. She couldn't stand to hear her own words, but they came anyway, all the manipulations of a woman scared her mate would leave the nest.

"You're not here for me, but the child we share inside me."

Yora put down his book, losing his place in the process. The candlelight flickered on his face, shadowing the lines, making him look just a little older. "What are you talking about?" he asked harshly, but sincere.

"Do you just come here when you're lonely? Is it just for the baby?"

He took a deep breath, then let it out. The candle highlighted the muscles of his topless back as he stood up from his seat by the bed and stretched his neck. She wanted an answer out of him, but he didn't show any sign of wanting to give her one. Suddenly her mind brought up the thought that she might not be the only woman he was seeing. He could be out lying with other women, prettier ones. How could he do this to her? Torture her with his silence.

Then she saw one of the scars on his back. She'd seen it many times but had never asked him about it. It was just one of those things that came with a man of war. With that thought came the image of his spirit, a ghostly picture of himself standing like a sad face in front of a foggy mirror. There were scars on the spirit that didn't show on the body. They showed his dead wife, his sickly son, and, looking too closely at this image conjured by her mind, she saw her own name scratched on his side.

Denaiah.

She was part of what was breaking him, wasn't she? Part of a gradual chiseling. She wanted to stop herself but couldn't.

"Yora, I hate living this lie."

Yora finished his stretch, blew out the candle and returned to her side, prostrating himself on the covers next to her. Tenderly, he put a hand over her womb.

Calmly, thoughtfully, he stroked the small dome that housed his child. "I can't be like my brother. I can't abandon my father or my people."

"Is your betrayal any better than his?"

"Worse. The wall will be my penance. I believe the warnings my teacher brought us that night in the palace were real. I've trained my whole life to become the man who will wield that sword. Perhaps I won't make a great king. Perhaps I am not a man of honor. But I can stand at that wall. That's all that matter."

"Where am I in this picture?" Denaiah felt her blood boiling. "Where is your honor to me?"

"I'm here," he said, frustration trying not to mount over his stupid emotional walls, walls that were bigger than whatever might be erected around the stupid valley, walls of a man. "You matter to me. You're part of what I must defend."

If you really loved me, you would take me away from here. You would make me your queen in another place. But she didn't want that, did she? She wanted him where she could control him. That was the craziest of the thoughts racing through her mind. She wanted control. Control meant she could trust. Trust was vanishing from her palace world. The king kept ranting about Cash Rivers. Yora didn't see any of this. Armies from the East, armies from the West, infidelity in the king's court.

Consorts were a sure casualty in this sort of mess.

"I've heard things," Denaiah said, "about the army on its way, not in the East but about Cash Rivers. He's ruthless and unpredictable, a more real threat than imaginary enemies from far away. I've seen men like him before, killers in my father's house. He killed the killers in my father's house. You give a man like him an army, he will use it against you. He will use it to gain more power."

"What would I do about him? His men will follow him. Alone, he accomplished the greatest military victory of our generation."

"What about your great victory?"

"I...The people love him more than my father, even more than me. I even liked him the day we met. He seems like he should be my friend more than my enemy. What does he have to do with us?"

Denaiah took Yora by the face, moving her palms over the stubble on his cheeks. Bringing him close, she looked him in the eyes through the darkness between them. "He killed my father, Yora. If you love me, you will not be his friend. If you love your father, you will not be his friend. You don't see what's happening, but I do. There is a great rift traveling here from Ashra City, and someone is going to die."

58

Arty imagined what her crew would have done, if in the middle of space on the *Marshall*, someone showed up in the mess hall and asked to see the captain. A number of questions would fly around the crew. How did the person approach unnoticed? How did they get in? Are they the enemy? She and her crew would have locked the person in the brig, tested them for contaminants, interrogate them till they went insane, and work to shore up whatever holes in their security let the intruder slip through.

So, she wasn't surprised when the soldiers of the encampment did the same to her.

Bound and waiting on a stool till nightfall, she studied their appearance. They were undersupplied and underclothed. Less clothes meant less rank. The light rain battered their skin, their wagons, and their tents.

The camp also seemed diverse. Not everyone seemed to come from one specific group. There were some who spoke broken Standard, and others who spoke it fluently, but still with varying accents. There was another language she didn't understand spoken in a mix with Standard. Arty assumed those who spoke Standard most were Federacy-planted.

A man approached her. She first noticed his nicer shoes, laced with leather and fastened with plastic she wouldn't expect to find in the wilds of a broken civilization. Farther up from the shoes, past durable cargo pants of rough, tactical cloth, she saw a thigh holster with a pistol and the barrel of a long, old-fashioned-looking rifle with a large, rudimentary scope. He held the rifle slung over his shoulder. There was an image of a Greek lyre carved into the butt of the gun at the level of her face.

"You want to tell me what possessed you to land a ship so close to here? That fireball almost caused a religious uprising." His voice was a low drawl, slow and deliberate, with a bit of a mumble. There was some kind of leaf pouched under his lip.

"I came from the *Pantheon*, same as you," Arty said.

"I don't recognize you," the big man said, "and your armor looks...different. I've been down here for years but I would recognize armor like that."

"It's a long story," Arty said, "but Captain Jameson sent me. I'm Lieutenant Arty Sato, I served on the *Marshall* and was taken to another universe."

The man didn't know how to react. He paced around her, checking the bonds behind her back. "Forgive me if I don't believe you."

"Forgive me if I don't have time to care." She broke the bonds and jumped to her feet. The man reached for his pistol but she took his wrist before he found it. Her hand burned hot and he stepped back, gasping. A red shape of fingers started to form itself on his skin.

"What is that?" he winced.

She didn't mean to burn him, but she stayed focused. "Part of the long story you don't believe. Who are you?"

"I'm Sergeant Flint. Part of a generational force multiplier mission. Gods, that hurts. Many of these friendlies were raised in Federacy land, taught in our schools. Others were picked up along the way. You'll recognize the new ones. They dress in bright clothes and are a devil to herd."

"Are you in charge?"

"As far as our interests are concerned. But there's a local group drafted to head up the op. They seem to think this is some kind of big score, running things more like a gang than an army. Their head honcho is calling himself the Outlaw King."

Arty dusted herself off and rubbed her wrists, finishing taking off the braided leather bonds. Sergeant Flint watched her. He looked like he was trying not to check her out, strength and all.

"Well," she said, ignoring the wander of his eyes. "Let's go see him."

The Outlaw King's tent was pitched with many stakes, stretched out in the rain with furs and hides to block the rain. A young woman stood outside the front with a large gun under a flap of thick hide. She chewed on something and chatted with a pair of large young men who looked the same in the dark. One of them said something in the other language and the woman laughed and punched him in the arm.

"Someone here to see the big man inside," said Flint. "He in there?"

"Yeah," said the woman, "but who is fancy clothes here? You step out of a picture book, lady?"

One of the identical silhouettes next to her made a foreign comment that sounded vulgar. His identical companion laughed.

Arty didn't say anything. She couldn't decide how much of her origin and abilities she wanted to reveal. It was interesting that Captain Jameson didn't have a direct representative in charge. The worry that her people might escalate any conflict into something that would damage the planet's real estate must have been a galaxy-stretching mandate. Win the war, but don't interfere beyond hired guns and raw influence. Arty would have to ask Flint more about these schools.

The closer of the moons was already waning, and for whatever reason, so was Arty's patience to stand in the rain. She hadn't experienced real rain before. It was cold and she wanted under the woman's tent flap. Arty tried to figure out what she could tell the woman to get her to let her inside and see this Outlaw King.

"She's one of our people," spoke Flint. "She's a warrior he'll want on our team."

"Works for me," the guard woman said. "Make sure you wipe your feet. The man's always been a little particular."

Arty wiped her armored shoe on some clean-looking grass and stepped under a flap. One of the men was holding it. Light from inside lit up his face. Sure enough, Arty saw that both men really were twins.

The inside of the tent was a cavort of torchlight. A man knelt down an aisle of tiny fires burning in oil on standing lamps. There were tables and maps around him, but he closed his eyes on a rug in front of a mirror. His face looked calm, wise, reminding her a little of a younger but still seasoned Captain Worley. On the floor next to him was a hat that reminded her of old cowboy legends.

"Judge!" the twin said behind her. "You've got a hot visitor."

The Outlaw King opened his eyes and sighed. "Alright, Eimos, but tell Abe no more till morning."

"That's some story," said Judge. "I almost believe you."

Arty and Sergeant Flint had tried to tell him she was also from the *Pantheon*. She blinked, thinking. The two soldiers sat on stools while the outlaw paced above them.

"They come here trying to look like us," said Judge. "They even try to speak our language. It's fine. But you're different. There's an aura about you, something... something spiritual yet not. You're like a big pool in the light. You take up too much of it."

Sergeant Flint gave Arty a look that seemed to say, *He gets like this.*

"I was sent here by Captain Jameson," Arty said. "I'm here

to help you with your mission."

"I don't believe you, because you're too different," said Judge, pacing over her. "You two don't know each other, and I don't think you trust each other either. You also came to see me without anything to say, which makes me think you're here out of more of a compulsion than a responsibility."

Arty pursed her lips, not caring to push her half-made-up story anymore. The truth was the captain had only given her a mandate to find Seth, not interfere in her conscripted local army.

"See that look right there?" Judge pointed at her while addressing Sergeant Flint. "That's a 'well the truth is' look. You're having a moment of self-honesty. Could you share it with the room? Beating it out of you would take the fun out friendship."

Arty's tongue was still tied. She heard Kami in the back of her mind, nudging her to say something.

"But what?" she said out loud.

"But?" said Judge. "Alright, I won't ask you to open up without a little reciprocation." He pulled another stool from a map table and sat on it right in front of her. "People call me Judge. They always have. I used to be an outlaw in a city run by rich people named Ashra City. I got by swindling those rich people. Once, I decided to raise the kid of some people I met living in the wild. That kid grew up to be someone really special, right up until he shot one of the rich people for keeping some enslaved children in his basement."

Judge waited, seeing if anyone had anything to say. They didn't.

"Pop!" he shouted. "The rancher fell down, bleeding all over the floor, a fancy floor of white, serene carpet. Suddenly that carpet looked like my whole life, my whole childhood innocence soaked in the blood of people. Not of my boy, Cash, that was his name. No, Cash was a good man. The right kind of killer. No, I realized I'd spent my entire life getting used."

Sergeant Flint cocked his head to the side. "You haven't told me this story before, Judge."

"It wasn't one you needed to hear." Judge looked Arty in the eye, searching for something.

"Say, Sergeant," he turned to Flint, "I've got a few bottles of old shine in the back of that room over there. Do you mind grabbing a couple? This is a conversation that needs integrity."

Arty shrugged. "I haven't had a drink in three hundred years."

The sergeant slapped his gloved hands on his knees. The red mark was still on his wrist. "This conversation is getting a little weird for me anyway. I'll still be listening, though. Don't leave me out of the good parts."

"People like the sergeant," Judge said, "they use you. They keep your family in the community they made and tell you to fight for them, promising things for your efforts. You know they tried to hide the fact they were from space?"

"Makes sense to me, though," said Arty. "Maybe the threat they want you to fight is real. Maybe what they do and teach you is for the best."

"I've been where they want us to fight," said Judge, throwing up a hand. "It's a grand sort of place with architecture and innovation of true human wonder. It's no house of demons. I left that boy there, the one I was talking about. They wanted to use him for their own fight. He had blood owed in Ashra City. His parents were killed there, and he needed a war. You know how great men are. And I bet he's winning that war, too. My boy Cash."

The Sergeant came back with three bottles. Judge laughed and they each opened one. Arty got hers popped without the corkscrew or a knife. It was her first real moment of honesty in front of Judge. He noticed, but didn't say anything about it.

"So," he drank and continued, "My story is almost over, I promise. Me and mine, we're trekking through truly wild country. The kind with beasts I've never seen before, and a biting, gnawing, humid cold that none of us had ever experienced. One of the youngest loses an ear to frostbite, and I think my Lady was going to die. We don't even know why we keep going on. "But then we found them. Your Federacy. I figured out who they were before long. I have my ways." He looked at the rug where he had been meditating when Arty walked in. "We took up with them. Though I should actually more rightly say they found us. Ushered us in from the cold. They'd somehow restored an old city. Schools, shared wealth. I had to read about that kind of government to figure out a name for it. Socialism. You familiar?"

"Of course," said Arty. "I was born in it."

"Me too," said Flint.

"It's sure different than the resource trade in Ashra City. People there will kill for what you have because they want more. It's amazing what people will do for shiny stones out of the ground, but your Federacy... They're different. Idealistic, but for all their resources they'll still deal for your soul. They'll make you lead one of their armies if you impress them too much."

"Is that why you're here? They didn't impose it on you, did they?" Arty said.

"If I wanted their protection, a good home for my Lady," Judge got up again, waving his bottle, the effects of the drink starting in on him. "I don't trust them, but I have to do right by them. I'm used. Of course they imposed. What do you even know about humanity?"

Arty took a long draught of the "shine," wondering how the little Bosions within her might handle it. They might prevent her from getting drunk. She wasn't sure if that was such a bad thing. The cold liquid poured into her stomach, burning a little at her throat. A small buzz tickled at the back of her brain, making her smile. It reminded her of a long time ago when something dark dragged her into a psychedelic coma, events from another universe that looked now like images from a hijacked dream.

"If you want their protection," Judge said again, his cheeks flushing, "you must serve. In other words, what?"

"You have to be used," said Flint.

"You have to be used," Judge affirmed. "I may not be a space warrior, but I know people. You two are both used. Just like me."

"The Federacy has been good to me," Arty said.

"If they haven't made you do terrible things by now, they will," said Judge. "That's the business of governments."

"I know what I signed up for," Flint sighed.

The rain on the tent pattered like fingers on keys, fingers recording a testimony.

Judge continued, "They hooked me up to lead this thing, 'drafted' a free spirit." He bowed. "Will I win? Will I sack the Valley? Of course. I've been inside that palace. I know its weaknesses, and I'm a good commander on the ground. I led a good gang in my day. I did terrible things before then, too."

Arty just watched him, her first acquaintance with a native on Kardu. She thought he looked sad, and very honest for a man who called himself the Outlaw King. Perhaps that was the nature of outlaws in this world. The governments told lies, dealt in death and proxy fighting, but the outlaws ignored them and lived as nations unto themselves. Depending on the government available to them, maybe being "outlaw" made for the life of most integrity. She could see that Judge was a force of nature, not law. He fought for people and for himself, not causes.

"Now, I've been honest, fancy clothes, Lieutenant Sato. Arty, you said? Arty. Who in jelbete are you?"

Arty held the bottle, feeling a little courage from its bittersweet aftertaste and pungent air. "You know my name." She raised the bottle. "I am somewhere over three hundred years

old, in a manner of speaking. My ship picked a fight with a superior race over your skies before this world burned. A woman
named Ashetarai, the Mother, destroyed my ship by bending
space. I fell out into the void and flew into another universe.
Everyone I know died, their bodies trapped to float forever toward a hole in spacetime, or until that hole disappears."

Judge pulled the air with his hand, like beckoning a symphony. She couldn't tell if he understood her or just basked in
her confession. What she said to him didn't seem to matter as
long as it was true. She didn't feel the need to lie, anyway. Her
newfound strength made her too brave to lie.

"I was rescued by a machine entity. Beings of light that call
themselves Bosions."

"You were rescued by what?" Sergeant Flint started.

Judge cut him off, "Shut up. I don't understand any of this
but I want to know it."

Arty went on, "Not those Bosions. Though I met them, too.
These were weirdly benevolent. One of them, she's a consensus
of some of them and Botistems from the *Libertas*... it's confus-
ing, don't worry. I think she actually built herself as a reflection
of my unconscious mind, but...she calls herself Kami. She made
herself into a ship and brought me back here, changed and
unageing. I don't know for what purpose. I'm not sure if I have
a purpose except for wanting to make this world my home."

Judge took her hand. She let him study it. He seemed fa-
ther-like, in a way, even though they'd only just met. "What did
Captain Jameson send you here for?"

"To find an immortal man named Seth Caeso who might be
her enemy."

"Immortal like you?" Judge asked.

"Yes," said Arty.

"I've met him," said Judge.

Sergeant Flint's drink was getting the better of him. He
swayed and the end of his rifle stuck in the ground, balancing

him somewhat upright.

Judge laughed at him and dropped Arty's hand. "We'll be lucky if he remembers any of this. That's strong shine."

"We'll be luckier if he doesn't."

He sighed, smiling with his eyes at her. "Never apologize for honesty. That's what I miss most about my boy Cash."

"If you left him in the Valley, you'll meet him soon enough."

"That's a bridge I hope I haven't burned."

They sat, listening to the rain typing on the tent.

At last, Judge spoke again. "Finding this Seth should be your purpose. Not for anyone else but yourself. You may think you still serve your government, but I know an outlaw when I see one. Take it from an old one like me. A goddess like you should never be alone."

59

—.—

Mya saw Cash riding under the fanfare of music and flower petals with his officers. Returning at the bloom of spring looked good on the army. The people rained blossoms on the soldiers in a torrent of colors. The reds and browns of Cash's sweaty horse glistened in the clear sunlight. Breeze off its hooves brushed the flower petals into little flights that reminded Mya of butterflies, fluttering like the nerves in her stomach when she thought about meeting him.

Cash rode at the front of the group surrounded by his lieutenants: men and women from the Valley, the Kona Tribe, and Ashra City, each to lead their own soldiers in large companies. She recognized an older and wiry man named Jayce at his side. Of the whole parade, Cash and Jayce looked the most haggard. Cash waved at the crowd with a glare of grief in his eyes that spoke to her own, like a secret they already shared.

She stood on a raised platform with her parents and Yora. Denaiah wasn't present. Her sickness with the pregnancy had gotten the better of her. So she said, anyway. It was probably for the best. As they watched the approaching small parade of soldiers, Mya couldn't help but feel how small her family was without Ran and Tais. She wondered if she would ever see Ran again, and if their kingdoms would be friends or enemies.

As thoughts raced through her mind, Cash rode in, a captain and an idea all under a military cap, a cap that her brother had given him. She felt nervous for the moment he would notice her. The muscles in her thighs and backside clenched as she thought about her posture. Lift the chest, tighten the core.

As he drew closer, he did notice her. His eyes locked with hers for a long moment from under his cap. He stopped waving at the crowd when it happened, and it was like he met her through the blossoms, his hips and shoulders swaying with the saunter of his horse. The smile he gave the crowd dimmed the way someone might look at something they can't have. He hadn't answered her letter; maybe that was why.

You can come to me, she thought to him. *I don't know what you've seen, or what you've done, but I'll meet you where you are. You have a beautiful soul and I want to help you find it again.* There were a lot of paths to cross before Ran's obvious idea of marriage could be considered but, as far as she was concerned at this point, Cash was an ally she needed. No, that wasn't a fair way to think. She wanted to be his friend. She had so little of those in her princess world. A captain like him, a young man like him, could make such a good friend.

But it would all be so much easier if he'd bothered to write her back. Even prior to meeting him, Mya was already mad at him. If that wasn't the beginning to a Praylum relationship, she didn't know what else could be.

Off his famous horse and wearing a pleasant soldier's expression, Cash ascended the platform by way of the carpeted stairs. Mya heard her father curse under his breath as Cash drew near, but he played the part Mya had advised. With Cash's deeds having such a hold over the people, he made a better ally than rival for the moment. The king gave Cash a special spear.

Holding the spear in both hands, Cash gripped the shaft as though it held meaning. He spoke loudly to the king so others could hear, "I will use this in defense of our land, my Lord." Then he turned, and presented the gift to the crowd. Hundreds cheered. They knew what he had done with such a weapon before.

Chills ran down Mya's neck, beginning at her head and running down her spine in the antithesis of an embrace. She saw war in the hand that held the spear. Invisible and clutched in her own fingertips, she imagined a scroll.

Yora fiddled with his food at the revel to celebrate Cash. His mother's best chefs had presented their finest work, but food had a way of tasting like war. In the texture of the palate and the color of the meat he could see things he often didn't want to remember. And then, when the flavor was just right, he remembered Vonica and the way she liked to cook. She cooked as an artistic expression, a manifestation of her feelings for him. She was dead. He abandoned her and she died. Everything tasted like regret.

He got daily dispatches from the Eastern front. With the melting snow, small groups of the bright-clothed warlords had surfaced. None seemed willing to parley, but a few prisoners had divulged information. There was an army marching westward as Seth the Teacher had predicted. According to the prisoners, the army had driven them from their lands, demanding they serve the interests of the marching army or leave. Yora thought they might be herded this way as fodder for Valley guns, a way to whittle at his defenses. He needed to get scouts out there, but now he had to worry about Ran's replacement captain. Ran had picked a great time to be himself. The food tasted like a future without his brother.

"Can I sit here?" It was Cash, knocking Yora out of his thoughts.

"Has my father's table bored you?" Yora answered him.

Don't be his friend, he heard Denaiah say.

Your fate is aligned with his, he heard another. *He is not weak. I'm going crazy. I need to get back out there.*

"No," said Cash, "but I thought we should talk."

Yora looked at the younger man taking a seat across the table. Cash looked different. He was older, and had let more hair grow on his face. Not a lot, but the scruff made his features look a little more defined and less green. He stood upright and strong with the bearing of a warrior, not only an outlaw.

"I congratulate you on your success, Cash. You saved a lot of riders' lives by doing what you did."

"I did it for the men for whom it was too late."

"I know."

Cash hadn't finished his plate either. Both men played with their food in the awkward space between conversation, the one where words could be understood but not heard because they were unspoken.

Cash forced a fork full of peas into his mouth. It seemed to break the ice for him and he spoke again. "Ran wanted me to take his place all along?"

Yora made himself bite down on a yuka root, trying to show more strength. "Not until he knew who you were."

"An outlaw from Ashra City?"

"A highborn." Ran hadn't told Yora all of his plans. He suspected Ran wasn't sure about staying in Ashra City until he realized what kind of state he would leave the place in if he didn't.

"I don't really know what that is."

"No one really does. The idea of them is something of a specter, a ghost in your blood that gives you abilities and an affinity to kill. It means you're descended from the Mother."

"I wonder why Judge kept this from me."

Both men chewed the food they didn't want.

Yora pointed his table knife around the room. "Everyone knows now. Ran told me a while ago. I didn't say anything, but the papers are printing it all over the Valley. What will Captain Rivers do?"

Cash's face didn't give anything away to Yora. He stayed

cold. "I'm not more special than anyone else."

"Your history speaks otherwise. Your actions speak otherwise."

"What do you think I'm here to do?"

The buzz of noise of other conversations of the dozens in the large room didn't distract Yora from trying to stare into Cash's soul. He still wanted to like him, deep down. His father hated the idea of him, Denaiah held a complicated grudge for Cash's killing her father, but Yora had no opinion to form yet. His instinct told him to hold onto his first impression.

But Yora couldn't tell if he was looking at a destroyer or a builder. Cash's life had to be a hard one. Raised without parents by a high-minded rogue, forced to live as someone with no nation, no moral code except for the good of the gang. He grew up killing, didn't he?

The people in the hills came to Yora's mind. He saw the mangled body of his sister, the dismembered piles of dead from his retribution. He could taste the powder from the automatic. He could hear the muffled terror between the shots.

"I think you're here to judge all of us," Yora finally said.

Cash picked at the bone of a large bird, its torn wing and charred flesh. He didn't seem to want it, but he still ate it. "Ran told me the kingdom is mine if I want, that you would understand why."

Yora's thoughts went to Denaiah, to his child. "Because you're highborn?"

"Maybe," Cash said, "but I don't want what's yours. I can tell you're a good prince and a better captain. I respect you."

Yora sighed. He didn't know if it felt like relief, or just a further degree of despair. Whatever the case, he had enough to make up his mind. "With your achievements, Ran gave you what you deserve. I look forward to commanding alongside you, Captain Rivers. We'll leave soon for the wall. I don't think I'll enjoy food again till we do."

Cash tossed the bone and laughed. No one had to say what for.

Cash kept smiling. He hadn't felt like it at the king's table. The queen was stuffy, the food was too fancy, the noise too full of sounds that made him uneasy, and then there was a girl that he hadn't written back. Mya stared at him a lot. Somehow, he knew that in her wide eyes was written an invitation to talk to her, but also in those eyes were windows to parts of himself he would rather hate for now. His head and heart weren't in the right place for pleasantries. A few days, a few weeks, months, sometime soon he would have to fight again. He would have to lose again, and he wasn't sure how a wide-eyed, beautiful princess could fit into his already complicated life.

He couldn't stop thinking about her, though. Techa.

Sitting with Yora was a gamble, but Cash still felt the same kind of bond with him that he had when he met him outside the gate. Yora could be a kindred spirit, a friend if Cash were allowed to have one. However, he knew that he had to stay vigilant. Without Ran and outside of his men, Cash didn't know who to trust, even as they celebrated his success on their behalf. He held the favor of the people and the army of outsiders that would keep their wall from falling. Other than that, he was a threat to their power.

Cash smiled at the ironic taste of his food again. He'd grown a lot since passing through Shadow Pass. Now he thought in politics.

Yora knocked on the table. "Have you come to join us, little sister? Cash and I were just discussing our next moves."

Trying not to wince out loud, Cash looked up and saw her. She had her family's dark hair, though not her brothers' face, but her mother's sharp features instead. He couldn't guess her age, but she seemed younger than she was old, like him. She wore clothes of the court, worlds away and above anything Cash had ever known. If anything, she was too beautiful for him. Here she was staring at him with those eyes again. They looked at each other for moments of silence. Cash couldn't get himself to speak.

"I'll leave you both to it," Yora said, entering the frame one more time. He left his unfinished plate on the table and vanished from the nervous cloud that clung to Cash's vision.

Mya sat down, not asking permission. It was her banquet, after all. "We haven't officially met yet," she said.

"No, my lady, I suppose we haven't."

"Please just call me Mya."

"I'm sorry." He wiped his mouth with a napkin.

"For having manners?"

"No." Cash put two fingers through a pocket on the shoulder of his uniform. "I kept meaning to write you back." Huh, he hadn't meant to bring it up so quick. Well, it was done. He pulled out her letter, worn through miles of desert and mountain.

She blushed faintly through the darkness of her freckled cheekbones. "I'll forgive you, Captain."

"So easily?"

"No, not easily at all. You'll have to take me somewhere."

Cash found himself blushing now. He had enough composure to hide it, enough sun in his face to conceal it. He thought he did, at least. "What will your father say?"

A mischief surfaced as she bit her cheek and then her lip. "It's not like he would need to know about it."

Another half-smile escaped his face, but this time with a rush of excitement. This country of assertive women got better all the time. He took a large bite of bread. It was sweet.

60

—·—

"We've got something," Kami said.

"Well, what is it?" asked Arty.

"This mind reading can go both ways, you know."

Arty pulled up the results, a strange energy reading in the center of a broken city. "Let's see if it's our man."

They stole into the upper atmosphere, far from the eyes of witnesses. It was strange to fly over a people who didn't know about space travel, about all the seeds of humanity spread out over parsecs of invisible sea. What could be heard for miles, like distant thunder, was Kami's utter crushing of the sound barrier above the clouds.

Passing over a mountain range, ship and pilot descended over the wreckage of an old city. Arty thought it looked strange, like a window into what she imagined places on Earth might have looked like once abandoned. The planet was swallowing the destruction now, making ruins into soil over the course of what would take thousands of years in any other world that wasn't full of life.

"Somewhere in the universe, a defeat for everyone," Arty said. She set down in the middle of the city where the readings were the strongest, and also the place where the ruins were all but gone. A large pack of dogs ran away from her landing zone, and Kami landed in a cloud of dust and pollen.

"Not the stealthiest landing," Kami said. "So be careful, he may also sense my presence here."

Arty leapt out of the cockpit and slid down the wing. Her armor graced down the seamless plating with little sound. The ground at the bottom was soft, kept alive by the passage and life of deciduous vegetation. She hadn't gotten used to the beauty of this world yet. She didn't think she ever would.

Some of the trees, waking from winter slumber, had blossoms that emitted a strange smell. She tried to like it, but it wasn't a pretty odor. Instead, it had a kind of locker room quality to it, a bit like the gym on the *Marshall* on a crowded day when the air filters needed love. All the same, the flowers were beyond what a girl from tin cans in space could wish for in a new life. They were a joy just like everything else.

"What am I looking for?" she asked Kami, pulling out a mobile she'd been issued by the *Pantheon* quartermaster.

"You're looking for signs of a half-machine god."

"I don't know what that looks like."

"It looks like you, but male, and perhaps older. He hasn't been quickened in a while."

"The energy readings from before are gone. The strange mix of radiation that we detected has diminished. I don't think he's here anymore, if any of that was him."

"Maybe you're relying on the wrong tools."

Arty thumbed the mobile, looking at the display. "It's the only tool I have, besides you."

"Think of what's inside you."

Arty nodded to the trees. Of course. She should use her mythical light powers. Using them was always a trip, though, kind of intimate. "Okay, what do I do?"

"Connect to the life around you. That's a big part of your purpose in our partnership. You are alive in ways that I am not. You connect with the living universe in ways I cannot."

"Okay. Okay."

Arty rolled her neck, listening to the sound of the trees, the hum of insects and the trickling of streams. She found that the more she focused, the more she leaned into the abilities without trying to think of her human limits, she could process more of her surroundings. The forest was incredibly alive, scarily alive. She heard an animal rustling in the brush. The bristles on its tail scraped against the decaying leaves that mulched the forest. It was eating some kind of large nut. She could hear the shape and imagine the color.

Next she moved on to a larger animal, a bear. It foraged at a thoughtful pace, finding food in the unlikely places. The pads beneath its claws were soft, and it moved in a way that told Arty it existed in harmony with its environment. The bear belonged in this forest.

Maybe I need to look for sounds that don't keep with the rhythm and step of the other sounds.

Soon enough, she picked out the noise of heavy breathing. The sound was human. She also picked up from this source the faint tingle of kindred light, akin to what she experienced in the presence of the Mother, even more like what she had felt when she heard the sound of a commander's voice. Wait, that was it. The sleeping breathing belonged to a man. If she was right, that man was Seth Caeso.

"I've got something, Kami."

"Let me know how it goes. I'll be here when you're ready."

Arty moved through the thickness of dead undergrowth and low-hanging branches. Twice, she rolled her ankle in rodent holes but she kept moving, light on her feet for someone who lived her entire adult life in artificial gravity.

Stopping to listen to the breathing, she could hear it louder than before, more distinguishable from the sounds of nature.

She inched forward. It should be right about...she tripped and almost fell over a foot. It was armored, just like her own, but black.

Instant fear rushed through Arty, slapping her with the realization that she'd just stumbled into one of the most dangerous men in the galaxy. She took a few steps back and unholstered a rail pistol. The fat power supply of it didn't feel like much all of a sudden. She didn't feel so confident in her own powers either, powers that Kami would say didn't need a pistol.

The foot didn't move, nor did the rest of the man who belonged to it. He was lying face down on the other side of a thick coniferous tree. Arty circled him and the tree. Okay, why not? She nudged his abdomen with her foot.

He coughed.

Arty jumped and almost shot him.

He moaned, waking up. Putting his hands under him, he pushed up and she got a better look at his face. He looked older. That was strange.

"Don't move," she said stepping into his view. "I'll shoot."

Seth looked at her, his expression shifting from confused, to focused, to confused again. He muttered something that sounded like a curse. "Who are you?"

"I'm Lieutenant Sato, currently assigned to the FSV *Pantheon*."

Seth rose the rest of the way to his feet, put his hands in the air, and looked her up and down. "That's not a Federacy uniform."

She lowered the pistol a little. "This was a gift from the Mother."

"Why would she – No, let's start again. Who are you, really?"

"I'm Lieutenant Sato," she emphasized her name again, "of the FSV *Marshall*." Emotion she didn't mean to give away leaked from her voice.

Seth closed the distance to her gun in a flash, surprisingly limber from someone with the body of an upper-middle-aged man. In a moment she was standing in front of him with no gun and he was holding it. "Wow, I haven't seen something like this in a very long time." He said, twirling it like a gunfighter.

She started forward, wanting it back.

He held up a hand. "I wouldn't do that."

She came at him anyway. He stepped to the side and avoided her. Out of instinct, Arty shoved her arms toward him and light came out, blasting the old man backward through the needled limbs of the tree. Her turn for a surprise. She heard him land, but didn't find him. Seth was gone. The gun was left on the ground. She bent to pick it up.

Hands took her down. As she hit, Arty felt herself make a noise she hadn't made before, grunting an embarrassing high pitch from the force of the impact. She tucked to roll away but Seth's arms pinned her so she couldn't move.

"I don't think you're here to kill me," Seth said, "and I have questions. Leave the weapon on the ground and let's talk, officer to officer."

He waved the word officer in the air like a badge he could pull out whenever he liked. "*Officer*," she mocked, choked from his knee pressing her stomach. "Were you acting like an officer when you left us all to die?"

Seth let go, easing back into a standing position, ready for her to try anything. Arty considered it, but she couldn't see the rail pistol.

"You really are from the *Marshall*?"

"Yes. I was there when your mother tore a hole in space and everyone died."

"I'm not convinced."

"She was there, on the *Tecumseh*. I watched her touch the captain, influencing him. Then I was there when the commander fired."

Seth looked her over. "That armor is like mine."

"I already told you how I got it, bastard." She got to her feet. She was shorter than Seth. Kami hadn't made her *that* tall.

Seth held up his hands. "Tell me your story. The universe moves slower here than what we're used to. We've got time."

"So," Arty said, "we don't have as much time as you might think."

Seth took a handful of leaves and debris from the ground, then looked for any sign of the Iola. Not really Iola, the spirit he had embraced not moments before Arty came. He wanted to shout for her, beg for some sign to illuminate his path. All he saw were visions of clashing allegiances. His mother, the only being like him, and a noble galactic government he had fought for. Arty had come to haunt him.

With the Federacy, he had held back hordes of animalistic machines. He hadn't known their relation to his own people, his Mother, or about the strange, Shangri La-type place that Arty spoke of that might bring him clues to his own origins. There was too much to think about. Where was the voice of his guide, the illumination in the darkening forest? He had the sense she had pulled away. He felt sick. The whole palaver had been such a weird experience. It made sense at the time, but with a clear head it was hard to make sense of.

"Hello?" said Arty.

Oh, yeah, her. "I do remember you. I saw you that day. You impressed me. What happened to the *Marshall*, the *Tecumseh*... shouldn't have happened."

"It doesn't matter now," Arty said. "I just don't know what to do. I don't know where I belong or who I should follow. Part of me wants to blame you."

"Welcome to immortality. Everyone needs you, and all you want is a reason. To live or to die, it doesn't matter."

He stopped. A wave of pain hit his abdomen again. The pain was more frequent. He wasn't eating enough. Something malignant needed a little more energy to squash, maybe. Seth felt the color leaving his face.

Arty came closer to him, looking like she wanted to grab his shoulder. "Are you alright?"

Seth shook it off, embarrassed he'd let weakness show. "Don't let yourself be separated from your ship; you might be frightened of what you'll become without her. What's her name?" He sat on a fallen log, aware of scurrying insects he frightened when he did.

Arty folded her arms, seeming to forget his question. "Is that a good idea?" she asked. She was talking to her ship. He recognized her expression.

He interrupted the conversation he couldn't hear. "Can I see your ship?"

Arty looked at him again. "Kami was just asking to see you."

Walking to where Kami rested in a field, Arty began to let in the feelings of strange familiarity with Seth. She remembered the admiration she felt aboard the *Marshall* when they first encountered the *Libertas*. She had so many emotions associated with his face and his voice. He horrified her, yet he also seemed so beautiful. He must have experienced extreme horrors and struggle here on this world. Arty wanted to ask him why he looked older, but didn't yet feel a strong enough acquaintance.

They walked in silence until the sight of Kami amidst the trees.

Seth marveled at the ship, striking and new in his world of ruins. The gap of centuries in his memory shrank into insignificance. Seeing a child of Libertas like Kami gave him sparks of hope, hope for a coming day when he could fly home, a day like today. He tried to reach out to the ship in his mind.

"She says she came here for you on behalf of another like you," said Arty behind him. She walked to the ship, feeling the lining of the fox's jaw.

"You saw Pegassos?" Seth said. "Mother must have had a reason for sending you here."

"She didn't have to throw me."

"Theatrics." Seth waived off the complaint. "She manipulates that way. It's often more love than anything else."

Arty closed her eyes, like she was listening. "Kami has a gift for you."

Seth stepped forward, a nervous pull in his gut almost holding him back. Reaching forward, he approached Kami with a slow hand, sensing the power within her. She knew Pegassos. She knew part of him. "I accept your gift, Kami."

He placed his hand on the metallic skin of Kami's wing. A surge of power and life surged out of her almost immediately. Light enveloped him, blinding him to all but the sensation of change through every cell of his body. The process would have been painful, a billion microsurgeries and infusions of incomprehensible energy, but Kami was in his mind, calming him, assuring him, numbing away all discomfort. Somewhere in the corners of his awareness, he heard Arty's astonishment.

When it was done, Seth slumped unconscious into Kami's shadow. The gray on his temples was gone. The lines on his face and the leather of his hands were now filled with new skin, soft and young. His eyes were clear and his breathing sound. Kami had given him the gift of full strength, and the old man who had walked Kardu in mystery and sorrow was gone. Seth the Immortal had returned.

61

— · —

Mya sat near Cash. Their backs rested against a slanted rock under an ascending hillside. The moon rose above them, illuminating the curve of Cash's face. He didn't look like the fighter everyone knew him to be. His features were mellow, too kind. Everything about his appearance spoke to his youth. Yet, here next to her was a man who had won her brother a kingdom, a man who fought for her home as readily as his own. She tried not to build him up in her mind, to get to know the real him that had rode by her side through the hills and into the night, but she couldn't help but fantasize, to romanticize the legend.

"Why do you think we love the stars?" he asked after long moments of silence.

She answered him, stealing a look at his face gazing at the sky, "Would it be enough just to say that they're beautiful?"

"But why are they beautiful?" He dropped a hand to his side, keeping one behind his head, and rested it on his leg near his military hat. She felt far too aware of it.

"Maybe it's the way we long for them. The same reason we find trees and water beautiful. There's a part of us that calls to things we wish for, places where we can feel safe."

He looked at her, his eyes searching her face, lingering in a way that made her heart race. "The same probably applies to how we see people."

"What people?"

"The ones we find beautiful."

They both looked away to gaze at the stars. Mya felt Cash's hand reach for hers where she kept it waiting in her lap. She took it and laced her fingers into his. His hand didn't feel like a legend. It felt like it belonged to a boy. Just a boy.

Cash made a surprised noise, a burst of profane Joropa under his breath. She couldn't tell what was wrong.

"Cash, are you–"

"Mya, get down."

The rock above their heads shattered into splintered pieces of dust and stone showering in the sound of ricochet over their heads. Cash threw himself over her. The rock broke a few more times. She didn't know what was happening. The dim light turned into a blur.

"Cash, what is it?"

"Stay down," he said sharply. He took a knee and drew his pistol. Mya realized someone was shooting at them.

She crawled away toward the brush, not knowing where else to go. The rocks and roots were rough on her elbows and knees, but she couldn't notice. All she felt was the approaching teeth of bullets, like invisible monsters in the dark of a nightmare. She looked back to see Cash firing his two pistols into the darkness. He had dropped to his stomach, his body still except for the shots from his guns.

The enemy stopped for a moment, and Cash turned to look at her. She could see his mind calculating with calmness in the intensity. "Keep crawling," he said, and he sprang into the cover of the woods. Bullets traced the ground behind him like feet stomping over his tracks. As they bounced off the ground, the bullets sounded a bit like rocks against a water tank.

She didn't hear anything until more lights of muzzle flashes illuminated the trees. Fear paralyzed her in the brush, but she forced herself to look, to see what might be happening. She imagined evil men with bright clothes in the brush waiting to grab her, to have her as their hostage or worse. Cash would get them before they got her. She knew the legend. He wouldn't let anything happen to her. In this moment, she loved the killer.

Mya saw him as the sounds of the gunfire grew farther apart, like a drifting thunderstorm, far into the edge of the clearing. The noises ceased, and he appeared from behind a large, knotted tree dragging someone by the hair. Cash threw the man on the ground as Mya came running. Closest to him seemed like the safest place to be. The man grunted, trying to get up, but Cash thrust the hot muzzle of his pistol into his sternum and the man relented, keeping on his back. Cash knelt one knee on his crotch.

The man wheezed, quick, hyperventilating breaths. His eyes blinked out quick tears that streaked down his dirty face.

"Who sent you?" Cash said in a hushed tone.

The man started to laugh, a whimpering, gruff sound that Mya wished would stop as soon as it started.

"His clothes are from here in the Valley," Mya found herself saying. They weren't the clothes of a wild man. Not the clothes of the people who killed Tais.

Cash's eyes flicked in her direction. He winced, as if he was remembering she was there and wished that she wasn't.

"Who are you?" He turned back to the man, but picked up his knee and moved it to the man's stomach.

The man grunted, pushing at the knee but not able to move it. "No highborn will rule the High...Valley."

Cash pressed harder. Mya put her hands over her mouth, as if she could catch shock of the moment escaping her breath. Someone from her sweet Valley had tried to kill them, here, where she had always felt safe. She had never felt the need for guards, the daughter no one thought of.

"Your friends are dead," Cash said. "Your bounty is lost. Tell me who wants to kill me, and I might let you go."

"Cash, he's got a knife."

The man pulled out a small glint of silver that the moonlight barely caught. Instead of going for the knife, Cash hit the man between the eyes with the grip of the pistol. The man dropped the knife and reached for his nose. Mya watched the knife land near her feet. She picked it up. The leather on the hilt felt right. She had trained with such weapons before.

"Don't get smart," said Cash. "I'm running out of mercy. You just put someone I care about in danger. You've attacked a captain, the captain with the biggest army in the Basin. Talk." He pressed the gun into the man's clavicle.

Mya knew she would replay what he just said later.

"The king," the man said through bloody hands.

"What?" Mya and Cash said at the same time.

"The king sent us. We're part of his guard. You killed king's guards, you ignorant sack of piss."

Mya and Cash looked at each other, incredulous, horrified. The betrayal shook her.

Cash let the man get to his feet. "Why would the king turn on me?"

"I will not serve a highborn," the man started to say, preparing to rush at Cash again. "And I will certainly put down an outlaw."

An instinctive, visceral rage blazed within Mya. Knife in hand, she sprang, throwing herself down on the king's guard, thrusting the blade above his chest plate and through the skin at the base of his neck. The man took her hands into his. She felt the blood on them. Shaking, he tried to breathe, but the knife was blocking his airway. Mya pulled the knife out of his grasp and the wound was left open, air and blood gurgling from hole. Gasping, pleading without discernable words, he lowered his head and met his next life.

Mya had never killed before. She should have thought about that. She should have found another way. Cash saw her kill. Cash saw her defile herself. She started to panic, and her hands started to curl.

Cash caught her before she fainted from breathing too hard and let her down with gentle kindness. The forest started to spin as she put her head in his chest.

"My father..." she started to say.

"I know."

"What are you going to do?"

"I'm going to get you somewhere safe. I'm sorry. Mya, this isn't your fault. I'm so sorry."

62

— · —

Cash wasn't alone. He rode with a train of loyalty, spilling out behind Red's pounding hooves against the sienna road. He took 150 riders with him, enough to overpower any guard. He had already handled four of them earlier tonight. What was fifty more? As his men closed on the palace gates, the guards let them through. No shots were fired, nothing was spilt except for fear that billowed into the air like smoke out the aorta of heart filled with fury.

Dismounted, Cash ascended the steps, torches from his men illuminating the palace halls. The flickering lights were like demons pushing the shadows, forcing their way to take their due. There were more guards at the final door. They were less willing to let Cash's men through. His men subdued them with ether.

Denaiah's palace was taken. The king was Cash's prize now. He was Ezra. He was Fala. He was just another old man in the way.

Cash wondered if the old man could sleep, knowing he sent men after him while he courted the old man's daughter. Cash wondered if the king knew how much danger his goons had put her in, what the ordeal put her through. He'd find out.

The king woke with Cash's blade at his throat. Denaiah screamed, but kept to her side of the bed. He'd caught them both while they slept. The way he felt right now, he'd have entered in whatever state he might have found them in. There was no law here, only Captain Rivers.

The king babbled something, trying to call for his guards.

"No one's coming," said Cash calmly. The knife felt good where it was.

"You're a dead man," growled the king.

"Use your eyes," Cash sneered back. "I'm so very much alive."

"Then do what you came to do, swine," the king said. "It's what outlaws like you live for. It's what highborn like you were bred for."

"Who gives a shit what I am." Cash saw the blood vessels he held the knife against throbbing.

"You're a damn pestilence," the king seethed. "I know more about your heritage than you do. I know your very disposition. You are not fit to lead my armies. You're not worthy of my daughter, of my line."

"Why won't anyone leave me alone? I did not make myself the killer. It's men like you that wake the monster in me. Here I am, *Lord.*"

The king started to laugh. His movement drew drops of blood from the edge of Cash's knife. "There aren't many like you anymore. They were all hunted down in their time, gifted men and women with powerful sight and talent for battle. War is the scourge Seth brought to Kardu. You represent it. That's one of the first things the wise come to know."

"Why kill me?" Cash let up the knife a little. He heard De-naiah start to cry, small sobs into her palm. "I'm commanding your armies. I've given you everything I have."

"You've given me nothing!" the king spat at him. "You and my sons have taken everything! I even know that the thing growing inside my wife is not my own." Drool dripped into his beard, clinging in froth.

Denaiah stopped crying.

"Kill me, don't kill me," the king said. "Go win your war.

Marry my daughter. With you alive, my time is spent. I know I'm finished. Don't take me for a fool just because I am old. Your friend knew that, too. He knew he couldn't keep someone like you around. You're not someone who can be ruled."

Cash felt sweat dripping from his forehead, falling on the knife and the spoiled man underneath it.

"I wasn't going to kill you," Cash breathed. Finding a piece of the man's collar, he cut it off. The king looked at the cloth, and Cash could tell the old man saw his life in it. Finished, Cash pocketed the cloth and turned to leave.

As he reached the door, he heard a pistol slide into action behind him.

"Finish it."

It wasn't the king's voice he heard, but Denaiah's.

"Kill him," she said.

Cash turned around to see the king's second wife pointing a shaking pistol at him. The terror and madness in her eyes conveyed a language he could almost understand. Her tears streamed down to where she left them undisturbed as they fell into her bed, becoming part of the fabric.

"You killed my father," the pregnant woman said like it was an idea.

Cash didn't say anything.

"Kill my husband," she choked.

Cash adjusted his hat.

"I'll love you."

Many men Cash had met had called Denaiah the most beautiful woman in the valley. She carried an air of sensuality with her grace. Cash had met whores a bit like that. He had always felt sorry for them. Their life wasn't a fight, it was a surrender. In contrast, his life had always been a fight.

I'll love you. Her words buzzed his mind like a bottle of old shine, in spite of all his best judgment. She would just throw herself at him like that. She didn't see herself, a queen, as anything more than the woman of an old, lamented profession.

He turned his thoughts to Mya. Her smile was like an eastward dawn in front of him, full of hope. This woman's eyes held only despair. Cash didn't want despair. He wanted hope. He knew what his decision had to be as clear as that smile.

"In this house, I choose peace," he said. "Your fight is your own. I will not find fault with your decision."

"To the wall?" Jayce asked him as Cash mounted Red outside the palace.

"Yeah," Cash agreed. "I'm done with civilized people."

Denaiah trembled. She knew in her heart that she was dead.

"Now you know that I know," the king said. "Put that thing away and get some sleep. The royalty growing in the bloody walls of your treachery is still my heir."

She obliged, putting the pistol back into its place in the drawer of the table next to her bed. Her hands shook, and her spirit felt like a prisoner, a prisoner to her body and the men who used it.

She had a knife in the drawer as well. Her hands had taken hold of it without conscious decision, and brought the blade up, inspected by her eyes. She looked back. The king faced away from her. He was already starting to fall asleep.

The knife was long and slender, beautiful with jewels at the hilt. She never had a use for it before. It was too ceremonious to cut bread.

Cash should have killed him.

"I am not a wife," she whispered, and she raised herself up, aiming for the king's temple. "I am a queen."

She brought her full weight down with the blade, right as the king turned his face. Her strike met his eye. The knife pushed through. It stopped as the hilt reached his brow. The blade had bent against the other end of his skull, and she had pierced him so deeply that she couldn't draw it out.

The king's surprise held on his face. The eye behind the knife was split like an onion.

Denaiah shook, unable to look away, unable to hide. By the time the waking guard found her she was a curled-up mess on the ground. She wanted to be rescued, but no one would come for her. The vessel had lost its value.

63

"Have you seen her?" his sister asked him. Yora had just come from the palace.

"Yes," he said. "They're keeping her there. She's beside herself."

"I don't believe it." Mya was done crying, but the sadness in her eyes hadn't lifted.

Yora clenched his right fist, not sure of what part of the room he wished to put it through. "He never told me he was going after Cash. I can't believe he would have instructed those men to go after him while he was with you."

"It was the most alone they could have found him."

"I'm surprised they only sent five guns after him. He took out an entire fortress on his own."

"I try not to think about that," Mya said.

"You should," said Yora. "That kind of blood wears at a man. I should know." He thought of the bright clothes of the wild men and the carnage he wrought on them with his automatic.

"It's different, isn't it? A life taken in war, or a life taken in spite."

"War is just a lot of people fighting over someone else's spite. The people you kill are still faces you carry."

Mya let out a single sob, a quiet one, but he saw it. Yora knew she had killed a man when she was attacked. He wasn't sure if she needed to talk about it yet.

Yora paced the court of his mother's palace. It was deserted except for the two of them, brother and sister trying to make sense of their father's murder. His blood was cold from anger toward his father, but it was anger he couldn't express, that couldn't get past all the memories. There were better parts of the king, the ruler who kept the Valley safe, who gave him all he needed to be the captain at the wall.

Mya repeated herself, "I don't believe it."

"That father is dead, or that Cash is the one who killed him?"

"Cash."

"He's executed powerful men before." Yora knew more than he let on, he just wasn't sure when to show Mya the letter in his pocket. Maybe now would be best. She needed truth. They all needed truth.

Mya took out a cloth and wiped her nose. "He takes his position seriously. He told me he's found himself in service to our people. I believe him. You should see the way he wears his uniform, his hat. He won't let it out of his sight."

Yora took out the letter, a little creased from his quick ride from Denaiah's palace. It was unsealed, and he had read it. Whether an invasion of privacy or not, the letter contained truth he needed for himself.

He took Mya's hand. "You need to read this." He put the letter in her fingers next to the cloth.

She unfolded it, not seeming to care that her brother watched her. He remembered the words.

Sweet Mya, I'm sorry I have to leave like this. I'm aiming to leave for the Eastern Wall tonight. I'm afraid my company won't be safe until I fight the war for which I was commissioned. Ran trusts me to win this battle, and I don't intend to let him down. This is a fight that needs a mind like mine, one that thinks outside of conventional parameters. I was born to do this, I'm convinced of that now. Every-thing in my life has happened for a reason, and I wouldn't be any kind of man to deserve a woman like you if I didn't see this through.

It's funny how much of a soul can be poured into written words, isn't it? To say I love you in person would be hard for me outright, especially for all the sweet moments we'll have to miss, moments when love can blossom as fruit of peace, not of longing. I don't know if we'll get those moments. I'm going to fight, and fighters don't get to count their tomorrows. So, I'll say it right now, Mya. I love you.

Yora could tell Mya must have reached that part. The smile that curled up from her lips behind the cloth, and the happy tears that pooled between her eyelashes told him she returned the sentiment.

I left your father a message. I hope you'll forgive me for it, but I don't want to have to watch my back while I fight his battles. He's not the person I'm riding out there for, anyway, just his daughter and her sweet vision of peace in the land. That's a dream I could live for.

On a sour note, I'm worried about the queen Denaiah. She pulled a gun on me and told me to kill her husband. That's not the kind of person I am, despite all the blood on my hands. I could not justify killing a king that I do believe has his people's security in his heart, even with all his flaws. Just know, I guess, that there is trouble in that house, and I don't want to be a part of it. I hope to make peace with your family. I like the Praylum legacy.

Take care, and don't hesitate to write. As a frontline captain now, I've got riders to spare for personal dispatches. With love, Captain Rivers (just because I like how that sounds)

Mya seemed to lose a grip on her bearing and surroundings. She leapt, squealing like the little girl she used to be, back when the world was full of less worry. Yora smiled with her, or at least tried to. So many things that should have made him happy now hit with a bad memory. That was why he needed to have this conversation with her.

"My men gave me that message after I saw Denaiah. It's how I know she did it. I know she killed our father."

Mya stopped smiling, her cloud of bliss scattered by cold fog. She sat on a bench. The legs made a sound that echoed through the hall. She looked again at Cash's letter. "He didn't know she would kill him herself. Could she have done it?"

Yora sat next to her and looked at his callous hands. "I think anyone can kill, when driven enough. She hated father for her own reasons."

"I never understood why she married him in the first place."

"It was the option he gave her," Yora said. "He was selfish. He said she could be part of the Valley if she became his second queen, if she would bear him more children. Ran and I couldn't be enough for him as sons."

"And he couldn't abide his daughters carrying his legacy."

"He was complicated."

"That's kind," said Mya.

"His time is over."

Mya folded the letter. He could tell she was resisting reading it all over again in the middle of their conversation.

Yora put a hand on her knee. "I'm happy for you, Mya. He's a good, honest man. Perfect for an honest, good woman like you."

They listened to their thoughts in the hall for a moment. Then Mya spoke again, "Denaiah was my friend. I can only imagine how you feel, Yor."

"She was my friend, too," he said. "I betrayed father's trust for her, for myself. I was so lost, mourning my wife. I fear that in my grief I put Denaiah in a position that drove her to murder. That's something I think I'll always carry with me."

"What will you do? Mother wants you to take up the mantle and be king. You could marry her now. You both could be happy."

Yora wiped his hair from his eyes.

"No," he said.

Mya looked like she understood.

"The throne is yours," he said. "I won't sit on a throne built on framing Cash for a murder he didn't commit. It was never meant to be mine, anyway. I..." He trailed off, not sure how to say what he meant.

"You still love Vonica."

"Yes," he said, emotion cracking his voice. "I miss her more every day. The way it was when we were like you and Cash. I... I betrayed our family. I betrayed Father. I betrayed the memory of a woman I hadn't yet buried. My redemption is at the Eastern wall. I cannot be king."

The echo of his broken words hit back at him from the walls. He didn't like it, but he went on anyway, "Be the ruler the people need, Mya. I'll be your captain, your bear at the front line. If I live, I'll send for Yora II when it's time and Ran's boys, too, if they want to come. We'll live at the ranch, and I'll be the father I didn't have, the one I think my teacher intended me to be. I don't need to be king like Father or Ran. I don't need to break any more parts of me. I want to heal."

Mya shed more tears for him. They fell like notes of a song both happy and sad in light rain. "That's the bravest thing I've ever heard, Yor."

The sun brightened the hall a little more, or maybe the darkness in his head just lifted for a second. The palace looked a lot better now that he knew it wouldn't have to be his.

64

—·—

Arty had the still-unconscious Seth in the hold of her fighter. There was a surprising amount of room in there. She could have put him in the small space behind the cockpit, but he was asleep. It would have been weird. Kami had told her he needed time to put his body back together, that the regenerative process would be the most extensive and painful of his long life. She had given him light from herself and Libertas. He would be his old self again, younger. He could stay in the hold for that.

Arty wished his transformation meant more to her than it did. When he didn't wake up, she did what the Federacy soldier in her said to do. She scooped him up and planned to take him back to the *Pantheon*. As a Federacy officer, he could answer for what happened to the *Marshall*.

She wished that meant something, too. All she had now were pools of guilt, guilt for having survived, guilt for not being human anymore, guilt for kidnapping a sleeping galactic warrior, a lot of things. In her old life, she could have visited a ship's counselor, a psychologist who could break her problems into simple steps.

"Hey Kami, remember when you tried to look like a psychologist?"

"Yes, you attacked me."

"Still no regrets."

The ship broke away from the atmosphere. Faded stars appeared behind the firmament of fading blue. They looked like home, except for the now-blinding sun. She turned her ship so she wouldn't have to look at them directly.

"I have a prisoner for you," she told Captain Jameson as she saluted. The hangar was almost empty, but Arty could see wary sentries posted in the catwalks.

"So I heard." The captain shook her hand. "How'd you manage grabbing him? We've never been able to find him."

"He submitted willingly." It was a half-truth, or maybe a quarter.

"I'll make a note of that in my report."

Empty conversation took them to the AIC, the captain's command center. The equipment was newer than the *Marshall*. She had to keep getting used to that.

"Lieutenant Sato, this is Commander Re'ez."

"I had a grandmother on the *Marshall*," the middle-aged woman said, giving Arty another reason to feel strange.

"Oh, I probably knew her."

"Perhaps. She was a Marine."

"While you debrief us, Lieutenant," Jameson said with hands behind her back, "Commander Seth Caeso will be placed in the brig under special guard. If he cooperates, he may become our best asset to understanding the enemy."

"Do you mean his mother, or the people in the Basin?" Arty saw a young lieutenant working the Detections station, her old sandbox. She missed her job, gathering intel, interpreting information. She wouldn't have that kind of work here. Command would send her to the ground again...

"I need you back down there, Sato." There it was.

"Yes ma'am."

Leaving the monstrous ship where it hung in its orbit over Kardu, Arty couldn't help but wonder about how Kami never questioned her motive to take Seth back to the *Pantheon*, even after giving him the gift of youth. Questions of morality seemed to be Arty's burden in their partnership. That seemed fair, and a good reason for a machine to choose a pilot.

65

Compared to the western side, the Eastside mountains of the valley were hills. Still tall, still impassable in most places, but more forgiving when it came to finding passage through them. Spring's snow had finished melting off the peaks, and Cash had his army shoring up the wall. The wall stretched much like the gate at Shadow Pass, connecting the mountain so that all canyons had an obstacle. He was afraid it wouldn't be enough, and so were his officers. Cash, Jayce, a Kona chief, and several Ashran and Valley officers considered the wall on horseback.

Jayce, his appointed second – a pretty big promotion all things considered – agreed with him. "Ancient stone won't hold up if the enemy's bringing guns anything close to ours." He referred to the artillery.

One of Cash's new lieutenants, a stocky man named Nim, agreed, "If we post up in there, we'll be set up to fall as soon as the enemy takes the wall. If we were throwing sticks at each other, we'd be unbeatable, but we're not."

"I'd hate to knock it down, though," said Cash. "It's old and massive, a monument to people history might forget without it."

"And by our remembrance the dead live on." Lieutenant Nim was a religious man to his core.

Even though he didn't share all the man's beliefs, Cash found his earnest qualities refreshing. "Let's make it a decoy. Spread out one company of Kona men with straw dummies.

It's an old bandit trick. We can look like we're occupying the wall, but we'll hide most of our people in smaller patrols and trenches. As a fallback, we'll keep guns on this side, bottlenecking whoever comes through."

The Kona chief looked concerned beneath his pointed beard.

"Are you fine with that?" Cash asked him.

"Did you really see this enemy?"

"I've seen their light beyond the hills coming for weeks now. Months if you count the time before I left for Ashra. Yora will—"

"Then we will trust your eyes, highborn. I'll place good men at the wall. They'll light torches at night to enhance the illusion." The chief flexed a few of his huge muscles as he talked.

"Fantastic," Cash replied.

He had met a number of Kona men on his travels through the Basin. They were a different breed of person. All of them he had met were strong and loyal to their people. The catch in dealing with them was that they always expected something in return for passing through their land. Judge had spent years cultivating a rocky but mutual respect with them. Ran must have done the same. Cash's association with both helped him now. In many ways, he had a hard time imagining how anyone but a former outlaw like him could get these three armies from isolated nations to work together. In that way, Ran had been a prophet in recruiting Cash, but he liked to remind himself that everything he had now was earned through acts of valor. He would just have to keep being brave, and he could do some good with the power given to him.

They returned to headquarters. The engineers had built a compound for Cash and the senior officers on level ground in sight of the foothills. Cash and his advisors coordinated from the central building. Dispatches arrived day and night. He wondered if one would come today about his attack on the king, good or bad. He expected his men would protect him here, but he figured the ordeal wasn't over.

He arrived at his command building to find a full squad of the king's guard, different than the usual single rider delivering the mail.

"Captain Rivers."

"Captain." Cash didn't recognize any of them, but he assumed they'd all been knocked out by his men when he took over the palace.

The captain of the guard hesitated, then saluted. "Sir, I've come to inform you that the King is dead."

"He's what?" It must have been Denaiah. She did it. He didn't believe she would. "What happened?"

"We don't know," the captain complained. "When we awoke, Queen Denaiah Praylum informed us you had killed the king. We expected to be dispatched to arrest you."

"My men will vouch for me. I didn't kill anyone."

"You weren't there when we woke up, and were our immediate prime suspect. However, the new queen has instructed us to aid your effort, as penance for attacking you both."

"New queen?" Jayce spoke up behind him.

"Mya Praylum has claimed the throne."

Cash blinked.

"Wow," Jayce said. "Your lady is the most powerful woman in the world. I'll go ahead and make myself the father-in-law. When's the wedding?"

66

—·—

Denaiah wished she could see him, but Yora didn't come. She hadn't expected him to. She knew what it was to hate someone for killing family, even someone as dreadful as her father, but Yora should have come. One day, she might forgive him, but not now. He had left her to a dreadful exile.

The wagon bore her from her palace, her baths and library and sweet luxuries. The wheels under her carriage bounced her back and forth as if in mockery. *Take one last look. You're going back to where you came from, consort.* Whore.

The child inside her stirred a little. He or she would grow up away from this place. They wouldn't know the life she planned. They wouldn't grow up to inherit a throne. All of it gone for a passionate thrust of a thin blade. She would never be able to get her husband's last look of despair out of her mind, or the final peel of his eye where she had stabbed him.

The banishment wasn't all cruel, however. Ran dispatched and said her father's estate awaited her in the protection of Ashra City. She was also told that as her father's only heir, she should have it by right. He had always seemed like a kind, although wild man. She would have to pay him back with a visit.

"Don't worry, little one," she told the growing child within her womb. "Mother will always make everything alright."

67

— · —

The moment arrived. Days of digging, planning, second guessing, moving troops, drilling and keeping peace all came to a long moment of sightings. To Cash, it was like watching the tide. When the water rolls back the farthest, you know the greatest waves are coming. First had come those fleeing the approaching army. Yora and Seth had fought them. Now came the real tide, men from a world away seen in scouting groups.

Cash had no idea what to expect, but he knew everyone counted on him to pull the impossible out of his tactical mind. After all, he was famous for well-timed victories. If the hands of fate had helped him then, perhaps they would keep helping him now. Confidence was a part of command he was learning to master.

He knelt on a rug in his quarters. To most of the army, rooming by himself must have looked like a luxury, but no one knew the weight of command on young shoulders. They had passed the burden to him. Yora, Ran, even the king; no one really wanted the responsibility for the preservation of culture. Therefore, he needed time alone. He employed the silence of his room as a tool, a space for his mind to spread out and break imaginative barriers.

Judge would have meditated on a moment like this, sought out the spirit of nature for guidance. He had always told Cash he would one day have a need to find it for himself. This could be the moment. *Toss logic to the wind, Cash. Find Yurasema. Find*

Cash Rivers in the branches of the great tree.

He let his thoughts wander.

First, he thought about Mya. She always occupied the first rooms in his mind's house of thought. She was a fantasy for the child in Cash, a friend and an attraction. His dreams were wrapped in her aura. He wasn't trying to think of her now, however. He let her stay in his mind, but strived to look deeper, to clear conscious thought for outside inspiration. Judge had taught him all of this, but even Cash himself didn't know he'd been listening.

A sanctuary came to his mind, a mountain meadow that didn't belong to anyone. The meadow was clothed in rolling clouds. The clouds rolled into the sky where sunlight had broken a storm. He had thought he saw someone in the light, a woman, stretching out a hand away from everything he had known. She faded as the sun retreated behind the clouds, away from the veil of his mortal eyes. He was a boy then. That was the day Judge took him as his own, the birth of Cash as he knew himself. He didn't remember a lot from those first days, but he did remember the woman in the storm.

The door opened.

"Cash," Jayce's voice broke the meditation. "I don't know how to say this. There's a small party here, definitely not from the Valley. They're waiting at the wall on horseback, demanding to see you, specifically. They come from the direction of the approaching army, and they say they know you."

"Who?"

Judge looked a little older, and a little thinner, and Cash couldn't believe it was him. Yet, here they were, standing in a tent below the outer edge of the wall, and all of his life seemed to have come full circle. Seeing Judge and his friends at one end, with him and his captains on the other made his stomach sick, like he had found himself standing in manure. Fresh, grass-fed manure.

"It's good to see you," said Abelnora. She stood next to Judge with the twins right behind her. Cash and the woman he kissed last fall didn't greet with the embrace any other occasion like this would have warranted. On her march, she must have had time to prepare for this moment, but she didn't have to lie. It wasn't good to see her. Not here, not when he'd been content enough just to miss her, to move on from the gang that left him behind.

"Let's sit down," Cash said. He and Judge took the heads of the table in the shade of a large tent. They were on Cash's turf, but Judge and his people were in no danger. Jayce and Lieutenant Nim stood behind Cash as his advisors, each listening to Judge's story with interest and wariness.

"The winter was hard," Judge finished explaining to him. "We lost the boys. Chip and Ringer died of overexposure. Lady lost the tip of two of her fingers." He kept pleasantries open in his face, but Cash detected the anger in his voice, the strain of hardship.

"And you took in with the people you found."

"Yes," Judge said. "But they won't keep us for free. Lady's health won't last on the road anymore. So, anything I do here, in the spirit of full disclosure, is for her, for her long life."

Techa, Judge. Have you changed this much, or have I? "If these people, these 'space' people, mean so well, why would they make you fight for them?"

"Aren't your new people doing the same to you?" said Abelnora. "Would they have any need for you otherwise? Any kindness?" She still looked pretty, and still looked like she could kill with the right look.

Months of hard memory tried to erase itself in their company, his family, but Cash knew he had to hold back. Something still wasn't right. They had marched an army up to a land he'd sworn himself to defend.

"My valor," Cash said, "is a unique currency. I fight for all the Basin. No one is using me except myself."

"That's admirable, son," said Judge. "Look at you! The leader of the greatest army this side of the broken world has ever seen. Abe, didn't I tell you we'd find him here?"

Abelnora didn't say anything, but she tried to smile.

"I don't suppose, Cash, that I could persuade you to join with us?" Judge asked, an earnestness in his voice.

"You're free to cross the line, too, Judge," answered Cash. "Plenty of room for good fighters over here."

"I just need you to answer me. Because to do what I have to do, I need to know where you stand."

"I stand where I've always stood."

Abelnora left the room. She had to pass him to reach the door. He could feel her, almost reach out to her. Familiarity had dug roots hard to kill.

Cash wanted to go to her, mend some bridge that probably didn't exist anymore, but he couldn't. Mya held on to him somehow, holding fast in the grip of his own parting words. He had to let his old love go to embrace the new.

Everything about this meeting hurt.

"I understand."

The two parties were few in the tent. Judge had brought a small entourage of riders, each of varied cultural appearance. Some wore bright clothes, like the people Yora had described. Others wore clothes more similar to the Basin people, but matted, like they had crossed countless miles.

"Do you have supply lines?" Cash asked.

"We're well-supplied," Judge said. "Don't be fooled by our appearance."

"I would never make that mistake."

They both laughed uncomfortably.

Judge's face grew serious. "If you surrender, your people

will be treated well. The *Pantheon* wants us to invade your land, divide your forces, and prepare your people for its... influence, plain and simple. All cards on the table. We can't go home until their flag hangs in the king's fancy palace and Ashra City Square."

"That's a strange way for a new power to introduce itself," said Cash. "From our hills, it looks real unfriendly."

"Our duty is to the scroll and the spear of the great Mother," said Jayce at Cash's side. "We won't give up our heritage."

"That's what's at stake, isn't it?" said Judge. "Do you know about your heritage, Cash?"

Cash thought about his answer, then spoke, "I'm your son."

"He's highborn," said Lieutenant Nim.

"None of you have a problem with that?" said Judge.

No one on Cash's side of the table answered.

"I never did. I raised you right, son. I raised you away from that identity. Your parents never could have done that."

"I love you for it, Judge," said Cash. "It's too bad our loyalties couldn't be the same in the end."

"Indeed. Yurasema, let this be a fast war."

68

—·—

Yora arrived to the theater of war in the hills where he had seen his destiny, and the first thing he did was eat. Food out in the field was good. Wagons brought daily fresh ingredients, and the men were looking strong. His ride out from the Valley was long and hot, with the humidity of spring making him and his horse sweat. The light suffering made the meal even more delicious. Only a soldier could know how good any biscuit could be after a day's hard traveling.

He met Cash in the mountain trenches over the wall. They were dug out at the base with the great hills rising behind them. They were still at high ground over rolling foothills. There was a lot of dead space where the enemy couldn't be seen. Much of that area was covered by guns and artillery positioned behind and above them in natural watchtowers in the rocks.

"Your post is ready," the new, high-ranking captain told him. There wasn't much of a difference between his and Cash's ranks, but Cash had the bigger army. Yora was happy to defere to Cash. A place at the front would be fine for now. Penance.

"It's a good position," said Yora, admiring the engineering of the trench.

"I just told them where to dig, your men did the rest. Their morale is good. They want to fight with you."

"What's that hole for?" Yora pointed his foot at a hole dug into the front of the trench under slabs of wood holding up the wall.

"We don't know what kind of explosives the enemy might have," said Cash. "One of your younger riders thought of it. If someone throws in something with a fuse, you can kick it into the hole. Might save your life."

They talked more tactics, fallback points and gun positions. Yora had requested the construction of this kind of position, and Cash obliged, making sure he had the best odds of holding back the enemy he could get. The enemy would have to be fools to try and take these hills from them, assuming they didn't just leave the Valley and try to go around.

"They would have a hard time of it," said Cash. "Engineers are out there, sealing any pass they can. Judge will come here while he still has the supply lines and strong numbers he needs. He'll try to take the Valley before he moves west."

"It's a good thing you know him," said Yora.

"He'll fight like a bandit," Cash said. "All in. Let's hope I thought of everything."

That night, guns popped in the distance, deep in the darkness where Yora and his men couldn't see.

"Do you see it?" said Lieutenant Brooks. "I can't see anything."

"Brace!" Yora shouted, and the men threw themselves at the ground. The first rounds hit behind them and were answered by the Valley guns even further back. The guns talked, great cannons in conversation across the mountain. The continuous barrage lasted for what felt like a long time. Yora could taste and smell the powder in the air.

His stomach ached with the anticipation. The enemy would come soon, the air was getting hazy. He'd already felt most of the night's fear. Yora and the men had shared it, slept with it. Now he just wanted the fight, to face the waves of enemy. He craved the moment like a dog pointing to a flock of birds.

More pops resounded in the distance, this time like drumming. Yora heard the rush of wind. The rounds were coming closer.

"Brace!"

Explosions shook the ground in front of the trench. Hits behind, hits in front, the enemy was zeroing in, calibrating their guns to break Yora's line. The trench roof would have to hold.

"Brace!"

The trench held, for the most part. A few men and one woman were wounded as shrapnel and shockwaves rattled through the openings, concussions through the walls and the meat of the people inside them. Anyone holding onto the walls had the worst of injuries.

The third barrage was as exhausting as it was disorienting.

Yora shook off the shock and called out to his lieutenants, "Get me a readiness report. Who's injured, who's dead, and what's the damage. I need it now before–"

Another barrage came, but this time it was smoke. Whatever they hit them with this time, it almost completely cut off their ability to see. The smoke brought Yora's senses the true feeling of excitement now; it crawled through his skin and clung to his clenched jaw. The only reason the enemy would try to blind them like this would be to hide the fact they were almost on top of them.

"Knives! Spears!" Yora yelled. "Don't wait to run out of ammunition before you start cutting."

Then they waited, holding back for the moment that was surely coming. The smoke in the air was filthy, as was the lust in their bones. Then the enemy wave came, bizarre like an animal cascade through the line. Gunshots from entrenched Valley men burst out of the trench in succession, leading closer and closer to Yora's position. His attention was so focused on the direction of the approaching shots on his right that he almost didn't notice the wild attacker diving onto him through his opening. The forceful leap knocked him back but not down.

Yora gripped the knife in his hand and pushed it through the bare midriff of his attacker. It was a woman, bright-colored clothes, and she squealed, her own bloodlust halted before she'd made any progress for her cause. Yora took back his knife from where he had it placed and rushed to the next, a big man on top of one of his best riders. The man had a bloody mouth. Yora's rider no longer had an ear.

In an instant, Yora had tangled with five more of the foreign attackers, and the battle as he perceived it flowed in blood and haze. Time didn't speed up for him; it rather slowed down. He didn't tell his body what to do. His lifetime of training and practice worked through him, kill after kill until the dead piled the trench so high his legs couldn't find a place to stand. He slashed and fired, bit and spit, stomped his enemy with ferocity that couldn't find a match.

Rise, bearer of my mark, a cold voice breathed through the crest of the wind. *You are strong.*

The night was as desperate as it was awful, but Yora became lost to the want of comforts. The enemy warriors collapsed the roof of the trench and poured onto Yora and his remaining men. The air was thick, like the souls of the dead lingered there with them, bound to the battle as atmosphere. He felt connected to the air. It was life for him, as was the warm spring water of the valley.

At last, Yora's pistols were gone, and his rifle a splintered mess. He had taken a long-curved blade out of the pile of dead and started using it. The sword was heavy and bone-breaking. Attacker after attacker found the sharp edge tearing into flesh and nerve as they threw themselves into the riotous trench.

"These are the last of them!" Yora heard a young woman's voice cry.

He didn't know what she meant, but he kept fighting, kept slashing. Two warriors fell at the same time to his feet, one feeling his throat and the other his thigh, fainting. Yora made sure the man wouldn't get back up with a boot to the back of his head. The crunch and sink of the body woke an exhaustion in Yora and he finally sighed. He smelled blood in his breath.

"Don't faint," Yora told himself. "Stay in the moment. Fight. Last breath."

In the haze of his fatigue, Yora lost focus. His vision clouded in pulsing, edgeless shapes. Someone was crawling toward him over the bodies. The person raised a sword, or was it a club? Yora picked up his own and cut through their belly, sliding it first down their sternum until it found the right spot without a bone in the way. He slid the blade until he and the crawling corpse were face to face. Sweat stung Yora's eyes. He didn't know if it was his own.

Yora left the sword and collapsed onto his back. Regaining some focus, he saw two men retreating out of the trench. What was strange was how they actually appeared to be one person, but wearing different things. One had a long jacket, the other an interesting hat, but both had the same face, like twins. Yes, twins. The one in the long jacket had a pistol in his hand, an old kind. He turned, noticing Yora looking at him. He pointed the gun at Yora and pulled the trigger. Yora didn't flinch, expecting his world to go fully dark. But the gun didn't fire as the hammer fell. The other twin grabbed his brother's arm and led him out of the trench.

Going to see them again, Yora thought. *Kindred spirit.*

"It's over, sir." Yora awoke with a hand on his shoulder. "I'm glad you're alive."

He had passed out. His mind had shut off without warning him first. Touches of dawn ignited the hills, paving light over the shadows. The temperature was cool spring, good enough to take Yora II for a ride. He crawled to the edge of the trench, the bodies under him high enough he could see over without trying to stand. Their stink should have shocked him, but he was acclimated. Dead men and women dotted the landscape. Some of them were friendly. Most were not. The automatics had trimmed their numbers in high degree before the lucky ones climbed into the trench. There must have been thousands of them, scattered and spoiled in upturned fields.

"Get me a dispatch to Captain Rivers," Yora said to the man who woke him. "We're going to need more guns, fresh soldiers, sanitation..." He trailed off to look at all the blood on his body, pain materializing with his awareness. "If any of this is mine, I think I might need a doctor."

— · —

Part 3

Four Months After the Attack on the Eastern Wall

But these lay dead on the ground, far dearer now to the vultures than to their wives.
      —Homer

69

Seth did his best to process new surroundings. As far as he could tell, he was in space. He didn't prepare himself for returning to space.

"I should have known," he said to the plastic and metal. "This is the only way she'd have got me in here."

He disconnected the intravascular needles the Federacy technicians had stuck in him and pulled out the feeding tube. That was unpleasant. Someone had intended to keep him under for some time. Delusional. His body would wake him up when it wanted to, drugs or no drugs. The metamorphosis he underwent at Kami's hand was unexpected. For the first time in centuries, he felt surprised and renewed at the same time. Not only did his body feel young, his humor was waking up, too.

Arty must have brought him here right away. He wasn't sure if that was a betrayal or not. She traded him a prison of body for a prison of walls. He could break walls. That meant he could still thank her for the body. The old pain in his stomach, the ever-gnawing hunger of a marooned god was gone.

"Thank you, Arty, wherever you are."

He wanted a mirror.

The machines he'd been hooked up to were sounding alarms. Someone should come running soon enough. The question was what he should do about them when they came through the door.

On cue, the door slid open. Equalizing pressure from the

outside blew in his face. Recycled air. That was another sensation he hadn't had in a long while. The stale wind blew in two medical officers, an older man and a younger woman, each wearing concerned looks on their faces. Behind them, Seth noticed the feet of a security team staging outside. They were afraid of him, and he couldn't blame them. He was there when a ship about this size was torn apart without a shot, and he'd also spent the last three centuries or so in a violent world after its apocalypse, remolding that world with his violence as much as his kindness. If he were to be most honest, he would have to say that he was scared, too, not of them but of himself and his new, powerful body.

He held up two youthful hands in surrender. "I'm not here to hurt anyone," he said.

The medical officers seemed to relax a little. The man spoke first. "Commander Caeso, my name is Doctor Charles and this is Doctor Teems. We've been keeping you–"

"Sedated," Seth said.

"I was going to say alive."

Seth shook his head. "I'm awake now. Take me to your captain."

"The captain is here now."

The woman in charge, Captain Jameson of the FSV *Pantheon*, stepped through the door. Seth could hear the quiet protests of some of the security team. Another woman accompanied her. She had a lot of freckles, and was built like a tan k."Captain," Seth said, standing up. "Commander Caeso of the Echo Front reporting for duty."

"Cute," said Captain Jameson. "The Echo Front was centuries before my time." Her bleached blond hair was glued to her head like a helmet. It looked fireproof.

Seth hesitated at the sarcasm but saluted anyway. "I'm not sure what you've heard of me, ma'am, but I promise I have every intention to honor the statutes and laws of the Federacy."

"Spare us, Caeso, I've seen what's left of the *Marshall*."

Seth sat on the edge of the bed where he'd been lying, deciding to give equal regard to protocol as the captain. "Captain," he said, "I was there. Commander Worley fired on Libertas. She retreated. It was a horrific event where I was the victim as much as anyone else."

"You made it out alive."

"I made it out a monster."

"I'm not sure I want to know what you mean."

"I'm sure you don't."

"Let me show you what's happened in the months you've been... indisposed."

Months. He'd been asleep for months. The two officers took him to a small briefing room.

The war on the surface of Kardu had taken a toll on all sides. The Federacy had drafted surrounding communities under the lure of enlightenment. They had rebuilt cities on the eastern side of the continent and promised Federacy protection and membership if the people could take Seth's Valley for themselves. They'd recruited a man Seth had met once who called himself Judge, or more recently, the Outlaw King, as part of that army. He'd climbed to the top of it through some vague intrigue, possibly murder, and had Federacy personnel herding his growing army across the continent and to the Valley, his first target in the Basin. Captain Jameson supported him because he seemed like someone who'd finish the job.

"Wow," Seth said. "I miss Captain Meskin."

"He's part of a wormhole now," said the freckled woman. "With my grandmother."

Seth didn't look at her. Temporally speaking, her grandmother would be outside the wormhole, stuck, space-mummified. Wormholes made by Libertas didn't follow conventional relativistic understanding. But he shouldn't make that comment right now.

"Like it or not, we're going to tear up the roots of your precious 'Basin,'" Jameson said, bringing her face closer to him. He was much taller.

"So I'm your prisoner of war," he said to the top of her head. "This is why you kept me asleep. Why didn't you kill me?"

The two women didn't answer. "You didn't kill me. I see this flagship still has some principles. Those get a little thin on the frontier, don't they?"

"Don't mistake the stay of my hand for mercy," said Captain Jameson, "and don't mistake this ship for a prison."

"Then what are you offering me? I could end that war right now. If you let me out of here, I will." Seth pointed at a table displaying a hollow map of the mountains around his valley. Armies were depicted on them, fighting in both the East and the South.

"Stay off the planet, Commander," said Captain Jameson. "Remember the oath you swore to the Federacy. Let the fight play out on the ground, as we are, and let the better side win."

"What if my people win?"

"Then we will withdraw. The Federacy has lost too much in the pursuit of this planet already."

"And if you win, I withdraw."

"Yes, you and your mother." Captain Jameson kept her stern eyes on him, but he saw the faltering faith.

"How am I supposed to believe you? The Federacy will only send more ships. Who are we both kidding?" said Seth. "The arm of the galaxy is here. This is only going to get more complicated. Hell, I forgot how small this world is from up here."

"How do I know you won't try to break out?" said Jameson.

"The same way I know you won't put more of your own soldiers on the ground?"

"And how do you know that?"

"I really don't."

70

Arty had a horse, the most beautiful, lady-like, and loyal smoky-white horse. She spent most of her time with her now and named her Liza. The war was far away, and the country of her own upon which she played seemed much wider without it. That isn't to say the Federacy didn't come call every now and again. Here they were, in a small cargo shuttle, landing with big plumes, scorching the green of her landscape. Liza reined back and protested, so Arty dismounted and let her go. Liza thundered her hooves through the green and spit large specs of spongy dirt from out behind her iron shoes before settling in the distant pasture, flicking the flies and nerves from her legs with her hooves. Some of Judge's blacksmiths had helped her get outfitted before Arty brought her over.

The cargo shuttle powered down as four soldiers disembarked and formed a perimeter, kneeling down with their thick armor and rifles pointed outward in security. Each of them moved with aggressive posture, treating the land itself like an enemy, not the beautiful home Arty had begun to make of it over the past months.

There's no one here, you idiots, she thought.

The air grew thick with the scorched vegetation and the punch of foggy air hissing out of the hydraulic landing gear. Arty knew someone would come for her eventually. She'd made herself a protesting servant, all for good reasons. Nevertheless, as Commander Re'ez stepped off the ramp next, waving for Arty to come over, she obliged, but not without some reluctance.

"Lieutenant, you haven't been answering your comms," the commander yelled a little while the engines continued to spin down. "Because I didn't want to," Arty answered back.

They walked a short distance away, the engines calming and starting to cool.

Re'ez said, "We need you back at the front. We lost Lieutenant Flint. He was our last liaison with enough rapport with the Outlaw King."

"I told you I'm done." Arty waved her off.

"The Federacy still needs you."

"Well, maybe I don't need the Federacy."

Re'ez furrowed her brows. They were bushy and hard not to notice. "We need you, Sato. Caeso is awake."

That meant they really did need her. They couldn't keep him unconscious forever. Arty felt certain they would have tried. "So, what? Do you want me to win the war before he decides to steal a ship and finish your people off first?"

"That is a concern."

"Why don't you kill him? The Federacy seems to like killing people in this century."

"He's an officer."

"Are you sure your interest isn't scientific?"

The bushy eyebrows raised again. They wouldn't answer something that was classified outside of Arty's need to know.

Arty looked off into the sun-kissed horizon. The brightness reflected off the grass in colors of false hope. The more she got to know this place, the less she wanted to participate in anything that would defile it. The grass didn't look like it wanted war. "I can't, Commander."

"Why not?"

"Back when I was a new officer, deep in civilization's systems-wide bubble, the principles of the Federacy made sense to me. They were my traditions, and my ticket to better pursuits."

"What changed?"

"I don't believe in making other people kill for me. This may be hard to see from orbit, where men and women look like pieces on a chessboard. But I don't think these people should be fighting each other. They should be building, not tearing each other down for politics light-years away from them. I know it may seem like my abilities make me the perfect weapon, but my hands wish to build, to ride. I can't be part of your war, not now."

Re'ez handed her a mobile, ignoring Arty's concerns. "Just in case you lost the one you won't answer. Listen, I don't care what your delicate conscience might tell you. The stakes of this war are real. The *Libertas* will show up again out of whatever void she's nesting in, and when she does, she's not going to find any civilization of followers with that scroll and spear on their chests. She's going to find a Federacy-controlled world, and fleets of ships to defend it. We are doing the right thing. No matter the sacrifices. If you can't get on board with that soon, you'll be our next hunt. Do you understand what I'm telling you?"

Arty sensed every bit of herself that was stronger than this woman. "Yes, I do."

"Yes ma'am."

"Yes," Arty said again, "I do."

71

— · —

Cash saw his reflection. He didn't often get to that much before. His hat looked right, his boots, vest, gloves; he looked like a captain. He felt like a captain, too. He had to. A lot of people continued to depend on him outsmarting the world's most sly of kings: The Outlaw King. Cash laughed at the thought, one of the kinds of laughs he made when he didn't have any words.

He studied his face in the tall mirror. The eyes seemed different, tired, like all the focus had given them permanent sadness. "Don't keep score," he told his reflection. "One day, one meal at a time."

That was something he told his men. "Live like you're poor. If you've made it to the next meal, it's a victory. Celebrate by eating. Earn the food of the Valley by not dying." And of course, they knew that not dying meant fighting better than the enemy.

The enemy hadn't been real until so recently. People of the Basin had spent so long under the traditional thought that no other community had survived fallout past the end of old civilization. Of course that didn't make sense. How could anyone assume they were ever alone, ever unique? He wondered what must have given Judge that assumption when he set out east with no guidance except spiritual prompting from his imaginary tree and a few rumors. Seeing him again, seeing him as the Outlaw King was almost enough to give Cash faith. Everything lined up for this. There existed strange powers in the workings of Yurasema that wanted to see this great struggle happen.

Do they want me to win? Are they picking favorites, casting lots?

"I like when you do that," said Mya. She was behind him, sitting in his chair by his maps and reports.

"Do what?" he asked, still looking in the mirror.

"When you make that face in the mirror."

"What face?"

She got up and reached her arms around his waist, looking into the mirror from behind him. "This one." She made a smirk.

"I don't do that."

"Yes you do."

"Fine, maybe I do."

"I think you look good, too," she said.

"'Too' because I think I look good first?"

"Exactly," she laughed.

"Well, neither of us is wrong."

She punched him in the arm.

"Ayquwe."

She laughed again. Cash could tell Mya liked squeezing Joropa phrases out of him like that. He liked it, too. He was learning how to be himself around her, the part that wasn't a captain or an outlaw. Just a man who liked a woman.

"I'm afraid I've got to leave you this morning," he said.

"I'm sorry I won't be here when you get back," she replied.

They were two busy leaders. Young, but busy. He was glad they could see each other today, though. One of the perks of her being queen is he couldn't say no if she said she was coming, even if otherwise he would have thought it unsafe. The battle lines were well-defined in the mountains, not moving by anything worth measuring over the course of months, but that didn't mean enemy patrols couldn't make it through unseen passes and strike anywhere. That's why he had to go patrol himself at times, not wanting to pull too many resources from the main line.

"See you again soon," he said. "Yora should be back once his relief gets to his fort. He's making all the difference there."

"Bye." She gave him a kiss on the cheek.

He wondered what that kiss would grow into someday.

"Captain."

"What is it?" Cash was looking across waves of grass over an abandoned field. The family here had evacuated and moved deeper into the valley. Now, the field was untamed and overgrown, nature already trying to take it back into her chaotic sense of balance.

A young rider had crawled to his position where he knelt in the cover of some brush. "All teams are blue on ammo, negative casualties. They're good to go."

"Are they blue on water?"

"Yes, sir."

"Good."

Cash couldn't see the enemy well. They were trying to keep low in the grass and were walking their horses. "We'll have to assume there are more we can't see," said Jayce, kneeling nearby.

"I'm glad you're with me on this one, my friend."

Jayce was chewing on a long stalk of the grass. "I do my best work away from the sand tables."

"Same here," said Cash.

Jayce took a long breath through his nose. "They're *your* sand tables."

Cash snorted as he continued to scan the countryside. The enemy hadn't come out this far in a long time. Judge was changing tactics. There were drawn battlelines in the passes, with the great wall barring them, but most of the fighting had started happening in smaller patrols, like Judge wanted to keep the greater force behind and jab at Cash's defenses over wider spreads. This time, a prisoner had informed one of Cash's special teams that a group of unknown numbers was coming to sabotage the gate at Shadow Pass. As Cash didn't want to take too many of his people away from the main fight, the places he thought Judge would send a stronger assault, he led a small but well-armed group here to the gate to intercept.

"Looks like they're ready for a climb," said Cash.

"That's what I would do," said Jayce. "Send in a small team to strike where it's least expected."

"Let's hope they're as few as they look."

As shadows of the mountains shifted and clouds trekked like covered wagons overhead, a soft billow of seed spores from a tree distracted Cash as it flew past. It seemed to move independent of any breeze, stepping up and down as though in a mindless trance of visible music. A vision came with it, and notes from almost a year before pirouetted through Cash's mind in the form of a memory. He saw falling leaves, a strange man with discolored eyes playing a tall stringed instrument with a bow, and he felt the sorrow of a woman's first and last kiss: Abelnora's farewell.

"What's the plan, sir?" the young rider asked him, eager to return to his squad and deliver instructions.

"She's here," said Cash to himself.

"What's that, sir?"

"Nothing. Tell everyone to wait. We'll follow them to the cliffs. They'll be easier to take with their backs to a wall."

"Yes, sir."

Cash turned back to the tall grass. He couldn't see her, but something told him she was there. Though hard to believe, he couldn't ignore the strange throbbing ache of an omen in the back corners of his mind. Finding faith was starting to hurt.

72

Yora finished a meeting about sanitization of battlements in the front with a, "Thank you, gentlemen." He thought it was strange that even the battle's front had tedium and rooms where lives were numbers and casualties were statistics. They had good plans to improve conditions, however. The new fortifications would give them an edge, higher ground and a lot less exposure to carnage.

"Can I talk to you, sir?" a sergeant asked him. The man had a young face but receding hair that made his age hard to guess.

"Yes, Sergeant, what's on your mind?"

"It's Lieutenant Brooks. The doctors are saying he won't make it past tomorrow. He's got the rot."

"You want me to visit him?"

"Yes, sir."

Yora sighed. Brooks had more than proven himself at the wall and had proven to be a valuable leader. When Yora found out he had been rejected by Ran from being his second, he had expected more mistakes, but the pressures of war had forged something strong out of the boy. This was a great loss.

"Let's go," Yora said.

The hospital had grown a lot since the start of the war. The engineers kept building more rooms until a compound made more sense. Most of the staff were women, each of them skilled in all arts of medicine and sterilization. Brooks was in the largest building in the middle, the oldest and most haunted.

"My lord," exclaimed the nurse. "I'm sorry, we weren't expecting you."

"Just keep doing what you're doing," said Yora. "How is the lieutenant?"

"Brooks?"

"Yes."

"The infection's gone septic. I'm afraid there isn't anything left to do. Did you get our dispatch regarding the antibiotics?"

"They're working on it back home," said Yora. "You'll know before I do when you'll have more."

"We have to triage," said the doctor, her brown eyes stale. "Brooks is too far gone. We already took the one leg."

"I understand, just let me see him"

"This way."

Yora wanted to feel worse, to be horrified by what he saw, but the nerves meant to shock him at the sight of a poor young man's tragedy refused to fire. He knew he wouldn't process this sight until it followed him home. He would sleep and dream the emotions. They would keep him from eating, from feeling any measure of peace again. But he was here, at the bedside of a dying son of his Valley, and he could only leave the heartache for a different day. Today, Brooks needed his strength and Yora knew he could give it to him.

"Have you seen her?" Brooks said. He smelled like vomit and rotten meat.

"Seen who?" Yora asked, taking the boy's hand.

"The spirit dancing in the fields. She's in all of us. Just like the dead. Inside us. An emissary."

Yora felt the boy's forehead. He was cold, the sepsis taking him, taking his mind.

Brooks screamed and coughed. A nurse standing with a cloth in her hand began to cry. It wouldn't have been the sight of the dying that made her lose it. Maybe it was him. She was touched by Yora's visit. She had seen too much of this.

"Tell me more about her, son," said Yora.

"She has flaming red hair, shining at the tips with power like the sun. She is the water..." He trailed off. His eyes searched where there was nothing. Then he spoke again, "The water. She is flame on the hills and water of the seas. She is the trees that reach the light and those that die in the darkness. She is the balance of all of them."

Yora took a spare towel from a rack and used it to wipe tears from Brooks's eyes, and he listened. The boy reminded him of Vonica as she passed, and the peace Yora had hoped she would find.

"She asks me what I know of souls."

The sergeant stood near the door, a deep scowl on his face, watching his platoon leader whisper nonsense. Yora turned to him. The sergeant nodded with respect.

Brooks tried to sit up, but Yora and the others held him down. He babbled words that didn't make sense, and then he lay back, exhaling a faint whisper. "I don't want her to take me."

"Where does she want to take you?" asked Yora.

"I don't know," said Brooks. "But now she is a bear. She's taken the shape of a bear."

"Welcome to the wall," said the Kona Chief. His name was Arapu Sandu, and he was an intimidating man, so Yora liked him.

Yora nodded in response.

"You are not like your brother," Arapu said.

"I'm taller," said Yora.

"You think more before you speak, but he's the poet."

"Give me some time," said Yora. "I can turn a phrase."

"No," said Arapu. "Leave the sweet talk to your brother."

They ascended a spiral stairway up the backbone of the wall. The structure spanned from slope to slope. The skeleton of it was ancient, and the rest reinforced by valley engineers. Cash had wanted it to be imposing but not the main defense. The passage before it was a mess of craters, big and small, where the engineers had explosively made the roads impassable by horse or carriage. Because of the terrain, artillery only covered the wall from behind. In the case of a hasty retreat, those guns would obliterate the wall and the canyon floor around it. The enemy would get bottlenecked and torn to unrecognizable pieces. It seemed like a foolish place to attack.

Nevertheless, some of the well-armed of the enemy had carved themselves a small road just out of range and were starting to test the defenses.

"I've brought you a platoon," said Yora.

"I asked for a company."

"When we have one to spare, you'll get it."

A Kona lookout called out from above, "Chief! I see two men on foot. Twins. It must be the Hawks."

"Twins?" Yora climbed up the ladder to the lookout's perch.

There they were. The infamous Hawk brothers. As Cash had briefed everyone on the four members of his gang leading the enemy, Yora recognized them from his encounter with them at the end of the enemy's first push. One of them had pointed his empty pistol at him and pulled the trigger. Since then, Yora had seen them only a few times, and each time people died.

Reaching the perch, Yora took a telescope from the lookout and saw the twins on horseback. They were small in the lens, but unmistakable. "That's them," Yora said. "Prepare your men for imminent attack and see if any of your sharpshooters can get a hit."

"Not at this range," Arapu said. "We should save the ammunition."

Yora examined the terrain. The small craters dotting the canyon were made to stop artillery from being able to roll in. Horses would have a difficult time, as well. He looked back for the twins, but didn't see them. They vanished into the cover of twisting, knotted trees.

"It's said those men hold Old Man Death on a chain," the lookout said. "He goes where they tell him to go."

Arapu leaned on his long rifle as if it were a spear, or a walking stick. He shrugged, "Death is not unfriendly. If we meet, we meet. Greater worlds await as fruits of higher branches."

A younger Yora might have thought that was a nice thought.

To Yora, the most difficult part of this war wasn't the fighting. He hated the waiting. Suspense and boredom played inside his emotions like children fighting over a rope. "Come on," he said, the telescope to his eye. "Come out of your hiding places."

Vegetation hadn't grown too much since they cleared the field before the wall. The engineers had it burned to get rid of dead space for the automatics. No one could sneak up unless they climbed the jagged face of the mountains at either side of the wall. They waited all day watching it, Yora, Arapu, and ancient stone filled with fighting men for two twins and whomever they brought with them.

But Yora hadn't expected a tunnel.

The noise began with the automatic pop of rotating barrels. The lookout stood in front of where Yora sat in the close quarters of the perch. In an instant, the lookout's right arm and head separated from his body. Blood splattered all over the perch. Yora threw himself to the floorboards.

"Enemy fire!" he shouted.

At first no one came. Another volley of shots circled the perch and rang off the stones of the wall.

"Someone get up here!"

Yora wrestled open the trapdoor and tumbled down the ladder face-first, swinging himself off the rungs to try and land on his feet. His feet hit first but he landed hard on his rear. That was going to hurt later. He groaned and stretched the back of his pelvis as best he could.

When he was ready, he started down the stairs, hobbling a little at the stiffness in his tailbone.

Entering the next level down, Yora noticed dead men at the automatic gun positions pointing to the East. Some of the guns were damaged. Everyone was yelling, half in Joropa.

"There's a gunman downstairs," Arapu shouted at him. Yora caught up to the chief. He was holding his thigh where a bullet had grazed off a chunk of flesh. A Kona woman was trying to tie it off with a cloth, but the chief kept moving and barking orders.

"How did he get in?"

"A tunnel, how else?"

"There's automatic fire outside," Yora said.

"I know, my men spotted a nest in the cliffside. They must have dug their way up there as well."

Yora made his way downstairs, following the shots and commotion. The two gunmen had to be the twins. The attack was well-coordinated and just two shooters. He had to find the one inside the wall first. Then they could access the tunnel and seek out the other. If they didn't execute in time, the gunmen would have the entire wall distracted enough to be vulnerable to attack.

The commotion died down before Yora reached the bodies. The gunman had been thorough. The sight reminded Yora of how the scene must have looked at Cash's munitions depot. Corpses had fallen in all kinds of positions. It was very hard to believe one person could have reaped such carnage.

"Fire! There's a fire on the third floor!"

"Put it out!"

The floor and walls shook from an explosion above. The fire must have found powder. Yora kept running. He couldn't afford to get distracted from eliminating the greater threat.

He reached a trapdoor leading into a cellar underground. The gunman must have come from there. Inside, there was a fresh hole in the cobbled stones and a small trail of blood leading into the darkness. The light from the cellar door didn't reach the bottom. An uncanny odor came from inside, smelling like a bad idea.

Ashran soldiers piled outside the cellar, some of their faces visible through the trapdoor.

"Make me a torch," Yora told them. "Give me five for an assault."

Five Ashran soldiers joined him, sporting condemned faces for a gauntlet of darkness.

73

Judge looked a little older, and Arty could see the lines in the squint of his eyes more pronounced, like all the focus of leading his war had chiseled them to permanence. He was showing her his sand tables.

"This wall is where we're making our biggest push. Cash turned over the land too much for us to bring our guns there, but that's where the Hawk twins were able to extend the tunnel they found. All we need is the right breach. A good place for us to push the lines back into the Valley."

"How are your supply lines? Reinforcements?" Arty asked.

"It's going to be Fall again soon. What little I get will be cut off once the cold stops the wagons from coming," said Judge.

"You need your victory now," she said.

Judge folded his arms, staring at the models of canyons, mountains, and walls dug into the dirt. "Yes," he said. "Why don't you open this wall for me?"

"The twins can't handle it?"

"I haven't heard if they've succeeded."

Arty shook her head. "I'm an explorer, Judge. Not a warrior."

"You could be," Judge said. "You'll find your price. We all do. Every man and woman is a fighting whore waiting to be bought."

Arty changed the subject. "Who do you have out West? That's spread a little thin, isn't it?"

Judge looked to where Arty was pointing. He smiled,

"That's Abelnora. My top lieutenant. She's got the idea that she can climb the cliffs with a few small fighters. She should be getting to the gate soon. If they can take it, it would spread Cash's forces out enough to give us an advantage. We could cut off their main supply that way."

"Sounds like you might be able to win, after all. Then what?"

Judge rubbed his eyes. He looked like he never slept. His hands were coarse, hands that had traveled far and built and destroyed. "Walk with me," he said.

The camp was a mess of tents and activity, multiple languages intonating at their own rhythms and intensities. A pair of men walked past her, whispering to each other in hushed tones and glancing at her armor. They were also holding hands.

Judge took her to the commissary for a bite to eat. He stopped at the main water pump to wash his hands. Arty lit up the light within her and sanitized her skin that way.

Judge whistled. "That's a magic I don't think I'll be able to understand or get used to seeing."

"Me either," said Arty. "Some of us were just born different, I suppose."

"Here they would call you highborn."

"What does that mean?"

Judge shrugged his shoulders. "At one point it must have been a compliment. Now most see it as a curse. It's a catch-all for someone born with special abilities that come from being descended from space people. It's not an advantage. To be different is to be a danger."

"I'm not afraid of these people."

Judge laughed, "I sure am."

They got in line for the food. It was being served by Federacy cooks with hollowed-out circles in their eyes. Everyone was tired of fighting here.

"What kind of world do you see yourself building when this

is over?" said Arty.

"I'm not a builder," said Judge. "I exploit, and I take, and I do what needs to be done for those who find themselves in my protection. In the end, I wouldn't call myself good or bad, I just exist."

"You survive."

"Exactly," said Judge. "I survive. Your special space Federacy, they're the ones who want to do the building. They just want to do it without that evil space lady out there – what was her name?"

"Ashetarai, but most just call her the Mother. I've met her."

"You've met her," exclaimed Judge. "You've seen the imperfect face of God herself. Tell me, was she a *woman*?"

"How do you mean?"

"Never mind."

They got food from the camp's cooks. One of them gave her a look that gave more a vibe of disgust than curiosity. The food he scooped onto her wide, wooden bowl was a hash of roots and wild vegetables that Arty was unfamiliar with. She only nibbled at her meal as they sat at a table at the end of the open-air commissary and the flies buzzed in her ears.

"There's one thing I haven't understood," said Arty, "and you tell me that you're honest, so I expect a real answer. The Federacy sent you here to fight for them in exchange for refuge for your loved ones, but how did you end up in charge of the army? How are you, a latecomer, the Outlaw King?"

Judge sloshed the hash around with his spoon, then took a big bite. He chewed on it for a moment, not showing pleasure or aversion to its contents. He stared off into the distance, and then answered her question. "The same way anyone acquires an army of followers."

"What's that?"

"I killed the right man."

"Somehow that doesn't surprise me."

"Why?"

"How else does a man get a name like Judge?"

"Excuses never amount to the price of taking a person's life. That's the tragedy of our lives in this world of ours. But the original commander of this army was especially cruel. He was a space man, no real claim to this fight. Somehow, he seemed to believe that anything he did was justified. He cited our blood as the price of civilization. Naturally, the army was in disarray when I got to it. Many of the wildest of the bunch had left, gone ahead to run away from him, take a piece of the Valley for themselves. Turns out most of those who ran ahead were killed by someone the survivors called Lipande Olon."

"I don't know what that means," said Arty.

"Bright eyes," said Judge. "It's an old legend, a monster to imagine in the dark corners of the wilderness."

Arty fought to keep her mouth from gaping. Bright Eyes must have been Seth.

"Your space prince killed thousands of people," said Judge.

"Justified by the price of civilization," Arty quoted.

"Yes. You would think the great tree of the universe would be too big for people to fight over a speck of dirt. But the powers must play their game. Those of us with a life-stake in it have to play."

"Aren't you here, spilling blood to pay for your version of civilization?"

Judge took another big bite. He spoke with his mouth half-full but didn't spit anything. "That's astute. And yes, I killed that commander from space, representative of the *Panth eon*... because I believed I could do a better job. Captain Jameson agreed with me. I sympathize with this people, and once I've finished my violence, I can go home to my lady."

"You'll have earned your civilized life."

"For someone."

Arty stood up, leaving her food with a young woman with

her arm in a sling. "I'll be sure to pass along your report to the captain of the *Pantheon*."

"Just one more thing," said Judge.

Arty waited for him to slurp down the last of his meal. Some of it slipped out and clung to his short beard. He wiped it carefully. "Tell her that if these last endeavors don't work, I'm out of resources. If she wants the Basin, she'll have to come get it herself and use some of her big guns she supposedly has up there."

Arty turned, making her way back to Kami, sitting alone in the waving grass.

"Will you let the Federacy aid his army?" the ship asked.

"More than they already have? I don't know," said Arty.

"The *Pantheon* would destroy this place. How much of this world do you think they're willing to burn to get what they want?"

Arty felt sick at the thought. "I want to talk to Seth."

74

Seth ran his finger along the complex polymer of the wall of his cell. He could feel energy in it, a shielding bond that made the material even stronger. For added measure, there was also an energy barrier warbling at the door. There was a physical door, and a shield. They really didn't want him to break out if he got bored.

Too late, he was bored.

The ship turned beneath him. A glass of water on the thick, plastic, bolted-down table shifted. To his perspective, the glass didn't move, but the surface of the water tilted like a saucer, elongating its plane. It moved because inertial dampening of artificial gravity couldn't completely compensate for a mega flagship like the *Pantheon* changing course. He wondered if they were leaving orbit for some reason. Someone on the ground might notice if they did. One of the many satellites still orbiting the planet from a bygone, short-lived space age would change its course like a moving star might if it were alive. It was strange to think that this ship and others had been in the sky for much of the time he was stuck on the planet. They never came to rescue him. That was their first bad move.

He tested the polymer in his fingers. Yes, it would break if he applied enough force, but it still might take him a while. Seth would play the captain's game for now. Escaping would mean killing a lot of good people. Inside, he hoped his new body could be a sort of baptism, a sort of fresh start. Old Man Seth killed large multitudes. Perhaps he could leave the blood of the past in the clearing where the old man went away. An immortal's curse was to live long enough to see himself become a monster: Lipande Olon.

In a way, though, long life was also a blessing. Seth had a lot of time to run away from the deep haunt of memory. In a sense, he could live the redemption of Dorian Gray, never having to catch a full glimpse of his painting because he had the ability to throw it away.

At least Seth hoped he could. For now, he felt the walls of an energized polymer cell in the prison of his own pulsating conscience, the only thing protecting this ship from a one-man judgment. Conscience was a fire that could turn outward, however, if the Federacy kept provoking him.

The ship moved again, this time a faster turn, more than a course correction. Something had to be happening outside.

He turned away from the wall and looked into a mirror he had requested. Having his young face back had given him something of a Narcissus complex. Not that he was in love with himself, he just couldn't believe he had undergone such miraculous change. Okay, he was a little in love with himself and the miracle that changed him.

A blue glimmer caught his attention. It was like a tiny flame within his eye, blue. He wiped his eye with the back of his hand, thinking he might have imagined it. What was that?

It was still there. He had only seen that kind of flame from the Spirit of Kardu, a voice that he thought had left him. It was the same that lit the trees and had enveloped him. It had something, everything, to do with her.

"Spirit of Kardu, are you still with me?"

75

—·—

"We'll wait until they're hooked in," Cash had told his squad. "I'm not sure if they'll be abandoning their horses or if they've assigned someone to take the long trip around again and take them back."

"I'd bet on that," said Jayce, squinting his canyon eyes in the sunlight. "Horses aren't something you can steadily supply, like food."

The plan was set, the teams in place; now Cash just had to make sure nothing messed up capturing the enemy squad alive. If she was here, as he expected, Cash wanted to take Abelnora prisoner. There were at least three females in the group of climbers, but he couldn't tell if she was one of them.

"Are you ready for this, Cash?" Jayce asked him. They were prone on a riverbank. The river was low, at the end of summer season, and they had room to conceal themselves. The river covered their sounds as well.

The enemy was in front of them, tiny individuals sorting ropes and rigging harnesses for the ascent. Their plan seemed to be to take Shadow Pass by surprise from above. It didn't seem like a great plan, but it might work. The few guards left at the Pass weren't looking up, and there weren't many there. The assaults to the east took all of Cash's manpower. The longer the war drew on, the more ground a single unit had to cover.

But Jayce was talking about Abelnora.

"Yes," Cash said. "I'm committed to our fight. My old gang

chose their allegiance. I've chosen mine."

"Tell me why you side with us," Jayce said.

"I've told you before."

"Tell me again, one more time."

Cash counted the clips of rounds on his vest while he thought about his answer. Then he said, "I imagine a better world. A world with large buildings that pierce the skyline. Of boundless supplies and energy. Judge would think it's a foolish idea, that people will always kill each other before they cooperate, that the achievements of our ancestors could never happen again."

"I'm inclined to agree. I've seen more evil than good in people," said Jayce.

Cash continued, "The price of this war we're fighting now has to buy us something. Think of what we've won. Ran leads Ashra City. Mya leads the High Valley. They are two fundamentally good people who want to see progress. Arapu Sandu, he's good people, too. With all of these working together, we can root out the bad in our land. We can become a great civilization."

Jayce half-smiled at the thought and then shook his head. "That's why we have young commanders," he said. "You can see the bright future that I can't. Call it the astigmatism of wisdom."

"Oh, that's good. I like that. But, to answer your question," said Cash, loading a whistling dart into his rifle, "I'm here because we're going to win. Each of us is a piece of the artist's hand sketching the portrait of a peaceful era. Who wouldn't I kill before they crossed the line of our foundation?"

Cash fired the dart. It whistled in the air to signal his men. They rode in like thunder on a storm, capturing the climbers with ease.

Abelnora wasn't there. Cash wasn't surprised, but his hunch, the feeling, had been that she would. His nerves could

have been to blame. He grew more nervous about a confronta-
tion with her as the months trailed on. At one time, not even
that long ago, she was his best friend. Cash, Judge, Abelnora
and company against the world. He didn't feel as apprehensive
about facing the Hawk twins, however. They were the bandit
half of the gang, the dark, violent side of his past.

His men ordered the prisoners to give up their arms before
they ascended the cliff further. They climbed down in surrender. Most spoke some dialect or another of Joropa. One had
panicked and gone to draw his pistol. He was still hanging from
the cliff, blood dripping from his boots. No one had yet seen
a need to cut him down, as high as he was. He hung with his
mouth open to the flies.

"How many are there?" Cash asked.

"I count twenty, him included," one of his team leaders said,
pointing at the hanging dead man with his lips.

"That's a round number, think we got them all?" said Jayce.

One of the riders grabbed the face of a climber, squishing
the man's lips together. The rider demanded of him in Joropa,
"How many of you were there?"

The man didn't answer. But he smiled, his lips working
their way out of his captor's fingers.

Cash didn't like the man's confidence. He must have missed
something. One rider from each of his teams was pulling security at half right angles. Visibility wasn't great at this spot,
though. The enemy horses were gone, too. Cash never had a full
count of the enemy. That was his mistake.

"Techa," he murmured.

"Enemy on my left!"

"Enemy on my right!" Both of his security were screaming,
opening fire.

"Hit the dirt!" Jayce cried.

Automatic rounds rang off the stone of the cliff in odd tones,
and two of Mokoi team's men dropped before they could react.

The prisoners dropped to the ground as well, each of them with hands tied behind their backs. All of them had been disarmed, but there were twenty of them. Cash's people were exposed on all sides, included within their circle.

The automatic rounds were relentless. None of the Valley soldiers could lift their heads to see.

"Return fire!" Cash yelled through the commotion. "Full ahead. Meet them with a wall of lead or I'll shoot you myself."

His men fired into the trees and brush. The automatic backed off.

"Petei team, with me to right flank at the river. Mokoi, keep up the fire but talk your guns. Shift fire at my flare. Jayce, stay here."

"You got it, boss."

Several of the prisoners tried to get up to run. Cash didn't want them to add to the enemy. He shot them as they bolted. They fell, faces sliding in the prickling sage.

He and the team ran for the river. Two of them fell before they got there. He had three soldiers left to assault an unknown threat. There could be several waiting for them. There could be a hundred. All he could do was attack and meet them head-on. Bullets kicked up dirt around the revolution of his legs against the ground. The riverbank and the cover it provided were near. He just had to keep running.

Someone moved to his left. He fired with his left hand. A pained cry echoed back from his shot.

He threw himself down the bank and turned to see if anyone had made it with him. One soldier tumbled down after but was holding the small of his back. Blood seeped out from between his fingers. Spinal.

Cash, the commander of armies, would have to assault alone.

Taking a moment to catch his breath, he took the flare and shot it into the air. Orange smoke trailed after it from a fine powder. The bullets from Jayce's team kept firing, but if they did their job they would have shifted away from where Cash would run.

Leaping out of the bank, he fired five quick shots from his repeater into the cover of trees, where he could see some of the exposed backs of the enemy. He imagined that each one hit a mark, but he couldn't be sure because he'd already hit the ground himself. The longer he stayed upright, the more likely it was he'd get shot.

Getting back up again, Cash took another few bounding steps, firing each time, then he dove back into a prone position. This time he took a rock right to his groin, but he was too focused to care, too battle driven. He rolled onto his back and loaded another extended clip. The taste of the dust and the spent powder was in his mouth and the smoke burned his lungs. Getting up, he kept firing, kept diving, kept reloading, until he reached the enemy's position where they had turned toward him. There were more barrels than he could count.

They were going to kill him. Without time to go prone again, he just started pulling the trigger, lighting into as many as he could identify in the space between pulls.

"Cash, Cash, cease fire!" he heard Jayce yell. It was faint against the sound of the rounds leaving his gun and the whiz of those in the air around his face, but he stopped right as Jayce and his men swept through the enemy position in front of him. They took care of the rest, some firing from the rounds they had left, others using either their rifles as clubs or the knives from their vests.

The afternoon traded the sounds of battle for the cries of the dying. The remainder of the soldiers pulled security while Jayce and Cash made sure all who should have been incapacitated weren't feigning injury before another strike. They took the weapons from each of the bodies, taking note of injuries as they made their way.

"Take inventory of your men," Jayce told the one remaining team leader. "Both teams."

"Yes, sir."

Old branches cracked under Cash's feet as he surveyed the aftermath. He realized he should check himself for injuries. There were grazing tears in the leather of his vest in the front and back. He'd come very close to dying. His armor had done its job, and he hadn't taken anything head on.

"Cash," a small, choked murmur came from somewhere. "Cash."

He tried to figure out who it was. It sounded like a woman.

"Cash, I'm... I'm down here." Coughing.

Techa fio.

He found her lying on her back, blood and dirt soaking her clothes in the shade of the trees.

"Abe," he said, panic and horror plucking his throat and stomach. He lowered himself to her, instinctively searching for the source of the blood, somewhere to put pressure. "No, Abe."

"What a game we're playing, huh?" she said, shaking.

Jayce called for him from a few trees away, "Cash, are you alright?"

"It's Abe. It's...she's...get the medic."

Jayce and the squad's medic knelt beside them. Another soldier tried to see what they were doing.

"Stay on security!" Jayce shouted at him.

Cash couldn't stop the tears from reaching his eyes. They sprang out of a well he'd been keeping in the crevasse of his soul, cut off by damn ambition. Beautiful Abelnora, the girl who looked after everyone, the girl who loved bioco and had teased him since they were little. She was the girl he first loved and never told. She was here, and she was dying. He took her in his arms. She could hardly hold herself, each piece of her heavy and limp, and wet. Fresh, warm snot strung on his lips as he failed to swallow the quiet sound of his sorrow.

"Cash," she said again, her voice faltering.

He heard himself shake, muttering more words in Joropa than he had said at once in a very long time. *Don't go like this.* "I'm here, Abe. You're gonna be okay."

"I can't do anything," the medic said. "There are multiple entry wounds. Her liver is punctured, and her stomach, too, large-scale organ damage. I'm sorry, but this is it. I'll leave you alone."

Jayce put his hand on Cash's head and left him to mourn.

Abelnora swallowed, her own tears beginning to flow, though there was a strange peace about her, an aura he could feel, like more than just Cash were keeping her company.

"I wish I'd stayed with you," she said. "I thought about... I should... miss..."

"I'll stay with you now." He stroked her hair from her face and pulled her close, holding her. She felt like a piece of himself he'd just found again, like a memory of spring runoff. She was a river of peace to him, always in the back of his thoughts. With her there, as incredulity marred his place in the shade of trees, war and his part in it vanished in the space of a feeling. Yurasema had turned herself back for him. He was a little boy holding his friend.

"Father of all living," he said in his people's tongue. "Take this woman into the boughs of your song. Forgive us all who make war." His father had said something like that once. He couldn't be sure where.

The shadows grew as the sun moved and one of the moons rose overhead. Jayce came back, his feet breaking old leaves on the battle-stained country. "We've got the dead taken care of. It didn't take long. We're moving out. Red will stay with you. Find us when you can. Your people will keep the fight going. The princess... the queen..." he started to say. Cash didn't turn to him, but he knew his second well enough to know when he was scuffling with battle's wear, when tears were all a man had to give, but his pride stood ground. "You're the best man I know, Cash. Fuck it. You'll know what to do."

"Hey," Cash said, when all the soldiers were gone, though the stench of death still clung to the field.

Abelnora didn't answer. The color was fading from her face. Her eyes focused on horizons that weren't for Cash to know. The last light of her aura dispersed. It didn't fade. He couldn't believe her essence could be gone from the world, not when she'd become the wedge in his heart. He'd killed her, hadn't he? Or had Judge? He would say that she knew where her own feet took her. She had followed her path in the way of the universe, her branch in the great tree.

Damn you for bringing her back here, old man.

But this moment shouldn't be about him. Cash kissed Abelnora's lips, catching whatever might have been left of her last breath gracing the air of her beautiful world.

He took her to the river. From his saddlebags on Red's back, he drew a small shovel. Abelnora's cold vessel rested on his bedroll while he dug into the bank. She really did look at peace. Her troubles had ended with the rush of lead and the tumult of Cash's dark crusade, but she wasn't an outlaw anymore. She wasn't a mercenary for forces of war anymore. He'd dedicate this place to her. This was her river. As he reshaped the world, no one would drink from these waters again without a piece of Abelnora.

When he finished, he placed her in the ground, at peace beneath the roots of trees and rustling brush, giving the beauty of her hallowed corpse to the valley waters. Covering her with stones, he whispered to the river who she would become.

"Abe, I'll make this worth it. I'll kill him. I promise."

76

—.—

Yora crouched at the rear of the small six-man column down the dark tunnel. There was no light except for his torch and another from the man leading on point. The problem with using the torch was the twins would see them coming. The problem with not using the torch was they would have no way to see.

The walls of the tunnel reminded him of the ancient walls of the palace, the passages where warm waters had flowed for hundreds, if not thousands, of years. The enemy must have uncovered the tunnels and dug them out, using the old reinforcement for support. With enough labor it wouldn't have taken them much time to make it work. He wondered why they only sent two men this way. Just one of them in the wall caused enough of a massacre. Maybe one Hawk is all the sky would need for the birds and mice to scatter.

The tunnel smelled like a mix of urine and rotten eggs.

"Techa fio, that's awful," said one of the Ashran soldiers. The sound of his whisper echoed off the walls. Another soldier put a hand on his back and a finger in front of his lips.

"Stay focused," Yora whispered, wanting to gag. The smoke from the torch made the smell a little better, but not much.

The tunnel ended at an old concrete shelf. Above it was a rusted metal trapdoor, left open.

One of the soldiers, a small and stocky man a little older than the rest pointed at the hinges. The door had been ripped off of them. Yora signaled to all of them that he would go first and passed the torch to the stocky soldier. Taking his pistol in one hand, he climbed the shelf and raised himself through the door, sliding on the front of his vest. He kept his eyes and head pointing into the darkness ahead as the five climbed up and took position around him. They elected to kneel.

Just then, gunfire broke loose. Yora heard groans and shouts from his men and he opened fire in the direction of the muzzle flashes. They were close. He emptied his clip into the darkness, seeing in the flash the outline of a large man crouched around a corner. He couldn't tell if he hit him, or if the shape was one of the twins.

Yora scrambled for a different position and looked behind him. The torch illuminated the dead and torn face of the stocky soldier. Someone was moaning. He didn't have time to help, he had to finish the fight first.

More shots hit the walls and thumped into already dying bodies. Yora answered back with a few of his own. The noise was deafening to the point of hurting his ears. He coughed as some of the dust tried to make its way into his lungs.

"Eimos, I'm out!" said the gunman.

He heard some indeterminable shouting from far away. The twin on the gun on the hillside must have been Eimos, and this one Teeg. Cash said they were almost impossible to tell apart. Maybe it didn't matter which name belonged to either one. Yora just knew he had to kill both of them or take at least one prisoner. He felt half certain they'd been gunning for him for a long time, ever since he repelled their first assault.

Suddenly a hand was at his throat, lifting him off the ground just above where his knees would scrape the rocks. It was Teeg. He had a wild look in his eye behind curly hair that tumbled down his forehead. An outlaw-style hat with a bloody handprint on the brim clung to the side of his sweat-grimed face. The dying light of the torch made him look like a kind of ghost with yellow teeth.

Yora dropped his gun on the floor as his hands reacted to the loss of air.

"Found you," said Teeg.

Yora choked in response, a gagging, desperate sound. One hand flailed around his vest while the other tried to ease the iron pressure of the blood-raged man's grip. His eyes bulged from the pressure. He hadn't fainted, though, so he knew he had time.

His hands found the knife and he slashed at Teeg's torso. The big man screamed and dropped Yora to his knees. Yora took the knife to the man's legs next, but Teeg threw himself on top of him in a sprawl. They tossed around, wrestling for the knife in Yora's hand. He cut Teeg again and again – once on the back of the hand, many times on the forearm. Teeg bit at Yora's neck as they rolled into the torch. It fell through the trapdoor. All was darkness.

Without being able to see, Yora felt Teeg tire. He had already been wounded before the fight. There had been a bloody trail leading into the tunnel in the first place. There was a second twin somewhere, though. Yora tightened his grip on the knife.

Teeg had him from behind, both of them on the ground and Yora on top. Teeg's legs were wrapped around Yora's waist. If he could twist just right, he'd have room to finish with the weapon. He took a deep breath and thrust his right leg under his left, twisting himself inside Teeg's grip to face him. He pressed up on his legs, pushing his back end into the air to make room with his arm. Then he plunged the knife into Teeg's belly, once, twice, three times.

Teeg groaned and then went limp. He wouldn't fight ever again.

Yora felt the bite on his neck with his hand. There was warm blood, but nothing to worry about for now. He found the torch still burning on the shelf.

"That was Teeg," he said out loud. "Let's see about Eimos

and his big automatic."

Wait a second, Yora realized as he started up the tunnel. They were brothers. He wouldn't have to go looking for the other. He could find him here, at Teeg's body. Eimos wouldn't know where the body was, though. All he heard was Teeg yell that he was out of ammo. Yora could set a trap for him when he came looking.

"Are any of you still breathing?" Yora asked.

None of the Ashran soldiers responded. Passing the torch over their faces, he could tell they were dead. There were only four bodies, though; one must have run back to the wall.

"Can't blame you," he said.

Teeg's body was heavy. Yora dragged it to the middle of the tunnel and turned it facedown next to the torch. At last, in much-needed rest, he lay himself near the shell of Teeg in the mess of other bodies and pretended not to breathe.

"Teeg," a familiar-sounding voice whispered. "Teeg."

Eimos felt his way on a string on the wall. Yora took note to remember it was there because the torch was dying.

"Teeg, where are you?"

The last of the twins crept into the light. Seeing his brother lying on the ground, he rushed to his side.

"No, no, no, no," he said amidst a smoke plume of ancient curses. "No!" Eimos screamed, picking up the torch. He started toward Yora and the other bodies, then softened and went back to his brother.

Yora waited, close enough to smell him.

Eimos lifted Teeg to turn him over. The body rolled and Eimos whimpered under the weight. Yora sprang to a sitting position and fired ten shots into his back without stopping.

Slumping forward, Eimos grunted and flopped, reaching for his pistol. Yora got up and fired two more times with a different pistol, hitting Eimos in the chest. The dying outlaw wheezed and raged, blood seeping from the corners of his mouth.

"Sweet mother in the sky, how much can you take?" Yora was on his feet now, his pistol aimed between Eimos's eyes.

Eimos fired at Yora with a surprise twitch of the wrist near his waist. The bullet hit the buckle on Yora's thigh holster. The holster fell loose and hung off his leg as Yora blasted one good shot into the man's brain. The outlaw's back arched as if he would get up again, but then his body gave up, all synapses done firing, and he died in the stench of bloody filth and horrid old cave.

The torch, as if in harmony with the end of a saga, went out, and Yora could no longer see.

He found the string. He had searched what he thought was the right wall for a long time but had to move on to another one on his hands and knees to find it. He didn't know the twins well enough to call them smart, but at least they weren't stupid. This string might save his life once he completed his mission.

The string led him up old staircases and ladders into the mountain. Much of the passage looked like old caves dug out for a different purpose. He wondered what the ancients must have used it for. The ladders were new, but the structure was old. The rock formations inside the cave must have been beautiful for someone with a light. For now, Yora couldn't see a thing, and it made his skin crawl. Imaginary, disfigured corpses of the twins seemed to be reaching for his legs like monsters that would scare Yora II from under his bed at night.

After a long climb along the string, Yora found he could see a little. The light grew into full visibility of the brown and black rocks around the ladder. When he reached the top, he laughed despite the sound of gunshots and mayhem coming from the end of the upper tunnel. At the scene of the sound, he found slits in the wall of the mountain leading outside and two automatic guns loaded with belt feeds.

Through the window, hordes of enemy soldiers were attacking the wall. It was a massacre of Arapu and his men.

Yora fumbled for the automatics. They seemed to work the same as guns from the Basin, but the safeties and levers were different. He pulled the trigger at the first gun and it jammed. Finding a lever that must have been the rack, he cranked it a few times to clear the rounds from the chamber and feed the belt. It worked. He pulled the trigger again. Nothing.

The friendly automatics on the wall weren't firing. The enemy was filling the ditch and working out new ways to get more of them over the wall. There were so few shots coming from the friendly side that Yora didn't know if his people were leaving it behind or if not enough of them had ammunition. They might be all dead. He continued working on both the guns.

Finally, he got the first one to work. He shot into the enemy's rear flank as they climbed the wall. As long as he had the rounds, he wouldn't let them through. He grinded the gears of death's belt-fed factory as bodies fell into piles of carnage. The panic and fear in his heart poured into the mechanism of his weapon. When the barrels melted and the pins wouldn't strike, he moved to the next and served down again his passionate defense.

He shouted no words, but dished the retribution of a prince's vengeance behind the shouts of the enemy's gun used against them.

Some of them tried to scale the cliff but failed, but soon enough the last gun went dry anyway and Yora had nothing but his pistols and cartridges he took from the dead Ashran soldiers. As he thought about using them, even at this range, distant sounds of Valley artillery stopped him.

The shells from the cannons hit the great wall. It crashed down in giant blocks of rubble onto the rushing enemy, dozens of them wailing as they were crushed by debris and the stampede of the crowd.

The mountain shook above Yora and stones poured down the cliff face like flour from a shaken spoon. In just seconds the rocks covered his opening and sucked away his light. He scrambled back to avoid further collapse. Darkness closed in on him like it was alive. The friendly guns hadn't just shelled the wall, they'd brought down part of the mountain. He was in that mountain.

Exhausted and in the agony of a war-drenched soul, he felt desperately for the string but couldn't find it.

The panic of that moment hit him with the most horrifying revelation since he survived getting mauled by a bear. In spite of all thoughts to the contrary over the months and years spent in the sweat of his life's problems, now, in the dark, entombed within the Eastern mountains that had once called for his soul, Yora had no wish to die.

77

The light was low in Mya's court. Of all the things to have a shortage of, candles were in a top list of inconvenient. All manufacturing was spent on the war effort. Guns, ammunition, clothing, food, whatever they might need – even candles for Cash and the other commanders for late-night planning. She limited herself to one, and she used it for emergencies.

This was an emergency.

Ran, she wrote, *I don't need to tell you as a sister how your absence has affected our family. We are broken. Mother won't come out of her suite, Father is in a tomb, and Yora seems to place himself in every engagement. What's more, with Father's murder at the hand of Denaiah, I feel like I've lost another sister. Now I'm Queen and I'm barely holding the Valley together. Our supplies are stretched ever so thin.*

Where are you?

Where is my brother who won himself his own kingdom? I need you now. Yora has gone missing and I'm afraid he perished beneath the East wall. The men had to knock it down. Cash hasn't returned either and I fear the worst for him. Come back, Ran, help us finish this fight.

Don't just shut yourself away in your own kingdom. Now is not the time to be like Father....

She paused before penning more words. These would cut deep, she was sure. Ran never wanted to be anything like his father, to the point where he went out of his way to not inherit anything from him. He would come to himself after reading those words. The Valley didn't just need his supplies, or his reinforcements. The people needed him. One more hero to rally victory out of the long summer.

She heard a sound in the echoes of the walls around her, someone shutting the large double doors into her empty court.

"Is it time?" she asked the captain.

"Yes, my lady," he replied.

We are abandoning the palace today. Find us in the fields defending what is still your home. I have faith in you, brother, in all of us. We can win this fight. We can expel the invaders and welcome an era of prosperity. You've given us supply and manpower. Be man enough to give us your strength, or your new country is surely next.

She would have written "an era of peace," but she believed Ran would understand "prosperity" a little better. "Have this sent to Ran. Tell your riders to push their horses to death if they have to."

"I'll see it done."

"Mother," Mya said, placing a hand on her mother's shoulder from behind.

The older woman sat facing the arched window of many glass panes. The hand-crafted glass distorted the view a little but brought in light breaking through a sky full of light rain. The rain brushed the window. Her mother had always loved the rain.

"My sweetest daughter," the old queen said. She took Mya's hand in her own, reaching up without taking her eyes off the raindrops.

They looked at them, pattering at the window and the garden trees, until Mya could feel the tension from the soldiers in the hall. "It's time to go now," she said.

"I know."

The soldiers rushed them to closed-topped carriages outside, where all the staff of the court and the palace would flee with Mya's guard to Shadow Pass and out to a hidden fortified camp in Kona territory. The carriages looked solemn in the rain. The horses shook the water from their eyes and seemed prepared for the burden of delivering their masters to safety.

Her mother sighed as they removed their coats and sat on the couches. "You are an unlikely blessing to our people, Mya."

Mya chose not to respond. She just listened to the rain.

"Mya."

"Hmm?"

"Your Cash, can you see him as our king?"

Mya looked at her mother. Her eyes sat behind gray shadows, like iron shackles of grief. She still wore clothes of mourning, for the king, for her lost daughter, and for her sons at war. "Yes," Mya told her. "I can see him being whatever he wants to be."

"Because he's highborn?"

"Because he's himself. Cash isn't like other men. There's a kindness, an empathy behind his actions, and an air of integrity that wins any alliance. His enemies fear just his name, and his people rally behind his bravery."

"It seems as though his followers knew what he'd become before himself."

Mya found her lips forming a smile. "Yes, that's also true."

"He's already a prince," her mother said. "A prince of the wild lands. When you two are wed, you will both have to tell me about his adventures in the roughest parts of the Basin."

Mya blushed. "We haven't talked about marriage. We still haven't known each other for very long."

The old queen pulled a book out of a small leather bag she carried. She thumbed through the pages. "You're bonded through war and grief," she said. "Yours is a love even a lifetime couldn't recreate. His duty will be always to you. If he doesn't see it now, the clarity of his troubles will bring him back."

Mya's heart skipped into a faster rhythm, like it wanted to dance in the rain, dance and run back to Cash and be with him. She knew it was her duty to stay behind, to lead the effort from home, but the more she thought of him, the more she wanted to be where he was. Her anxiety turned to worry. He might die. The war that brought them together might tear them apart.

"Just promise an old queen something, Mya," her mother said.

"Yes, anything."

"When the flame of young hope turns into the ashen coals of wisdom in your lover's eyes, don't let him become your father. Don't let him slip away from you."

"Mother, Cash is nothing like Father."

Her mother continued to turn the pages, like she was trying to read, or pretending. Mya recognized the old woman's handwriting from younger days. The aging woman took a breath as if she might say something, and then let the air go. Her breath fell into the words of her book like fog steeping the glass of a cool garden window.

Mya saw the rain in a different way. "Mother," she said, "I think I know what I have to do."

78

—·—

After a while, all biological beings become predictable. That was something Arty would never admit to Kami, biological "programmer," but she knew it was true. That's how she knew that the blip of life signs, metal, and energy coming from a separate orbit than the *Pantheon* was where she could find Seth. The many orbiting bits of old space trash around the planet still surprised her. There almost seemed to be more monuments to collapsed society in space than there were still left recognizable on the ground, at least in the places where Arty had wandered so far.

"Planets are big when you look at them up close," said Arty.

"I agree," said Kami.

"I'm bringing us into docking range. It's time I face my... what would he be to me? Cousin? Peer? Ancient nemesis?"

"Boyfriend?"

"No, absolutely not," said Arty.

"Your elevated heart rate would say otherwise."

"Ugh, no boundaries with us, are there?"

"Even as I am a part of your physiology, I have yet to understand human motivations," said Kami.

Arty pressed at the twittering dance of fairies inside her stomach. "What can I say? It probably goes back to the cavewomen of Earth. There's just something about a bad boy..."

And soon enough, there he was, where she expected to find him, sitting on a shuttle in the middle of nowhere, where

Jameson thought he couldn't hurt the *Pantheon* if he thought to escape.

"I thought you'd have broken out of here by now," Arty told him. She was inside his cell, which was, in a way, more of a lab.

"The captain and I have a bit of a wager that I found fair," he said. "She seemed set on fairness. Somehow, I think one of the only things stopping her from orbital bombardment or full troop measures is the fact she has me hostage. It's good to see you." He looked lighter than she had seen him before, less burdened.

"You look young for someone who grew old," Arty said.

"My soul still has a few scars, but my body's brand new."

"It sure is," she said under her breath.

"What?" Seth asked.

"Nothing." She fought to keep a good poker face. "I'm glad you were able to wake up. Captain Jameson told me you were going to stay under until the war was over."

"What, did she try to inject me with the virus?"

"I think they tried just about everything short of decapitation." Arty didn't know why she was being this honest. Judge's strange philosophies had rubbed off on her.

Seth didn't look surprised, but he did look a little hurt. "Where were you this whole time?"

"Silently protesting."

"You brought me here."

"I did my duty," Arty corrected him. She paced the room while he sat on a shelf sticking out from where his bunk made part of the wall. "I've been at odds with this war. I don't think it's necessary. It isn't what Captain Meskin and everyone aboard the *Marshall* wanted. We wanted peaceful interaction with a society that we didn't even know was going to genocide itself. But we were so scared, so scared of you and your mother that we forgot who we were for five minutes. Do you know what that cost us?"

Seth pressed his smooth hands together under his chin and then his lips. Then he rubbed his eyes and ran fingers through his hair. "I've never known anyone like you, Arty."

Arty lost track of her rant but found a clever comeback just in time. "Have you known many other unwittingly immortal conscientious objectors?"

"Well," Seth said, getting up off the bed, "have you seen my mother fighting anywhere lately?"

An awkward stammer sifted between them.

"Let's actually not go there," Arty said.

"Right," Seth said. "Let's not."

Arty didn't want to like this man. She barely knew him, but the bond of kinship seemed to be growing in her heart anyway. In her mind, she imagined an island at sea, except this island wasn't green surrounded by blue, it was copper and reds surrounded by an infinite sea of light in a strange world that had started to feel like a lost home. Seth was standing on that island.

Seth's expression changed for a moment. She couldn't tell what it was, but he seemed to be considering her for the first time. "Why did you come here, Arty?"

"I..." She didn't know how to put her thoughts into words. "I don't... I don't know who I am."

Seth stepped closer to her and put his hand on her shoulder. She thought he would embrace her for a moment, but he retracted and put his hands behind his back, turning to the wall of his cell. "I don't either. No matter what I do, I feel like I'm standing on the wrong side of a genocide. I think the captain saw me getting anxious. She moved me onto a different ship."

"I know what you mean," said Arty. "History is so ugly up close."

"What have you learned?"

"Judge, the commander for the Federacy's... people... on the ground, he's out of ideas. They're making one last push right now. They've entered the Valley but they're out of resources. The Valley held him off long enough for Winter to be a major obstacle. He seems to know he can't hold out in the Valley's capital for forever. The Valley has guns that make the walls look like a kid's toy. I think this is it. If the *Pantheon* wants the Basin, she'll have to take it herself. Unless Judge can make a push for Ashra City, but that's looking unlikely."

"She's going to burn it," Seth said.

"Burn what?"

"Jameson can glass the whole Basin if she wants to. Snuff out the people. That's the real game we're playing up here. We're waiting for her to lose patience."

"Now you know why I'm here," Arty said softly.

"I can't let it happen." Young Seth looked like his older self for a moment.

"Tell me what to do," said Arty. "I don't know what part the universe wants me to play in this."

Seth put his hand on the wall. To Arty's astonishment, a blue flame began to lick away at the elements. The blue flame didn't look Botistem, but a different source of power. "It's time for us to appeal to the woman behind the curtain. It's time for us to find my mother. I think I'm done with this game."

Arty kept staring at the flame in amazement. With all that the Federacy doctors had done to try and suppress the Botistem power within him, they hadn't succeeded with whatever this was.

Seth smiled. "It's nice to know you are, too." The wall exploded, and the entire ship began to scream. Seth stayed calm, standing between glowing pieces of cell wall. "Do you mind driving?"

79
— · —

Cash followed Abelnora's river. He needed to turn Red's head the other way, but he couldn't keep himself from mourning. She should have been taken prisoner, not killed. At times, he was angry with her, at other times, he was angry with himself. In the end, he was angry with the universe, with the indifferent trees and the rolling hills, mountains of bone and remorse.

Light breeze blew a strange melody through the wilderness. Cash didn't know when it began, but the sound of it grew with the breeze as the day settled into evening with the sun low and his spirits somber. Red heard it too.

"What is it, boy? I swear I've heard it before."

Red turned to follow the music. The instrumentation was low, somber notes that carried atop invisible waves in the atmosphere. Red marched through thickets and branches, stepping over small tributary streams until he found the spot, an arch of branches leading underneath a canopy like a giant bird nest. An old man sat there under the shade, and as he came into view Cash recognized him, the strange wooden instrument, and the music he played as something he saw a year ago after he kissed Abelnora goodbye. The man had a blank and colorless stare in one eye, as though lost in a memory of sometime long ago, younger days.

I've thought that phrase before, too, Cash realized. Something about younger days.

"Thank you for bringing him here," the man said, continuing to play.

"My horse?"

"Thank you, horse, for bringing the boy."

Cash dismounted and took Red by the rein.

"No," said the man. "Let him wander. You and I must talk."

Cash flipped the rein behind Red's ear and the horse walked away to stand at the edge of the small clearing under the canopy and eat bits of grass. The horse bit the blades with a gentle pull, cutting the plants down but saving the roots for growth.

"I know you," Cash said. "I saw you near an orchard once."

"Are you sure you saw me? Are you sure you're seeing me now?"

"Yes?"

"Good," said the man. "My spirit is drawn to souls afflicted with loss and love. You, my friend, are very interesting to me."

"Spirit?"

"There is another, awake for some time now. She is War." Thunder flashed in Cash's mind, and he was reminded of the woman in the storm, the woman in his vision. He felt her. She seemed to always be there in every breath of longing.

"So you've seen her too." The man nodded and stopped his music.

Cash found a log near the man. He should have felt frightened, but his soul connected with the man like someone he had known his entire life. Maybe all this was just happening in his mind.

"I've lost it, haven't I?"

"That could mean a lot of things."

Cash sat on the log. It felt real enough and hurt on all the right bruises.

"My name is Orpho," said the man.

"Sounds mysterious."

"I brought you here."

Cash looked at the canopy, the way the branches twisted and grew into each other, the greens and red fruits that made their burden. Smells of nature hung in the canopy air, and soft wisps of cotton drifted in the light breeze like snow. "I think I came to know your strange music. Why are you here again now?"

Orpho smiled with half his face and drew his long horsehair bow across the strings of his instrument. "Do you know what this is?" he asked in accompaniment to the long note.

"No," said Cash. "I've never seen an instrument like that before."

"In one tongue, long ago, it was called a cello."

"It makes a nice sound."

"It does," said Orpho. "I find it serves as a voice for memory, and a compositor of thoughts words could not otherwise express."

He took to his notes, weaving pictures and scenes that Cash couldn't comprehend. Cash tried to listen, to see if the music could speak to him in some way.

"You're not listening properly," said Orpho.

"What is the proper way?" said Cash.

"Listen in the way you would feel a loved one's embrace."

Cash tried to think of Abelnora, but she was not in this music. Then he imagined Mya, how it felt to hold her, to see her smile as a haven, a sheltering rock in the heart of a storm. He thought of her laugh, the way any day with her would help him face the hardships of his present and escape the pain of his past. He lost himself to thoughts of her, all as the cello wove its story in solemn prayer of song.

The song led his thoughts until he saw something. A building of white marble and dark trim. Round pillars held up a high arched ceiling. At the far side, an enormous window opened to a night sky with stars unlike any he had ever seen. He approached the window as one floating in a dream so he could look at the view. As he reached the window, the building disappeared and he found himself among the stars, suspended in endless night.

The stars moved and formed themselves into a giant branched structure that resembled a great tree. Their connection was a vein of movement, other stars flowing through the branches in rivers of illumination. The tree was liquid in form and solid in appearance. As the branches grew in small, miniature forms of the greater tree, they stretched themselves to reach all around him. In front of his eyes, Cash witnessed the birth of two worlds. One, he recognized as his home. The other, somewhat different but similar in appearance, the music told him was called Earth.

"What does this mean?" he asked Orpho.

The vision faded before Cash could understand. He missed the beauty but let himself reorient to the wooded plane he recognized. Feeling his eyes, he found that they had spilt a few tears without him knowing.

"It doesn't mean anything," said Orpho. "It's just a nice song." He kept playing his music. Cash thought he could see the cotton and the vines sway, as though the old man could bring life to them with only a cello.

"Show me more."

"I'm still playing. You just have to listen."

The music changed to a faster rhythm. The vision returned and the two planets changed, lights appearing as life on them evolved. Artificial light appeared first on Earth, illuminated as the world spun. During the day, it looked as before. At night, there were lights that spanned the continents. But before long, the lights faded and the fruit of Earth dimmed from view, retreating into the branches of the tree. As this happened, other lights appeared on Yurasema, his world, like humanity moved from one to the other. He saw also other lights that traveled up into the tree, lost to his vision. Cash felt as big as a planet and small as a germ. By the look of the lights on his world, a germ could be a fitting description. Humankind was a luminescent germ on the face of grander beauty.

"That is not truth," said Orpho. "You are not the disease. All life has purpose in the way, the flow. Each light plays a part in the fractal growth of the universe."

"What do you mean, fractal?"

"All things are the same, all things are unique."

"The smallest branches are a type of the greater tree," said Cash.

"Yes," said Orpho.

"So what is my purpose?" asked Cash.

The tones of the cello took to a higher key. The vision changed and Cash saw his own world, Kardu, Yurasema, as it once was, after the arrival of humanity, as his ancestors made it, with flying airplanes and floating ships, vehicles that skimmed over the ground at three times Red's fastest pace. Buildings touched the clouds, and there were rockets placing satellites in the sky. Cash had read about many of these things, and he had words for them, but they didn't seem any less miraculous than watching magic.

He saw wars, distrust, and prejudice tearing apart the great family of humanity. The scene hurt to watch because the music mirrored his own battles. He sympathized with the plight of the under-trod and mourned as they would ascend to replace the despots. Cycles of chaos and order, the descent of man. There were weapons that could level cities and burn the air. He didn't know if he was looking at the past or the future. It didn't seem to matter.

In the depths of the sorrow in the song, another harmony found the melody, unlikely and remote in its nature, but Cash felt the relief of the movement, like from somewhere beyond would come a break in the circle. "I've never heard anything like this," said Cash. "What could offer any relief? All nature is built to destroy."

"The same way you save an olive tree," Orpho said. "Keep listening to the graft in the song."

Cash saw Libertas. Small in the distance but beautiful, luminescent, transcending reality. She looked far grander than any artistic depiction that hands in his world could make. Although she didn't move, she seemed alive. "My other ancestors," Cash said.

As Libertas came, Cash saw Orpho playing a piano, playing navigational music for a woman equal in greatness only by her ship.

"The Mother."

"Yes," said Orpho, "the Mother."

"Is that you playing her the music?"

"Yes."

"I don't understand."

Orpho stopped playing. "All for you to understand, child of the stars, child of Yurasema, is that there is a design. You will be a builder in the end, young Cash. I need you to know this now."

Cash settled back into the wooded place where Orpho played, his thoughts unable to grasp all that he saw and heard.

"Orpho," Cash said.

The old man got to his feet.

"I've killed a lot of people. I just killed my best friend."

Orpho took a breath of the late-summer air, a breath of peace. "If you're wondering what happens to souls," he said. "I am not the spirit to give you an answer. My songs are only for the living. My songs are for those in search of a home."

80
— · —

Blindness, not darkness. Yora couldn't wave a hand in front of his face or catch the rocks and slags before they struck him as he stumbled along. The string left by the twins ended some time ago, and the way into the wall was shut. If the wall was overrun, no one would come looking for him. Yora wandered the halls of an extensive tomb. He had no company but the scurrying of animals he couldn't see. Somehow, though, he could feel their eyes.

"This isn't darkness, it's blindness."

He found that talking out loud calmed him more than listening to the panting breaths shaking themselves out of his lungs. Forward, forward into nothing, forward beyond the wall and home and life and family. He had met a blind man once who held his hand as he talked with him, like he needed to know Yora's engagement with him through touch, touch being the only sense he could trust.

Yora wished he had a hand to hold now, and he was ashamed that the hand he thought of belonged to Denaiah.

"She's my curse," he told the cave walls. His voice didn't tremble as much as it had, being used to the darkness now. "I was an unhappy man, a stranger in my own country with my own family. Here was a woman who gave cold comfort to my sorrowed wounds. Still, in her arms... ah, okay, I was still unhappy."

The cave turned damp, water passing down tiny cracks in

the stony ground to reach him. He lapped up the drops and washed his face. The taste didn't kill him, but he had to stop often to relieve himself. His stomach hurt.

He stumbled onward, continuing his thoughts, unobserved to the outside world. "She loved me and still killed my father. No good path for her there, no smart finish. She could have let my father live and endured the lashing of a lie. She didn't, she made the brave choice, still... How do I forgive her? How do I let her raise my child in a far-off place, the murderer of the child's own grandfather?"

The cave against his hand was cold; he withdrew the hand and stuck it in the armpit of his vest. He slid down the wall and onto the ground, spent to surrender. "When I finish this fight, I'm going to go to her. I'm going to know all my children."

Small rocks tumbled down the side of the tunnel next to him. He reached out a hand to shove away whatever rodent might have disturbed them. He found a handful of clothing instead. He screamed out loud and scurried backward, cursing in every language and dialect he knew.

"Great, now I'm hallucinating, aren't I?"

Nothing answered. He was too scared to feel that way again.

"I want to live," he said for perhaps the hundred-thousandth time. "I just want to live." He turned to face the same direction he'd been walking, but kept on for a while in a crawl.

"Live," he said again. "I'm going to live."

Behind him, he thought he could hear someone sharing his journey, walking or crawling where no one should be. For now, the hallucination seemed like a friend. All the same, he kept a hand on his pistol.

Time didn't do Yora any favors in the dark. His hunger felt like a panic and started to drain him. What little food he had in his pockets was gone, and he didn't think he absorbed much anyway. The bad water had made him sick. The next shipment of antibiotics out of Ashra City had better arrive soon. He'd left a trail of what felt like chunks of his insides for far greater distance than what should have been possible for a man this starved.

The walls were closer together now. He stayed upright, hand over hand. As far as he knew, he still followed the tunnel that would lead him to wherever the twins had entered, but the darkness made him uncertain. He could very well have managed an endless loop in the same space.

The noise of his mysterious follower surprised him again. He screamed out, "Whoever you are, just show yourself." He swung his arms but couldn't find anyone. He just heard footsteps, footsteps and breathing. It made his skin crawl with the sensation of a dozen insects.

"Help me," he pleaded. "Help me survive this. I want to see my family again." He lowered himself to his knees, tired and hungry. Beaten. He didn't resist when the footsteps reached the space in front of him. He could feel the brush of the fabric against his hair. The follower lowered to his level. There was breath there. Female.

Her hand touched his face. Yora knew the scent. His breath staggered and choked as the hand pulled him into an embrace. Where there had been fear, the sweet palm brought relief. Familiarity and the strange mixed like oil and water in his mind. This was not a hand of this world.

"Vonica?" he asked the arms that held him.

The apparition didn't answer but placed his eyes inside its feminine palm and closed them. The world was just as dark as when his eyes were open, but he felt peace welcome him behind the doors of his eyelids. He held them shut for a time and let himself feel the embrace until the shape moved away, wordless, and left him alone.

When he opened his eyes, he noticed a small glow in the

distance. He felt his way toward it. The glow was a sky-colored blue, shimmering around a corner. Summoning the courage to face the light and whoever was behind it, Yora snuck around the corner. When he saw where the light originated, he laughed.

The walls, floor and ceiling were painted with a kind of bioluminescence, a mold with the inner candle of a firefly, small flames of many colors.

For the first time in days or weeks, Yora summoned the courage to run. He ran through the bio-lit passageways, letting them guide him through the maze. His feet, though starved of food and proper hydration were propelled by the steam of hope. With all certainty, Yora knew in the base parts of his soul that a door was at the end of his spirit-given light. Hope was his strength, and love was his guide, love for his son, for Vonica, for Denaiah, for his Valley soldiers he would bring this new flame.

The light brought him to a hatch. He touched it, just to make sure it wasn't an illusion. The wheel that held it in place was hard, but not impossible, to turn. He pushed the door open and let sunlight find his face again on the other side. Looking back underground for one last second before climbing out, he couldn't see anyone with him. Vonica, or whatever his hallucination had been, was nowhere in sight. The light of the tunnel had also faded. Darkness was the last testament that it had ever been there.

"Thank you, my love. Let me go win a war for you."

81

— · —

Seth watched from behind Arty as they, within Kami, approached the wormhole. In front of them somewhere in the distance, the *Marshall* continued its slow decent and Libertas drew power inside the shadow between galaxies.

"Hold here," he said, putting a hand on Arty's shoulder.

Kami decelerated and assumed a far-out orbit.

"Can you establish a link with Libertas?"

"I don't know... I–" began Arty.

Kami opened a channel herself. Seth's mother appeared on the screen. She was standing, looking through the Eye of Libertas as though expecting the call.

"Mother," he said.

"I can't see you," said Mother.

"We aren't close," said Seth, feeling a double meaning. "It's time. A Federacy ship is about to bombard our people in the Valley."

"You've done it, haven't you?" said Mother, smiling.

"Yes, but one battle remains."

Mother hesitated. She looked the same, much different than how he felt. Centuries carving desert and mountain floor with his feet had left him weathered. She looked untarnished, as if only months had passed, months with a purpose he couldn't imagine. He felt resentment waxing in his heart. He recognized it as a son's resentment, a juvenile antipathy reserved for the abandoned son.

"There's a place waiting for you," he said. "Thousands of good people are waiting for your guidance. They wear your spear and scroll on their armor."

"Oh, Seth," she said.

Arty started to say something, but Seth shook his head.

"Mother, I don't think I can stop the *Pantheon* for you. You don't know what I've had to do. You left me here to do the worst in your name. I have done my best to fulfill that purpose for the sake of good souls."

"Is Arty Sato with you?" Mother asked.

"I'm right here," said Arty. "There has to be a peaceful solution to this conflict."

"If there is one to find," said Mother, "you'll be the one to carry it out. Don't think like a soldier. You're immortal like us now. Think like a god."

The transmission started to fade. The light on Kami's hull above them faltered.

"You both have what you need, Ares and Athena. Fight your battle in the sky. I have to stay here."

"What is it, Mother? Why won't you resurface?"

His mother sighed, "The Bosions are here, children. I should have seen it. There was always this work to do. Seth, of the sword. Arty, of the scroll, antithesis paired. Finish your fight as quick as you can. The greater foe is at the door. In spite of the centuries between us, we will all be gods of war before the end. Ashetarai Areios. I... I see."

The transmission ended.

"Oh, no," Arty whispered.

Seth felt his gut sink. "If Libertas can't hold out, if the Bosions get through the barriers and get to Kardu, this world will die." He sat back and rested the back of his head in his hands, looking no further than the reach of his thoughts. *How?* Echo Front, where Seth had fought the machines long ago, was beyond far from this place.

"It was me, wasn't it?" said Arty.

But then Seth stopped thinking about old enemies and co-incidence. Hope rang like the hum a bell makes after the tone is finished, the faint hum that tingles the soul. He recognized that feeling. It was more than simple familiarity.

"Seth," called a voice in tones of thought. Arty couldn't hear them, but Seth was immediately distracted from her conversation.

"Do you think they followed me from the other universe? It seems like too much of a coincidence. How can this be happening now?" Arty continued.

Seth ignored her.

He felt something he hadn't in... wow, so long. The feeling supported him, normalized his... No, it couldn't...

"Seth, look outside," the voice said.

"Pegassos!" Seth launched for the hatch over the wing.

"Wait, what?" said Arty, raising herself in the seat to look around.

An eagle-shaped fighter pulled up beside them.

"Let me out," exclaimed Seth.

Arty cupped her hands over her mouth. "Look at her! How did she sneak up on us like that? She's beautiful, isn't she?"

"She is," Seth agreed, palming the hatch window. His old friend, his lost ship was little more than a shadow in this light, but he knew her, he could feel her. "Not a decade too soon. She's the sign we need. It's time to finish this fight."

"I'm with you, Ares," Arty told him. Looking back from her seat, her eyes looked clear and bright like the stars outside. They smiled with the roundness in her face. He hadn't noticed her dimples before. Well, he had, but not quite this way.

Her eyes then turned into a glinting tease. "Kami's only got room for one, anyway."

Seth snorted and pushed into the small airlock. The air cycled and he flung himself out into the vacuum.

Pegassos looked different, like she had grown. His breath held and under the stress of cold space, Seth quickly found a grip on her hull and pulled himself inside. Everything looked the same, smelled the same, felt the same. Her air was warm, and everything was the way he had left it. She was newer and stronger, but still his.

"Finally!" he shouted.

The ship chirped in his mind, faster thoughts than he could comprehend in his own excitement. "We'll have time to catch up soon, old girl," he said. "I have some posterity to save."

The two ships turned their course sunward and pulled space like swimmers in deep water.

"Yes," Seth said, "I had a few kids. Yes, I liked your gift. Had no idea you could make me feel this young again. What? No. I don't have a picture of when I was old."

Arty laughed through the comm. Of course, Pegassos and Kami had left the channel open.

82

Denaiah sat on one of her father's old couches in a room without carpet. It had been removed sometime after the Keepers who occupied it decided the stain of his brains on the floor weren't the right ambience. She stared at the spot sometimes, imagining it and all the other bleeding liquid masses stuck to the floor the day Cash Rivers came to talk cattle.

She felt the lump on her belly that was the child of her lost love. "Glad you aren't a Rivers baby," she told it gently.

Her baby would come soon. She needed the poor thing out; her body couldn't handle being sick with it any longer. As much as she loved the little monster, she wanted to hold it as a person in her arms and not as a parasite kicking her bladder. Was that wrong for a mother to think? It wasn't the worst thought she'd had in her time of misfortune. One of those thoughts landed her back here. Denaiah Steele, from palace to graveyard ranch.

She missed her old baths.

One of her servants, a redrafted survivor of her father's old estate entered the room. "Ma'am, King Praylum is here to see you."

"I wish you wouldn't call him that."

"Nevertheless, an important man is here."

"Send him in."

Ran clopped his boots into the room. "Hello, in-law," he burst through clapping hands. "I'm happy to see you're still well."

"Careful, Ran, all that noise and the baby might not want to come out," Denaiah said.

Ran laughed and found himself a chair across from her couch. It was her father's old chair. She wondered if it carried his headshot curse.

"You do look ready to explode or combust," he told her. "Is it too hot in here?"

"It could never be cool enough."

"That's a fair statement. Ashra's humidity is taking a little getting used to. It's not much more than the High Valley, but I do notice it. Especially on the horse."

"What have you got to gloat about today?" she asked, fanning herself with a woven fan from her late mother's closet.

Ran pulled a letter from his pocket. "Well," he said, taking his time to open it. "It seems the Valley's war is about to pay off."

"Why should I care? I'm an exiled queen living at the edge of sanity in the walls of my nightmare and living at the mercy of the son of a man I killed."

"And brother to the man whose heart you broke. Were you just taking a breath or did you forget that part?"

Denaiah stopped fanning. Her heart quickened and her face went hot. "Did Mya tell you?"

Ran furrowed his brow as though confirming a suspicion. "No, but I have a good idea what she would tell me. That's why I keep you around. That baby is worth a lot to me. Royal blood of any variety is worth protecting."

Denaiah tried not to shudder. "Tell me about the war."

"Mya says it's time for me to join the fight. Sending men isn't enough. She says if I don't go myself, I am too much like my father."

Denaiah took a wet cloth from a tray at her side and put it on her forehead. It was cool, but not enough, never enough. "I don't want to talk about him."

Ran pressed the issue all the same. "Do you think I am like my father?"

"No."

"Why not?" he asked.

"In what way do you think you're like him? You wouldn't have come here to talk about it if you didn't see something of him in your reflection."

"No, I'm inclined to agree with you. We're nothing alike. I've done everything I can in my life to distance myself from his legacy. I even conquered a kingdom for myself to get away. But Mya says if I don't go rescue her kingdom, the one I purposefully left in the hands of another, I am like my father. That gets to me."

"Do you think because I was married to him, that I'm qualified to make a judgment?"

Ran leaned forward in his chair, his elbows pressed to his knees, the letter between his fingers. "You're my best bet at an honest answer."

"My honesty ended that marriage."

"Just tell me."

Denaiah sighed and thought about an answer. "Your father cared about the Valley more than he cared for anyone else. That was his defining trait, strength and weakness bound in a royal ring on his finger. He thought if he could close off the rest of the world, that his people would have the best chance for safety. That was a part of why I married him, to be part of his safe world."

Ran looked down at the floor, his eyes tracing the place where her father's blood had left its mark.

"You're not like him in that way, Ran, but maybe you will be someday. You're young, your heart is set to conquer and influence. You're trying to find your reach. I believe you want a better world, but you haven't lived long enough to see your flaws. That's the difference between you and Tarsus Praylum.

You're the legacy of a father's overabundance of caution. He had you too late in his life for you to see yourself in his actions."

Seriousness bubbled behind Ran's face. He looked his age, for once, and thoughtful, the walls of indignancy falling to the floor. She saw not a king, but a man reflecting on home and fatherhood. Then, she did see the resemblance to Tarsus in him, and in Yora.

"Thank you," he said, standing.

"It's all my pleasure," she said, not rising at all to see him off. "Picking up the broken pieces of Praylum men. Let me know when you want to fall in love with me."

Ran shook his head, ignoring her. "I'll go save my home. Not for him or anyone else, but because I think the world needs to know I'm that kind of king."

"Whatever you say," she said. "Just don't expect me to.... But..." she tried to find words for something she didn't want to say out loud. The mask she was trying to show Ran started to crack.

I hate this family.

"Don't worry," Ran said. "When I see him, I'll tell Yora you still care."

She opened her mouth, then closed it again. A few words did find their way out before Ran left, but they weren't right. "Tell him I... tell him his child will want to know him. Tell him I'll be a good mother."

83

— · —

Cash found maybe a third of the army, now pulled back from the wall, and mobilized them as fast as possible. He sent most of them back to regroup, the underequipped ones that were on foot or too weak to keep pace. The rest, he took to the enemy in fly-by raids.

His best prize in these hunts would be to find Judge, who must have been somewhere among the enemy patrols. They were pushing for the palace, each patrol keeping Cash's people spread out to where they couldn't accomplish enough damage. The right guns couldn't be moved fast enough. Cash had thought Judge's army seemed big before, but now his ranks appeared numberless.

He couldn't think of anything to do but let Judge in. As painful as it was to let Judge's people into the capital and the palace complex, it was actually the better strategy. Mya had left the Valley, which was good, so Cash was free to do what he was doing now, riding with Red and hundreds of thundering hooves behind him, to press Judge's people to make the obvious choice: Head for the city. Take the old fortress. This patrol Cash was chasing was a large detachment. Bullets tore at the outside ranks, but the foreign host pressed on, fighting Cash's waves off like metal shavings from a drill bit. It didn't help that they had to conserve ammunition.

Cash led a platoon of riders up very close this time, aided by a distraction on another flank. Red pounded out such speed that it was hard to hold on.

"Just get me close, boy," he yelled over the thundering hooves. Red was having the best time of his life under fire.

Close enough to spit on a frightened-looking man of rank whose horse drifted to the outside of the enemy's gaggle, Cash roped him like a running calf, slinging a lasso over the rider's torso, tangling his arms, and dragging him off his horse. The man sputtered behind him, hitting every brush and lump of dirt in the way between bounces. Cash knew the man might die on the flight back to camp, but he could at least try to interrogate him, to figure out the master plan of the great Outlaw King.

The man did live, and Cash's men gave him food and water, all with him tied to a tree.

"What's your name?" Cash said, looking at a strange image of a harp engraved on the man's rifle.

"Flint."

"I've never heard a name like that," said Cash.

"In case you haven't noticed, I'm not from around here," said Flint with a cough.

"More water?" offered Cash.

"Yes," said Flint.

A soldier gave Flint some water from a bladder. He guzzled it down, almost choking himself.

"Thirsty, isn't he? How about some shine?"

"Gods, no," the man sputtered mid-drink.

"Very well." Cash jabbed him in the sternum with the tip of the rifle.

Flint gasped and spewed water a yard in front of him. It dripped on Cash's boots.

"You're really tall," said Cash. "You have weird symbols, sophisticated weaponry, and your accent is all off. Where are you from?"

"East," said Flint.

Cash took the weapon and fired it at a berm. The rounds

repeated without any lever action and without much recoil. "Techa fio, this one is new. What's in the magazine?" He fumbled around the sides of the weapon, looking for a release. After hitting a button, the weapon steamed in his hand and the stalk and barrel cooled. It was made to look like wood but was actually some kind of powder-coated metal with something ceramic.

"It was a gift from one of the spacemen," Flint stammered.

Cash smirked, as did his lieutenants watching. "Sure, when they gave it to you in space, on your spaceship."

Flint shook his head and spit on the ground. His face was chapped and bruised. "You seem comfortable with the idea."

"I've seen things you wouldn't comprehend, and I've met someone from space before, my own kin."

"Then you're an abomination."

"Oh, yeah. A sick abomination. One that should scare you. What's the instrument on the engraving?" Cash swayed the rifle, letting it point now and again at Flint's face.

"It's a lyre, a tribute to Apollo Far-shot."

"Huh," said Cash. "Apollo. I'm sure it's in our libraries somewhere. We have some Earth books. Hey, Jayce."

"Yessir." Jayce stepped from the growing crowd of tired riders.

"Have this man sent to the forward camp. He'll know things we'll want to know. I'm not going to trust anything he says right now."

Jayce had Flint untied and taken away. The men had to carry him. His cuts and bruising were severe.

"You're all dead," Flint said, almost in a whisper. "You're going to die and you're not going to know what hit you."

Cash tried to imagine what he meant. An attack from above? The space people would have tried that by now. They seemed to choose instead to take on the role of vindictive gods, ones who play favorites and let the hardened men like Cash do the dirty work. Seth was here, but he was different. He was the Apollo Far-Shot of his mother. Cash laughed softly to himself, wondering if he'd gotten the reference right.

"Are we really going to let them take the capital, sir?"

Cash turned to see who spoke. It was Lieutenant Lakemeadows. "Lieutenant?"

"We should intercept them, cut them off in their path."

"We don't have the men."

"My family is still there, sir." The young officer was shaking in his boots.

So green, Cash thought. *How did he get promoted so high? How many men are left in my army of boys?* There was Jayce. Jayce was like a stubborn tree. Life just plowed around him.

Cash let a troubled look escape his demeanor. "They couldn't get out?"

"My sister doesn't walk. She's too weak to ride. Others stayed, too. They won't leave their homes."

The officer's words stung and Cash thought about Mya. He hadn't heard where she ended up, but he hoped she was safe. Dispatches were hard to coordinate without his old headquarters and supply lines.

"We'll keep hitting their numbers, keep them running." Cash put a hand on the man's shoulder. "Help me figure out a way to take the city again. For now, I won't consider artillery within the walls."

This wasn't the answer the lieutenant was looking for, but he knew the order of things. "Thank you, sir."

Cash had some difficult choices to make. Rounding the enemy up and killing them within the fortress of the city was the safest option, but Judge knew that. What was his plan?

"Will they harm the people in the city?" asked Lakemeadows.

Cash swung his new rifle over his shoulder. "Ask the spaceman."

He turned to walk away and take care of Red. Red didn't like stablehands as much as Cash's own attention, always the particular king of drama. He was nipping at one of them trying to brush him when Cash got to the makeshift corral. He grabbed a brush out of a bucket.

One of the many team leaders came running from one of the surrounding berms. "Sir, riders from the East."

"What? Who? Friendly?" Cash asked.

The sound of gunfire answered his question.

"Get me a few squads to flank them. Who's up on the rotation?" Something about this wasn't right.

"Riders north, and northwest, sir, large forces in for the kill."

"Techa, Judge," he said to no one. "You're splitting your forces now? Just take the city. I'm giving it to you." He threw Red's saddle to the ground.

Cash scrambled his riders. He needed covering fire and he needed eyes. Red smoke would mean the entire enemy force was bearing down on them, or enough of it to worry.

"Hold your positions!" his lieutenants echoed to anyone who wasn't mounted. "Die now or die later."

Cash watched riders break from the main group and circle around. They executed their maneuver well but lost many of their numbers before falling back. The enemy would surround them soon.

"Protect the horses, protect yourselves," he told his soldiers. "We can't take the city if we all die today."

Throwing himself onto a protective berm on his stomach, Cash tested his new rifle. It took down both horse and rider, zeroed to a range he'd never guessed possible. He also never had to reload. When the gun got hot, he'd flick the button and let it cool itself. But he couldn't cover all sides, and the enemy laid down a blanket of fire that his men couldn't suppress. Horses from down the field would roll over them soon.

Go take the city, Judge. I gave it to you!

He shot rider after rider, and man after man fell from his ranks. In a matter of minutes, Cash was losing way more than he was gaining by way of a trade. He shouldn't have set up camp here; he should have kept his people moving.

"Friendlies! Friendlies! Friendlies! Shift fire!" Lakemeadows was on his horse, shouting down the line. It was a risky move but at this distance and the decline of the terrain he didn't seem worried.

Another group of Valley, Ashran, and Kona soldiers were attacking the enemy's flank.

"Those aren't ours, are they?" Cash asked someone nearby. "I know what I see, but, wow."

"You'd know better than I would, sir," Lakemeadows said, his voice elevated and finding space between the gunfire. "Is that a woman leading them?"

Cash scanned the ranks of the new group. Sure enough, he saw who Lakemeadows saw. She had long dark hair and rode a white and brown pinto. Her horse charged the enemy host with others surrounding her, protecting her like they would a queen. The enemy turned to meet them head-on.

"Who do you think it is, sir?"

Cash jumped to his feet and grabbed a fresh horse that was minding its own without a rider. It was spooked but came to him as trained. "It's Mya! The queen. Counteroffensive, now!"

"Sir?"

On top of the horse, Cash turned to the soldiers who followed suit. He could feel the wildness in his eyes, the rage and thrill of a charge, the feeling in his trigger finger when he knew the game was his to win. Rifle propped on his shoulder, he felt suddenly serene, like destiny had lined up the breeze just right. "Does anyone else hear that song? It's like... finding home. She's always been there, hasn't she?"

The soldiers looked at him, confused but inspired. "Who?"

"My mother."

Cash aimed his horse up the berm, kicked its flanks, and charged with his rifle singing. Cassius Far-Shot clipped the enemy in multiples of ten as he rode at them head on. He left the greater part of his men behind. They couldn't match his vigor. He rode to meet his love and to destroy his enemy, all his purpose in youth fulfilled.

Judge's forces ahead lost all formation, and horses and riders turned loose. Cash bellowed his horse over root and hole, ringing the deep bell of death in echoes off the distant mountain. He ferried souls from Yurasema like a creature of myth. Those against him left standing their ground had no choice but to turn their guns solely on Cash or be cut down. Several enemy shots whizzed near his face.

He pressed on, charging into the dust and smoke. He felt invincible. The forces of the universe and the soul of his world were on his side. "You're going to be a builder," he heard Orpho's voice in his mind. A woman sang in accompaniment to the cello.

The enemy would take the city today, but he and Mya would lead the people to victory. Culling this force was only the beginning. Cash could see the end of the fight clear as he could see Mya leading troops into the battle now, saving his men. She needed his help though. He just had to ride like he'd never ridden. More bullets buzzed in his ear, like whining bugs. Irritating.

A single round caught his chest. His ear heard the crack as the bullet crashed into his armor. The sky rolled into view as his feet lost the stirrups in the force of the shot. The wind left his lungs, and his head struck the ground.

The song faded and the world turned white.

84
—·—

Yora had emerged from darkness to the far edge of a dirty secret.

Metal cages and dirty chains surrounded him. The hatch where he escaped the darkness wasn't far away. When he made his way into the camp, no one noticed him. Most of the guards seemed to have left. Stricken people sat in the cages, indifferent to him, as if he were just another guard. They wore bright clothes and reminded Yora of a boy he'd met many months before. The boy had run away, vaulting over the wall and into the valley as if he could find relief anywhere but behind him.

Yora was certain he found the missing piece of the psychology behind the war. Those who wouldn't fight were kept prisoner.

"Thank the Mother I wasn't born in the East," Yora said.

A guard heard him. Yora's time underground, he still didn't know how long, had made him forget that talking out loud meant people could hear.

"Who said that?" the man said in Joropa. He wore a yellow sash over a short band of cloth fastened around his waist. His shirt was tattered but at some point must have been blue. His hair curled behind his head in oil-drenched waves.

"Heads up," Yora muttered, and kicked the man hard in the face with the base of his shin, just above his foot. The kick stung a little for Yora, but the maneuver worked. The man was short and the art of the kick felt right. The man fell back with his feet swinging out in front of him. Yora grabbed a plank of wood and beat the man's head until the blood told him he could stop.

The people in the cages clamored in disbelief. "Quiet," Yora told them in Joropa. "How many more are there?"

"Hapu," a woman said. Five.

He maneuvered his way through the camp. A man was whistling. Yora ducked behind a cart full of food rations. The whistling man was relieving himself in the open. Finished, the man waddled passed Yora at the cart. Yora stabbed his knife through the back of the man's neck. His hair was sweaty against Yora's fingers at the hilt of the blade. Letting him down to the ground, Yora found keys and food in his pockets.

The next and last four men reeked of strong drink, unaware of anything around them and didn't see the blade of Yora's judgment before it tore open the flesh that kept their souls.

Yora took the keys and unlocked the cages one at a time. They creaked with rust and overgrowth, but they did open, so maybe the people inside weren't always kept under lock. At the last cage, a boy rubbed his eyes and called out for his mother. He looked undernourished, much like the rest of the enemy host.

Yora knelt to speak with him. "I met a boy like you once," he said. The boy stared at him. "He was older than you, but had the same hair, same eyes. He was very brave. Can you be brave, warrior?"

The boy curled his lips upward in a way that seemed to affirm, yes.

"You are a kind enemy," an older woman said.

"I regret the circumstances that make us enemies," Yora answered.

"You've killed many people like us?"

"Heh," Yora said. Yes.

She pulled out a kind of doll from the folds of her pockets. "Take."

"What is the gift?" Yora asked.

"It is a bear. A token of my people. If you find yourself in our lands, show it to the chieftains. They will view you as a friend."

Yora took the gift. The surface of it was rough, made of a plant he didn't know. "Avuy'ye," he said with reverence. Thank you.

"We will disrupt the supplies," she said. "The time has come for this war to end and for us to go home."

"How do you know it will be safe for you?" Yora asked.

"The moons have told us."

"Then go with the moonlight. Any resistance you can offer on the way is welcome."

"Goodbye, warrior-friend." She took the boy by the shoulders and took him away. Yora saw that there were horses corralled for them to take.

"It's almost over," he said. "We're almost done."

He took one of the horses, still clutching the doll. With ammo and weaponry from the men he killed, he set himself to go west, back to the fight. Once the hills drifted back in the night, he imagined Vonica there, waving to her lost lover on the road.

"Goodbye, dearest," she seemed to say. "Carry with you my embrace."

"I will. I don't know how else I could be whole."

85

Kami and Pegassos found their formation, a spaceflight duet that bowed space around their shared protection. Arty remembered learning about the *Marshall*'s use of high energy reactions, antimatter with matter, fusion, and some experimentation with quantum teleportation. But no matter how they got to the warp function, the ship's isolation was the same. The *Marshall* couldn't share the space between spaces with anything but itself. These ships could, Kami and Pegassos, two sisters licking the glass surface of the Dao like birds flying through thick forests.

"Seth, are we doing the right thing?" Arty said into the open comm.

"That's a loaded question," came his reply. "Why did you come and rescue me from my prison?"

"Because I came to believe that the Federacy is doing the wrong thing."

"Maybe that's your answer, then."

"I don't think two wrongs can make a right," she answered.

"The *Pantheon*'s mission has to be stopped," Seth said. "I owe that to my people in the Basin."

"How many of them are your family?"

Seth took a moment. "I suppose, with statistics in mind, quite a few of them."

Arty thought about what he said. "So that's how you did it, how you saved the human race on Kardu. You gave them your genes. You made a small group into a viable gene pool."

"Something like that. There's more of our kind in them than they would care to know. Sometimes, especially in the beginning, my genes would manifest themselves in the form of gifts. Strength, sight, immunity, to name a few."

"Lasers from their eyes?"

Seth laughed, already so much more the young man than the old man she'd first met. "No, not lasers. They don't have the light of the Botistems in them either."

"Could they? Could they be immortal like us?"

"That isn't a science I know anything about," said Seth.

"Honestly, that surprises me."

"Go around the galaxy and ask people how any given system in their body works and see if they know. Then tell me how I should know more about myself when there aren't any books about it."

"There wasn't anyone you could ask, either, was there?"

"You've met my mother," he sighed. "Maybe someday I'll be an equal in her eyes. Someday I'll find more answers about myself."

"I hope you do," Arty said.

"I found you," said Seth. "That's a start."

She let what he said hang in the Dao for a while, flying in silence. The Dao carried with it a sort of meditative induction. If she listened to herself breathe, let herself go in thoughtless flight, she felt the universe somehow with her, inside her, rejuvenating her spirit and mind.

Seth interrupted her zen. "I have this thing that I do."

She tried not to sound annoyed. Conversation with anyone other than Kami took getting used to, even though she'd many times craved just talking with someone. "What's your thing?"

"I view how people treat others. If they are kind and honorable, I try to listen to their interests. I try to spare them."

"And when they don't do that?"

"A lot of people die."

Arty lowered her voice. "Are you talking about the *Marshall*?"

Seth shot back quickly, "No. I was in negotiations that day. You know this. I'm talking about my time down on Kardu, about my time with the people there, helping them build their civilization."

"I think I know what you mean," Arty said. "I was taken prisoner almost as soon as I landed. That situation could have gone...differently."

"The 'right thing' is arbitrary. Time and perception change who and what can be right or wrong. Captain Jameson thinks she is right. She thinks that any expense, even innocent human life, is justifiable in the end. She operates under the firm belief that if my mother's technology touches this world, it will be like setting off a thousand nukes."

"Wow," Arty said. "Is she right?"

"In this type of case I think that only the victorious end up being right. They make the history books. They compose the music."

"So how do I know what to do?" Arty really wanted to know. "I'm caught between these worlds."

"I'm still trying to figure that out for myself. The universal constant, the principle upon which all civilizations should exist, is kindness. I don't see a way to find honor without decency," said Seth.

"The *Pantheon* imprisoned you. They tried to keep you unconscious. I'll bet money they tried to dose you with a virus aimed at your Botistems."

"They're planning ways to wipe out my people. That's the blatant violation of our agreement I'm worried about at this point," said Seth. "What they may or may not have tried to do with me didn't work. My power's intact."

Arty put her hand over her closed mouth and then raised it

to rub her eyes. Could she do it? Do things she feared, for a ship full of souls? "Is there any way we can show mercy?"

Seth didn't answer. Why should he? He had people on the planet below to protect. The Federacy hadn't shown them honor or any degree of kindness. The Federacy's assault was forced genocide, action out of fear.

"If there is a way," Seth said after a while, "it would be the right thing to do."

"I think I know," said Arty.

"Yeah, me too," said Seth.

"We can take command of the *Pantheon*. We can unseat Captain Jameson."

86

— • —

Cash didn't remember being shot. He woke up without any other sensation than a kiss. It wasn't Mya. The kiss was hairy, wet, heavy. Red. Red was waking him up. Above the horse he saw the walls of a tall canvas tent, and his ears picked up the sound of his favorite girl. He thought she'd left the Valley.

"He's awake," he heard Mya say. "Red, give him some space."

The horse didn't comply, but kept prodding his master with concern.

"Red," Cash muttered. "Boy, get off. Get off."

Then came a human embrace. Mya shoved Red's face out of the way. Red huffed in annoyance.

"Hey, you," Cash said with a grunt. "What's Red doing here?"

Mya kept hugging Cash's neck. "He fought his way past the stablehands when he realized you were in trouble. Then he stood watch over you until we were done fighting. He hasn't let us take him from your side since."

Cash reached up an arm to pat Red on the nose. "Ouch."

"Careful," said Mya. "Your chest is bruised. The round didn't go through your vest, but you were thrown from your horse and hit your head. I was so worried I..." She trailed off.

"I've had worse." Cash tried to sit up. "Ugh, techa, forget it. Where's a bucket?"

"Here you go."

Cash threw up some nasty rations into the bucket. "Yep, this is a concussion, isn't it?"

"Just lie down on the cot, Cash. Others can take the battle from here."

One of the captains came into view, with Jayce at his side.

"What's the word?" Cash asked them.

"Mya helped us finish off our attackers," said the captain. "She left the royal convoy and rallied some of our people who were spread out in the confusion of the enemy's advance. There's bound to be more out there, wondering where the fight is."

"How are our numbers to... to..." Cash struggled to think. The nausea and headache clouded his mind. The light hitting him in the eyes from the flaps of the tent made it worse.

Jayce seemed to read Cash's mind. "We're going to fire on the city."

"People are still inside," Mya said, "but if we don't take it now, I don't know if we ever will."

"I agree. Judge is desperate. He's pulling a stupid move," Cash said, vaguely proud of himself for having a coherent thought. "Can't figure out why. Some trick up his sleeve, or he's giving up. He wants..." *Me?*

"We're preparing what we have left of an army for an assault," the captain said. "With your approval, sir."

Cash struggled with the weight of the decision. "Do what you must. I'll be there."

Jayce and the captain turned and left. Red relieved his guts in place, indifferent to the solid, grassy waste he spilled in a hospital setting, still guarding his best friend.

Mya sat down on Cash's cot.

"Mya?"

"Yes, Cash."

"You weren't supposed to be out there, Mya."

"I'm queen. I do what I want."

"What if we lost you?"

"You weren't going to. I was making sure we didn't lose you."

Cash took her hand. "I love you."

"That's the swollen brain talking."

"No," Cash's voice cracked. "I'm telling the truth."

Mya stroked his hair, careful to avoid the bandage covering the swelling at the back of his head. "You always tell me the truth."

"I don't want to kill any more people."

He felt like a child. He couldn't help it. His emotional walls cracked. He'd lost a lot in the war, his entire sense of self was in flux, and now this confounded headache. Huh, confounded. That's something Judge would say. Abelnora would point it out.

"Cash, Cash." Mya held his face, her eyes close to his. Their green color bought him clarity. "I'm here, Cash."

"Could you ever walk away?" Cash asked. He wondered if he was going to start crying. His eyes were really dry.

"From my home? I can't do it. That's why I came back. I belong to this land, ruling over these people, and I belong with you. I'm not going anywhere."

"That's what I needed to know," Cash said. He closed his eyes, ready to sleep.

Maya stayed with Cash for a while, reluctant to leave. He rested with a frown on his face, like the care he felt for the people and the guilt he experienced in his heart couldn't let him free even in his dreams. She worried about the concussion. He would come out of it alright. He had to. She was going to make him her king. All the lights in her path pointed that direction.

As the day faded in the flaps of the tent, Mya bent to kiss his face. She must attend to strategy and Cash would understand. "You've done well, my Outlaw Prince."

The guards didn't salute her at the gate, as they might have. The standing order was to not salute anyone. The camp was in the open, and no one knew whether the enemy intended to stay in her stolen city for long. After such a push, she imagined they would. They would choose to stay there, tend the land, and have children. Someday those children would fight for her Valley with just as much claim as her people did.

She couldn't let that happen.

"I'm going to bed," she told her guard. "Tell me if anything changes with Captain Rivers, and inform the captains I expect a full battle plan by morning. They have my permission to do what is necessary to win. Take every initiative."

Sleep ignored her, but she made herself stay in her quarters until sunrise. When she left the tent, she headed first to the place she had left Cash sleeping. She hoped the sleep had been kind to his mind and he would wake up without the nausea. Sometimes concussions healed easily, other times the brain bled and left complications. To garnish the hardship, the war had also run out her supplies of antibiotics to almost nothing. The enemy could quite possibly beat her with infected paper cuts.

Arriving at the hospital tent, Mya knew immediately something was wrong. The staff was scrambling, not wanting to look her in the eye. When she got to his bed, she understood why, and every negative emotion she could have felt toward a man she'd grown to love fired off like a powder keg.

She didn't find him asleep. She didn't find him in the tent at all. His bedding was folded, his weapons gone. Red's prints led out the door. All Cash had left for her was a note, folded with the crease off-balance and the handwriting slanted from a man who couldn't see straight.

Give me some time. Judge might listen.

She crumpled the note, cursing that outlaw boy. "Someone find him and bring him back to me."

87

— • —

Now that night had fallen, Yora's legs wanted to do the same. They wanted to sleep. They wanted to heal. The horse he'd ridden from the enemy camp hadn't given them much rest. They wanted a full day out of the fight with fresh nutrients to build them back up, but he couldn't give them that. The best he could do was eat and drink the rest of his stolen rations on the go. His gut still felt sick from the bad water, but he kept it all down. His dehydration had improved, on a positive note, and his thoughts lined up in his mind with better coherence.

The water inlet to the city was his best bet to sneak in, but he had no way of knowing if the enemy would suspect that kind of maneuver, so he sat on the bank of the canal and spun the bear doll in his hand. The woman gave him the token for a reason, but using it the way he thought he should took some courage, some gut fortitude that he had to meditate out of himself.

"I'm going to do it." Yora pulled himself onto his tired legs using his tired arms. "Let's see what you can get me," he told the token.

Guards at the east gate held spears and rifles. Yora took a deep breath and strode up to meet them, holding up one hand as a sign of goodwill and the other with the token in plain view. "I've been sent here, I promise," he said.

The surprised guards pointed their weapons at him.

"It's alright," said Yora, his Joropa a little shaky from his exhaustion. "I'm on a mission."

Two of the guards approached him. "Get on your knees," one said. "Knees, now."

"What's your mission?" the other demanded. Both spoke in Joropa dialects that were hard for Yora to understand.

"What?" said Yora.

"What are you here to do?"

"I'm here to kill the Outlaw King."

One of the men took the doll. The other smiled and stared behind Yora. Yora turned. A man's huge fist smashed him in the nose, blinding him in pain. They took his guns and tied his hands behind his back.

"This was a bad idea," he said in the common language of the Basin.

The smiling one grabbed Yora's face with one hand by the cheeks. He pressed Yora's lips together and bruised the skin. He said another thing Yora didn't understand, and his friend laughed. They were talking too fast. The smiling one with his cheeks let him go.

Yora looked down at the ground and tasted a little blood that trickled down to the back of his lip.

One of them asked a question to the other one, again one Yora couldn't understand. He didn't realize the question could have been aimed at him until his face got nudged by the flat end of an ungentle, warped sword.

"You may have your chance, bear. If she has sent you, we won't interfere. We'll leave you your knife, bear-man, but we won't give you the city. It's ours to spit upon."

"Judge!" Cash called out from Red's saddle. The city gate stood in front of him at the end of the path arched with trees pruned for their summer shade. The leaves weren't falling yet but looked like they were about to turn. "Judge!"

His head hurt with the pain starting in the back of his neck and the top of his back. Inside, his brain felt like it had swelled enough to push out his eyes. Thank the cello-man he could get here while it was still dark. He imagined that if the sun reached his eyes, his head would at last explode and his mission remain unfulfilled.

"Red, not so fast. Ugh. You're killing me with the trot, bud. Hold up." Red's gait took on a sense of urgency. His nature dictated headlong rushes into battle. Usually, that's what made him a good horse for an outlaw-turned-commander.

"Judge, it's time we talked," Cash called. Raising his voice didn't feel much better than the bouncing stallion underneath him.

The gate opened as he reached it, and ten skeptical-looking men of ragged apparel met him. With steely eyes and cold hands, they pulled Cash off his horse. Red bucked and bolted, running out the gate.

"Leave his weapons. The king wants him as he is."

"That wasn't about to turn out well for any of you, anyway," Cash said through his throbbing injuries. It was true, though. He wouldn't have swung a fist, just filled the square with bullets.

"Come with us to the tower."

The tower was the place Seth didn't allow Judge to go the last time he was here. Made sense that's where he'd be. Cash walked on, trying to hide his pain. Feeling his new vest, he wondered if it was as sturdy as the last one, or if the soldier he took it from would miss it.

I'm coming, Judge. You want me. I'm here.

88

Seth scolded Pegassos, "I'm not rusty, you are."

"Have you two finished arguing?" Arty said through the comm. "Two more fighters coming hot from seven o'clock."

Seth spun his ship around and fired. Fast-flung mass and energy buzzed through the frequencies of one of the fighter's kinetic barriers and struck its thrusters. The ship turned in circles as the pilot tried to compensate. "I need you to yield," Seth told the pilot, hoping he hadn't scrambled his comms.

The pilot was on an open channel. "I yield," he choked under the force of his fighter's spin.

"Obliged," said Seth.

Arty disabled the other fighter. "Let's hope that's the last one. It's like Captain Jameson wants us to kill someone."

"You might be onto something there," said Seth, looking at the field of derelict ships floating around him. "She wants to vilify us, justify her next move."

"You'd think us breaking out of your prison shuttle would be enough."

"This is quite honestly the most merciful I've ever been."

Arty teased him, "That must mean I'm good for you."

Seth smirked and shook his head. "Let's take that flagship. Can you tell if she's fired on the planet yet?"

"It doesn't look like it," said Arty. "Judge seemed to think she would soon."

"What gave him that idea? I mean, she's obviously losing

patience with us on the board, but he shouldn't be clued into any of this."

"The guy's tapped into something. He meditates a lot."

"Maybe in another world, he and I would get along," Seth said.

As they sailed through quick miles of darkness, he pondered their next move. "The more we confront the problem of the *Pantheon*," he told Arty, "the more we accelerate her next move. This is a pressure game. Let's get closer. Jameson will show us her true motives then. If her head's in the right place, if she has a proper sense of human decency, she'll yield the ship to us as we demand it."

"I'm glad we can show her people mercy," said Arty. "That has to mean something."

"Whatever happens, we'll put it on her," said Seth. "Good or bad."

"As long as we don't get shot down first."

"That's something to think about."

Seth spun up more thrust. Pegassos purred around him. "I know people. The only real power they have over others is to kill. You can't control life, but you can control death. Call it the oldest temptation. Jameson is going to realize it's all she has left."

"Torpedoes incoming," said Arty.

"Yep, she's trying to kill us."

Cash looked up in the sky, flashes of movement in his vision. He saw moving lights in the forefront of otherwise motionless stars. In his life, Cash had often seen flashes of shooting stars or orbiting satellites of space debris of forgotten ages, but this time the lights were alive and engaged. They danced. He lowered his gaze back to the task in front of him and watched the palace creep toward him in steps of throbbing destiny.

That's Seth, he somehow knew. *The gods are at war now. How do you like it, immortals? How do you like finally having to choose sides? You have ships, you have long life, but you're no different than any of us. You live and die for someone else's scheme.*

Arty and Kami were learning to work together now more than before. Their last space battle with the Dark Bosions was spent with Kami managing and Arty tossed and seasick. Now, human and machine melded together in consensus of mind. Arty could feel the torpedoes and rockets. She could sense the patterns of the planet's gravity and the thrust of Kami's energy. Time appeared to distort itself as Arty experienced near-perfect flow with her companion ship, the dangerous mindfulness of two sentient creatures making one warrior in the void.

"I'm having trouble shaking this one," Seth said calmly in her ear. "Was Federacy guidance targeting always this good or have I just been out of the seat for a few hundred years?"

"It's both," said Kami to Arty.

"How would you know?" Arty asked Kami.

"Machine-level extrapolation," said her ship. "He has been out of the seat for a few hundred years. This ship could be many centuries newer than his last acquainted flagships."

Arty found it hard to think at Kami's level at the moment. Fighting was taking most of her energy.

"Has he ever fought the Federacy before?"

"I haven't asked him. He's an officer, though, so, probably not?" said Arty.

"Arty, I need you," said Seth.

"I've got you." Arty shot the torpedoes with bursts of Bosion power, flanking them from the left with tactics straight out of million year-old textbooks. "Flanked and burned. Derelict."

"Thanks," said Seth. "But don't rest yet, you've got three, four more on your six."

"Care to join me?" said Arty.

"Already ahead of you."

"I actually need you behind me."

Cash climbed the steps. He hadn't been up here since the day Seth took him and the royals up for some drama or another. Cash wondered if Seth really was one of the dancing lights in the night sky, fighting over his world. Seth seemed to care back then about the Valley and about Cash. For a while, Cash would fantasize about leaving the planet with him, becoming a spaceman. Those dreams happened less since getting with Mya. His feet seemed to belong more on the ground with her at his side.

Must be some girl. He had said that to Judge once. Different context. Techa. His head felt so weird, like no headache he'd experienced. This was probably why doctors told people to rest when they had concussions.

The steps wound and wound and made Cash dizzy until at last they met the top of the tower at a propped up, trapped door. He couldn't remember if that door had always been there. Through the hinged-open window, Cash could see the lights still dancing over the night. Something in the back of his mind told him again that Seth was there, fighting his own war in ethereal landscapes that looked like Cash's vision from Orpho's music.

Judge was slouching with his arms folded, looking over the palace, his back to Cash. Seeing him now was less of a shock than last time. The guards escorting Cash took positions around the room, enemy sentinels at the top of the tower, surrounding him. Next to Judge, on his knees with his hands tied behind his back was a silhouette Cash didn't recognize until his eyes focused.

"Yora," said Cash. "You're alive."

Yora smiled through dried blood that had come from his nose. "Haven't snuffed me yet."

Judge turned. He looked a lot older. The scar on his eye was a different color.

89

—·—

"Point defense cannons," Seth said, watching the lights of high-explosive rounds approaching Pegassos and Kami like a wall. As the distance closed between the immortals and the giant *Pantheon*, darting through the flagship's defenses was only going to get harder.

"I've always wondered what they look like from this angle," Arty said, wonder and fear in her voice.

"Yeah," said Seth. "This is right about that time we should run away. They're trying to limit our maneuverability."

"Why do I think it's so beautiful?"

"Maybe that's exactly what death is," answered Seth. "Beauty and light coming at you for one last explosive finish."

The point defence rounds were quite far away, perhaps a normal person wouldn't be able to see them very well, not without the right enhancements. But Seth could, and so could Arty. Then, for just a moment, Seth realized Cash might see something, too.

Arty moved her ship into action. "I'd rather live forever."

"Me too."

Seth stowed his reflections and shot into the fray of rocketing ordinance, spinning his ship like a corkscrew. His ship was one small but significant plume of light facing thousands of explosive rounds meant for fighting machines. Perhaps dozens, if not hundreds, of enemy fighters were out there, too, each one capable of doing great damage. Pegassos rode with all valor, following him like she always had. The synergy he had craved was between them.

"Stay close," he told Arty, "and follow my lead. I've done this kind of thing a lot."

"Got it."

Kami started firing as well, pushing a hole with all the expertise of a child of Libertas. The two ships shot around themselves in a shell, keeping the fire-clamped jaws of death at a healthy radius.

"Keep pushing," said Seth. "Don't lose focus. We're almost through."

Yora's knees ached against the stone floor. He shuffled them to try and alleviate the pain. Shockwaves of nerve irritation shot up his leg every time he did. He tried not to think about how long he had been awake since the battle at the wall. Sleep didn't come easy back in the tunnel with rats and ghosts for company.

Judge turned to meet Cash as he came farther into the room. The guards surrounded them from the sides, watching.

"Son."

"Judge."

Yora crept his fingers along his belt where the guards had placed his knife. These guards in this room probably didn't know about the conspiracy. He'd have to wait, for now, before he freed his hands. He saw that Cash still had his weapons, a long rifle slung on his back and a couple pistols holstered on his thighs. There was a long belt of ammunition around his shoulder as well.

"I heard about Abelnora," said Judge.

"I buried her. A spot near the river. You would like it," said Cash.

"I'm sure she would, too."

The two men looked beaten. Even though Judge had won

the city, his composure was torn up, like a man who lived a life he never wanted. Cash looked like every step he took was agony. Yora would know. Something bad had happened to his head. He had it bandaged but the pins were coming out and the back was wet with new blood.

Judge took a pacing step to the side toward Yora, stroking the hair on his chin. "Are we here to discuss your surrender and withdrawal, or is this a different kind of visit?"

"I don't know," said Cash. "I took a hard hit to the head. Maybe I want to defect."

Yora felt for the knife again.

"*Pantheon*, open your doors or you will be fired upon," said Arty.

Still no response. Arty opened more frequencies. She assumed the ship had to be listening.

"*Pantheon*, I'm running out of mercy."

Arty knew the problem she faced, and it was that the universe had given her too much power. Back when she was a mortal, proud, and low-ranking member of the Federacy food chain, her allegiances, her indoctrination and outlook, were all chosen for her. She was Lieutenant Sato, and she had given herself to the noble cause of exploration and spreading constitutional ideals. Her life had been its most simple then. But then she had to die, and Kami came along. Kami carried her to a mirror universe. Kami made her a god. That was really it, wasn't it? Arty wasn't Lieutenant Sato anymore. The words she found herself using weren't part of the chain. She'd broken free.

It was terrifying.

"Listen to me, Captain Jameson," Arty pleaded. "We know about the ground operatives' failure to take over the Basin. The Outlaw King is holding fast, waiting for your next move. We're here to make sure you don't interfere. Let us aboard and we can talk this out. I'm willing to accept Federacy loss. Don't turn against the principles Captain Meskin died for."

They flew quite near the *Pantheon* now. Seth had grown quiet, a resolved kind of quiet, like he didn't have anything else to say. She couldn't blame him. The *Pantheon's* solution to dealing with him had been to keep him silent, unconscious for as long as they could. Seth had even honored the captain's proposition at the time. He'd let the war play out and didn't escape until Arty came to him. In a way, so much of what was happening now was her fault, wasn't it?

What would have happened had she fought alongside Judge, had she been a good Federacy soldier? Would it really have been so bad to play the aggressor's part? Yes, it would have, but thinking a little on that side gave Arty a window into Captain Jameson's mind. All the captain had to do was win. If she won, history would remember her as the woman who tamed Kardu, who held back the threat of Libertas. History wouldn't be wrong either. It would just lack the context of this moment.

Okay, so Seth was in the right because he saved the human race on Kardu. He preserved civilization. His progeny had claim to the land by centuries of birthright.

Captain Jameson and the Federacy also felt a claim to the world. They'd given lives to defend it from machines, from interference, from the unknown factor of human and machine symbiosis.

What's my claim?

Arty really was the antithesis of both factions, wasn't she? Seth's mother had used that word. Maybe Ashetarai had meant that Arty was the scale tipper.

Underneath the flying ships, the unscathed wilds of Kardu looked helpless, like innocent forest that didn't know the disposition of a bolt of lightning. Judge's army was a tiny speck from up here. He couldn't have any idea how small he was in Captain Jameson's deck of cards.

"*Pantheon*, your war is over," Arty found herself speaking again. "Open the launch bay doors and prepare to be boarded. We will make this interaction as peaceful as you allow."

"Arty," said Seth, breaking his silence over the comm. "Arty, they're turning their guns on the planet."

"Dammit!"

"I know you too well for that, son," said Judge. "You won't defect. And I know what I deserve under the machinations of justice that exist inside your head. I let you keep your weapons. If you've come to kill me, you can do it now."

Cash looked at his old mentor, beaten in his seat of victory. "I'm not here to kill you, Judge. Stow the fatalism. I'm here because I'm done. My heart hurts more than my head. Do you know how that is?"

"You killed Abelnora. You killed the twins. You've killed a lot of people," said Judge. "Yes, I know how that is. I'm your father."

"How did we get here, Judge?" Cash didn't ask a rhetorical question. He wanted to know. He'd come to the only man he thought could answer.

The lights he saw in the stars grew brighter, closer together. Some of the lights hit the atmosphere and ignited, meteors to ruin something's day somewhere. They seemed residual, not deliberate. The guards were getting distracted watching them.

"I'll try to answer that if I can," said Judge. "For both of us. For all of us." He pointed to everyone in the room. One of the guards looking out the window snapped back to attention.

"Do you know the filthiest word in our language?" he said. "Keranu'umi. It means syncretism. You don't know that word either, do you? Maybe you do. You both live by it. You too, Yora. We all do, all of us who believe anything live in a palace made of the bones, stories lost to changing faces. These people who came from the sky can't force us to change, but they can add to what was already here. They can alter the face of the gods to win our devotion. That's what's happened to all of us. No one is innocent. These ancient foundations, built by conquerors. These new walls, conquerors. How much blood did they spill under them? What's in the brick mortar here? Guts and filth. Perseverance at the expense of neighbors, even the expense of family."

He was talking about Abelnora. Cash winced. His head. He wanted to lie down, perhaps just die. No, not die, just disappear.

"I've realized there's no winning this war," Judge went on. "Some god floating in her ship in the sky just wanted us to do the dirty work. She knows her only power, the only power humanity has truly ever been able to wield over itself. The power to kill. Cause a famine, or a drought, drop a plague or a mountain-sized bomb. Freeze the planet in nuclear winter. That's the ancestral lesson. If you want territory, if you want legacy, you have to cull herds, you have to tear out the meat. But leave the bones. The bones are the structure of what you build next, what the historical libraries will forgive you for. That spaceship, that orbital goddess in our sky. She's going to burn this Valley now. She's realized that's her power. That's her role in history, her legacy for the civilization she'll build here. We are the bones for her foundation."

Cash didn't say anything. That was the thing with Judge, he was never wrong.

"I'll wait here. You can join me, son. Wait out the burning. We'll go get my lady. We'll be a nation of our own again, and we can leave the rivers of blood and the lives we've taken behind us. What do you say, Cash? Can we be family again? Outlaws under the eye of Yurasema. Accountable only to nature, the great tree of the universe! I'll be anything but the hammer of syncretism any longer. Do what you came to do, Cash. No one will stop you."

Yora sprang from the ground, knife in hand, leaping for

Judge's back. Before he could reach him, the old man went limp, falling to the ground without any ceremony of posture. On the wall, there was blood and pink, sticky matter that dripped and clung to the brick and mortar.

Cash felt the steel grip of the gun in his hand and the smell of the smoke. For the moment, his head stopped hurting.

To Seth, Captain Jameson's desperation came out of prejudice. She operated under the urgency to finish the battle. At first, that meant shooting Seth and Arty down. Now, she'd given up on the idea, aiming guns for the Basin, sitting below them on the dark side of the planet, well in view for orbital bombardment.

"Arty, I'm not sure we can save them."

Arty's voice sounded helpless. "Are we talking about the people on the ground, or up here?"

"Does it matter?"

"It shouldn't, but maybe it does."

"I'm going in. Follow me if you will. I'm going to stop those guns."

"Seth, wait. Let's make a plan. How are we going to minimize casualties?"

I'm not sure we will, Arty. You don't see it now, but you will.

"Seth?"

Seth bore Pegassos down with weapons blazing with the fire of suns on a focused area of the *Pantheon*'s hull. Pegassos maneuvered to match the spin of the *Pantheon*'s great drum to keep her shots in one place. When the metal looked hot enough, Seth opened the cockpit and jumped. The air depressurized and launched him at great speed. All sound vanished from his ears. There was a feeling of invisibility to such silence. In the noiseless descent, even though he could see, he felt like he could not be seen.

That wouldn't be true, though. Every eye on the *Pantheon*

would be wide with terror watching him fall at them like a man-sized, streaking bullet of retribution. Death was with him at his heels. Her blue fire of war and memory was in his eyes.

The heated, torn scrap of *Pantheon* hull that Pegassos left for him to breach sped toward him. Remembering Pegassos, he turned for one second to watch her speed away. "Keep the guns busy. Take them out when you get a shot." He threw the thought at her.

"I'll be here when you need me."

"You've seen what I become when you aren't."

He smashed through the heated metal, tearing into the *Pantheon* interior with blue flame and burning white flashes that the architects of the *Pantheon*'s energy barriers never anticipated. In only a moment he'd torn through layers of redundant systems and mechanical apparatus like a dog through sodded grass. Crashing through to the main corridor, Seth leapt out of the floor with all ferocity. He was his old self and his new self all in one great and terrible form. He was Kardu and Libertas. He was Seth Caeso, founder and destroyer, god of broken civilization.

There wasn't a jawbone in his hand this time, but he would find something. Those who broke his mercy in this arena would taste something just for them.

Yora watched Judge fall under him in surprise and quick, engrossing panic. Warm brains had squirted onto the left side of his face, blocking part of his vision. The guards around the room held their breath in disbelief at the brazen simplicity of what they'd witnessed. Cash stared at Judge on the ground and the gun in his hand, infinite potential for more death in his palm. He looked up at Yora, a question in his eye.

Yora nodded to answer, pressing down the urge to get Judge's last filth off his skin and clothing. Cash's eyes reflected

Yora's own instinct. Kill now, question later. Cash swung the pistol in his right hand and shifted his weight while drawing the second at his left. Yora took the knife and went right. Together they swept the room. Cash with bullets, Yora with a slashing blade, throat for throat. Cash, with the faster weapon, killed the most.

Each guard died before firing a shot or throwing a fist. More blood and brain for brick and mortar.

Panting, Yora held up a hand as Cash still held his pistols forward. Tears without sobs spilled out both of Cash's eyes.

Yora wiped his face with a cleaner part of his arm. "Alright, what's the plan now?"

"Huh?" Cash said.

"What's the plan? What do we do now?"

"I don't have a... I don't..."

Yora cut him off. "We're here, we've got the tower. Can you use that rifle?"

Cash's mind was deteriorating, no thought in his brilliant head. "Rifle?"

"Forget about it. You cover the door. We're going to have visitors after all that noise. Shoot anything or anyone who pops their head through there while I block the way. But first, I'm going to unsling this rifle from your back, okay?"

"Okay."

"Cash. Put away your pistols first. I don't want you to shoot me."

Consciousness returned to Cash's face. "Yeah. Sorry. I got it."

Carefully, Yora unslung the rifle from Cash's shoulder. The wound on the back of his head looked bad. *Think about that later, Yora.*

Yora stacked bodies against the trapdoor, dropping their limp, bloodied forms like bags of sand with appendages. Furniture would have been nice, too, but there wasn't any worth using. Bodies would do the trick. He took position in front of one of the slit windows. "You good there, Cash?"

"Uh, I threw up. No worries, though. Not my first concussion."

"Not your first? Okay. Just let me know when they start coming through the trapdoor on the floor right here.. I'm going to start some havoc at the windows and make them think twice about coming up."

"You let me know when you want to switch. That gunf...rifle... is as fun as... as..."

Cash didn't finish the sentence before Yora was already blasting into leaderless masses on the ground below the tower. Cash was right. The special rifle was fun.

"Ugh," Arty moaned. "No, no, no, no, no." She struggled to follow where Seth entered the spinning drum of the *Pantheon*. "Can you get me in there, Kami?"

"Certainly. Are you feeling conflicted, Arty?"

"I'm feeling like I want a peaceful solution while everyone around me insists on behaving like animals."

"Many animals are known for their rather complex territorial disputes."

"Get me inside that ship!"

"Matching velocity with Seth's point of insertion," Kami said as machine-like as possible.

"Sometimes I can't tell if you're trying to be ironic," said Arty.

"Exit now, Arty."

The cabin depressurized and Arty flew with less grace than she hoped for, tumbling through metal and ceramic. The fall was a good test for her armor and her lungs. She pulled herself up through the floor. The hole in the ship was now underneath her. The *Pantheon* used a lot of spin gravity even in combat, which was an impressive feat of engineering. She would have wanted to learn more about the process if she had to worry less about how to prevent a wild, ageless man from blowing it up.

"Seth, I know you can hear me," she called through her comm, still regaining her breath. "Remember the plan. We can remove Captain Jameson."

He didn't answer.

She could tell where he went from the bend and wear on the floor and walls. "Wait for me. I'm on my way."

90
— · —

Mya held her anxious, white horse next to Ran's. He showed up with an impressive compliment of Ashran men and women, as well as many young Kona fighters. His work on alliances before, during, and after the war had paid off. Ran didn't look any different, even after the year since she'd seen him, but he did look more himself. He was free.

"Think we can do this?" she said, staring off into the flickering lights.

"I think our boy is fighting from up in that tower." He passed her his telescope. "See the muzzle flashes?"

"We have to do this now, Ran. I can't lose him."

"Not after Yora," Ran agreed.

"He's not dead," Mya said. "Many of our troops are unaccounted for. More show up every day. I don't believe he died at the wall. People saw him go underground."

"You're right. If anyone can find his way out of the dark, it's our brother. But we'll take our vengeance now. For Tais, for all whose blood sits beneath our feet in this sacred valley."

"Well said, Ran. I'm glad you came."

"Wish we could have brought more. I don't think any army has crossed the Basin faster than we did."

Mya gave the telescope back to her brother. "Let's signal the guns."

A sort of battle hum sounded in Mya's veins at the reverberation of a gong, flushing her cheeks and standing the hair on her neck. She lifted her rifle and shot a screaming dart into the sky. Many more darts answered hers around the flanks of the city. Over their heads, cannon artillery shot shells into the walls and onto the battlements. When the barrage ended and the walls were down, the horses charged waves of violence in the shape of a death cry.

"Stick with me, little sister," Ran said, and shot off down the field behind the ranks of other riders.

Mya caught up with him, pushing the line into the city. "I'm coming, Cash."

Seth felt Arty come up behind him, an unspeakable flutter, a touch to his deeper sense that he couldn't describe, like when he drew near to Pegassos, or even his mother. The stuff that made his soul, the consensus of warm blood and hot machine, reached from within him toward her in strange chemistry. Right now, the sum of this equation spelled sensations of dread.

He heard her steps slow. He knew she could see him where he stood, facing dozens of soldiers wearing body armor and pointing energy weapons at his chest. "Stay back, Arty," he told her, gripping the rod he'd taken from the metal framing. There was blood on the tip. It was a good thing she hadn't come a few minutes earlier.

"Seth," she pleaded.

"We don't have time for that now," he replied.

"No, you don't," said Captain Jameson, stepping out from the reeds of gun barrels.

The AIC, the captain's command center, was packed with enough arms to back Seth down. He'd never tested his immortality that way. Firing squad at point-blank by trained Federacy soldiers wasn't something he'd thought of practicing.

"You can die, can't you?" asked Captain Jameson. "I mean, we know enough now that it would take more than a few bullets, a few burns. But your consciousness is tethered to this world by the same thread of the fates as ours. We eliminate your body, and you die, just as the rest of us."

Seth looked at the soldiers' faces. Some were scared, others jaded and cold. Each person in this room had a story. Each had a reason to point the sting. Each had a reason Seth should kill them.

"Seems fair," he said. "I've never pretended the trip was forever."

"Lieutenant Sato," said Jameson with hands behind her back. "I'm disappointed you came back. Your first death was enough. You should have stayed in the other world. A hero's death looked better for you than that of a traitor in this one."

"You should look at what you're betraying, Captain," said Arty, stepping into Seth's peripherals at his side.

He turned to look at Arty. She wore terrifying beauty in her expression. Her eyes were lit from the inside in manifestation of her new power. Captain Jameson talked of fate, but she couldn't know what it felt like, what Seth felt like now, looking at someone like him, but also wondrously different. Arty was the best of them both. Athena to his Ares.

Arty turned, noticing him staring. The apprehensive determination in her eyes told him stories, told him hopes that he couldn't share. *I want to trust you*, her eyes said.

He answered them out loud. "Arty, it's too late."

Cash was on his feet, shooting from the tower position with the rifles of fallen guards. Though his aim stayed true, the greater battle happened in his mind as he worked to keep focused on the task of two-man war. His thoughts wanted to drift. His consciousness wanted to sleep, to lay on the floor and let the elements pass away, onward until the flesh of all became dust, became like Judge.

He'd killed his father. Judge had predicted that. The old wise outlaw had always known what was coming.

Techa. I just want to sleep. I want it all to go away. Abe, Judge. Eimos and Teeg. Brick and mortar. Bones.

"They're at the wall, Cash. Do you see them? It's our people. They're getting through. Just keep the enemy scrambling, brother. Hey!" Yora's arms wrapped around Cash's shoulders. The rifle had left his hands. How did it get down there?

"Come on. Come on," Yora commanded in a prince's best tone. "Don't sleep. You should do anything but sleep right now. I've got to get back to the window...just... just hang tight there. Stay awake. Stay alive."

Faint gunshots tried to wake Cash out of the fall. His body went to the ground, but the world around him spun him into a drowning sensation. But someone was coming, someone he loved, maybe. She had a pretty face and comforting arms. Mya. He came here for Mya, didn't he? Maybe none of this was about Judge or Abelnora. They were the past.

"Yora," Cash found himself saying.

Yora kept shooting at the window.

"Yora."

"Stay with me. Stay awake, okay? You're my brother, Cash, you're..."

"Tell Mya she's the best part... the best... she's..."

A white haze took his vision. Then he saw faint stars over shades of nothingness. Echoing lights in a cave.

Arty saw the hurt in Seth's eyes, a burden of years that the new, rejuvenated body couldn't hold back.

"It's too late," he said again.

Arty didn't want to understand. "I don't want to be that person."

"What person?" said Jameson. "You've lost. We hold the

AIC. You're going to die, and we're going to reshape that valley. It'll make a nice glass monument for a planet-sized museum."

Arty turned back to the captain. "What authorizes you to turn your guns onto innocent people? Are you planning on killing all of them? What about your army? They're still down there."

Jameson spat as she answered. Her words were coffin nails. "I am the Federacy. You missed a lot while you were getting armed by the real enemy. Bosion forces are advancing galaxy-wide. The Federacy needs worlds like this. This world is hope and a future all wrapped up in one green and blue blanket. How lucky were we that most of the people here wiped themselves out? This isn't about ideals. This is about territory. On this planet, our people can have babies, build universities and cities. We can learn how to create our own Earth-like worlds. The only thing standing in the way is a so-called 'Queen of the Heavens' that no one has heard from in centuries. If we move now, we beat the galactic gold rush. We win. I kill your people, and you won't have a reason to be here anymore. What's the difference, if I do it from here, or an Outlaw King does it down there? What's the difference in the end?"

"There are people down there," Arty said, taking a step forward. "You are not a voice for them."

One of the many soldiers raised his weapon to Arty's face. "Don't move another step, Lieutenant."

Captain Jameson held out her hands. "I will not let you, or the unspeakable anathema that is your race, inhabit this planet. I will destroy all that this world is before I let that happen. My people stand with me."

Arty turned back to Seth, who remained silent, resolved. "Help me."

"We don't have a choice anymore," he told her.

Arty tried to think about who she cared about. Anyone from her past had long since died. Anyone from her present was a fleeting acquaintance. She longed for the Federacy she signed up for. She longed for the officers who taught her good principles. Captain Jameson belonged to a different generation, a different Federacy.

"I'm here, Arty," said Seth. "You won't be alone."

Captain Jameson retreated back into the forest of guns. "Kill them. Kill their people. Our campaign has failed."

"But ma'am," one of the junior officers protested from the terminal.

Jameson took her sidearm and shot him. Arty winced, feeling her eyes and muscles twitch. She watched the dead officer slump, spreading something red down the terminal. His body landed on the floor, robbed of housing the *Pantheon's* last bit of conscience.

"My simple directive is to establish a liaison with the citizens of this world," Captain Jameson said, "and to cultivate trust. If trust is impossible, I'll remake the world into one where it isn't. Gods know I won't be the first. Shoot the traitors, fire on the populations, or meet the same fate as your colleague. History won't need to forgive us for a loss it won't remember."

Arty took Seth's hand. "Okay."

Seth returned Arty's grip, and the flow of time on the ship slowed down. Energy and life rushed into her. Arty wouldn't have called the feeling euphoric or stimulating. The connection was nothing but simple consensus, unconscious agreement between two entities and their adjoining cells, their inter-network of machine and biology. It was the most calm, resolute experience of her life. She knew what had to be done, not just for the people they would save on the planet, not for the Mother, not for Kami or Seth, but for herself. Arty chose, with Seth at her side, to not be alone. She chose a side.

"It's strange," she told Seth as energy built between them, time pulling in much like Libertas in front of the *Marshall*. "Indecision is no kind of peace, and inaction is no kindness."

Arty felt him sigh. "When this is over, and we hate our-selves," Seth said, "let's remember that."

Regular rhythm in the thrum of reality restarted with a surge of energy built out of Seth's and Arty's union. White light with tips of blue flame overcame the host of guns with the grace of a blade through silk. The AIC dissolved. The captain and her officers, the security teams and the junior staff, all misted into shadows on the wall. Arty didn't let herself feel the kill, only the harmony with Seth, with the Dao from which her soul could derive strength.

As the AIC and its crew fell, so did the barriers of the ship.

"We have to go," said Seth, and he took Arty by the arm. "Are you still with me?"

"Yes." Arty shuddered. "It has to be this way."

They set out to the halls. More security from other parts of the ship found them, and Seth took upon them with nothing but scraps of metal. Arty took an energy weapon off one of the fallen and joined him.

"Hangar's this way," she called.

"Pegassos is starting her attack."

"Kami, too."

"Let's go meet them."

The concentration of security soldiers diffused as the im-mortals fought their way outward. Arty shot at men and women because they were shooting at her. She couldn't think about their guilt or innocence anymore. Her decision gave her peace, for the moment. She only saw muzzles that could hurt her or hurt the people she'd chosen to save. As her weapon flashed and the bodies went down, Arty thought about Judge and the sadness in his eyes when he spoke about a boy named Cash.

A lot more death still stood in the way of the hangar. A lot of hallway to try and feel nothing. The Federacy soldiers, numbering in thousands of independent souls, were fighting for their lives. They had chosen a path where Arty couldn't save them. She followed Seth and kept hoping it was all for the best.

Yora led Mya through the piles of carnage and burning buildings. She found Cash at the top of the tower, his head resting against the body of a faceless man. He looked asleep. His hands were cold.

At the breach of the walls, the enemy that didn't surrender died or fled. No one chased them. Mya ordered that they should be free to choose their own way.

The war was over, but the ache in Mya's heart had just begun.

As he cut his way through the ship, Seth tasted the old rage inside himself, but he also felt Arty fighting alongside him, and with both feelings together in his heart, he felt complete enough to go on. They made for the hangar that was at the center of the drum, the hub of the spinning wheel where gravity was weakest. Pegassos was making her way there, too, if she hadn't arrived already.

"All hands," a woman's voice came over the radio. "This is your acting captain. The prisoners must not be allowed to leave the ship. I repeat, the prisoners must not be allowed off the ship. If they escape, we will all surely die."

"For your wrongs," Arty said, "you have brought death to your house already."

"I'm sorry it's come to this, Arty," said Seth. "Not long ago you seemed like a nice kid."

She turned her rifle around a corner, keeping the muzzle aim in such a way that she could clear each part of the turn like slices off a pie. He saw her Federacy military training in all of her steps.

"Hallway clear," she said. "I choose this, Seth. You're a good man. I've come to see that. If I'm going to navigate a galaxy of change, I need a constant. I need a teacher and a friend."

"What is it?" Seth asked.

"Can you be that for me?"

"Your teacher?"

"And my friend."

Seth prepped himself to rush at new gathering enemy at the end of the next turn. "Arty, I think there's a lot more you can teach me."

Arty smiled, a sad but honest curve in her mouth. "Let's go. This ship is nothing but a bad memory."

Seth saw a cart up ahead, abandoned where someone had run away before they arrived. If they could get it to go fast enough, it would be a better alternative than fighting the next wave. "Let's take that cart."

Arty jumped into the front seat and handed Seth her gun. "I'll drive."

"Is he still breathing?" Yora asked Mya. Yora tried not to project the extent of his exhaustion. His clothes and hair were stained with blood.

"Yes," Mya said, starting to cry again. "Thank you for saving him, Yora. Thank you for coming back. I knew you had to be alive."

Yora bent down and picked up Cash, cradling him with care. "Let's get him to the medics. At least he can be comfortable."

"He's not going to die," said Mya, wiping her nose with a dirty cloth. She looked like she saw her own decent share of the battle. She had led a good charge. "I didn't lose you and I won't lose him."

"I believe you, my queen." Yora took her love, his brother in combat, into his arms and descended the stairs. He whispered into the young captain's ear. "Cash, if you can hear me, I need you to stay with us. I don't think this family can take another broken heart. You're right. My sister is the best of all of us, and you aren't allowed to leave her."

The *Pantheon* groaned in its ribs and spine and tossed in futile efforts to remain intact. Now in the hangar, Arty kicked off a handrail and flew over fallen men and women in the destruction she and Seth paved. She had never witnessed a real, prolonged battle before this. During her short time on Kardu, she'd avoided violence as much as she could. But as much as she had objected, Arty had always known what she was capable of. She had become a soldier for something.

"Kami, I'm ready now," she called out. "I know the woman I'm meant to be."

"Then I know the vessel I've chosen is the right one," Kami answered.

Kami caught her and pulled her into the cockpit. She looked out the window. Seth had found Pegassos. Pegassos the noble eagle, carrier of a god of war.

"Time to end this," Seth's voice said in her ear. Pegassos began firing into the guts of the ship. "Follow us down, Arty?"

"I'm... we're with you."

She turned her ship into the belly of the *Pantheon* and opened Kami's wrath, ripping through the structure. "I hope the people of the Basin, and the people of all the cities of Kardu make this worth it."

"They will," said Seth. "They've been given the chance now. We were all led to that place by more than ambition."

The ships broke free and waited at a distance to watch as everything burned. The *Pantheon* buckled and lit like a small star in orbit around the world. Pieces of her fell into the atmosphere along with no small number of escape craft, tumbling into the atmosphere without guidance.

"Will any of them live?" asked Arty.

"I doubt it," said Seth. "Maybe we should have given more of them a chance."

"I don't want to think about it," said Arty. "We made the decision we could with what we were given."

"Spoken like a true commander," said Seth.

"Just like one I used to know."

The ships sat in silence for a moment.

"Let's go back," said Seth. "I need to see what's left of my people."

91

---•---

The three surviving children of Tarsus Praylum surrounded a sleeping Cash Rivers. Mya sat on the ground by his cot, her legs out to the side, her pants still filthy from the charge. Ran stood beside her. Yora sat on the next cot, eating a hot meal for the first time since the wall was breached days before. He stirred the broth of his soup around in contemplation. They listened to the sounds of Cash's faint breaths as his body struggled to stay alive in spite of the brain swelling inside his head.

Mya stroked Cash's face and hair. The swelling wasn't going down.

"He's a good kid," said Ran. "Better than any other officer we could have brought up. It had to be him."

Yora sighed, putting away the rest of the soup. "He gave everything he had. Even when he knew what it would cost."

Mya kissed her sweet boy's face. He looked young and kind when you took the battle and strain away. Her family had put the world on his back, but in the end he was just a boy who cared enough about a better world to fight for it.

"He'll be remembered for all he did and more," Ran said. "His legend will grow, even in death. They'll build churches for him. Remembrance to last centuries."

In the corner of her eye, Mya saw Yora continue to stir the broth. She could see pain in every stir, but peace as well. He was going to be okay. Maybe he could learn to love again.

She couldn't feel such hope for herself. Cash had been more

than a good captain, more than just a lover. She'd loved him more during their short time than she could ever allow herself to love again.

"We're with you, Mya," said Ran. "I'm sorry, truly."

"Everyone always is," she said. "Everyone is sorry. But this time I'm not. I'm glad he was mine."

Hours turned into miles of somber goodbye. All of them stayed with Cash, waiting to witness his soul pass into another world.

"It doesn't feel real," Mya told Cash softly. "I don't believe you're really going." He had been hers, not for long, but time enough to change her world, to build with his violence a future of hope.

She had the sudden sensation of a mountain field after the snow melted into many springs. The cool of the wind on the water and its deep breath through the branches of budding white trees. She could see Cash in one of those fields, the sunlight gleaming on the lightest parts of his sandy hair. He had a father's look in the line of his mouth and the tilt of his jaw. For a moment, she could feel his child inside her. Not now, but perhaps what could have been.

"Pardon me, my queen, my lords. A man and a woman are here to see you," one of the nurses interrupted. The happiness of the field turned back to the somberness of a hospital tent.

"I don't want to see anyone right now," whispered Mya with some bitterness.

"He said you would know him as the Teacher."

"What?" said Ran. He took his feet off the bench next to him and dropped a blade of grass from his mouth.

"He said Teacher?" Yora rose to his feet. He looked at Ran, who nodded.

"He told me you would know him," said the nurse.

"Send him in," said Yora. "Mya, it's fine. Trust me."

Mya turned and saw a man and a woman approach in

strange, yet beautiful armor. The man knelt beside her. "Mya. You're older than when I last saw you."

"I don't know you," she said.

"You should have known me," said the man. "My name is Seth. I knew your father and your brothers. And I know Cash."

"Can you help him?" said Mya with a breath of irony.

Seth looked at the woman he came with. "Let's see what we can do, Arty."

"Oh, I've never... I don't know what I'm doing," said the woman. "What are we doing?"

"Just put a hand here and help me," said Seth.

The two strangers put a hand each on Cash's chest, and Seth scooped his hand under the wound on Cash's head. Light came out of their hands as both strangers closed their eyes. Yora bowed his head.

"Are you healing him?" asked Ran.

"It's just a small gift," said Seth. "The world isn't done with Cash Rivers."

The light went into Cash for a long moment, glowing like a touch of magic. Mya cupped her hands over her mouth. "Cash, Cash, are you there?"

The strangers took their hands away and Cash kept still. His breathing quivered, then relaxed into long breaths.

Mya's heart sank into a brief spiral of hopelessness, like not even the light of the strangers could help him.

But her fear had been wrong, and Cash opened his eyes. His irises were clear and glowed a little in the shadowed light of the tent.

"I understand," Cash said.

Seth cocked his head and whispered to his companion. "That's new."

Mya hugged her man. She would never let him go. His heart beat next to hers and she would keep it there, protected. "Cash?"

"Yes?" His eyes were still glowing. His body was warm and full of life. He returned her embrace.

"How would you like to be King?"

— · —

Epilogue

Cash took Red to Abelnora's river. The fall leaves were back, and the breeze off the water cooled his face like a silk pillow. Red bent to drink from the water. Cash did the same. The clear and white stream through the rocks had a tranquil taste.

"I'm sorry it's been a while," he told the swirling water. "I've had a lot going on in the Valley. Mya's pregnant again and, well, you know kids. They're born outlaws."

He laughed and took off his hat to stroke the back of his neck. The sandy colors of his hair had turned a little more brown. He gripped his hat tight. It was the first hat he got when he arrived at the High Valley.

"Yora's still sending books from around the continent. He's really something of an archaeologist. You wouldn't have known it, had you even met him, but what he's done has set us forward by miles. There's talk about building railroads soon. I can't even believe it, and I've seen some crazy things."

He sat on a rock, setting his hat on the flat surface next to him. "Sweet Abe, the things I could show you."

The sun descended and lit the water like tiny memorial candles, each lightfooting on the running glass. The river seemed to smile at him, soaking in the beauty and radiating in the autumn glow. He imagined his childhood friend, sitting with him and watching the world be its truest self.

"They say there's nothing so peaceful as a river," said Cash. "But I think I know better than that. The closer you are, the more the water rages. The waves overwhelm you and the air you need to breathe is hard to find. When you swim in it, you can't hear anything, say anything, you just... you survive."

He sighed, trying to excavate thoughts from behind tired scars.

"From far away, a river is only peace. You watch it like you would read a book. Maybe a book is a river. Maybe our story is a river. A little sad, a little peaceful when you see it from far away enough. But this river I'm treading still hurts. I'm still finding it hard to breathe."

Red nudged his shoulder. His mouth was still wet from the water. Cash grabbed his face and pulled him close. "You used to tell me this horse was too much for me."

They watched the water together, a man and his horse to remember a friend.

"I've got to head out already, Abe." He picked the hat back up, wanting to throw it into the water. He sighed. "I guess I'll keep this for now. Can't let go just yet."

The stars began to appear, hanging over the colorful leaves with two little streaks of light making their way into distant expanse.

"Are we really leaving?" said Arty from her ship.

"Yes," said Seth from his. "We couldn't put it off forever. My mother will need us now. But we'll be back."

"How do you know?"

"I think I'm taking a piece of Kardu with me. Not sure if it's borrowed."

We everlasting gods... Ah, what chilling blows we suffer, thanks to our own conflicting wills, whenever we show these mortal men some kindness.

—*Homer*

ACKNOWLEDGEMENTS

There are too many wonderful people to mention, but I'll try to get it out quickly.

First, a shout to all the ancient writers of the East and West whose works survived the dust and wind long enough to capture my imagination since before I could read. You gave me my love for epic stories.

Next, I've served with many brave and inspiring heroes. They're the voices behind Jayce and Ran, and the grit of Cash's initiative. If anyone asks, Combat Engineer is the coolest job anyone can ever have. Thank you to all my veteran brothers and sisters who taught me the way of the warrior.

I would also like to acknowledge the people of Paraguay. Much of the language spoken by Cash and his gang came from Guaraní.

I owe most all to my family and loved ones, especially Carol Pratt Bradley, who has mentored me as a creator ever since I was a kid. She's read every word I've written and is probably the main reason I will ever finished anything. She's one brilliant author. And Hannah, who has always believed in my best self even when I haven't. She's the world's best editor, best friend, and best hand to hold.

To those who are a part of my civilian life, I apologize for the language and violence I included. To those from my military and emergency services life, I apologize for all I did not. As one additional disclaimer, sometimes writers are faced with choices of science and narrative. If there's something technical or cosmic that doesn't add up with a scientific journal, chalk it up as author imperfection. But in my defense, theories are meant to be disproven anyway. Fiction lasts because it never pretended to be anything else.

There are many more people to thank, even ones who would rather remain nameless and off the printed page, but I would be remiss if I didn't thank you, reader, who made it this far. The songs played and sung out of the depths of Kardu's mystery are still alive in my imagination, and many more adventures are on the way. For any news and additional content, you can follow the journey at dbradleyexplores.com. I promise you a fun and exciting universe.

Till the next story,

Dan

About the Author

Daniel Bradley is a science fiction novelist with a military combat arms, emergency services, and linguist background. Writing at the steps of the Rocky Mountains, Daniel explores humanity's connection with nature and the greater cosmos through characters and events inspired by old mythology. When he isn't writing, he's hiking, performing in local theater, or on his way to a large body of water.